By Larry McMurtry

Dead Man's Walk
The Late Child
Streets of Laredo
The Evening Star
Buffalo Girls
Some Can Whistle
Anything for Billy
Film Flam: Essays on Hollywood
Texasville
Lonesome Dove
The Desert Rose
Cadillac Jack
Somebody's Darling
Terms of Endearment
All My Friends Are Going to Be Strangers
Moving On
The Last Picture Show
In a Narrow Grave: Essays on Texas
Leaving Cheyenne
Horseman, Pass By

By Larry McMurtry and Diana Ossana

Pretty Boy Floyd

Dead

SIMON & SCHUSTER

New York   London   Toronto   Sydney   Tokyo   Singapore

Man's Walk

a novel by

Larry McMurtry

SIMON & SCHUSTER
Rockefeller Center
1230 Avenue of the Americas
New York, NY 10020

SIMON & SCHUSTER and colophon are registered trademarks
of Simon & Schuster Inc.

Designed by Eve Metz

Manufactured in the United States of America

10 9 8 7 6 5 4 3 2 1

Library of Congress Cataloging-in-Publication Data
McMurtry, Larry.
  Dead man's walk : a novel / by Larry McMurtry.
    p.   cm.
  I. Title.
PS3563.A319D38   1995
813'.54—dc20   95-21011   CIP
ISBN 0-684-80753-X

For Sara Ossana
très belle
très claire
très fidèle

part

I

1.

MATILDA JANE ROBERTS WAS naked as the air. Known throughout south Texas as the Great Western, she came walking up from the muddy Rio Grande holding a big snapping turtle by the tail. Matilda was almost as large as the skinny little Mexican mustang Gus McCrae and Woodrow Call were trying to saddle-break. Call had the mare by the ears, waiting for Gus to pitch the saddle on her narrow back, but the pitch was slow in coming. When Call glanced toward the river and saw the Great Western in all her plump nakedness, he knew why: young Gus McCrae was by nature distractable; the sight of a naked, two-hundred-pound whore carrying a full-grown snapping turtle had captured his complete attention, and that of the rest of the Ranger troop as well.

"Look at that, Woodrow," Gus said. "Matty's carrying that old turtle as if it was a basket of peaches."

"I can't look," Call said. "I'll lose my grip and get kicked—and I've done been kicked." The mare, small though she was, had already displayed a willingness to kick and bite. Call knew that if he loosened his grip on her ears even slightly, he could count on getting kicked, or bitten, or both.

Long Bill Coleman, lounging against his saddle only a few yards from where the two young Rangers were struggling with the little mustang, watched Matilda approach, with a certain trepidation. Although it was only an hour past breakfast, he was already drunk. It seemed to Long Bill, in his tipsy state, that the Great Western was walking directly toward him with her angry catch. It might be that she meant to use the turtle as some kind of weapon—or so Long Bill surmised. Matilda Roberts despised debt, and carried grudges freely and at length. Bill knew himself to be considerably in arrears, the result of a persistent lust coupled with a vexing string of losses at cards. At the moment, he didn't have a red cent and knew that he was unlikely to have one for days, or even weeks to come. If Matilda, who was whimsical, chose to call his debt, his only recourse might be to run; but Long Bill was in no shape to run, and in any case, there was no place to run to that offered the least prospect of refuge. The Rangers were camped on the Rio Grande, west of the alkaline Pecos. They were almost three hundred miles from the nearest civilized habitation, and the country between them and a town was not inviting.

"When's the next payday, Major?" Long Bill inquired, glancing at his leader, Major Randall Chevallie.

"That woman acts like she might set that turtle on me," he added, hoping that Major Chevallie would want to issue an order or something. Bill knew that there were military men who refused to allow whores within a hundred feet of their camp—even whores not armed with snapping turtles.

Major Chevallie had only spent three weeks at West Point—he left because he found the classes boring and the discipline vexing. He nonetheless awarded himself the rank of major after a violent scrape in Baltimore convinced him that civilian life hemmed a man in with such a passel of legalities that it was no longer worth pursuing. Randall Chevallie hid on a ship, and the ship took him to Galveston; upon disembarking at that moist, sandy port, he declared himself a major and had been a major ever since.

Now, except for the two young Rangers who were attempting to saddle the Mexican mare, his whole troop was drunk, the result of an incautious foray into Mexican territory the day before. They had crossed the Rio Grande out of boredom, and promptly captured a donkey cart containing a few bushels of hard corn and two large jugs of mescal, a liquor of such potency that it immediately unmanned several of the Rangers. They had been without spirits for more than a month—they drank the mescal like water. In fact, it tasted a good deal better than any water they had tasted since crossing the Pecos.

The mescal wasn't water, though; two men went blind for awhile, and several others were troubled by visions of torture and dismemberment. Such visions, at the time, were not hard to conjure up, even without mescal, thanks to the folly of the unfortunate Mexican whose donkey cart they had captured. Though the Rangers meant the man no harm—or at least not much harm—he fled at the sight of gringos and was not even out of earshot before he fell into the hands of Comanches or Apaches: it was impossible to tell from his screams which tribe was torturing him. All that was known was that only three warriors took part in the torturing. Bigfoot Wallace, the renowned scout, returned from a lengthy look around and reported seeing the tracks of three warriors, no more. The tracks were heading toward the river.

Many Rangers thought Bigfoot's point somewhat picayune, since the Mexican could not have screamed louder if he had been being tortured by fifty men—the screams made sleep difficult, not to mention short. The Great Western didn't earn a cent all night. Only young Gus McCrae, whose appetite for fornication admitted no checks, approached Matilda, but of course young McCrae was penniless, and Matilda in no mood to offer credit.

"You better turn that mare loose for awhile," Gus advised. "Matty's coming with that big turtle—I don't know what she means to do with it."

"Can't turn loose," Call said, but then he did release the mare, jumping sideways just in time to avoid her flailing front hooves. It was clear to him that Gus had no intention of trying to saddle the mare, not anytime soon. When there was a naked whore to watch, Gus was unlikely to want to do much of anything, except watch the whore.

"Major, what about payday?" Long Bill inquired again.

Major Chevallie cocked an eyebrow at Long Bill Coleman, a man noted for his thorough laziness.

"Why, Bill, the mail's undependable, out here beyond the Pecos," the Major said. "We haven't seen a mail coach since we left San Antonio."

"That whore with the dern turtle wants to be paid now," one-eyed Johnny Carthage speculated.

"I've never seen a whore bold enough to snatch an old turtle right out of the Rio Grande river," Bob Bascom said. In his opinion, it had been quite unmilitary for the Major to allow Matilda Roberts to accompany them on their expedition; though how he would have stopped her, short of gunplay, was not easy to say. Matilda had simply fallen in with them when they left the settlements. She rode a large grey horse named Tom, who lost flesh rapidly once they were beyond the fertile valleys. Matilda had no fear of Indians, or of anything else, not so far as Bob Bascom was aware. She helped herself liberally to the Rangers' grub, and conducted business on a pallet she spread in the bushes, when there were bushes. Bob had to admit that having a whore along was a convenience, but he still considered it unmilitary, though he was not so incautious as to give voice to his opinion.

Major Randall Chevallie was of uncertain temper at best. Rumour had it that he had, on occasions, conducted summary executions, acting as his own firing squad. His pistol was often in his hand, and though his leadership was erratic, his aim wasn't. He had twice brought down running antelope with his pistol—most of the Rangers couldn't have hit a running antelope with a rifle, or even a Gatling gun.

"That whore didn't snatch that turtle out of the river," Long Bill commented. "I seen that turtle sleeping on a rock, when I went to wash the puke off myself. She just snuck up on it and picked it off that rock. Look at it snap at her. Now she's got it mad!"

The snapper swung its neck this way and that, working its jaws; but Matilda Roberts was holding it at arm's length, and its jaws merely snapped the air.

"What next?" Gus said, to Call.

"I don't know what next," Call said, a little irritated at his friend. Sooner or later they would have to have another try at saddling the mare—a chancy undertaking.

[16]

"Maybe she means to cook it," Call added.

"I have heard of slaves eating turtle," Gus said. "I believe they eat them in Mississippi."

"Well, I wouldn't eat one," Call informed him. "I'd still like to get a saddle on this mare, if you ain't too busy to help."

The mare was snubbed to a low mesquite tree—she wound herself tighter and tighter, as she kicked and struggled.

"Let's see what Matilda's up to first," Gus said. "We got all day to break horses."

"All right, but you'll have to take the ears, this time," Call said. "I'll do the saddling."

Matilda swung her arm a time or two and heaved the big turtle in the general direction of a bunch of Rangers—the boys were cleaning their guns and musing on their headaches. They scattered like quail when they saw the turtle sailing through the air. It turned over twice and landed on its back, not three feet from the campfire.

Bigfoot Wallace squatted by the fire—he had just finished pouring himself a cup of coffee. It was chickory coffee, but at least it was black. Bigfoot paid the turtle no attention at all—Matty Roberts had always been somewhat eccentric, in his view. If she wanted to throw snapping turtles around, that was her business. He himself was occupied with more urgent concerns, one of them being the identity of the three warriors who had tortured the Mexican to death. A few hours after coming across their tracks he had dozed off and dreamed a disturbing dream about Indians. In his dream Buffalo Hump was riding a spotted horse, while Gomez walked beside him. Buffalo Hump was the meanest Comanche anyone had ever heard of, and Gomez the meanest Apache. The fact that a Comanche killer and an Apache killer were traveling together, in his dream, was highly unpleasant. Never before, that he could remember, had he had a dream in which something so unlikely happened. He almost felt he should report the dream to Major Chevallie, but the Major, at the moment, was distracted by Matilda Roberts and her turtle.

"Good morning, Miss Roberts, is that your new pet?" the Major inquired, when Matilda walked up.

"Nope, that's breakfast—turtle beats bacon," Matilda said. "Has anybody got a shirt I can borrow? I left mine out by the pallet."

She had strolled down to the river naked because she felt like having a wash in the cold water. It wasn't deep enough to swim in, but she gave herself a good splashing. The old snapper just happened to be lazing on a rock nearby, so she grabbed it. Half the Rangers were scared of Matilda anyway, some so scared they would scarcely look at her, naked or clothed. The Major wasn't scared of her, nor was Bigfoot or young Gus; the rest of the men, in her view, were incompetents, the kind of men who were likely to run up debts and get killed before they could pay them. She sailed the snapper in their direction to let them know she expected honest behaviour. Going naked didn't hurt, either. She was big, and liked it; she could punch most men out, if she had to, and sometimes she had to; her dream was to get to California and own a fine bordello, which was why she fell in with the first Ranger troop going west. It was a scraggly little troop, composed mostly of drunks and shiftless ramblers, but she took it and was making the best of it. The alternative was to wait in Texas, get old, and never own a bordello in California.

At her request several Rangers immediately began to take off their shirts, but Bigfoot Wallace made no move to remove his, and his was the only shirt large enough to cover much of Matty Roberts.

"I guess you won't be sashaying around naked much longer, Matty," he observed, sipping his chickory.

"Why not? I ain't stingy about offering my customers a look," Matilda said, rejecting several of the proffered shirts.

Bigfoot nodded toward the north, where a dark tone on the horizon contrasted with the bright sunlight.

"One of our fine blue northers is about to whistle in," he informed her. "You'll have icicles hanging off your twat, in another hour, if you don't cover it up."

"I wouldn't need to cover it up if anyone around here was prosperous enough to warm it up," Matilda said, but she did note that the northern horizon had turned a dark blue. Several Rangers observed the same fact, and began to pull on long johns or other garments that might be of use against a norther. Bigfoot Wallace was known to have an excellent eye for weather. Even Matilda respected it—she strolled over to her pallet and pulled on a pair of blacksmith's overalls that she had taken in payment for a brief engagement in Fredericksburg. She had a tattered capote, acquired some years earlier in Pennsylvania, and she put that on too. A blue norther could quickly suck the warmth out of the air, even on a nice sunny day.

"Well, we've conquered a turtle, I guess," Major Chevallie said, standing up. "I suppose that Mexican died—I don't hear much noise from across the river."

"If he's lucky, he died," Bigfoot said. "It was just three Indians—Comanches, I'd figure. I doubt three Comanches would pause more than one night to cut up a Mexican."

About that time Josh Corn and Ezekiel Moody came walking back to camp from the sandhill where they had been standing guard. Josh Corn was a little man, only about half the size of his tall friend. Both were surprised to see a sizable snapping turtle kicking its legs in the air, not much more than arm's length from the coffeepot.

"Why's everybody dressing up, is there going to be a parade?" Josh asked, noting that several Rangers were in the process of pulling on clothes.

"That Mexican didn't have no way to kill himself," Bob Bascom remarked. "He didn't have no gun."

"No, but he had a knife," Bigfoot reminded him. "A knife's adequate, if you know where to cut."

"Where would you cut—I've wondered," Gus asked, abruptly leaving Call to contemplate the Mexican mustang alone. He was a Ranger on the wild frontier now and needed to imbibe as much technical information as possible about methods of suicide, when in danger of capture by hostiles with a penchant for torture.

"No Comanche's going to be quick enough to sew up your jugular vein, if you whack it through in two or three places," Bigfoot said. Aware that several of the Rangers were inexpert in such matters, he stretched his long neck and put his finger on the spot where the whacking should be done.

"It's right here," he said. "You could even poke into it with a big mesquite thorn, or whack at it with a broken bottle, if you're left without no knife."

Long Bill Coleman felt a little queasy, partly because of the mescal and partly from the thought of having to stick a thorn in his neck in order to avoid Comanche torture.

[19]

"Me, I'll shoot myself in the head if I've got time," Long Bill said.

"Well, but that can go wrong," Bigfoot informed him. Once set in an instructional direction, he didn't like to turn until he had given a thorough lecture. Bigfoot considered himself to be practical to a fault—if a man had to kill himself in a hurry, it was best to know exactly how to proceed.

"Don't go sticking no gun in your mouth, unless it's a shotgun," he advised, noting that Long Bill looked a little green. Probably the alkaline water didn't agree with him.

"Why not, it's hard to miss your head if you've got a gun in your mouth," Ezekiel Moody commented.

"No, it ain't," Bigfoot said. "The bullet could glance off a bone and come out your ear. You'd still be healthy enough that they could torture you for a week. Shove the barrel of the gun up against an eyeball and pull—that's sure. Your brains will get blown out the back of your head—then if some squaw comes along and chews off your balls and your pecker, you won't know the difference."

"My, this is a cheery conversation," Major Chevallie said. "I wish Matilda would come back and remove this turtle."

"I'd like to go back and have another look at them tracks," Bigfoot said. "It was about dark when I seen them. Another look couldn't hurt."

"It could hurt if the Comanches that got that Mexican caught you," Josh Corn remarked.

"Why, those boys are halfway to the Brazos, by now," Bigfoot said, just as Matilda returned to the campfire. She squatted down by the turtle and watched it wiggle, a happy expression on her broad face. She had a hatchet in one hand and a small bowie knife in the other.

"Them turtles don't turn loose of you till it thunders, once they got aholt of you," Ezekiel said. Matilda Roberts ignored this hackneyed opinion. She caught the turtle right by the head, held its jaws shut, and slashed at its neck with the little bowie knife. The whole company watched, even Call. Several of the men had traveled the Western frontier all their lives. They considered themselves to be experienced men, but none of them had ever seen a whore decapitate a snapping turtle before.

Blackie Slidell watched Matilda slash at the turtle's neck with a glazed expression. The mescal had caused him to lose his vision entirely, for several hours—in fact, it was still somewhat wobbly. Blackie had an unusual birthmark—his right ear was coal black, thus his name. Although he couldn't see very well, Blackie was not a little disturbed by Bigfoot's chance remark about the chewing propensities of Comanche squaws. He had long heard of such things, of course, but had considered them to be unfounded rumour. Bigfoot Wallace, though, was *the* authority on Indian customs. His comment could not be ignored, even if everybody else was watching Matilda cut the head off her turtle.

"Hell, if we see Indians, let's kill all the squaws," Blackie said, indignantly. "They got no call to be behaving like that."

"Oh, there's worse than that happens," Bigfoot remarked casually, noting that the turtle's blood seemed to be green—if it *had* blood. A kind of green ooze dripped out of the wound Matilda had made. She herself was finding the turtle's neck a difficult cut. She gave the turtle's head two or three twists, hoping it would snap off like a chicken's would have, but the turtle's neck merely kinked, like a thick black rope.

"What's worse than having your pecker chewed off?" Blackie inquired.

"Oh, having them pull out the end of your gut and tie it to a dog," Bigfoot said, pouring himself more chickory. "Then they chase the dog around camp for awhile, until about fifty feet of your gut is strung out in front of you, for brats to eat."

"To eat?" Long Bill asked.

"Why yes," Bigfoot said. "Comanche brats eat gut like ours eat candy."

"Whew, I'm glad I wasn't especially hungry this morning," Major Chevallie commented. "Talk like this would unsettle a delicate stomach."

"Or they might run a stick up your fundament and set it on fire —that way your guts would done be cooked when they pull them out," Bigfoot explained.

"What's a fundament?" Call asked. He had had only one year of schooling, and had not encountered the word in his speller. He kept the speller with him in his saddlebag, and referred to it now and then when in doubt about a letter or a word.

Bob Bascom snorted, amused by the youngster's ignorance.

"It's a hole in your body and it ain't your nose or your mouth or your goddamn ear," Bob said. "I'd have that little mare broke by now, if it was me doing it."

Call smarted at the rebuke—he knew they had been lax with the mare, who had now effectively snubbed herself to the little tree. She was trembling, but she couldn't move far, so he quickly swung the saddle in place and held it there while she crow-hopped a time or two.

Matilda Roberts sweated over her task, but she didn't give up. The first gusts of the norther scattered the ashes of the campfire. Major Chevallie had just squatted to refill his cup—his coffee soon had a goodly sprinkling of sand. When the turtle's head finally came off, Matilda casually pitched it in the direction of Long Bill, who jumped up as if she'd thrown him a live rattler.

The turtle's angry eyes were still open, and its jaws continued to snap with a sharp click.

"It ain't even dead with its head off," Long Bill said, annoyed.

Shadrach, the oldest Ranger, a tall, grizzled specimen with a cloudy past, walked over to the turtle's head and squatted down to study it. Shadrach rarely spoke, but he was by far the most accurate rifle shot in the troop. He owned a fine Kentucky rifle, with a cherry-wood stock, and was contemptuous of the bulky carbines most of the troop had adopted.

Shadrach found a little mesquite stick and held it in front of the turtle's head. The turtle's beak immediately snapped onto the stick, but the stick didn't break. Shadrach picked up the little stick with the turtle's head attached to it and dropped it in the pocket of his old black coat.

Josh Corn was astonished.

"Why would you keep a thing like that?" he asked Shadrach, but the old man took no interest in the question.

"Why would he keep a smelly old turtle's head?" Josh asked Bigfoot Wallace.

"Why would Gomez raid with Buffalo Hump?" Bigfoot asked. "That's a better question."

Matilda, by this time, had hacked through the turtle shell with her hatchet and was cutting the turtle meat into strips. Watching her slice the green meat caused Long Bill Coleman to get the queasy feeling again. Young Call, though nicked by a rear hoof, had succeeded in cinching the saddle onto the Mexican mare.

Major Chevallie was sipping his ashy coffee. Already the new wind from the north had begun to cut. He hadn't been paying much attention to the half-drunken campfire palaver, but between one sip of coffee and the next, Bigfoot's question brought him out of his reverie.

"What did you say about Buffalo Hump?" he asked. "I wouldn't suppose that scoundrel is anywhere around."

"Well, he might be," Bigfoot said.

"But what was that you said, just now?" the Major asked. "It's hard to concentrate, with Matilda cutting up this ugly turtle."

"I had a dern dream," Bigfoot admitted. "In my dream Gomez was raiding with Buffalo Hump."

"Nonsense, Gomez is Apache," the Major said.

Bigfoot didn't answer. He knew that Gomez was Apache, and that Apache didn't ride with Comanche—that was not the normal order of things. Still, he had dreamed what he dreamed. If Major Chevallie didn't enjoy hearing about it, he could sip his coffee and keep quiet.

The whole troop fell silent for a moment. Just hearing the names of the two terrible warriors was enough to make the Rangers reflect on the uncertainties of their calling, which were considerable.

"I don't like that part about the guts," Long Bill said. "I aim to keep my own guts inside me, if nobody minds."

Shadrach was saddling his horse—he felt free to leave the troop at will, and his absences were apt to last a day or two.

"Shad, are you leaving?" Bigfoot asked.

"We're all leaving," Shadrach said. "There's Indians to the north. I smell 'em."

"I thought I still gave the orders around here," Major Chevallie said. "I don't know why you would have such a dream, Wallace. Why would those two devils raid together?"

"I've dreamt prophecy before," Bigfoot said. "Shad's right about the Indians. I smell 'em too."

"What's this—where are they?" Major Chevallie asked, just as the norther hit with its full force. There was a general scramble for guns and cover. Long Bill Coleman found the anxiety too much for his overburdened stomach. He grabbed his rifle, but then had to bend and puke before he could seek cover.

The cold wind swirled white dust through the camp. Most of the Rangers had taken cover behind little hummocks of sand, or chaparral bushes. Only Matilda was unaffected; she continued to lay strips of greenish turtle meat onto the campfire. The first cuts were already dripping and crackling.

Old Shadrach mounted and went galloping north, his long rifle across his saddle. Bigfoot Wallace grabbed a rifle and vanished into the sage.

"What do we do with this mare, Gus?" Call asked. He had only been a Ranger six weeks—his one problem with the work was that it was almost impossible to get precise instructions in a time of crisis. Now he finally had the Mexican mare saddled, but everyone in camp was lying behind sandhills with their rifles ready. Even Gus had grabbed his old gun and taken cover.

Major Chevallie was attempting to unhobble his horse, but he had no dexterity and was making a slow job of it.

"You boys, come help me!" he yelled—from the precipitate behaviour of Shadrach and Bigfoot, the most experienced men in the troop, he assumed that the camp was in danger of being overrun.

Gus and Call ran to the Major's aid. The wind was so cold that Gus even thought it prudent to button the top button of his flannel shirt.

"Goddamn this wind!" the Major said. During breakfast he had been rereading a letter from his dear wife, Jane. He had read the letter at least twenty times, but it was the only letter he had with him and he did love his winsome Jane. When the business about Gomez and Buffalo Hump came up he had casually stuffed the letter in his coat pocket, but he didn't get it in securely, and now the whistling wind had snatched it. It was a long.letter—his dear Jane was lavish with detail of circumstances back in Virginia—and now several pages of it were blowing away, in the general direction of Mexico.

"Here, boys, fetch my letter!" the Major said. "I can't afford to lose my letter. I'll finish saddling this horse."

Call and Gus left the Major to finish cinching his saddle on his big sorrel and began to chase the letter, some of which had sailed quite a distance downwind. Both of them kept looking over their shoulders, expecting to see the Indians charging.

Call had not had time to fetch his rifle—his only weapon was a pistol.

Thanks to his efforts with the mare, the talk of torture and suicide had been hard to follow. Call liked to do things correctly, but was in doubt as to the correct way to dispatch himself, should he suddenly be surrounded by Comanches.

"What was it Bigfoot said about shooting out your brains?" he asked Gus, his lanky pal.

Gus had run down four pages of the Major's lengthy letter. Call had three pages. Gus didn't seem to be particularly concerned about the prospect of Comanche capture—his nonchalant approach to life could be irksome in times of conflict.

"I'd go help Matty clean her turtle if I thought she'd give me a poke," Gus said.

"Gus, there's Indians coming," Call said. "Just tell me what Bigfoot said about shooting out your brains.

"That whore don't need no help with that turtle," he added.

"Oh, you're supposed to shoot through the eyeball," Gus said. "I'll be damned if I would, though. I need both eyes to look at whores."

"I should have kept my rifle handier," Call said, annoyed with himself for having neglected sound procedure. "Do you see any Indians yet?"

"No, but I see Josh Corn taking a shit," Gus said, pointing at their friend Josh. He was squatting behind a sage bush, rifle at the ready, while he did his business.

"I guess he must think it's his last chance before he gets scalped," Gus added.

Major Chevallie jumped on his sorrel and started to race after Shadrach, but had scarcely cleared the camp before he reined in his horse. Call could just see him, in the swirling dust—the plain to the north of the camp had become a wall of sand.

"I wonder how we can get some money—I sure do need a poke," Gus said. He had turned his back to the wind and was casually reading the Major's letter, an action that shocked Call.

"That's the Major's letter," he pointed out. "You got no business reading it."

"Well, it don't say much anyway," Gus said, handing the pages to Call. "I thought it might be racy, but it ain't."

"If I ever write a letter, I don't want to catch you reading it," Call said. "I think Shad's coming back." His eyes were stinging, from staring into the dust.

There seemed to be figures approaching camp from the north. Call couldn't make them out clearly, and Gus didn't seem to be particularly interested. Once he began to think about whores he had a hard time pulling his mind off the subject.

"If we could catch a Mexican we could steal his money—he might have enough that we could buy quite a few pokes," Gus said, as they strolled back to camp.

Major Chevallie waited on his sorrel, watching. Two figures seemed to be walking. Then Bigfoot fell in with them. Shadrach appeared on his horse, a few steps behind the figures.

All around the camp Rangers began to stand up and dust the sand off their clothes. Matilda, unaffected by the crisis, was still cooking her turtle. The bloody shell lay by the campfire. Call smelled the sizzling meat and realized he was hungry.

"Why, it's just an old woman and a boy," he said when he finally got a clear view of the two figures trudging through the sandstorm, flanked on one side by Shadrach and on the other by Bigfoot Wallace.

"Shoot, I doubt either one of them has got a cent on them," Gus said. "I think we ought to sneak off across the river and catch a Mexican while it's still early."

"Just wait," Call said. He was anxious to see the captives, if they were captives.

"I swear," Long Bill said. "I think that old woman's blind. That boy's leading her."

Long Bill was right. A boy of about ten, who looked more Mexican than Indian, walked slowly toward the campfire, leading an old white-haired Indian woman—Call had never seen anyone who looked as old as the old woman.

When they came close enough to the fire to smell the sizzling meat, the boy began to make a strange sound. It wasn't speech, exactly—it was more like a moan.

"What's he wanting?" Matilda asked—she was unnerved by the sound.

[26]

"Why, a slice or two of your turtle meat, I expect," Bigfoot said. "More than likely he's hungry."

"Then why don't he ask?" Matilda said.

"He can't ask, Matilda," Bigfoot said.

"Why not, ain't he got a tongue?" Matilda asked.

"Nope—no tongue," Bigfoot said. "Somebody cut it out."

2.

THE NORTH WIND BLEW harder, hurling the sands and soils of the great plain of Texas toward Mexico. It soon obliterated vision. Shadrach and Major Chevallie, mounted, could not see the ground. Men could not see across the campfire. Call found his rifle, but when he tried to sight, discovered that he could not see to the end of the barrel. The sand peppered them like fine shot, and it rode a cold wind. The horses could only turn their backs to it; so did the men. Most put their saddles over their heads, and their saddle blankets too. Matilda's bloody turtle shell soon filled with sand. The campfire was almost smothered. Men formed a human wall to the north of it, to keep it from guttering out. Bigfoot and Shadrach tied bandanas around their faces—Long Bill had a bandana but it blew away and was never found. Matilda gave up cooking and sat with her back to the wind, her head bent between her knees. The boy with no tongue reached into the guttering campfire and took two slices of the sizzling turtle meat. One he gave to the old blind woman—although the meat was tough and scalding, he gulped his portion in only three bites.

Kirker and Glanton, the scalp hunters, sat together with their backs to the wind. They stared through the fog of sand, appraising the boy and the old woman. Kirker took out his scalping knife and a small whetstone. He tried to spit on the whetstone, but the wind took the spit away; Kirker began to sharpen the knife anyway. The old woman turned her sightless eyes toward the sound—she spoke to the boy, in a language Call had never heard. But the boy had no tongue, and couldn't answer.

Even through the howling of the wind, Call could hear the grinding sound, as Kirker whetted his scalping knife. Gus heard it too, but his mind had not moved very far from his favorite subject, whores.

"Be hard to poke in a wind like this," he surmised. "Your whore would fill up with sand—unless you went careful, you'd scrape yourself raw."

Call ignored this comment, thinking it foolish.

"Kirker and Glanton ain't Rangers—I don't know why the Major lets 'em ride with the troop," he said.

"It's a free country, how could he stop them?" Gus asked, though he had to admit that the scalp hunters were unsavory company. Their gear smelled of blood, and they never washed. Gus agreed with Matilda that it was good to keep clean. He splashed himself regularly, if there was water available.

"He could shoot 'em—I'd shoot 'em, if I was in command," Call said. "They're low killers, in my opinion."

Only the day before there had nearly been a ruckus with Kirker and Glanton. The two came riding in from the south, having taken eight scalps. The scalps hung from Kirker's saddle. A buzzing cloud of flies surrounded them, although the blood on the scalps had dried. Most of the Rangers gave Kirker a wide berth; he was a thin man with three gappy teeth, which gave his smile a cruel twist. Glanton was larger and lazier—he slept more than anyone else in the troop and would even fall asleep and start snoring while mounted on his horse. Shadrach had no fear of either man, and neither did Bigfoot Wallace. When Kirker dismounted, Shadrach and Bigfoot walked over to examine his trophies. Shadrach fingered

[29]

one of the scalps and looked at Bigfoot, who swatted the cloud of flies away briefly and sniffed a time or two at the hair.

"Comanche—who said you could smell 'em?" Kirker asked. He was chewing on some antelope jerky that black Sam, the cook, had provided. The sight of the old mountain man and the big scout handling his new trophies annoyed him.

"We picked all eight of them off, at a waterhole," Glanton said. "I shot four and so did John."

"That's a pure lie," Bigfoot said. "Eight Comanches could string you and Kirker out from here to Santa Fe. If you was ever unlucky enough to run into that many at once, we wouldn't be having to smell your damn stink anymore."

He waved at Major Chevallie, who strolled over, looking uncomfortable. He drew his pistol, a precaution the Major always took when he sensed controversy. With his pistol drawn, decisive judgment could be reached and reached quickly.

"These low dogs have been killing Mexicans, Major," Bigfoot said. "They probably took supper with some little family and then shot 'em all and took their hair."

"That would be unneighborly behaviour, if true," Major Chevallie said. He looked at the scalps, but didn't touch them.

"This ain't Indian hair," Shadrach said. "Indian hair smells Indian, but this don't. This hair is Mexican."

"It's Comanche hair and you can both go to hell," Kirker said. "If you need a ticket I can provide it."

The gap-toothed Kirker carried three pistols and a knife, and usually kept his rifle in the crook of his arm, where it was now.

"Sit down, Kirker, I'll not have you roughhousing with my scouts," the Major said.

"Roughhousing, hell," Kirker said. He flushed red when he was angry, and a blue vein popped out alongside his nose.

"I'll finish them right here, if they don't leave my scalps alone," he added. Glanton had his eyes only half open, but his hand was on his pistol, a fact both Bigfoot and Shadrach ignored.

"There's no grease, Major," Bigfoot said. "Indians grease their hair—take a Comanche scalp and you'll have grease up to your elbow. Kirker ain't even sly. He could have greased this hair if he wanted to fool us, but he didn't. I expect he was too lazy."

[30]

"Get away from them scalps—they're government property now," Kirker said. "I took 'em and I intend to collect my bounty."

Shadrach looked at the Major—he didn't believe the Major was firm, although it was undeniable that he was an accurate shot.

"If a Mexican posse shows up, let 'em have these two," he advised. "This ain't Indian hair, and what's more, it ain't grown-up hair. These two went over to Mexico and killed a passel of children."

Kirker merely sneered.

"Hair's hair," he said. "This is government property now, and you're welcome to keep your goddamn hands off it."

Call and Gus waited, expecting the Major to shoot Kirker, and possibly Glanton too, but the Major didn't shoot. Bigfoot and Shadrach walked away, disgusted. Shadrach mounted, crossed the river, and was gone for several hours. Kirker kept on chewing his antelope jerky, and Glanton went sound asleep, leaning against his horse.

Major Chevallie did look at Kirker hard. He knew he ought to shoot the two men and leave them to the flies. Shadrach's opinion was no doubt accurate: the men had been killing Mexican children; Mexican children were a lot easier to hunt than Comanches.

But the Major didn't shoot. His troop was in an uncertain position, vulnerable to attack at any minute, and Kirker and Glanton made two more fighting men, adding two guns to the company's meager strength. If there was a serious scrape, one or both of them might be killed anyway. If not, they could always be executed at a later date.

"Stay this side of the river from now on," the Major said—he still had his pistol in his hand. "If either of you cross it again, I'll hunt you down like dogs."

Kirker didn't flinch.

"We ain't dogs, though—we're wolves—at least I am. You won't be catching me, if I go. As for Glanton, you can have him. I'm tired of listening to his goddamn snores."

Gus soon forgot the incident, but Call didn't. He listened to Kirker sharpen his knife and wished he had the authority to kill the man himself. In his view Kirker was a snake, and worse than a snake. If you discovered a snake in your bedclothes, the sensible thing would be to kill it.

Major Chevallie had looked right at the snake, but hadn't killed it.

[31]

The sandstorm blew for another hour, until the camp and everything in it was covered with sand. When it finally blew out, men discovered that they couldn't find utensils they had carelessly laid down before the storm began. The sky overhead was a cold blue. The plain in all directions was level with sand; only the tops of sage bushes and chaparral broke the surface. The Rio Grande was murky and brown. The little mare, still snubbed to the tree, was in sand up to her knees. All the men stripped naked in order to shake as much sand as possible out of their clothes; but more sand filtered in, out of their hair and off their collars. Gus brushed the branch of a mesquite tree and a shower of sand rained down on him.

Only the old Indian woman and the boy with no tongue made no attempt to rid themselves of sand. The fire had finally been smothered, but the old woman and the boy still sat by it, sand banked against their backs. To Call they hardly seemed human. They were like part of the ground.

Gus, in high spirits, decided to be a bronc rider after all. He took it into his head to ride the Mexican mare.

"I expect that storm's got her cowed," he said, to Call.

"Gus, she ain't cowed," Call replied. He had the mare by the ears again, and detected no change in her attitude.

Sure enough, the mare threw Gus on the second jump. Several of the naked Rangers laughed, and went on shaking out their clothes.

3.

IN THE EARLY AFTERNOON, still carrying more sand in his clothes than he would have liked, Major Chevallie attempted to question the old woman and the boy. He gave them coffee and fed them a little hardtack first, hoping it would make them talkative—but the feast, such as it was, failed in its purpose, mainly because no one in the troop spoke any Comanche.

The Major had supposed Bigfoot Wallace to be adept in the tongue, but Bigfoot firmly denied any knowledge of it.

"Why no, Major," Bigfoot said. "I've made it a practice to stay as far from the Comanche as I can get," Bigfoot said. "What few I ever met face-on I shot. Some others have shot at me, but we never stopped to palaver."

The old woman wore a single bear tooth on a rawhide cord around her neck. The tooth was the size of a small pocketknife. Several of the men looked at it with envy; most of them would have been happy to own a bear tooth that large.

"She must have been a chief's woman," Long Bill speculated.

"Otherwise why would a squaw get to keep a fine grizzly tooth like that?"

Matilda Roberts knew five or six words of Comanche and tried them all on the old woman, without result. The old woman sat where she had settled when she walked into the camp, backed by a hummock of sand. Her rheumy eyes were focused on the campfire, or on what had been the campfire.

The tongueless boy, still hungry, dug most of the sandy turtle meat out of the ashes of the campfire and ate it. No one contested him, although Matilda dusted the sand off a piece or two and gnawed at the meat herself. The boy perked up considerably, once he had eaten the better part of Matilda's snapping turtle. He did his best to talk, but all that came out were moans and gurgles. Several of the men tried to talk to him in sign, but got nowhere.

"Goddamn Shadrach, where did he go?" the Major asked. "We've got a Comanche captive here, and the only man we have who speaks Comanche leaves."

As the day wore on, Gus and Call took turns getting pitched off the mare. Call once managed to stay on her five hops, which was the best either of them achieved. The Rangers soon lost interest in watching the boys get pitched around. A few got up a card game. Several others took a little target practice, using cactus apples as targets. Bigfoot Wallace pared his toenails, several of which had turned coal black as the result of his having worn footgear too small for his feet—it was that or go barefooted, and in the thorny country they were in, bare feet would have been a handicap.

Toward sundown Call and Gus were assigned first watch. They took their position behind a good clump of chaparral, a quarter of a mile north of the camp. Major Chevallie had been making another attempt to converse with the old Comanche woman, as they were leaving camp. He tried sign, but the old woman looked at him, absent, indifferent.

"Shadrach just rode off and he ain't rode back," Call said. "I feel better when Shadrach's around."

"I'd feel better if there were more whores," Gus commented. In the afternoon he had made another approach to Matilda Roberts, only to be rebuffed.

"I should have stayed on the riverboats," he added. "I never lacked for whores, on the riverboats."

Call was watching the north. He wondered if it was really true that Shadrach and Bigfoot could smell Indians. Of course if you got close to an Indian, or to anybody, you could smell them. There were times on sweaty days when he could easily smell Gus, or any other Ranger who happened to be close by. Black Sam, the cook, had a fairly strong smell, and so did Ezekiel—the latter had not bothered to wash the whole time Call had known him.

But dirt and sweat weren't what Bigfoot and Shadrach had been talking about, when they said they smelled Indians. The old woman and the boy had been nearly a mile away, when they claimed to smell them. Surely not even the best scout could smell a person that far away.

"There could have been more Indians out there, when Shad said he smelled them," Call speculated. "There could be a passel out there, just waiting."

Gus McCrae took guard duty a good deal more lightly than his companion, Woodrow Call. He looked at his time on guard as a welcome escape from the chores that cropped up around camp—gathering firewood, for example, or chopping it, or saddle-soaping the Major's saddle. Since he and Woodrow were the youngest Rangers in the troop, they were naturally expected to do most of the chores. Several times they had even been required to shoe horses, although Black Sam, the cook, was also a more than adequate blacksmith.

Gus found such tasks irksome—he believed he had been put on earth to enjoy himself, and there was no enjoyment to be derived from shoeing horses. Horses were heavy animals—most of the ones he shoed had a tendency to lean on him, once he picked up a foot.

Drinking mescal was far more to his liking—in fact he had a few swallows left, in a small jug he had managed to appropriate. He had kept the jug buried in the sand all day, lest some thirsty Ranger discover it and drain the mescal. He owned a woolen serape, purchased in a stall in San Antonio, and had managed to sneak the jug out of camp under the serape.

When he brought it out and took a swig, Call looked annoyed.

"If the Major caught you drinking on guard he'd shoot you," Call said. It was true, too. The Major tolerated many foibles in his troop, but he did demand sobriety of the men assigned to keep guard. They were camped not far from the great Comanche war trail—the merciless raiders from the north could appear at any moment. Even momentary inattention on the part of the guards could imperil the whole troop.

"Well, but how could he catch me?" Gus asked. "He's trying to talk to that old woman—he'd have to sneak up on us to catch me, and I'd have to be drunker than this not to notice a fat man sneaking up."

It was certainly true that Major Chevallie was fat. He outweighed Matilda by a good fifty pounds, and Matilda was not small. The Major was short, too, which made his girth all the more noticeable. Still, he was the Major. Just because he hadn't shot the scalp hunters didn't mean he wouldn't shoot Gus.

"I don't believe you was ever on a riverboat—why would they hire you?" Call asked. At times of irritation he began to remember all the lies Gus had told him. Gus McCrae had no more regard for truth than he did for the rules of rangering.

"Why, of course I was," Gus said. "I was a top pilot for a dern year—I'm a Tennessee boy. I can run one of them riverboats as well as the next man. I only run aground once, in all the time I worked."

The truth of that was that he had once sneaked aboard a riverboat for two days; when he was discovered, he was put off on a mud bar, near Dubuque. A young whore had hidden him for the two days— the captain had roundly chastised her when Gus was discovered. Shortly after he was put off, the riverboat ran aground—that was the one true fact in the story. The tale sounded grand to his green friend, though. Woodrow Call had got no farther in the world than his uncle's scratchy farm near Navasota. Woodrow's parents had been taken by the smallpox, which is why he was raised by the uncle, a tyrant who stropped him so hard that when Woodrow got old enough to follow the road to San Antonio, he ran off. It was in San Antonio that the two of them had met—or rather, that Call had found Gus asleep against the wall of a saloon, near the river. Call worked for a Mexican blacksmith at the time, stirring the forge and helping the old smith with the horseshoeing that went on from dawn till dark. The Mexican, Jesus, a kindly old man who hummed sad harmonies all day as he worked, allowed Call to sleep on a pallet of nail sacks in a small shed behind the forge. Blacksmithing was dirty work. Call had been on his way to the river to wash off some of the smudge from his work when he noticed a lanky youth, sound asleep against the wall of the little adobe saloon. At first he thought the stranger might be dead, so profound were his slumbers. Killings were not uncommon in the streets of San Antonio—Call thought he ought to stop and check, since if the boy was dead it would have to be reported.

It turned out, though, that Gus was merely so fatigued that he was beyond caring whether he was counted among the living or among the dead. He had traveled in a tight stagecoach for ten days and nine nights, making the trip from Baton Rouge through the pines of east Texas to San Antonio. Upon arrival, his fellow passengers decided that Gus had been with them long enough; he was in such a stupor of fatigue that he offered no resistance when they rolled him out. He could not remember how long he had been sleeping against the saloon; it was his impression that he had slept about a week. That night Call let Gus share his pallet of nail sacks, and the two had been friends ever since. It was Gus who decided they should apply for the Texas Rangers—Call would never have thought himself worthy of such a position. It was Gus, too, who boldly approached the Major when word got out that a troop was being formed whose purpose—other than hanging whatever horse thieves or killers turned up—was to explore a stage route to El Paso. Fortunately, Major Chevallie had not been hard to convince—he took one look at the two healthy-looking boys and hired them at the princely sum of three dollars a month. They would be furnished with mounts, blankets, and a rifle apiece. Departure was immediate; saddles proved to be the main problem. Neither Gus nor Call had a saddle, or a pistol either. Finally the Major intervened on their behalf with an old German who owned a hardware store and saddle shop, the back of which was piled with single-tree saddles in bad repair and guns of every description, most of which didn't work. Finally two pistols were extracted that looked as if they might shoot if primed a little; and also two single-tree rigs with tattered leather that the German agreed to part with for a dollar apiece, pistols thrown in.

Major Chevallie advanced the two dollars, and the next morning at dawn, he, Call, Gus, Shadrach, Bob Bascom, Long Bill Coleman, Ezekiel Moody, Josh Corn, one-eyed Johnny Carthage, Blackie Slidell, Rip Green, and Black Sam, leading his kitchen mule, trotted out of San Antonio. Call had never been so happy in his life—overnight he had become a Texas Ranger, the grandest thing anyone could possibly be.

Gus, though, was irritated at the lack of ceremony attending their departure. A scabby dog barked a few times, but no inhabitants lined the streets to cheer them on. Gus thought there should at least have been a bugler.

"I'd blow a bugle myself, if one was available," he said.

Call thought the remark wrongheaded. Even if they had a bugle, and if Gus could blow it, who would listen to it, except a few Mexicans and a donkey or two? It was enough that they were Rangers—two days before they had simply been homeless boys.

Bigfoot Wallace, the scout, didn't catch up until the next day—at the time of their departure he had been in jail. Apparently he had thrown a deputy sheriff out the second-floor window of the community's grandest whorehouse. The deputy suffered a broken collarbone, an annoyance sufficient to cause the sheriff to jail Bigfoot for a week.

Gus McCrae, a newcomer to Texas, had never heard of Bigfoot Wallace and saw no reason to be awed. Throwing a deputy sheriff out a window did not seem to him to be a particularly impressive feat.

"Now, if he'd thrown the governor out, that would have been a fine thing," Gus said.

Call thought his friend's comment absurd. Why would the governor be in a whorehouse, anyway? Bigfoot Wallace was the most respected scout on the Texas frontier; even in Navasota, far to the east, Bigfoot's name was known and his exploits talked about.

"They say he's been all the way to China," Call explained. "He knows every creek in Texas, and whether it's boggy or not, and he's a first-rate Indian killer besides."

"Myself, I'd rather know every whore," Gus said. "You can have a lot more fun with whores than you can with governors."

Call had seen several whores on the street, but had never visited one. Although he had the inclination, he had never had the money. Gus McCrae, though, seemed to have spent his life in the company of whores—though he had once mentioned that he had a mother and three sisters back in Tennessee, he preferred to talk mainly about whores, often to the point of tedium.

Call, though, had the greatest respect for Bigfoot Wallace; he intended to study the man and learn as many of his wilderness skills as possible. Though most of the older Rangers were well versed in woodcraft, Bigfoot and Shadrach were clearly the two masters. If the company came to a fork in a creek or river while the scouts were ranging ahead, the company waited until one of them showed up and told it which fork to take. Major Chevallie had never been west of San Antonio—once they left the settlements behind and started toward the Pecos, he allowed his accomplished scouts to choose a route.

It was Shadrach who took them south, into the lonely country of sage and sand, where the two boys were now crouched behind their chaparral bush. In San Antonio there had been talk that war with Mexico was brewing—early on, the Major had instructed the troop to fire on any Mexican who seemed hostile.

"Better to be safe than sorry," he said, and many heads nodded.

In fact, though, the only Mexican they had seen was the unfortunate driver of the donkey cart. In the western reaches, no one was quite certain where Mexico stopped and Texas began. The Rio Grande made a handy border, but neither Major Chevallie nor anyone else considered it to be particularly official.

Mexicans, hostile or otherwise, didn't occupy much of the troop's attention, almost all of which was reserved for the Comanches. Call had yet to see a Comanche Indian, though throughout the trek, Long Bill, Rip Green, and other Rangers had assured him that the Comanches were sure to show up in the next hour or two, bent on scalping and torture.

"I wonder how big Comanches are?" he asked Gus, as they peered north into the silent darkness.

"About the size of Matilda, I've heard," Gus said.

"That old woman ain't the size of Matilda," Call pointed out. "She's no taller than Rip."

Rip Green was the smallest Ranger, standing scarcely five feet high. He also lacked a thumb on his right hand, having shot it off himself while cleaning a pistol he had neglected to unload.

"Yes, but she's old, Woodrow," Gus said. "I expect she's shriveled up."

He had just consumed the last of his mescal, and was feeling gloomy at the thought of a long watch with no liquor. At least he had a serape, though. Call had no coat—he intended to purchase one with his first wages. He owned two shirts, and wore them both on frosty mornings, when the thorns of the chaparral bushes were rimmed with white.

Just then a wolf howled far to the north, where they were looking. Another wolf joined the first one. Then, nearer by, there was the yip of a coyote.

"They say an Indian can imitate any sound," Gus remarked. "They can fool you into thinking they're a wolf or a coyote or an owl or a cricket."

"I doubt a Comanche would pretend to be a cricket," Call said.

"Well, a locust then," Gus said. "Locusts buzz. You get a bunch of them buzzing and it's hard to hear."

Again they heard the wolf, and again, the coyote.

"It's Indians talking," Gus said. "They're talking in animal."

"We don't know, though," Call said. "I seen a wolf just yesterday. There's plenty of coyotes, too. It could just be animals."

"No, it ain't, it's Comanches," Gus said, standing up. "Let's go shoot one. I expect if we killed three or four the Major would raise our wages."

Call thought it was bold thinking. They were already a good distance from camp—the campfire was only a faint flicker behind them. Clouds had begun to come in, hiding the stars. Suppose they went farther and got caught? All the tortures Bigfoot had described might be visited on them. Besides, their orders were to stand watch, not to go Indian hunting.

"I ain't going," Call said. "That ain't what we were supposed to do."

"I doubt that fat fool is a real major, anyway," Gus said. He was restless. Sitting half the night by a bush did not appeal to him much. It was undoubtedly a long way to a whorehouse from where they sat, but at least there might be Indians to fight. Better a fight than nothing; with no more mescal to drink, his prospects were meager.

Call, though, had not responded to the call of adventure. He was still squatting by the chaparral bush.

"Why, Gus, he is too a major," Call said. "You saw how the soldiers saluted him, back in San Antonio."

"Even if he ain't a major, he gave us a job," he reminded his friend. "We're earning three dollars a month. Long Bill says we'll get all the Indian fighting we want before we get back to the settlements."

"Bye, I'm going exploring," Gus said. "I've heard there's gold mines out in this part of the country."

"Gold mines," Call said. "How would you notice a gold mine in the middle of the night, and what would you do with one if you did notice it? You ain't even got a spade."

"No, but think of all the whores I could buy if I had a gold mine," Gus said. "I could even buy a whorehouse. I'd have twenty girls and they'd all be pretty. If I didn't feel like letting in no customers, I'd do the work myself."

With that, he walked off a few steps.

"Ain't you coming?" he asked, when he heard no footsteps behind him.

"No, I was told to stand guard, not to go prospecting," Call said. "I aim to stand guard till it's my turn to sleep.

"If you go off and get captured, the Major won't like it one bit, either," Call reminded him. "Neither will you. Remember how that Mexican screamed."

Gus left. Woodrow Call was stubborn—why waste a night arguing with a stubborn man? Gus walked rapidly through the cold night, toward where the wolf had howled. It irked him that his friend was so disposed to obey orders. The way he looked at it, being a Ranger meant you could range, which was what he intended to do.

He thought best to cock his gun, though, in case he was taken by surprise. He had heard men scream while dentists were working on them, but in his experience no one undergoing dentistry had screamed half as loud as the captured Mexican.

After strolling nearly twenty minutes through the sandy country, Gus decided to stop and take his bearings. He looked back to see if he could spot the campfire, but the long plain was dark. Thunder had begun to rumble, and in the west, there was a flicker of lightning.

While he was stopped he thought he heard something behind him and whirled in time to spot a badger, not three feet away. The badger was bumbling along, not watching where it was going. Gus didn't shoot it, but he did kick at it. He was irritated at the animal for startling him so. It was the kind of thing that could affect a man's nerves, and it affected his. Because of the badger's intrusion Gus felt a strong urge to get back to his guard post. Walking around at night didn't accomplish much. It was annoying that Woodrow Call had been too dull to accompany him.

On the walk back Gus tried to think of some adventure he could describe that would make his friend envious. The campfire had not yet come in sight. Probably the Rangers had been too lazy to gather sufficient firewood, and had let the fire burn down. Gus began to wonder if he was holding a true course. It was hard to see landmarks on a starless night, and there were precious few landmarks in that part of the country, anyway. Of course the river was in the direction he was walking, but the river twisted and curved; if he just depended on the river he might end up several miles from camp. He might even miss breakfast, or what passed for breakfast.

While he was walking, the wolf howled again. Gus decided it was probably just a wolf after all. The boredom of guard duty had caused him to imagine it was a Comanche. He felt some irritation. The wolf had distracted him with its howling, and now he was beginning to get the feeling that he was lost. He had always believed that he had a perfect sense of direction. Even when he was put off on a mud bar in the middle of the Mississippi River, he didn't get lost. He walked straight on to Dubuque. Of course, it was not hard to find Dubuque—it was there in plain sight, on its bluff. But there were willow thickets and some heavy underbrush between the river and the town. If he had been drunk he might well have gotten lost and ended up pointed toward St. Louis or somewhere. Instead he had strolled straight into Dubuque and had persuaded a bartender to draw him a mug of beer—it had been a thirsty trip, on the old boat. That Iowa beer had tasted good.

Now, though, there was no Mississippi, and no bluff. He could walk for a month in any direction and not find a town the size of Dubuque, or a bartender willing to draw him a mug of beer just because he showed up and asked. He had only owned his weapons for three weeks and so far had not been able to hit anything he shot at, although he believed he might have winged a wild turkey, back along the Colorado River. He might walk around Texas until he starved, due to his inability to hit the kind of game they had in Texas. It was skittery game, for the most part—back in Tennessee the deer were almost as docile as cows, and almost as fat. He had killed two or three from the back porch of the old home place, whereas here in Texas, deer hardly let you get within a mile of them.

Gus stopped and listened for a bit. Sometimes the Rangers sang at night—there had been plenty of whooping and dancing the night they drank the mescal. He felt if he listened he might hear Josh Corn's harmonica or some other music. Black Sam sometimes let loose with his darky hymns, when he was in low spirits; Sam had a full voice and could be heard a long way, even when he was singing low.

But when Gus stopped to listen, the plain around him was absolutely silent—so silent that the silence itself rang in his ears; the night was as dark as it was silent, too. Gus could see nothing at all, except intermittently, when the lightning flickered. It was because of the lightning that he had spotted the offensive badger that had managed to affect his nerves.

He took a few steps, and stopped. After all, it wouldn't be night forever, and he had not gone that far from camp. The simplest thing to do would be to wrap up good in his San Antonio serape and sleep for a few hours. With dawn at his back he could be in camp in a few minutes. If he kept walking he might veer off into the great emptiness and never find his way back. The sensible thing to do was wait. He could yell and hope Woodrow Call responded, but Woodrow had been too dull to move off his guard post; he might be too dull to yell back.

The lightning was coming closer, which offered a sort of solution. He could be patient, mark his course, and move from flash to flash. A few sprinkles of rain wet his face. He could tell from the way the sage smelled that a shower was coming—he could even hear the patter of rain not far to the west. For a moment he squatted, tucking his serape around him—if it was going to turn wet, he was ready. Then a bold streak of lightning split the sky. For a moment it lit the prairie, bright as day. And yet Gus saw nothing familiar—no river, no campfire, no chaparral bush, no Call.

No sooner had he wrapped his serape around him and got ready for the rain squall than he was up and walking fast through the sage. He had meant to wait—it was sensible to wait, and yet a feeling had come over him that told him to move. The feeling told him to run, in fact—he was already moving at a rapid trot, though he stopped for a moment to lower the hammer of his pistol. He didn't intend to shoot off his thumb like young Rip Green. Then he trotted on, just short of a run.

As he trotted, Gus began to realize that he was scared. The feeling that came over him, that brought him to his feet and started him trotting, was fear. It was such an unexpected and unfamiliar feeling that he had not been able to put a name to it, at first. Rarely since early childhood had he been afraid. Creaking boards in the old family barn made him think of ghosts, and he had avoided the barn, even to the point of being stropped for a failure to do the chores, when he was small. Since then, though, he had rarely seen anything that he feared. Once in Arkansas he had come across a bear eating a dead horse and had worried a bit; he was unarmed at the time, and was sensible enough to know that he was no match for a bear. But since he had got his growth, he had not encountered much that put real fear in him—just that Arkansas bear.

What had him breathing short and stumbling now was a sense that somebody was near—somebody he couldn't see. When he suggested that the wolf might be an Indian, he had just been joshing Call. He had felt restless, and wanted to take a stroll. If he turned up a gold mine, so much the better. He didn't seriously expect to kill an Indian, though. He had no desire to stumble onto a Comanche Indian, or any other Indian, just at that time. It had merely been something to twit Call about. He had never seen a Comanche Indian and could not work up enough of a picture of one to know what to expect, but he didn't suppose that a Comanche could be as large as that bear, or as fierce, either.

Now, though, he was driven to trot through the darkness by an overpowering sense that *somebody* was near, and who could it be but a Comanche Indian? It wasn't Call—being near Call wouldn't scare him. Yet he was near *somebody*—somebody he didn't want to be near—somebody who meant him harm. Shadrach and Bigfoot claimed to be able to smell Indians, and smell them from a considerable distance, but he didn't have that ability. All he could smell was the wet sage and the damp desert. It wasn't because he could smell that he knew somebody was near. It was a feeling, and a feeling that came from a part of him he didn't even know he had. What that part told him was run, move, get away, even though the night had now divided itself into two parts, the pitch black part and the brilliantly lit part. The brilliantly lit part, of course, was the lightning flashes, which came more frequently and turned the plain so bright that Gus had to blink his eyes. Even then the light stayed, like a line inside his eye, when the plain turned black again, so black that in his running he stumbled into chaparral and almost fell once when he struck a patch of deep sand.

It was just after the sand that the lightning began to strike so close and so constantly that Gus developed a new fear, which was that his gun barrel would draw the lightning and he would be cooked on the spot. There had been some close lightning three days back, and the Rangers, Bigfoot particularly, had told several stories of men who had been cooked by lightning. Sometimes, according to Bigfoot, the lightning even cooked the horse underneath the man.

Gus would have been willing now to risk getting himself and his horse both cooked, if he could only have a horse underneath him, in order to move faster. Just as he was thinking that thought, a great lightning bolt struck not fifty yards away, and in that moment of white brightness Gus saw the somebody he had been fearing: the Indian with a great hump of muscle or gristle between his shoulders, a hump so heavy that the man's head bent slightly forward as he sat, like a buffalo's.

Buffalo Hump sat alone, on a robe of some kind—he looked at Gus, with his heavy head bent and his great hump wet from the rain, as if he had been expecting his arrival. He was not more than ten feet away, no farther than the badger had been, and his eyes were like stone.

Buffalo Hump looked at Gus, and then the plain went black. In the blackness Gus ran as he had never run before, right past where the Indian sat. Lightning streaked again but Gus didn't turn for a second look: he ran. Something tore at his leg as he brushed a thornbush, but he didn't slow his speed. In the line inside his eyes where the lightning stayed, there was the Comanche now, the great humpbacked Indian, the most feared man on the frontier. Gus had been so close that he could almost have jumped over the man. For all he knew, Buffalo Hump was following, bent on taking his hair. His only hope was speed. With such a hump to carry, the man might not be fast.

Gus forgot everything but running. He wanted to get away from the man with the hump—if he could just run all night maybe the

Rangers would wake up and come to his aid. He didn't know whether he was running toward the river or away from it. He didn't know if Buffalo Hump was following, or how close he might be. He just ran, afraid to stop, afraid to yell. He thought of throwing away his gun in order to get a little more speed, but he didn't—he wanted something to shoot with, if he were cornered or brought down.

At the guard post behind the chaparral bush, Call alternated between being irritated and being worried. He was convinced his friend, who had no business leaving in the first place, was out on the plain somewhere, hopelessly lost. There was little hope of finding him before daylight, and then it was sure to be a humiliating business. Shadrach was an excellent tracker and could no doubt follow Gus's trail, but it would cost the troop delay and aggravation.

Major Chevallie might fire Gus—even fire Call, too, for having allowed Gus to wander off. Major Chevallie expected orders to be obeyed, and Call didn't blame him. He might tolerate some wandering on the part of the scouts—that was their job—but he wouldn't necessarily tolerate it on the part of a private.

When the rain came there was not much Call could do but hunch over and get wet. The bush was too thorny to crawl under, and he had no coat. The lightning was bright and the thunder loud, but Call didn't feel fearful, especially. The bright flashes at least allowed him to look around. In one of them he thought he saw a movement; he decided it was the wolf they had heard howling.

It was in another brilliant flash that he saw Gus running. The plain went black again, so black that Call wasn't sure whether he had seen Gus or imagined him. Gus had been tearing along, running dead out. All Call could do was wait for the next flash—when it came he saw Gus again, closer, and in that flash Call saw something else: the Comanche.

The light died so quickly that Call thought he might have imagined the Indian, too. In the light he had seen the great hump, a mass half as large as the weight of most men; and yet the man was running fast after Gus, and had a lance in his hand. Call fired wildly, in the general direction of the Indian—it was dark again before his gun sounded. He thought the shot might at least distract the man with the hump. In the next flash, though, Buffalo Hump had stopped and thrown the lance—Call just saw it, splitting the rain, as it flew toward Gus, who was still running flat out—running

[46]

for his life. Call fired again, with his pistol this time. Maybe Gus would hear it and take heart—although that was a faint hope. The thunderclaps were so continuous that he scarcely heard the shot himself.

Call raised his rifle, determined to be ready when the next flash came and lit the prairie. But when the flash did come, the plain was empty. Buffalo Hump was gone. The hairs stood up on Call's neck when he failed to see the humpbacked chief. The man had just vanished on an open plain. If he moved that fast he could be anywhere. Call backed into the chaparral, mindless of the thorns, and waited. No man, not even a Comanche, could get through a clump of chaparral and attack him from the rear—certainly no man who had such a hump to carry.

Then he remembered the lance in the air, splitting the rain. He didn't know if it had hit home. If it had, his friend Gus McCrae might be dead. Buffalo Hump might even have run up on him and scalped him, or dragged him off for torture.

The last was such an awful thought that Call couldn't stay crouched in the thornbush. He waited until the next flash—a fair wait, for the storm was passing on to the east, and the lightning was diminishing—and then headed for where he had last seen Gus. Once the thunder quieted a little more, he meant to fire his pistol. Maybe the Rangers would hear it, if Gus couldn't. Maybe they would come to his aid in time to stop the humpbacked Comanche from killing Gus, or dragging him off.

Yet as he waited, Call had the feeling that help, if it came, would come too late. Probably Gus was already dead. Call had seen the lance in the air—Buffalo Hump didn't look like a man who would let fly with a lance just to miss.

When the flash came, not as bright as before, Call saw that the plain was still empty. He began to walk toward the area where he had seen Gus—it was the direction of camp, anyway. He yelled Gus's name twice, but there was no answer. Again the hair stood up on his neck. Buffalo Hump could be anywhere. He might be crouched behind any sage bush, any clump of chaparral, waiting in the dark for the next unwary Ranger to walk by.

Call didn't intend to be an unwary Ranger—he meant to take every precaution, but what precaution could you take on an empty plain at night with a dangerous Indian somewhere close? He wished that he could have got more instruction from Shadrach or Bigfoot about the best procedure to follow in such situations. They had fought Indians for years—they would know. But so far neither of them had said more than two words to him, and those were mostly comments about horseshoeing or some other chore.

The lightning dimmed and dimmed, as the storm moved east. Call could see no trace of Gus, but of course, between the lightning flashes the plain was pitch dark. Gus could be dead and scalped behind any of the sage bushes or clumps of chaparral.

Call walked back and forth for awhile, hoping Gus would hear him and call out. He decided shooting was unwise—if he shot anymore, Major Chevallie might chide him for wasting the ammunition.

Heartsick, sure that his friend was dead, Call began to trudge back to camp. He felt it was mainly his fault that the tragedy had occurred. He should have fought Gus, if necessary, to keep him at his post. But he hadn't; Gus had walked off, and now all was lost.

It seemed to Call, as he walked back in dejection, that Gus should just have left him in the blacksmith's shop. He didn't know enough to be a Ranger—neither had his friend, and now ignorance had got Gus killed. Call was certain he was dead, too. Gus had a loud voice, louder even than Black Sam's. If he wasn't dead, he would be making noise.

Then, just as he was at the lowest ebb of dejection, Call heard the very voice he had supposed he would never hear again: Gus McCrae's voice, yelling from the camp. Call ran as hard as he could toward the sound—he came running into camp so fast that Long Bill Coleman nearly shot him for a hostile.

Sure enough, though, there was Gus McCrae, alive and with his pants down. A Comanche lance protruded from his hip. The reason he was yelling was because Bigfoot and Shadrach were trying to pull it out.

4.

THE LANCE WAS STUCK so deep in Gus's hip that Bigfoot and Shadrach together couldn't pull it out. It was a long, heavy lance—how Gus had managed to run all that way with it dangling from his hip Call couldn't imagine. Gus kept yelling, as the two men tugged at it. Rip Green tried to steady Gus as the two older men attempted to work the lance out. Rip alone wasn't strong enough—Bob Bascom had to come and help hold Gus in place.

Shadrach soon grew annoyed with Gus's yelling, which was loud.

"Shut off your goddamn bellowing," Shadrach said. "You're yelling loud enough to call every Indian between here and the Cimarron River."

"There wasn't but one Indian," Call informed them. "He had a big hump on his back. I seen him."

At that news, the whole camp came to attention. Bigfoot and Shadrach ceased their efforts to extract the lance. Major Chevallie had been peering into the darkness, but his head snapped around when Call mentioned the hump.

"You saw Buffalo Hump?" he said.

"He was the man who threw that lance," Call said. "I saw him in the lightning flash. That was when he threw the lance. I thought he missed."

"Nope, he didn't miss," Bigfoot said. "This is his buffalo lance. I'm surprised he wasted it on a boy."

"I wish he hadn't," Gus said, his voice shaking. "I guess it's stuck in my hipbone."

"No, it's nowhere near your damn hipbone," Shadrach said. He squatted to take a better look at the lance head—then he waved Bigfoot away, twisted the lance a little, and with a hard yank, pulled it out. Gus fainted—Rip and Bob had loosened their hold for a moment; before they could recover, Gus fell forward on his face. Bob Bascom had looked aside, in order to spit tobacco. He kept so much tobacco in his mouth that he was prone to choking fits in time of action. Rip Green had just glanced at his bedroll; he was suspicious by nature and was always glancing at his bedroll to make sure no one was stealing anything from it. Both Rip and Bob were startled when Gus fell on his face—Call was, too. He had not supposed Gus McCrae would be the type to faint.

But blood was pouring out of Gus's hip, and there seemed to be blood farther down his leg.

"Here, Sam," Major Chevallie said, motioning to his cook. "You're the doctor—tend to this man before he bleeds to death."

"Need to get him closer to the fire so I can sew him up," Sam said. He was a small man, about the size of Rip Green; his curly hair was white. Call was uncomfortable with him—he had had little experience of darkies, but he had to admit that the man cooked excellent grub and seemed to be expert in treating boils and other small ailments.

Sam quickly scooped some ash out of the campfire and used it to staunch the flow of blood. He patted ash into the wound until the bleeding stopped; while waiting for it to stop, he threaded a big darning needle.

Matilda walked up about that time, dragging her pallet. Gus's yells had awakened her, and her mood was shaky. She kicked sand at Long Bill Coleman for no reason at all. The Mexican boy was asleep, but the old woman still sat by the fire, silent and unmoving.

"Sew that boy up before he gets conscious and starts bellowing again," Shadrach said. "If there's Indians around, they know where we are. This pup makes too much noise."

"Why, they can mark our position by the fire—they wouldn't need the yelling," Bigfoot said. Gus soon proved to be awake enough to be sensitive to the darning needle. It took Matilda and Bigfoot and Bob Bascom to hold him steady enough that Sam could sew up his long wound.

"Why'd you kick that sand on me?" Long Bill asked Matilda while the sewing was in progress. He was a little hurt by Matilda's evident scorn.

"Because I felt like kicking sand on a son of a bitch," Matilda said. "You were the closest."

"This boy's lucky," Sam said. "The lance missed the bone."

"He might be lucky, but we ain't," Major Chevallie said. He was pacing around nervously.

"What I can't figure out is why Buffalo Hump would be sitting out there by himself," he added.

"He was sitting on a blanket," Gus said. Sam had finally quit poking him with the big needle—that and the fact that he was alive made him feel a little better. Besides that, he was back in camp. He felt sure he was going to survive, and wanted to be helpful if he could.

"I ran right past him, that's why he took after me," Gus said. "He had a terrible big hump."

Gus felt that he might want to relax and snooze, but that plan was interrupted by the old Comanche woman, who suddenly began to wail. The sound of her high wailing gave everybody a start.

"What's wrong with her—now she's howling," Long Bill asked.

Shadrach went over to the old woman and spoke with her in Comanche, but she continued to wail. Shadrach waited patiently until she stopped.

"She's a vision woman," Shadrach said. "My grandma was a vision woman too. She would let out wails when she had some bad vision, just like this poor old soul."

Call wanted the old woman to quiet down—her wailing had a bad effect on the whole camp. Her wails were as sad as the sound of the wind as it sighed over the empty flats. He didn't want to hear such disturbing sounds, and none of the other Rangers did, either.

Shadrach still squatted by the old woman, talking to her in her own tongue. The wind blew swirls of fine sand around them.

"Well, what now? What's she saying?" Major Chevallie asked.

"She says Buffalo Hump is going to cut off her nose," Shadrach said. "She was one of his father's wives—I guess she didn't behave none too well. Her people put her out to die, and Buffalo Hump heard about it. Now he wants to find her and cut off her nose."

"I'd think he had better things to do," the Major said. "She's old, she'll die. Why bother with her nose?"

"Because she behaved bad to his father," Shadrach said, a little impatiently. Major Chevallie's ignorance of Indian habits often annoyed him.

"I don't like it that he's out there," Long Bill said. "Once he cuts this old woman's nose off he might keep cutting. He might cut a piece or two off all of us, before he stops."

"Why, if you're worried, just go kill him, Bill," Bigfoot said.

"He's a swift runner, even with that hump," Gus informed them. "He almost caught me, and I'm fleet."

Major Chevallie kept pacing back and forth, his pistol cocked.

"Let's mount up and go," he said abruptly. "We're not in a secure position here—I believe it would be best to ride."

"Now, hold still," Shadrach insisted. "This is a vision woman talking. Let's see what else she has to say."

He went to the fire, poured some coffee in a tin cup, and handed it to the old woman. The Major didn't like it that Shadrach had ignored his order—but he took it. He sat down by Matilda, who was still in a heavy mood.

"I still don't see why he would go to so much trouble just to cut off an old woman's nose," he muttered, mainly to himself. Bigfoot Wallace heard him, though.

"You ain't a Comanche," Bigfoot said. "Comanches expect their wives to stay in the right tent."

Major Chevallie thought of his own dear wife, Jane. If it had not been for the scrape in Baltimore, he could be home with her right then; they might be nestled together, in a nice feather bed. How long would it be before he could return to their snug stone house in Loudon County? Would he ever return to it, or to his ardent Jane? He felt low, very low. It was too dusty in Texas. Every bite of food he had attempted to eat, all day, had been covered with grit. The large whore beside him was rough; she would never smell as good as his Jane. But Matilda was there, and Jane wasn't. Matilda was likable, despite being rough; the Major was feeling desperate. The Comanche war chief was within earshot of his camp. A minute's relief with Matilda would be helpful, but of course it was not a time to suggest to the troop that he was unmilitary. It was clear already that Bigfoot and Shadrach had a low opinion of his leadership. Chevallie was an old name, much respected in the Tidewater, but it meant nothing west of the Pecos. Ability was all that counted, in the West, in such a country, among such men—out West the ability to waltz gracefully did not help a man keep his scalp.

The fact was, he himself had no great opinion of his own military skills. His three weeks at the Point had involved little study, and none that touched on the fine points of warfare with Comanche Indians.

Call went over and sat down by Gus—his friend seemed relaxed, if a little gaunt.

"I seen you in the lightning," Call said. "I seen he was after you. I shot, but I doubt I hit him. He was after you hard."

"Yes, and he nearly got me," Gus said.

"I told you to stay put," Call reminded him, but in a low voice. He didn't want the Major to know that Gus had wandered off from his post, although if he hadn't they might never have known that Buffalo Hump was nearby.

"I didn't find no gold mine, just a badger and that big Indian," Gus admitted. "He was just sitting there on a blanket. What was he doing just sitting there with all that lightning striking?"

When Shadrach finished talking to the old Comanche woman, he seemed a little agitated.

"What's the news, Shad?" Bigfoot asked. He could tell there was *some* news. Shadrach had his rifle in his hand and he was looking north.

"Bad news," Shadrach said. "We need to watch our hair for the next few days. If we don't, we won't be wearing it."

"Why, Shad, I always watch my hair," Bob Bascom said. Ezekiel whooped when he said it, and Josh Corn smiled. The reason for their merriment was that Bob Bascom had almost no hair to watch.

He was bald, except for a few sprigs above his ears. Blackie Slidell was almost as bald—he had been heard to remark that any Indian scalping him would be mainly wasting his time.

"Old Buffalo Hump would need a magnifying glass if he was to attempt to scalp either one of us, Bob," Blackie observed dryly.

"That old woman says a war's coming," Shadrach said.

"Well, maybe she is a vision woman," the Major said. "General Scott has been talking about taking Mexico, I hear."

"No, not that war," Shadrach said. "She ain't talking about no white war. She says the Comanches mean to attack someplace down in Mexico—I guess that would be Chihuahua City."

"Chihuahua City? Indians?" the Major exclaimed. "It would take a good number of braves to attack a city that size."

"It might not take that many," Bigfoot said.

"Why not?" the Major asked.

"Comanches are scary," Bigfoot said. "One Comanche brave on a lean horse can scare all the white people out of several counties. Fifty Comanches could probably take Mexico City, if they made a good run at it."

"That old woman ain't talking about fifty, neither," Shadrach said. "She's talking about a passel—hundreds, I reckon."

"Hundreds?" the Major said, startled. Nobody, as far as he knew, had ever faced a force of hundreds of Comanches. Looking around at his troop—twelve men and one whore—he saw that most of the men were white knuckled with fear as they gripped their rifles. The thought of hundreds of Comanches riding as one force was nothing any commander would care to contemplate.

"That humpbacked man was there alone," Call said. He rarely spoke unless asked, but this time he thought he ought to remind the Major of what he had seen.

"It felt like fifty or a hundred, though, while he was after me," Gus said, sitting up.

"You said he was just sitting on a blanket?" Bigfoot asked.

"Yes, just sitting," Gus said. "He was on a little hill—I guess it was mostly just a hump of sand."

"Maybe he was waiting for Gomez," Bigfoot said. "That would explain my dream."

"No, that's wild," Shadrach said. "If he's got hundreds of warriors coming he wouldn't need to wait for no Apache."

"I've dreamt prophecy before," Bigfoot insisted. "I think he was waiting for Gomez. I expect they mean to take Chihuahua City together and divide up the captives."

"My Lord, if there's hundreds of them coming, they'll hunt us up and hack us all down," Long Bill said. He had been nursing a sense of grievance. After all, he had ridden off from San Antonio to help find a good road west, not to be hacked to pieces by Comanche Indians.

"There wouldn't need to be hundreds to take us," Bigfoot corrected. "Twenty-five would be plenty, and ten or fifteen could probably do the job."

"Now, that's a useless comment," Bob Bascom said, hurt by Bigfoot's low estimation of the troop's fighting ability.

"I expect we could handle fifteen," he added.

"Not unless lightning struck half of them," Bigfoot said. "I was watching you youngsters take target practice yesterday. Half of you couldn't hit your foot if your gun barrel was resting on it."

Shadrach conversed a little more with the old woman. When he finished, she began to wail again. The sound was so irritating that Call felt like putting cotton in his ears, but he had no cotton.

"She don't know nothing about Gomez," Shadrach said. "I think your dern dream was off."

"We'll see," Bigfoot said. He didn't press the issue, not with Shadrach, a man who trusted no opinions except his own.

Gus McCrae got to his feet. He wanted to test his leg, in case he had to run again. He walked slowly over and picked up his rifle. His hip didn't hurt much, but he felt uneasy in his stomach. When the lance stuck in his hip he saw it rather than felt it. He was even able to hold the shaft of the lance off the ground as he ran. Now, even in the midst of his fellow Rangers, the fear he felt then wouldn't leave him. He had the urge to hide someplace. Gus had never supposed he would run from any man, yet he felt as if he should still be running. He needed to get farther from Buffalo Hump than he was, and as fast as he could. He just didn't know where to run.

Matilda thought the tall Tennessee boy looked a little green around the gills. Though she was stiff with Gus when he importuned her, she liked the boy, and winced when the lance was being pulled out. He was a lively boy, brash but not really bad. Once or twice she had even extended him credit—he seemed to need it so, and a minute or less did for him, usually. She could occasionally spare a minute for a brash boy with a line of gab.

"Sit down, Gussie," she said. "You oughtn't to be exercising too much just yet."

"Let him exercise, it might keep that leg from stiffening up," the Major said. "It's a good thing that wound bled like it did."

"Yes, good," Sam said. "Otherwise he be dying soon."

"Comanches dip their lances in dog shit," Bigfoot informed them. "You don't want to get that much dog inside you, if you can help it. Better to bleed it out."

"Sit down, Gussie," Matilda said again. "Sit down by me, unless you don't like me anymore."

Gus hobbled over and sat down by Matilda. He was a little surprised that she had been so inviting. It wasn't that he didn't like her anymore, it was that he liked her too much; for a moment he had an urge to throw himself into Matilda's lap and cry. Of course, such an action would be the ruin of him, among the hardened Rangers. Rather than cry, he scooted as close to Matilda's comforting bulk as he could get without actually sitting in her lap. He gulped a time or two, but managed not to break down and sob. He saw old Shadrach mount his horse and ride off into the darkness. Shadrach said not a word, and no one tried to stop him or ask him where he was going.

"Doesn't he know that big Comanche with the hump is still out there?" Gus asked. He thought the old man must be completely daft, to ride into the darkness with such an Indian near.

Call, too, was shocked by Shadrach's departure. Buffalo Hump was out there, and even Shadrach would be no match for him. No one Call knew would be a match for him—not alone; Call felt sure of that, although he had only seen the man for a second, in the flash of a lightning strike.

But Shadrach left, with no one offering him a word of caution. Bigfoot didn't seem to give Shadrach's departure a second thought, and Major Chevallie merely frowned a little when he saw the mountain man ride away.

"What now, Major?" Ezekiel Moody asked. It was a question everyone would have liked an answer to, but Major Chevallie ignored the question. He said nothing.

Ezekiel looked at Josh Corn, and Josh Corn looked at Rip Green.

Long Bill looked at Bob Bascom, who looked at one-eyed Johnny Carthage.

"Now where would Shad be going, this time of night?" Johnny asked. "It's no time to be exercising your mount—not if it means leaving the troop, not if you ask me."

"I didn't hear Shad ask you, Johnny," Bigfoot said.

"That's twice today he's left, though," the Major said. "It's vexing."

Bigfoot walked over to the edge of the camp, lay flat down, and pressed his ear to the ground.

"Is he listening for worms—does he mean to fish?" Gus asked Call, perplexed by Bigfoot's behaviour.

"No, he's listening for horses—Comanche horses," Matilda said. "Shut up and let him listen."

Bigfoot soon stood up and came back to the fire.

"Nobody's coming right this minute," he said. "If there were hundreds of horses on the move, I'd hear them."

"That don't mean they won't show up tomorrow, though," he added.

"Why tomorrow?" several men asked at once. Tomorrow was only an hour or two away.

"Full moon," Bigfoot said. "It's what they call the Comanche moon. They like to raid into Mexico, down this old war trail, when the moon is full. They like that old Comanche moon."

Major Chevallie knew he had only about an hour in which to decide on a course of action. Of course the old woman might be daft; there might be no plan to raid Chihuahua City and no great war party, hundreds of warriors strong, headed down from the Llano Estacado to terrorize the settlements in Mexico and Texas. It might all simply be the ravings of an old woman who was afraid of having her nose cut off.

But if what the old woman said *was* true, then the settlements needed to be warned. That many warriors moving south would threaten the whole frontier. All the farms west of the Austin–San Antonio line would be vulnerable—even half a dozen warriors split off from the main bunch could burn homesteads, steal children, and generally wreak havoc.

The devil of it was that they were just at the midpoint of their exploration, as far from the settlements to the east as they were from the Pass of the North. Striking on west to El Paso might be the safest option for his troop—the war trail ran well east of El Paso. On the other hand, Buffalo Hump already knew they were there, and knew he was only up against a few men. If he had a large force at his disposal, he might pursue them simply for his pleasure. He no doubt knew that the two scalp hunters were with them. Scalping a scalp hunter was a pursuit that would interest any Indian, Comanche or Apache.

Turning east would mean the end of their mission—and they were only a week or two from completing it—and would also take them directly across the path of the raiders, if there were raiders. They would have to depend on speed and luck, if they turned east.

What was certain was that a decision had to be made, and made soon. He had no shackles on his men—Rangers mostly served because they wanted to; if they stopped wanting to, they might all do what Shadrach had just done. They might just ride off. The youngsters, Call and McCrae, would stay, of course. They were too green to strike out for themselves. But the more experienced men were unlikely to sit around and wait for his decision much past sunup. The sight of the buffalo lance sticking out of Augustus McCrae's hip was vivid in their minds. They wouldn't be inclined to play cards, or solicit Matilda, or shoot at cactus pods, not with a big war party swooping down the plains toward them.

The Major sighed. Going to jail in Baltimore was beginning to look like it might have some advantages. He walked over to Bigfoot —the tall scout was idly chewing on a chaparral twig.

"That old woman's blind," the Major said. "Do you think she was right about the raiding party? Maybe Shadrach misunderstood her about the figures. Maybe she was talking about some raid that took place thirty years ago."

Bigfoot spat out the twig. "Maybe," he said. "But maybe not."

Bigfoot was thinking about how lucky the two young Rangers were—young Gus particularly. To walk right up on Buffalo Hump and live to tell about it was luck not many men could claim. Even to have *seen* the humpbacked chief was more than many experienced men could claim. He himself had glimpsed Buffalo Hump once, in a sleet storm near the Clear Fork of the Brazos, several years earlier. He had stepped out of a little post-oak thicket and looked up to see the humpbacked chief aiming an arrow at him. Just as Buffalo Hump loosed the arrow, Bigfoot stepped on an ice-glazed root and lost his footing. The arrow glanced off the bowie knife stuck in his belt. He rolled and brought his rifle up, but by the time he did, the Comanche was gone. That night, afraid to make a fire for fear Buffalo Hump would find him, he almost froze. The large feet that produced his nickname turned as numb as stone.

Now the Major was stumping about, trying to convince himself that Shadrach and the old Comanche woman were wrong about the raiding party. The men were scared, and with good reason; the Major had still not been able to think of an order to give.

"Damn it, I hate to double back," the Major said. "I was aiming to wet my whistle in El Paso."

He mounted and walked his sorrel slowly around the camp for a few minutes—the horse was likely to crow-hop on nippy mornings. Shadrach came back while he was riding slowly around. Settling his horse gave the Major time to think, and time, also, to ease his head a little. He was prone to violent headaches, and had suffered one most of the night. But the sun was just rising. It looked to be a fine morning; his spirits improved and he decided to go on west. Turning back didn't jibe with his ambitions. If he found a clear route to El Paso, he might be made a colonel, or a general even.

"Let's go, boys—it's west," he said, riding back to the campfire. "We were sent to find a road, so let's go find it."

The Rangers had survived a terrifying night. As soon as they mounted, warmed by the sun, many of them got sleepy and nodded in their saddles. Gus's wounded hip was paining him. Walking wasn't easy, but riding was hard, too. His black nag had a stiff trot. He kept glancing across the sage flats, expecting to see Buffalo Hump rise up from behind a sage bush.

The scalp hunters, Kirker and Glanton, rode half a mile with the troop, and then turned their horses.

"Ain't you coming, boys?" Long Bill asked.

The scalp hunters didn't answer. Once the pack mules passed, they rode toward Mexico.

5.

"THERE AIN'T MANY SOLDIERS that know what they're doing, are there, Shad?" Bigfoot asked. "This major sure don't."

"I doubt he's a major, or even a soldier," Shadrach said. "I expect he just stole a uniform."

They were riding west through an area so dry that even the sage had almost played out.

Bigfoot suspected Shadrach was right. Probably Major Chevallie had just stolen a uniform. Texas was the sort of place where people could simply name themselves something and then start being whatever they happened to name. Then they could start acquiring the skills of their new profession—or not acquiring them, as the case might be.

"Well, I ain't a soldier boy, neither," Shadrach said.

"Was you ever a soldier?" Bigfoot asked. He was looking up at a crag, or a little hump of mountain, a few miles to the north. In the clear, dry air, he thought he saw a spot of white on the mountain, which was puzzling. What could be white on a mountain far west of the Pecos?

Shadrach ignored Bigfoot's question—he didn't answer questions about his past.

"See that white speck, up on that hill?" Bigfoot asked.

Shadrach looked, but saw nothing. Bigfoot was singular for the force of his vision, which was one reason he was sought after as a scout. He was not careful or meticulous—not by Shadrach's standards—but there was no denying that he could see a long way.

"I swear, I think it's mountain goat," Bigfoot said. "I never heard of mountain goat in Texas, but there it is, and it's white."

He immediately forgot his vexation with the Major in his excitement at spotting what he was now sure must be a mountain goat—a creature he had heard of but never previously seen.

After a little more looking he thought he spotted a second goat, not far from the first one.

"Look, boys, it's mountain goats," he informed the startled Rangers, most of whom were straggling along, half asleep.

At Bigfoot's cry, excitement instantly flashed through the troop. Rangers with weak visions, such as one-eyed Johnny Carthage or little Rip Green, could barely see the mountain, much less the goats, but that didn't weaken their excitement. Within a minute the whole troop was racing toward the humpy mountain, where the two goats, invisible to everyone but Bigfoot, were thought to be grazing. Only Matilda and Black Sam resisted the impulse to race wildly off. They continued at a steady pace. The old Comanche woman and the tongueless boy followed on a pack mule.

Gus and Call were racing along with the rest of the troop, their horses running flat out through the thin sage. Gus forgot the throb of his wounded hip in the excitement of the race.

"What do they think they're going to do, Sam, fly up that mountain?" Matilda asked. From the level plain the sides of the mountain where the goats were seemed far too steep for horses to climb.

Sam was wishing Texas wasn't so big and open—you could look and look, as far as you could see, and there would be nothing to give you encouragement. He had been in jail for dropping a watermelon, when Bigfoot happened to get locked up. He had picked a watermelon off a stall and thumped it, to see if it was

[61]

ripe; but then he dropped it and it burst on the cobblestones. The merchant demanded ten cents for his burst melon, but Sam had only three cents. He offered to work off the difference, but the merchant had him arrested instead. The cook in the San Antonio jail got so drunk that he let a wagon run over his foot and crush it, making him too sick to cook. Sam was offered his job and took it—he had known how to cook since he was six. Bigfoot liked the grub so much that he suggested Sam to Major Chevallie, who promptly paid the debt of seven cents and took Sam with him.

Now here he was, in the biggest country he had ever seen, with a horizon so distant that his eyes didn't want to seek it, and a sun so bright that he could only tolerate it by pulling the brim of his old cap down over his eyes; he was riding along with a whore after a bunch of irritable white men who had decided to chase goats. At least the whore was friendly, even if she did eat snapping turtle for breakfast.

The Rangers, young Gus in the lead, had raced to the foot of the mountain, only to discover at close range what Matilda had discerned at a distance: the little mountain was much too steep for horses, and perhaps even too steep for men. Now that they were directly underneath the crag they couldn't see the goats, either; they were hidden by rocks and boulders, somewhere above them. Also, their horses were winded from the chase; the mountain that in the clear air had looked so close had actually been several miles away. Many of the horses—skinny nags, mostly—were stumbling and shaking by the time the Rangers dismounted.

Call had never seen a mountain before, although of course he was familiar with hills. This mountain went straight up—if you could get on top of it, you wouldn't be very far from the sky. But they weren't at the top of it; they were at the bottom, near several good-sized boulders that had toppled off at some point and rolled out onto the plain.

Major Chevallie, like most of his men, had enjoyed the wild race immensely. After all the worry and indecision it was a relief just to race a horse at top speed over the plain. Besides, if they could bring down a mountain goat or two there would be meat for the pot. He had often hunted in Virginia—deer mostly, bear occasionally, and of course turkeys and geese—but he had never been in sight of a Western mountain goat and was anxious to get in a shot before someone beat him to the game. Several of the men had already grabbed their rifles and were ready to shoot.

Josh Corn got off his horse and vomited, to the general amusement. Josh had a delicate constitution; he could never ride fast for any length of time without losing his breakfast—it was an impediment to what he hoped would be a fine career in the Rangers.

"Boys, let's climb," Bigfoot said. "These goats ain't likely to fall off the hill."

Long Bill Coleman was the pessimist in the crowd. He was too nearsighted to have seen the goats—in fact, he could not see far up the mountain at all. His horse was in better shape than most because of his lack of confidence in the hunt. He had held the pony to a lope while the others were running flat out. Unlike the rest of the command, Long Bill had not forgotten that there were Comanches in the area. He was more interested in seeing that he had a mount fresh enough to carry him away from Comanches than he was in shooting goats. The latter, in his experience, were hard to chew anyway—worse than hard, if the goat happened to be an old billy.

Matilda and Black Sam came trotting up to the base of the cliff, where the hunting party was assembling itself. The only one to venture up the cliff was young McCrae, who had climbed some thirty yards up when his wounded leg gave out suddenly.

"Look out, he's falling," Bob Bascom said.

Call felt embarrassed, for indeed his friend was falling, or rather rolling, down the steep slope he had just climbed up. Gus tried to grab for a little bush to check his descent, but he missed and rolled all the way down, ending up beneath Major Chevallie's horse, which abruptly began to pitch. The Major had dropped his reins in order to adjust the sights on his rifle. To his intense annoyance, the horse suddenly bolted and went dashing across the plain to the west.

"Now look, you young fool, who told you to climb?" the Major exploded. "Now you've run off my horse!"

Gus McCrae was so embarrassed he couldn't speak. One minute he had been climbing fine, the next minute he was rolling. Call was just as embarrassed. The Major was red in the face with anger. In all likelihood he was about to fire Gus on the spot.

There was a funny side to the spectacle, though—the sight of

Gus rolling over and over set many of the Rangers to slapping their thighs and laughing. Matilda was cackling, and even Sam chuckled. Call was on the point of laughing too, but restrained himself out of consideration for his friend. Matilda laughed so loudly that Tom, her horse, usually a stolid animal, began to hop around and act as if he might throw her.

"Dern," Gus said, so stricken with embarrassment that he could not think of another word to say. Though he had rolled all the way down the hill, his rifle had only rolled partway. It was lodged against a rock, twenty yards above them.

"Get mounted, you damn scamp, and go bring my horse back, before he runs himself out of sight," the Major commanded. "You can get that rifle when you come back."

Several Rangers, Ezekiel Moody among them, were watching the horse run off—all of them were in a high state of hilarity. Rip Green was laughing so hard he could scarcely stand up. Everyone except the Major and Gus were enjoying the little moment of comic relief when, suddenly, they saw the Major's horse go down.

"Prairie-dog hole. I hope his leg's not broken," Johnny Carthage said. Before he could even finish saying it the sound of a shot echoed off the mountain behind them.

"No prairie-dog hole, that horse was shot," Bigfoot said.

Shadrach immediately led his horse behind one of the larger boulders.

"My God, now what?" the Major said. All he had taken off his saddle was the rifle itself—his ammunition and all his kit were with the fallen horse.

No one said a word. The plain before them looked as empty as it had when they had all come racing across it. There was no sign of anyone. Two hawks circled in the sky. The fallen horse did not rise again.

The Rangers, all of them ready to pop off a few shots at some mountain goats, were caught in disarray. Young Josh Corn, having just emptied his stomach, found that he needed to empty his bowels too, and walked down the slope some thirty yards to a little bunch of sage bushes; most of the Rangers had no qualms about answering calls of nature in full view of a crowd, but Josh liked a little privacy. He had just undone his britches when Gus rolled down the hill. But his call was urgent; he was squatting down amid the sage bushes when the Major's horse bolted. He heard the shot that killed the horse, but supposed it was only some Ranger, popping off a long shot at one of the goats. For a moment his cramping bowels occupied all his attention. Ever since gulping a bellyful of Pecos water he had been afflicted with cramps of such severity that from time to time he was forced to dismount and pour out fluids so alkaline that they turned white in the sun.

Josh kept squatting, emptying himself of more Pecos salts. He was in no rush to get back to the crowd—the cramps were still bad, so bad that he could only have walked bending over, which would have made him an object of derision to his fellows. Besides, he could tell from looking at the cliff that he was too weak to make it up very far. Unless he was lucky, someone else would have to shoot the goats.

Josh had just reached over to strip a few sage leaves to wipe himself with when he saw a movement in the sage some fifteen yards away. All he could see was the back of an animal; he thought it must be a pig, moving through the thickest part of the little patch of sage and chaparral. Josh reached for his pistol. The pig would come in sight in just a moment, and he meant to empty his pistol into it. The other Rangers could go scampering up the mountain to shoot at goats if they wanted to—he would be the one bringing home meat: pig meat. They had feasted on several javelinas on the trip from San Antonio. Some had been tough, others succulent. When there was time Sam liked to bury the whole pig, head, hide, and all, overnight, with coals heaped on it. By morning the pig would be plenty tender; Sam would dig it up and the Rangers would enjoy a fine meal.

Buffalo Hump had been watching the boy. When the young Ranger started to reach for his pistol, Buffalo Hump rose to his knees and fired an arrow just above the tops of the sage: Josh Corn saw him only for a split second before the arrow cut through his throat and severed his windpipe. Josh dropped his pistol and managed to get a hand on the arrow, but he fell sideways as he grasped it and didn't feel the knife that finished cutting his throat. Buffalo Hump dragged the quivering body behind him as he retreated through the sage. Kicking Wolf had just shot the Major's horse; all the Rangers were looking across the plain. They had forgotten the boy who was emptying his bowels amid the sage.

[65]

Buffalo Hump had his horse staked in a shallow gully. As soon as he got the dead boy into the gully he stripped him, cut off his privates, and threw him on the back of his horse. A curtain of blood from the cut throat covered the boy's torso. Buffalo Hump mounted, but kept low. He held the streaming corpse across the horse's rump with one hand. He waited, looking to see if the Rangers were inclined to mount and go investigate the sudden death of the Major's horse. He had watched the Rangers closely the day of the sandstorm and felt he knew what the capability of the little force was. The only man he had to watch was old Shadrach, known to the Comanches as Tail-of-the-Bear. The long rifle of Tail-of-the-Bear had to be respected. The old man seldom missed. Bigfoot Wallace was quick and strong, but no shot; Buffalo Hump regretted not having killed him the day of the great ice storm on the Clear Fork of the Brazos. The fat Major was a good shot with a pistol, but seldom used the rifle.

Buffalo Hump waited, while the blood from Josh Corn's corpse ran down his horse's rear legs and soaked his flanks. In their haste to kill mountain goats—in fact, two Comanche boys with goat skins over their shoulders—the Rangers had foolishly run their horses down. In their eagerness the Rangers had also outrun the old woman and the tongueless boy. He himself had already caught the old woman and notched her nose, to pay back the insult she had given his father. The tongueless boy he had given to Kicking Wolf, who would sell him as a slave. There had been much ammunition on the pack mule, too—the Rangers would soon be out of bullets, if they started shooting. He had slipped into the gully merely to watch the white men at close range, but then the careless young Ranger walked into the sage to empty his bowels. Taking him had been easier than snaring a prairie dog, or killing a turkey.

Once he was satisfied that the whites were not going as a troop to find the killer of the Major's horse, Buffalo Hump burst out of the gully. He yelled his war cry as loudly as he could and raced directly in front of the whites, still holding the bloody corpse across the rump of his horse. He saw a bullet kick the dust, well short of where he rode. Old Tail-of-the-Bear was shooting low. Even so, Buffalo Hump slid to the off side of his mount, one hand gripping the mane, one leg hooked over the horse. The old man would keep shooting and he might not always shoot low.

Then, in plain sight of the Rangers, Buffalo Hump regained his seat, took the corpse of Josh Corn by one foot, and flung it high in the air. Then he whirled to face the whites for a few seconds, screaming his defiance. When he saw bullets kicking dust at his horse's feet, he turned and rode slowly out of range.

At the base of the steep mountain, the Rangers were stunned, and in disarray.

"Where's that old woman?" the Major asked. He remembered suddenly that in their haste to get to the mountain they had run off and left the pack mule that was carrying the old woman and the boy; he remembered, too, that most of their ammunition was on that mule.

The Major looked around and saw that no one had even heard his question. All the Rangers had scrambled to take cover behind the few boulders or the scarce bushes. Gus and Call were huddled behind a rock, but it wasn't really a boulder and didn't hide them very well. Both of them looked around for a bigger rock, but all the bigger rocks had Rangers huddled behind them.

The Major himself got behind the other pack mule, the only cover available.

The cry that Buffalo Hump yelled as he raced across the desert was far worse, in Call's view, than the wailing of the old Comanche woman. Buffalo Hump's war cry throbbed with hatred, terrible hatred. When the Comanche whirled to face them and flung a naked white body streaked with blood up in the air, both boys were shocked.

"Why, he's kilt somebody," Gus said in a shaking tone.

Call was more shocked by how bloody the corpse was. Whoever it was—and he could see that it was a white man—had poured out a terrible lot of blood.

"Where's young Josh?" Bigfoot asked—he had a bad feeling, suddenly. "I don't see young Josh anywhere."

Ezekiel Moody gave a start—he and Josh Corn were best friends. They had joined up with the Rangers on a whim. Zeke looked around at the various Rangers, crouched behind such cover as they could get. He saw no sign of his friend.

"Why, he was right here," Zeke said, standing up. "I think he just walked off to take a shit—he's been having the runs."

"Foolish," the Major said. He couldn't spot the boy, either, and got a weak feeling suddenly in his gut.

"He's been poorly in his belly since he drank that alky water," Zeke protested. He was sure Josh wasn't doing anything wrong.

"I wasn't talking about Josh when I said it was foolish," the Major said. He had been talking about himself. One glimpse of a mountain goat—Bigfoot's glimpse at that—had encouraged them to make a wild charge and exhaust their horses. The thought of a hunt had been something to break the monotony of plodding on west. Well, there was no monotony now: the Comanches had *really* broken it.

Now they were backed against a cliff, his horse was dead, and possibly a boy, too.

"I think that was Josh he pitched up in the air," Bigfoot said. "I think that sneaking devil caught him."

"No, it can't be Josh!" Zeke said, suddenly very distraught. "Josh just went over in them bushes to take a shit."

"I think he caught him, Zeke," Bigfoot said, in a kindly tone. He knew the boys were friends.

"Oh no, all that blood," Zeke said. Before anyone could stop him he jumped on his horse and went riding off toward the spot where Buffalo Hump had thrown the body.

"Hell, where's that pup going?" Shadrach said. He came walking up, disgusted with himself for having been tricked into such a situation. He hadn't expected to hit Buffalo Hump when he shot, unless he was lucky, and he didn't intend to waste any more bullets in the hope of being lucky. He might need every bullet—likely would.

Just as he was walking up to the group, he thought he saw movement—the movement had been an arrow, which thudded into Bigfoot's horse. The horse squealed and reared. The arrow had come from above—from the mountain.

"They're above us!" Shadrach yelled. "Get them horses out of range!"

"Oh, damn it, it wasn't goats, it was Comanches!" Bigfoot said, mortified that he had been so easily taken in. He began to drag his wounded horse farther from the hill. Arrows began to fly off the mountain, though no one could spot the Indians who were shooting them. Several Rangers shot at the mountain, to no effect. Three horses were hit, and one-eyed Johnny Carthage got an arrow in his upper leg. Call had an arrow just glance off his elbow—he knew he was lucky. The horses were in a panic—he had no time to think about anything except hanging on to his mount.

The Rangers all retreated toward the patch of sage bush where Josh Corn had been taken. It was Call, dragging his rearing horse by the bridle, who spotted the bloody patch of ground where Josh had been killed. Call knew it must be Josh's blood because the shit on the ground was white—his own had mostly been white, since crossing the Pecos.

"Look," he said to Gus, who was just behind him.

At the sight of all the fresh blood, the strength suddenly drained out of Gus. He dropped to his knees and began to vomit, letting go of his horse's reins in the process. The horse had an arrow sticking out of its haunch and was jumpy; Call just managed to catch a rein and keep the horse from bolting. Long Bill and Rip Green were shooting at the Comanches on the hill, although they couldn't see their targets.

"Hold off shooting, you idiots," Bigfoot yelled. "You ain't going to hit an Indian a thousand feet up a mountain!"

Bigfoot felt very chagrined. He knew he ought to have been able to tell a goatskin with a Comanche boy under it from a living goat, and he could have if he had just had the patience to ride a little closer and observe the goats as they grazed. His lack of patience had led the Rangers into a trap. Of course, he hadn't expected the pell-mell rush to shoot goats, but he *should* have expected it: most Rangers would ride half a day to shoot any game, much less unusual game such as mountain goats.

Now one man was dead, several horses were hurt, a Ranger had an arrow in his leg, Zeke Moody had just foolishly ridden off, and no one had any idea how many Indians they faced. There were several on the mountain and at least two on the plain, one of them Buffalo Hump, no mean opponent. But there could be forty, or even more than forty. In his hurry to get to the mountain he had paid no attention to signs. At least Matilda and Sam had not been cut off. The fact that they had survived probably meant they weren't dealing with a large party. The loss of the ammunition that was on the other pack mule was a grievous loss, though.

The next worry was Ezekiel Moody, who was still loping off to locate the body of his friend. Bigfoot knew that Zeke would soon be dead or captured, unless he was very lucky.

"Damn that boy, they'll take him for sure," the Major said. All the Rangers, plus Matilda and Sam, were huddled in the little patch of sage. Shadrach saw the gully where Buffalo Hump had tethered his horse and found the bloody trail he had made when he dragged Josh Corn's body. Gus McCrae had the dry heaves. He could not stop retching. The sight of the Indian with the great hump reminded him of his own terrified flight; the smell of Josh Corn's blood caused his stomach to turn over and over, like a churn. Gus knew that Buffalo Hump had almost caught him—the sight of Josh's blood-streaked body showed him clearly what his fate would have been had the lance that struck his hip been thrown a little more accurately. A yard or so difference in the footrace, and he would have been as dead as Josh.

Gus finally got to his feet and stumbled a little distance from the blood; he needed to steady himself so he could shoot if the Comanches launched an attack.

Major Chevallie felt that he had decided foolishly—he should have followed his first instinct and headed east. More and more he regretted not taking his chances with the Baltimore judge.

Now he was caught in an exposed place, with only a shallow gully for cover and an unknown number of savages in opposition. Their best hope lay in the skills of the two scouts. Shadrach was calm, if annoyed, and Bigfoot was flustered, no doubt because he knew he was responsible for getting them into such a fix. His superior eyesight had not been superior enough to detect the trick and prevent the race.

The chaos involved in fighting such Indians bothered Randall Chevallie more than anything. In Virginia or even Pennsylvania, if quarrels arose, a man usually knew who he was fighting and how to proceed. But in the West, with a few puny men caught between vast horizons, it was different. The Indians always knew the country better than the white men; they knew how to use it, to hide in it, to survive in it in places where a white man would have no chance. No man in Virginia would ride around with a naked, bloody corpse bouncing around on the rump of his horse. No one in Virginia or Pennsylvania would yell as Buffalo Hump had yelled.

There was another shot from the hidden rifleman on the plain, and Zeke Moody's horse went down.

"I feared it, they'll get him now, the young fool," Bigfoot said.

Zeke was not hurt—he had heard no shot, and supposed his horse had merely stumbled. But the horse didn't get up—in a moment Zeke realized that the horse was dead. At once he turned, and began to run toward the mountain and the Rangers. But Zeke had scarcely run ten yards before Buffalo Hump loomed behind him, riding a horse whose sides were bloody with Josh Corn's blood.

"We better go help him," Call said, but old Shadrach grabbed his arm before he could move.

"All this damn helping's got to stop," Shadrach said. "We don't know how many of them are out there. If we don't stay together there won't be a man of us left."

"There's no chance for that boy anyway," the Major said grimly. "I should have shot his horse myself, before he got out of range. That way we could have saved the boy."

All the Rangers watched the desperate race helplessly. They saw that what the Major said was true. Ezekiel Moody had no chance. Old Shadrach raised his long rifle in case Buffalo Hump strayed in range, but he didn't expect it, and he didn't fire.

"I hope he remembers what I told him about killing himself," Bigfoot said. "He'd be better off to stop running and kill himself. It'd be the easiest thing."

Ezekiel Moody had the same thought. He was running as fast as his legs could carry him, but when he looked back, he saw that the Indian with the great hump was closing fast. Ezekiel's heart was beating so hard with fear that he was afraid it might burst. He had just come upon Josh Corn's body when his horse went down. He had seen the great red cap of blood where Josh's scalp had been. He had also seen the bloody arrow protruding from Josh's throat.

Yet he was afraid to stop running and try to kill himself. He was afraid the Comanche would be on him before he could even get his pistol out. Also, he was getting close enough to the Rangers that one of them might make a lucky shot and hit Buffalo Hump, or turn him. Old Shadrach had been known to make some remarkable shots—maybe if he just kept running one of the Rangers would get off a good long shot.

Then abruptly Zeke changed his mind and gave up. He stopped and tried to yank out his pistol and shove it against his eyeball, as Bigfoot had instructed. He knew the Indian on the bloody horse was almost on him—he knew he had to be quick.

But when he got his pistol out, he turned to glance at the charging Indian, and the pistol dropped out of his sweaty hand. Before he could stoop for it the horse and the Indian were there: he had failed; he was caught.

Buffalo Hump reached down and grabbed the terrified boy by his long black hair. He yanked his horse to a stop, lifted Zeke Moody off his feet, and slashed at his head with a knife, just above the boy's ears. Then he whirled and raced across the front of the huddled Rangers, dragging Zeke by the hair. As the horse increased its speed, the scalp tore loose and Zeke fell free. Buffalo Hump had whirled again, and held aloft the bloody scalp. Then he turned and rode away slowly, at a walk, to show his contempt for the marksmanship of the Rangers. The bloody scalp he still held high.

Ezekiel Moody stumbled through the sage and cactus, screaming from the pain of his ripped scalp. So much blood streamed over his eyes that he couldn't see. He wanted to go back and find his pistol, so he could finish killing himself, but Buffalo Hump had dragged him far from where he had dropped the pistol. He could scarcely see, for blood. Zeke was in too much pain to retrace his steps. All he could do was stumble along, screaming in pain at almost every step.

Shadrach sighted on the Comanche with the big hump, as Buffalo Hump rode away. Then he raised his barrel a bit before he fired. It was an old buffalo hunter's trick, but it didn't work. Buffalo Hump was out of range, and Zeke Moody was scalped and screaming from pain.

"Ain't nobody going to go get Zeke?" Matilda asked. The boy's screams affected her—she had begun to cry. In peaceful times, back in San Antonio, Zeke had sometimes sat and played the harmonica to her.

"Somebody needs to help that boy, he's bad hurt," she said.

"Matilda, he'll find his way here—once he gets a little closer we'll go carry him in," the Major said. "He oughtn't to have left the troop —if young Corn hadn't, he might be alive."

The Major was a good deal annoyed by the predicament he found himself in. The scalp hunters had defected, the two captives were lost, one young Ranger was dead, and another disabled; Johnny Carthage had an arrow in his leg that so far nobody had been able to pull out; besides that they had lost two horses, one pack mule, and most of their ammunition. It seemed to him a dismal turn of events. He still had no idea how large a force he faced—the only Indian to show himself was the chief, Buffalo Hump, who had spent the morning having bloody sport at their expense.

"Well, this is merry," Bigfoot said. "We've been running around like chickens, and Buffalo Hump has been cutting our heads off."

"Now, he didn't cut Zeke's head off, just his hair," Bob Bascom corrected. He was of a practical bent and did not approve of inaccurate statements, however amusing they might be.

"Zeke will have to keep his hat on this winter, I expect," Bigfoot said. "He's gonna scare the women, now that he's been scalped."

"He don't scare me, he's just a boy," Matilda said. She was disgusted with the inaction of the men—so disgusted that she started walking out to help Zeke herself.

"Hold up, Matty, we don't need you getting killed too," the Major said.

Matilda ignored him. She had never liked fat officers, and this one was so fat he had difficulty getting his prod out from under his belly when he visited her. In any case, she had never allowed soldiers, fat or otherwise, to give her orders.

Call and Gus knelt together, keeping a tight hold on the bridle reins of their two horses. Both of them could see Zeke, whose whole face and body were red.

"I expect he'll die from that scalping," Call said.

"I didn't know people had that much blood in them," Gus said. "I thought we was mostly bone inside."

Call didn't admit it, but he had the same belief; but from what he had seen that morning, it seemed that people were really just sacks of blood with legs and arms stuck on them.

"Keep close to me," Gus said. "There might be some more of them sneaking devils around here close."

"I am close to you," Call said, still thinking about the blood. Now and again, working for the old blacksmith, he had cut himself, sometimes deeply, on a saw blade or a knife. But what he had seen in the last few minutes was different. The ground where Josh had been killed was soaked, as if from a red rain. It reminded him of the area behind the butcher stall in San Antonio, where beeves and goats were killed and hung up to drain.

Now there was Zeke, a healthy man only a few minutes ago,

staggering around with his scalp torn off. Call knew that if Buffalo Hump had been a few steps faster when he was chasing Gus, Gus would look like Josh or Zeke.

In San Antonio every man on the street, whether they were famous Indian fighters like Bigfoot, or just farmers in for supplies, told stories of Indian brutalities—Call had long known in his head that Indian fighting on the raw frontier between the Brazos and the Pecos was bloody and violent. But hearing about it and seeing it were different things. Rangering was supposed to be adventure, but this was not just adventure. This was struggle and death, both violent. Hearing about it and seeing it happen were different things.

"We'll have to be watching every minute now," Gus said. "We can't just lope off anymore, looking for pigs to shoot. We have to be watching. These Indians are too good at hiding."

Call knew it was true. He had glanced over at Josh Corn just as Josh was taking his pants down to shit, and had seen nothing at all that looked worrisome—just a few sage bushes. And yet the same humpbacked Indian who had chased Gus and nearly caught him had been hiding there. Not only that, he had managed to kill Josh and mutilate him without making a sound, with all the Rangers and Matilda just a few yards away.

Until that morning Call had never really felt himself to be in danger—not even when he had sat around the campfire and listened to the tortured Mexican scream. The Mexican had been a lone man, whereas they were a Ranger troop. Nobody was going to come into camp and bother them.

Now it had happened, though—an Indian had come within rock-throwing distance and killed Josh Corn. The same Indian had caught Zeke and scalped him, as quick as Sam, the cook, could wring a chicken's neck.

Gus McCrae wished that his churning stomach would just settle. He wasn't confident of his shooting, anyway—not beyond a certain distance—and he felt he was in a situation that might require him to shoot well, something that would not be easy, not with his stomach heaving and jerking. He wanted to be steady, but he wasn't.

Another thing that had begun to weigh on Gus's mind was that so far he had actually only been able to spot one Indian: Buffalo Hump. When he looked up on the mountain he couldn't see the

Indians who had shot the arrows down on them, and when he looked across the plain he couldn't see the Indian or Indians who had shot the Major's horse, and then Ezekiel's, too.

For no reason, just as Gus was feeling as if he might have to dry heave a little bit more, he remembered the conversation Shadrach had had with the Major about the hundreds of Indians that might be coming down to attack Mexico. The thought of hundreds of Comanches, now that he had seen firsthand what one or two could do, was hard to get comfortable with. Their little troop was already down to ten men, assuming that Zeke died of the scalping. It wouldn't take hundreds of Indians to wipe them out completely. It would only take three or four Indians—maybe less. Buffalo Hump might accomplish it by himself, if he kept at it.

"How many of them do you think are out there?" he asked Call, who was squeezing the barrel of his rifle so tightly it seemed as if he might be going to squeeze the barrel shut.

Call was having the same thoughts as his friend. If there were many Comanches out there, they would be lucky if any of the Rangers survived.

"I ain't seen but one—him," Call said. "There must be more, though. Somebody shot those horses."

"That ain't hard shooting," Gus said. "Anybody can hit a horse."

"They shot them while they were running and killed both of them dead," Call said. "Who says that's easy? Neither of them horses ever moved."

"I expect there's a passel of killers up on that mountain," Gus said. "They shot a lot of arrows down on us. You'd think they'd have shot at Matilda. She's the biggest target."

To Call's mind the remark was an example of his friend's impractical thinking. Matilda Roberts wasn't even armed. A sensible fighter would try to disable the armed men first, and then worry about the whores.

"The ones they ought to try for are Shadrach and Bigfoot," Call said. "They're the best fighters."

"I aim to give them a good fight, if I can ever spot them," Gus said, wondering if he could make true on his remark. His stomach was still pretty unsteady.

"I doubt there's more than five or six of them out there," he added, mostly in order to be talking. When he stopped talking he soon fell prey to unpleasant thoughts, such as how it would feel to be scalped, like Zeke was.

"How would you know there's only five or six?" Call asked. "There could be a bunch of them down in some gully, and we'd never see them."

"If there was a big bunch I expect they'd just come on and kill us," Gus said.

"Matilda's about got Zeke," Call said.

When Matilda finally reached the injured boy, he had dropped to his knees and was scrabbling around in the dust, trying to locate his dropped pistol.

"Here, Zeke—I'm here," Matilda said. "I've come to take you back to camp."

"No, I have to find my gun," Zeke said—he was startled that Matilda had come for him.

"I got to find it because that big one might come back," he added. "I've got to do what Bigfoot said—poke the gun in my eyeball and shoot, before he comes back."

"He won't come back, Zeke," Matilda said, trying to lift the wounded boy to his feet. "He'd have taken you with him, if he wanted you." The sight of the boy's head made her gag for a moment. She had seen several men shot or knifed in fights, but she had never had to look at a wound as bad as Zeke Moody's head. His face seemed to have dropped, too—his scalp must have been what held it up.

"Come on, let's go," Matilda said, trying again to lift him up.

"Let me be, just help me find my pistol," Zeke said. "I oughtn't to have run. I ought to have just killed myself, like Bigfoot said. I ought to have just stopped and done it."

Matilda caught Zeke under the arms and pulled him up. Once she had him on his feet, he walked fairly well.

"There ain't no pistol, Zeke," she said. "We'll just get back with the boys. You ain't dying, either. You just got your head skinned."

"No, I can't stand it, Matty," Zeke said. "It's like my head's on fire. Just shoot me, Matty. Just shoot me."

Matilda ignored the boy's whimperings and pleadings and half walked, half dragged him back toward the troop. When they were about fifty yards from camp young Call came out to help her. He was a willing worker, who had several times helped her with small chores. When he saw Ezekiel Moody's head, he went white. Gus McCrae came up to assist, and just as he arrived, Zeke passed out, from pain and shock. Bringing him in went easier once they didn't have to listen to his moans and sobs. All three of them were soon covered with his blood, but they got him into camp and laid him down near Sam, who would have to do whatever doctoring could be done.

"God amighty!" Long Bill said, when he saw the red smear of Ezekiel's head.

Johnny Carthage began to puke, while Bob Bascom walked away on shaky legs. Major Chevallie took one look at the boy's head and turned away.

Bigfoot and Shadrach exchanged looks. They both wished the boy had gone on and killed himself. If any of them were to survive, they would need to move fast and move quietly, hard things to manage if you were packing a scalped man.

Sam squatted down by the boy and swabbed a little of the blood away with a piece of sacking. They had no water to spare—it would take a bucketful to wash such a wound effectively, and they didn't have a bucketful to spare.

"We need to give him a hat," Sam said. "Otherwise the flies will be gettin' on this wound."

"How long will it take him to scab over?" the Major asked.

Sam looked at the wound again and swabbed off a little more blood.

"Four or five days—he may die first," Sam said.

Shadrach looked across the desert, trying to get some sense of where the Comanches were, and how many they faced. He thought there were three on the mountain, and probably at least three somewhere on the plain. He didn't think the same warrior killed both horses. He knew there could well be more Indians, though. A little spur of the mountain jutted out to the south, high enough to conceal a considerable party. If they were lucky, there were no more than seven or eight warriors—about the normal size for a Comanche raiding party. If there were many more than that, the Comanches would probably have overrun them when they were strung out in their race to the mountain. At that point they could have been easily divided and picked off.

"I doubt there's more than ten," Bigfoot said. "If there was a big bunch of them our horses would smell their horses—they'd be kicking up dust and snorting."

"They don't need more than ten," Shadrach said. "That humpback's with 'em."

Bigfoot didn't answer. He felt he could survive in the wilds as well as the next man, and there was no man he feared; but there were quite a few he respected enough to be cautious of, and Buffalo Hump was certainly one of those. He considered himself a superior plainsman; there wasn't much country between the Sabine and the Pecos that he didn't know well, and he had roved north as far as the Arkansas. He thought he knew country well, and yet he hadn't spotted the gully where Buffalo Hump hid his horse, before he killed Josh Corn. Nor had he ever seen, or expected to see, a man scalped while he was still alive, though he had heard of one or two incidents of men who had been scalped and lived to tell the tale. In the wilds there were always surprises, always things to learn that you didn't know.

Major Chevallie was nervously watching the scouts. He himself had a pounding headache, and a fever to boot. The army life disagreed with his constitution, and being harassed by Comanche Indians disagreed with it even more. Half his troop were either puking or walking unsteady on their feet, whether from fear or bad water he didn't know. While he was pondering his next move he saw Matilda walking back out into the sage bushes, as unconcerned as if she were walking a street in San Antonio.

"Here, Matilda, you can't just wander off—we're not on a boulevard," he said.

"I'm going to get Josh," Matilda said. "I don't intend to just leave him there, for the varmints to eat. If somebody will dig a grave while I'm gone I'll bring Josh back and put him in it."

Before she had gone twenty yards the Indians appeared from behind the jutting spur of mountain. There were nine in all, and Buffalo Hump was in the lead.

Major Chevallie wished for his binoculars, but his binoculars were on the horse that had been killed.

Several of the Rangers raised their rifles when the Indians came in sight, but Bigfoot yelled at them to hold their fire.

"You couldn't hit the dern hill at that distance, much less the Indians," he said. "Besides, they're leaving."

Sure enough the little group of Indians, led by Buffalo Hump, walked their horses slowly past the front of the Rangers' position. They were going east, but they were in no hurry. They rode slowly, in the direction of the Pecos. Matilda was more than one hundred yards from camp by that time, looking for Josh Corn's body, but she didn't look at the Indians and they didn't look at her.

Call and Gus stood together, watching. They had never before seen a party of Indians on the move. Of course, in San Antonio there were a few town Indians, drunk most of the time. Now and then they saw an Indian of a different type, one who looked capable of wild behaviour.

But even those unruly ones were nothing like what Call and Gus were watching now: a party of fighting Comanches, riding at ease through the country that was theirs. These Comanches were different from any men either of the young Rangers had ever seen. They were wild men, and yet skilled. Buffalo Hump had held a corpse on the back of his racing pony with one hand. He had scalped Zeke Moody without even getting off his horse. They were wild Indians, and it was their land they were riding through. Their rules were not white rules, and their thinking was not white thinking. Just watching them ride away affected young Gus and young Call powerfully. Neither of them spoke until the Comanches were almost out of sight.

"I'm glad there was just a few of them," Gus said, finally. "I doubt we could whip 'em if there were many more."

"We can't whip 'em," Call said.

Just as he said it, Buffalo Hump stopped, raised the two scalps high once again, and yelled his war cry, which echoed off the hill behind the Rangers.

Gus, Call, and most of the Rangers raised their guns, and some fired, although the Comanche chief was far out of range.

"If we was in a fight and it was live or die, I expect we could whip 'em," Gus said. "If it was live or die I wouldn't be for dying."

"If it was live or die, we'd die," Call said. What he had seen that morning had stripped him of any confidence he had once had in the Rangers as a fighting force. Perhaps their troop could fight well enough against Mexicans or against white men. But what he had seen of Comanche warfare—and all he had seen, other than the scalping of Zeke Moody, was a brief, lightning-lit glimpse of Buffalo Hump throwing his lance—convinced him not merely in his head but in his gut and even in his bones that they would not have survived a real attack. Bigfoot and Shadrach might have been plainsmen enough to escape, but the rest of them would have died.

"Any three of them could finish us," Call said. "That one with the hump could probably do it all by himself, if he had taken a notion to."

Gus McCrae didn't answer. He was scared, and didn't like the fact one bit. It wasn't just that he was scared at the moment, it was that he didn't know that he would ever be anything *but* scared again. He felt the need to move his bowels—he had been feeling the need for some time—but he was afraid to go. He didn't want to move more than two or three steps from Call. Josh Corn had just gone a few steps—very few—and now Buffalo Hump was waving his scalp in the air. He was waving Ezekiel's too, and all Zeke had done was ride a short distance out of camp. Gus was standing almost where Josh had been taken, too. Looking around, he couldn't see how even a lizard could hide, much less an Indian, and yet Buffalo Hump had hidden there.

Gus suddenly realized, to his embarrassment, that his knees were knocking. He heard an unusual sound and took a moment or two to figure out that it was the sound of his own knees knocking together. His knees had never done that in his life—they had never even come close. He looked around, hoping no one had noticed, and no one had. The men were all still watching the Comanches. The men were all scared: he could see it. Maybe old Shadrach wasn't, and maybe Bigfoot wasn't, but the rest of them were mostly as shaky as he was. Matilda wasn't, either—she was walking back, the body of Josh Corn in her arms.

Gus looked at Call, a man his own age. Call should be shaking, just as he was, but Call was just watching the Indians. He may not have been happy with the situation, but he wasn't shaking. He was looking at the Comanches steadily. He had his gun ready, but mainly he just seemed to be studying the Indians.

"I don't like 'em," Gus said, vehemently. He didn't like it that there were men who could scare him so badly that he was even afraid to take a shit.

"I wish we had a cannon," he said. "I guess they'd leave us alone if we was better armed."

"We are better armed than they are," Call said. "He killed Josh with an arrow and scalped Zeke with a knife. They shot arrows down on us from that hill. If they'd shot rifles I guess they would have killed most of us."

"They have at least one gun, though," Gus then pointed out. "They shot them horses."

"It wouldn't matter if we had ten cannons," Call said. "We couldn't even see 'em—how could we hit them? I doubt they'd just stand there watching while we loaded up a cannon and shot at them. They could be halfway to Mexico while we were doing that."

The Comanches were just specks in the distance by then.

"I have never seen no people like them," Call said. "I didn't know what wild Indians were like.

"Those are Comanches," he added.

Gus didn't know what his friend meant. Of course they were Comanches. He didn't know what answer to make, so he said nothing.

Once Buffalo Hump and his men were out of sight, the troop relaxed a little—just as they did, a gun went off.

"Oh God, he done for himself!" Rip Green said.

Zeke Moody had managed to slip Rip's pistol out of its holster— then he shot himself. The shot splattered Rip's pants leg with blood.

"Oh God, now look," Rip said. He stooped and tried to wipe the blood off his pants leg with a handful of sand.

Major Chevallie felt relieved. Travel with the scalped boy would have been slow, and in all likelihood he would have died of infection anyway. Johnny Carthage would be lucky to escape infection him- self—Sam had had to cut clean to the bone to get the arrow out. Johnny had yelped loudly while Sam was doing the cutting, but Sam bound the wound well and now Johnny was helping Long Bill scoop out a shallow grave for young Josh.

"Now you'll have to dig another," the Major informed them.

"Why, they were friends—let 'em bunk together in the hereafter," Bigfoot said. "It's too rocky out here to be digging many graves."

"It's not many—just two," the Major said, and he stuck to his point. The least a fallen warrior deserved, in his view, was a grave to himself.

When Matilda saw what Zeke had done, she cried. She almost dropped Josh's body, her big shoulders shook so.

"Matty's stout," Shadrach said, in admiration. "She carried that body nearly five hundred yards."

Matilda sobbed throughout the burying and the little ceremony, which consisted of the Major reciting the Lord's Prayer. Both boys had visited her several times—she remembered them kindly, for there was a sweetness in boys that didn't last long, once they became men. Both of them, in her view, deserved better than a shallow grave by a hill beyond the Pecos, a grave that the varmints would not long respect.

"Do you think Buffalo Hump left?" the Major asked Bigfoot. "Or is he just toying with us?"

"They're gone for now," Bigfoot said. "I don't expect they'll interfere with us again, not unless we're foolish."

"Maybe the scalp hunters will kill them," Long Bill suggested. "Killing Indians is scalp hunters' work. Kirker and Glanton ought to get busy and do it."

"I expect we'd best turn back," the Major said. "We've lost two men, two horses, and that mule."

"And the ammunition," Shadrach reminded him.

"Yes, I ought to have transferred it," the Major admitted.

He sighed, looking west. "I guess we'll have to mark this road another time," he said, in a tone of regret.

The scouts did not comment.

"Hurrah, we're going back," Gus said to Call once the news was announced.

"If they let us, we are," Call said. He was looking across the plain where the Comanches had gone, thinking about Buffalo Hump.

The land before him, which looked so empty, wasn't. A people were there who knew the emptiness better than he did; they knew it even better than Bigfoot or Shadrach. They knew it and they claimed it. They were the people of the emptiness.

"I'm glad I seen them," Call said.

"I ain't," Gus said. "Zeke and Josh are dead, and I nearly was."

"I'm still glad I seen them," Call said.

That day at dusk, as the troop was making a wary passage eastward, they found the old Comanche woman, wandering in the sage. A notch had been cut in her right nostril.

Of the tongueless boy there was no sign. When they asked the old woman what became of him she wailed and pointed north, toward the llano. Black Sam helped her up behind him on his mule, and they rode on, slowly, toward the Pecos.

part

II

1.

"Where is Santa Fe?" Call asked, when he first heard that an expedition was being got up to capture it. Gus McCrae had just heard the news, and had come running as fast as he could to inform Call so the two of them could be among the first to join.

"They say Caleb Cobb's leading the troop," Gus said.

Call was as vague about the name as he had been about the place. Several times, it seemed to him, he had heard people mention a place called Santa Fe, but so far as he could recall, he had not until that moment heard the name Caleb Cobb.

Gus, who had been painting a saloon when the news reached him, was highly excited, but short on particulars.

"Why, everybody's heard of Caleb Cobb," he said, though in fact the name was new to him as well.

"No, everybody ain't, because I ain't," Call informed him. "Is he a soldier, or what? I ain't joining up if I have to work for a soldier again."

"I think Caleb Cobb was the man who captured old Santa Anna,"

Gus said. "I guess sometimes he soldiers and sometimes he don't. I've heard that he fought Indians with Sam Houston himself."

The last assertion was a pure lie, but it was a lie with a serious purpose, and the purpose was to overcome Woodrow Call's stubborn skepticism and get him in the mood to join the expedition that would soon set out to capture Santa Fe.

Call had four mules yet to shoe and was not eager for a long palaver. There had been no rangering since the little troop had returned to San Antonio, though he and Gus were still drawing their pay.

Idleness didn't suit him; from time to time he still lent old Jesus a hand with the horseshoeing. Gus McCrae rarely did anything except solicit whores; in all likelihood it was a pimp named Redmond Dale, owner of San Antonio's newest saloon, who had talked Gus into doing the painting—no doubt he had offered free services as an inducement. What time Gus didn't spend in the whorehouses he usually spent in jail. With no work to do he had developed a tendency to drink liquor, and drinking liquor made him argumentative. The day seldom passed without Gus getting into a fight, the usual result being that he would whip three or four sober citizens and be hauled off to jail. Even when he didn't actually fight, he yelled or shot off his pistol or generally disturbed the peace.

"Anyway, we need to join up as soon as we can," Gus said. "I think we have to go up to Austin to enlist. I sure don't want to miss this expedition. Would you take them damn horseshoe nails out of your mouth and talk to me?"

Call had four horseshoe nails in his mouth at the time. To humour his friend he took them out and eased the mule's hoof back on the ground for a minute.

"I still don't know where Santa Fe is," Call said. "I don't want to join an expedition unless I know where it's going."

"I don't see why not," Gus said, irked by his friend's habit of asking too many questions.

"All the Rangers are going," Gus added. "Long Bill has already left to sign up, and Bob Bascom's about to leave. Johnny Carthage wants to go bad, but he's gimpy now—I doubt they'll take him."

The wound from the Comanche arrow had not healed well. One-eyed Johnny could still walk, but he was not speedy and would be at a severe disadvantage if he had to run.

[88]

"I think Santa Fe's out where we were the first time, only farther," Call remarked.

"Well, it could be out that way," Gus allowed. He was embarrassed to admit that he didn't know much about the place the great expedition was being got up to capture.

"Gus, if it's farther than we went the first time, we'll never get there," Call said. "Even if we do get there, what makes you think we can take it?"

"Why, of course we can take it!" Gus said. "Why are you so damn doubtful?"

Call shrugged, and picked up the horse's hoof again.

"It's a Mexican town—it's just defended by Mexicans," Gus insisted. "Of course we'll take it, and take it quick. Caleb Cobb wouldn't let a bunch of Mexicans whip him, I don't guess!"

"I might go if I thought there would be somebody with us who could find the place," Call said. "Is Bigfoot going?"

"I expect he is—of course he'll go," Gus said, though someone had told him that Bigfoot Wallace was off bear hunting.

"I don't think you know anything," Call informed him. "You just heard some talk and now you want to go fight. Santa Fe could be two thousand miles away, for all you know. I ain't even got a horse that could travel that far."

"Oh, they'll furnish the mounts," Gus said. "They say there's silver and gold piled everywhere in Santa Fe. I expect we can pick up enough just walking around to buy ourselves fifty horses."

"You'd believe anything," Call said. "What about Buffalo Hump? If Santa Fe's in his direction, he'll find us and kill us all."

"I don't expect he'd care if we took Santa Fe," Gus said, though he knew it was a weak comment. The thought of Buffalo Hump cast a chill on his enthusiasm. Capturing Santa Fe and picking up gold and silver off the ground were fine prospects, but if it involved crossing the Comancheria, as probably it did, then the whole matter had a side to it that was a good deal less pleasant. Since returning with the troop, he and Call had not been more than a few miles out of town—once or twice they had gone a little distance into the hills to hunt pigs or turkeys, but they did not camp out. The week scarcely passed without the Indians picking off some traveler, often almost in the outskirts of town. When they went out to hunt, they went in a group and took care to be heavily armed. Gus wore two pistols now, unless he was just engaged in light work such as painting saloons. He had not forgotten what happened west of the Pecos —time and time again, in his dreams, he had seen Buffalo Hump. He remembered that Zeke Moody had dropped his pistol and been scalped alive, as a result. He carried two so that if he got nervous and dropped one, he would still have a spare.

One of his friend Woodrow's most annoying traits was that he kept producing information you didn't want.

"I've heard that some of the army's coming on this expedition," he said. "I doubt the Indians would want to interfere with us if we've got the army along."

"Buffalo Hump has an army, too," Call reminded his excitable friend. "If he can find ten warriors to ride with him, then he's got an army.

"Besides, he lives there," he added. "He's got his whole people. I expect he'll interfere with us plenty, if we try to cross his country."

"Damn it, ain't you coming?" Gus asked, exasperated by his friend's contrariness. "Wouldn't you rather be riding out on an expedition than staying around here shoeing mules?"

"I might go if we have enough of a troop," Call said. "I'd like to know more about this man you named—what was he called?"

"Caleb Cobb—he's the man who captured Santa Anna," Gus said. He didn't know that Caleb Cobb had done anything of the sort, but he wanted to pile on as many heroics as he could. Maybe it would get Woodrow Call in the mood to travel.

"They say there's enough gold lying around in Santa Fe to fill two churches," Gus said, piling it on a little more.

"Why would the Mexicans just give us two churches full of gold? It don't sound like any Mexicans I've met," Call said.

Though not unwilling to consider an adventure—shoeing mules was a long way from being his favorite occupation; it was mainly something he did to help old Jesus, who had been kind to him when he first came to San Antonio—the one Gus McCrae was describing seemed pretty unlikely. He would be trying to reach a town he had never heard of, led by a man he had never heard of, either. Who would command the Rangers, if the Rangers went as a troop, he didn't know, but it wouldn't be Major Randall Chevallie, because Major Chevallie had died of a fever not three weeks after returning from the failed expedition to El Paso. They had got into some wet

weather on their return—also, they had traveled hard. Major Chevallie took to his bed for a day or two, got worse, died, and was
buried before anyone had time to think much about it.

"You're too damn contrary," Gus said. "I've never known a person more apt to take the opposite view than you—you're too damn
gripy."

"I expect I've spent too much time with mules," Call said. "When
would we be to leave, if we go?"

"What's wrong with now?" Gus asked. "The expedition's leaving
any day—I sure don't want to get left. We'd be rich for life if we
could pick up a little of that gold and silver."

"I hope we can whip the Mexicans, if we get there," Call said.

"Why wouldn't we, you fool?" Gus asked.

"We didn't whip 'em at the Alamo," Call reminded him. "We
might get out there on the plains somewhere and starve—that's
another thing to think about. We could barely find grub for twelve
men when we were out on the Pecos. How will we feed an army?

"There ain't much water out that way, neither," Call added, before Gus could break in with a few more lies about the gold to be
picked up in Santa Fe.

"Why, we'll be going across the plains—it's plenty wet up that
way," Gus said.

"You could shoe one of these mules if you don't have anything
else to do," Call suggested. "Once we get these mules shoed I might
be more interested in capturing Santa Fe."

Gus at once rejected the suggestion that he help shoe the mules.
He saw that Call was weakening in his opposition to the trip, and
his own spirits began to rise at the thought of the great adventure
that lay ahead of them.

"I say leave the mules—I want to get started for Austin," Gus
said. "Redmond Dale can find someone else to paint his saloon. Of
course we might have time for a visit to the whorehouse, if you ever
get tired of working."

"I can't afford the whorehouse—I'm saving up for a better gun,"
Call said. "If we're going out there into the Indian country, I need
to have a better gun."

He had visited the whorehouse, though, with Gus, several times
—he didn't scorn it as a pastime. Matilda Roberts was employed
there while waiting for passage to the west. She had taken a liking

to young Call. Gus too had his likeable side, but he was overpersistent, and also a blabber. There were times when Matilda could put up with persistence easier than she could with blab.

Young Call, though, seldom said two words. He just handed over the coins. Matilda saw something sad in the boy's eyes—it touched her. She saw after a few visits that her great bulk frightened him, and put him with a young Mexican girl named Rosa, who soon came to like him.

Call often thought of Rosa—she taught him many Spanish words: how to count, words for food. She was a slim girl who seldom smiled, though once in awhile she smiled at him. Call thought of her most afternoons when he was working in the hot lots behind the blacksmith's shop. He also thought of her at night when he was sleeping on his blanket, near the stable. He would have liked to see Rosa oftener—Gus had not been wrong to recommend whores, but Gus was reckless with his money and Call wasn't. Gus would borrow, or cheat at cards, or make promises he couldn't keep, just to have money for whores.

Call, though, could not bring himself to be so spendthrift. He knew that he wanted to be a Ranger once the troop went out again, which meant that sooner or later he would be fighting Indians. This time, when the fight came, he wanted to be as well equipped as his resources would permit. Neither of the cheap guns he owned was reliable. If he ever had to face the Comanche with the great hump again, he wanted a weapon that wouldn't fail him. Much as he was apt to think of Rosa, he knew that if he wanted to survive as a professional Ranger, he had to put guns first.

Once he felt assured that his friend was going to come with him on the new expedition, Gus relaxed, located a spot of shade under a wagon, stretched out full length, put his hat over his face, and took a long, serene nap while Call labored on with the mules. The last little mule was a biter—Call cuffed him several times, but the mule bared his teeth and demonstrated that he had every intention of using them on Call's flesh if he could. Call was finally forced to rope the mule's jaws shut before he could finish his work. Gus had a snore like a rasp—Call could hear the snore plainly when he wasn't hammering in a horseshoe nail.

Just as the last shoe was nailed in place, there was a clatter in the street. Call looked up to see Long Bill Coleman, Rip Green, gimpy

Johnny Carthage, and Matilda Roberts come loping up. Matilda was mounted on Tom, her large grey gelding.

"Saddle up, Woodrow—it's Santa Fe or bust," Long Bill sang out. He was wearing a fur cap he had found in a closet in the whorehouse.

"Dern, Bill, I thought you'd left town," Call said. "Ain't it a little warm for that hat?"

He himself was drenched in sweat from shoeing the four mules.

"That cap's to fool the grizzlies, if we meet any," Long Bill said. "I'm scared of grizzlies, and other kinds of bears as well. I figure if I wear this fur bonnet they'll think I'm one of the family and let me alone."

"That cap belonged to Joe Slaw; they hung the son of a bitch," Matilda said. "I guess he considered himself a mountain man."

Gus McCrae, hearing voices, suddenly rose up, forgetting that he was under a wagon. He whonked his head so loudly that everyone in the group laughed.

"Shut up, I think my skull's broke open," Gus said, annoyed at the levity—he had only made a simple mistake. His head had taken a solid crack, though. He wobbled over to the water tank and stuck his head under—the cool water felt good.

While the group was watching Gus dip his head in the water, Blackie Slidell came racing up—he had been with a whore when the others left the saloon. The reason for his rush was that he feared being left, which would mean having to cross the prairies in the direction of Austin all by himself.

"So, are you with us, Woodrow?" Rip Green asked. Although Call was a younger man than himself, Rip considered him dependable and was anxious to have him with the group.

"I thought you was already gone, Bill," Call said.

"Why no, we've been collecting Rangers, but we can't find Bigfoot, and Shadrach prefers to travel alone, mostly," Bill said. "He's already gone up to Austin. I guess we'll have to leave Bigfoot. I expect he'll catch up."

With so many of his companions mounted and ready, Call hesitated no longer. His complaints and criticism had mainly been designed to annoy Gus, anyway. The urge to be adventuring was too strong to be resisted.

"So, who's leading the Rangers?" he asked when he untied the jaw rope and released the biting mule.

"Why, we'll lead ourselves, unless somebody shows up who wants to captain," Long Bill said.

"Whoa—I ain't rangering for Bob Bascom," Gus said. "I don't like his surly tongue—I expect I'll have to whip him before the trip is over."

Long Bill looked skeptical at this prediction.

"Take a good club when you go to whip him," he said. "Bob's stout."

"Take two clubs," Blackie said. "Bob's a scrapper."

"I didn't expect you'd want to go fight Mexicans, Matty," Call said, surprised to see Matilda with the Rangers.

"I'm needing to get west before I get old," Matilda said. "I've heard there's roads to the west from up around Santa Fe."

Call's possessions were few, though he did now have a coat to go with his two shirts. Gus McCrae, because of his urgent expenditures, had only the clothes on his back and his two pistols. When old Jesus saw that Call was leaving, he sighed. The thought of having to shoe all the horses and mules by himself made him feel a weariness. He had done hard work all his life and was ready to stop, but he couldn't stop. All his children had left home except one little girl, and his little girl could not shoe mules. Yet he could not blame Call for going—he himself had roved, when he was young. He had left Saltillo and come to the land of the Texans, but now he was weary and his only helper was leaving. There was something about the boy that he liked, too—and he didn't like many of the Texas boys.

"Adios," he said, as Call was tying his blanket and his extra shirt onto his saddle.

"Adios, Jesus," Call said—he liked the old man. They had not exchanged a cross word in all the time Call had worked for him.

"Let's ride, boys," Long Bill said. "Austin's a far piece up the road."

"We'll ride, but I ain't a boy," Matilda said, as they rode out of San Antonio. Gus McCrae had a headache, from rising up too quickly after his nap.

2.

"Boys, it's clouding up," Long Bill said late in their first day out of San Antonio. "I expect we're in for a drenching."

"I'd rather ride all night than sleep wet," Rip Green observed.

"Not me," Gus said. "If I have to be wet I'd just as soon be snoozing."

"There's plenty of farms up this way," Matilda said. "German families, mostly. If we could find a farm they might let us sleep on the floor. Or if they have some kind of shed for the stock, maybe we could crawl under it."

As the sun was dipping, Call noticed that the whole southwestern quadrant of the sky had turned coal black. In the distance there was a rumbling of thunder. At the horizon the blackness was cut through with streaks of golden light from the setting sun, but the light at the bottom only made the blackness of the upper sky seem blacker. A wind rose—it whirled Call's straw hat off his head and sailed it a good thirty feet, which annoyed him. He hated above all to lose control of his headgear.

Long Bill cackled at the sight.

"You ought to have a good fur cap, like I do," he said.

They crested a ridge and spotted just what Matilda had been hoping for—a little farm. There was only one building in the little clearing, but it was a sizable log building.

"It'll hold us all, snug, if the family is friendly," Blackie Slidell observed.

"I hope they're cooking pork, if they're cooking," Gus said. "I'd enjoy a good supper of pork."

Call retrieved his hat, but the wind had risen so that he saw no point in sticking it back on his head. All the men were holding their hats on by this time. They were a mile or two from the little cabin, and the darkness in the sky was swelling, pushing toward them. It abruptly extinguished the sunset, but the force of the sun left an eerie light over the long prairie ahead.

The rumblings of the thunder were deeper. Call had seen many storms, and paid them little mind, but this one caught his attention. It had been a sultry day—the wind coming out of the cloud wasn't cool. It was a sultry wind, and it blew fitfully, at first. Some gusts were so strong they caused his horse to break stride—of course, his horse was just a skinny nag that had been underfed for the last few weeks. It wouldn't take much of a wind to blow him off course.

"Why, look at that," Gus said. "That dern cloud is behaving like a snake."

Call looked, and saw that it was true. A portion of the cloud had formed itself into a column, or funnel, and was twisting through the lower sky in a snakelike motion.

"You damn young fools, that's a cyclone," Matilda said. "We better race for that cabin."

The snake cloud was dipping closer and ever closer to the ground, sucking up dust and weeds as it twisted. A hawk that had been skimming the ground looking for mice or quail rose, and sped away; Call saw two deer bolt from a little thicket and flash their white tails as they raced off, away from the twisting cloud. The cloud was roaring so loudly by then that the horses began to rear and pitch. They wanted to run away, like the deer.

"We won't make that cabin, we need to lay flat," Long Bill advised. "That's what you do when a cyclone hits. We best find a ditch or a gully or something, or we're done for."

"There's a buffalo wallow," Blackie said. "That's all I see."

"It ain't deep," Gus said. He had been feeling good, enjoying the thought of adventure, and now a dangerous cloud had come out of nowhere and spoiled his feeling. They were scarcely a mile from the cabin, but the spinning, roaring, sucking cloud was coming too fast. All day Gus had tensed himself and strained his eyes, looking for Indians. He didn't want to see the humpbacked Comanche charge out of a thicket with his lance raised. If Buffalo Hump showed up, or any hostile red man, he was prepared to run and shoot. The last thing he had expected was deadly weather, but now deadly weather was two hundred yards away. A bobcat burst from a thicket and began to run in the same direction as the deer.

The Rangers reached the little wallow and jumped off their mounts.

"What about the horses?" Call yelled, as the roar increased.

"The devil with the horses—get flat!" Long Bill advised. "Get flat and don't look up."

Call did as he was told. He released his rearing mount and flattened himself under the edge of the shallow wallow. The other Rangers did the same.

Gus was fearful of Matilda's chances—she was so big she couldn't really hide in anything as shallow as a buffalo wallow. But there was no time to dig—she would just have to hope for the best.

Then the roaring became so loud that none of them could think. Call's loose shirt billowed up—he thought the wind inside it was going to lift him off the ground. There was a kind of seething noise, like a snake's hiss, only louder—it was the sound of the sand being sucked up from the shallow wallow. It was pitch black by then—as black as a moonless midnight.

Gus was wishing he'd never come to Texas—what was it but one danger after another? He had been thinking about the cabin ahead, and the pork chop he hoped to eat, and now he had his face in the dirt, being pulled at by a cloud that was like a giant snake. In Tennessee clouds didn't behave like that. Besides, their horses were lost, though they had scarcely traveled half a day. Both his pistols were on his saddle, too—if he survived the storm and Buffalo Hump showed up, he would be helpless.

The sound of the cyclone was so loud, and the dust swirling up beneath them so thick, that some of the Rangers felt they were being deafened and suffocated at the same time. Blackie Slidell, who was limber, managed to bend his neck and get his nose inside his shirt, so he could breathe a little better.

But the whirling and roaring slowly diminished—when the Rangers felt it safe to lift their heads, they saw sunlight beneath the black edge of cloud, far to the west. The eerie light still hung over the prairie, a light that seemed hellish to Rip Green.

"I expect this is the kind of light you get once you're dead," he commented.

Matilda sat up, relieved. She had heard that cyclones took people up in the air and blew them as much as forty miles away. People who survived such removals were never again right in the head, so she had heard. Of course, being heavy, she herself was less likely than some to blow away, but then wagons sometimes blew away, and she was no heavier than a wagon.

"Are we all alive?" she asked. The grey light was so strange it made them all look different—most of them had been so scared while they were pressing themselves into the wallow that their voices sounded strange when they tried to talk.

"We're alive but we're afoot," Call said. Though unnerved, he hadn't really had time to be very frightened—the cyclone was a thing beyond him or any man. An Indian he could fight, but who could fight a roaring snake of air? His hat was gone—all the hats were gone, except Long Bill Coleman's fur cap, which he had stuffed beneath him as he clutched the sand.

"We ought to have tied them horses, somehow," Call added. "I expect they've run halfway back to San Antonio by now."

"I'd rather lose my horse than blow away," Gus said. "Them was just thirty-dollar horses anyway."

"I could spare the nag, but they took everything we own with them," Blackie said. "We'll have to hobble into Austin and hope they allow us credit."

"You boys are green—them horses ain't run far," Long Bill said. "They'll show up in the morning, or else we'll track 'em."

Now that he had survived the cyclone, Gus began to feel lively. The storm had scared his headache away, but not his appetite.

"I'm still in the mood for a pork chop," he said. "Let's go on to that cabin. They might just be sitting down to supper."

Having no other prospect to hand, the Rangers adopted the suggestion, only to find that the cyclone had obliterated the cabin where they had hoped to bunk. When they got to the ridge where it had been, there were only a few logs in place, and six unhappy people were stumbling around weeping and looking dazed—four children and a man and a woman. The man and the woman had lanterns and were shining them in the rubble, hoping to locate a few possessions to pile up. The four children had been scared into silence. One little girl was chewing on the hem of her dress.

Her father, a stout young man with a full beard, was inquiring about his roof in the bewildered tone that a man might use to complain about a mislaid hammer.

"Where's my roof, dammit?" the young man said. "It was here and now it's gone. I worked a week on my roof—now I guess it's blown plumb over into the woods."

"Well, we lost our horses," Gus said—a little callously, Call felt. The stout man with the beard had a family to house. Losing a thirty-dollar horse with a cheap saddle and blanket on it was not a loss on the same scale as the man's roof.

The area where the cabin had been was a wild litter. It was almost dark, but the Rangers could see that clothes and utensils and tools and animals were as jumbled as if they had all been hastily shoveled out of a wagon. A black rooster stood on one of the fallen logs, complaining loudly. Two shoats were grunting and rooting amid the mess, and several hens squawked.

No one paid much attention when Matilda and the six Rangers came walking up in the last of the light. The only person who seemed reasonably calm was the young woman of the house, and she was quietly picking up utensils and clothes and putting them in neat piles.

"Dern the luck—it's a pain to lose that roof," the stout man said. He didn't address the remark either to his wife or to the Rangers—he seemed to be talking to himself.

"That's enough cussing, Roy," the young woman said. "We got visitors, and the children don't need to hear you cussing just because the cabin got blown away. We can build another cabin."

"I can, you mean, Melly," the man said. "You ain't strong enough to hoist no logs."

"I said we got visitors, Roy—why don't you be polite and ask them to sit, at least?" the young woman said, with a flash of temper.

"You have to take weather as it comes," she added. "Cussing don't change it."

"Here, maybe we can help you pick up," Gus offered. He liked the looks of the young woman, Melly. Even in the dim light he could tell she was pretty. The husband seemed a rude sort—Gus felt it was a pity *he* hadn't been blown away. A young woman that pretty might entice him to give up rangering, if she took a notion.

"Well, men, I hope you ain't thieves, because our worldly possessions are spread out here for the picking of any damn thieves who happen to walk up," Roy said. He was still agitated by the loss of his roof.

The Rangers did what they could by lantern light to help the little family reassemble its scattered possessions. There were no pork chops, but the young woman did have some bacon and a little cornmeal. Long Bill Coleman was a master fire builder; he soon had a good blaze going in the ruins of the little chimney. They all ate bacon and corn cakes and talked about how curious it was to see an ordinary thundercloud turn into a cyclone.

"It sucked the dern bark off that tree over there," Roy said, pointing in the darkness to a tree nobody could see. "What kind of wind would suck the bark off an elm tree?"

"We're all alive, though, thank the Lord," Melly observed gratefully. She was sitting by Matilda Roberts. Though too polite to inquire, she was wondering what kind of woman would be traipsing across the prairies with six Texas Rangers. Of course on the frontier, things were less regular than they had been in eastern Missouri, where she was from.

Matilda, for her part, indulged in a little daydream in which she was married to a farmer with a beard, and had four tykes, some chickens, and a couple of shoats. In those circumstances she would have no need to accept whatever smelly ruffian came along with a dollar or two and a stiffness in his pants.

The little children, none of them yet five according to their mother, were curled up like little possums, asleep on a quilt that had escaped wetting. Long Bill Coleman brought out his harmonica —he never trusted it to his saddlebags but kept it about his person, and played a tune called "Barbara Allen." Call liked to listen to Long Bill play the harmonica. The old tune, clear and plaintive, made a sadness come in him. He didn't know why the music made him sad—or even what the sadness was for. After all, as the young woman said, they were all still alive, and not much worse off than they had been before the cyclone struck. The loss of the horses was a nuisance, of course, but it wasn't because of the horses that he felt sad. He felt sad for all of them: the Rangers, Matilda, the little family that had lost its roof. They were small, and the world was large and violent. They were alive and, for the moment, well enough fed; but the very next day another storm might come, or an Indian party, and then they wouldn't be.

"Well, I can't dance to that old song," Gus informed Long Bill. "I prefer tunes that I can dance to."

"Why then, here's 'Buffalo Gals,' " Long Bill said—he was soon playing a livelier melody. Gus got up and jigged around, hoping to impress Melly with his dancing. Rip Green joined him for a bit, but the others refused to dance.

"I'll be damned if I'll dance on the night my roof blew off," Roy said.

A little later Roy took his lantern and rummaged around until he found his whiskey jug, which he passed around freely. Long Bill Coleman soon put away his harmonica in order to drink, which annoyed Gus a little, because he wasn't through dancing. He was even more convinced that he would make a good husband for Melly —certainly a better husband than the surly Roy.

When dawn came, Roy found most of his roof at the edge of a little live-oak thicket, over a hundred yards from where the cabin stood. Long Bill was right about the horses—they were all found within half a mile of the buffalo wallow. There was no more bacon, but Melly made them a breakfast of corn cakes and chickory coffee.

Roy, realizing that he had an excellent labor force at hand, tried to persuade the Rangers to stay and help him rebuild his cabin. Gus McCrae wouldn't have minded. Melly had a peaches-and-cream complexion. She looked even prettier in the morning than she had in the dim dusk. But the other Rangers pleaded urgent business in Austin—they were soon mounted and ready to go.

"We're off to take Santa Fe," Blackie Slidell informed the homesteaders. "Caleb Cobb's our leader."

"Santa Fe?" Roy asked. "You mean Santa Fe, out in New Mexico?"

"That's the town—what of it?" Rip Green said, noticing that Roy wore a somewhat skeptical expression.

"Why, it's over a thousand miles from here," Roy said. "You could get there quicker if you started from St. Louis. There's a good trail from St. Louis. My pa was a trader on the Santa Fe trail, until he got murdered by a damn quick Mexican."

"Why'd he get murdered?" Johnny Carthage asked.

"No reason, much—the quick Mexican got the drop on him and shot him dead," Roy said. "I went to Santa Fe three times when I was growing up."

"Oh now, tell us about it," Gus said. "I hear there's gold and silver laying around for the taking."

"You heard an idiot, then," Roy said. "There's no gold, and you have to bargain hard for what silver you get. My pa did better with furs. The mountain men show up pretty regular with furs, or they used to. I got married to Melly and quit the trading life."

"Furs?" Gus said. "You mean like Long Bill's cap?"

"Oh, that's just a rabbit skin—I wouldn't call that a fur," Roy said. "I mean beaver, mainly. There's no beaver down here—you wouldn't know what I was talking about."

"Anyway, once we get there, we mean to annex New Mexico, I believe," Blackie Slidell said. "I expect the populace will be mighty glad to see us."

"The hell they will; they hate Texans—don't any of you boys have any experience at all?" Roy asked.

"Well, we ain't been to Santa Fe, if that's what you mean," Long Bill admitted. "I guess Caleb Cobb wouldn't be leading an expedition all the way to Santa Fe unless he had his facts down."

Roy looked at his wife in amusement. The little girl who had been frightened by the cyclone was still chewing on the hem of her dress. Two of the little boys were throwing rocks at one of the shoats, and the black rooster was still complaining.

"These men have been deceived," Roy said to Melly. "They think the Mexicans are just going to walk up and start piling gold and silver in their wagons, once they get to Santa Fe—*if* they get to Santa Fe. Caleb Cobb is a reckless rum-running scoundrel. What he'll do is get you all killed or captured, I expect.

"Of course, I doubt he can even find Santa Fe—maybe all that will happen is that you'll get lost," Roy went on. "Look for the Arkansas River, if you get lost up on the prairies. Once you find the Arkansas, you'll be all right."

The Rangers rode off, leaving the little family to sort through their soaked possessions. The troop's mood was somewhat dampened by Roy's pessimism.

"I expect it was a lie," Gus said. "The man's a farmer. He probably never set foot in Santa Fe."

"He sounded like he knew what he was talking about to me," Call said.

"No, you can't trust people from Missouri," Rip Green said.

"Why can't you? I'm from Missouri," Johnny Carthage said. "Missouri's as honest as the next place."

"Why would the man lie?" Call asked. "He's never seen us before."

Matilda Roberts let out a hoot. "Gus wouldn't think that's a reason not to lie," she said. "Gus lies all the time to people he's never seen before—gals, mostly."

The remark caused Gus to blush—he had been thinking the same thing himself, though of course he would never have said it. One of the main troubles with women was that they were always saying things that ought not to be said. Of course he lied freely to impress the girls, but what business was that of Matilda's?

"Look yonder, ain't that Bigfoot's horse?" Blackie Slidell said. "That's his big sorrel, I believe."

The mood of the whole troop lifted at the thought of joining up again with Bigfoot Wallace. Shadrach was a commendable scout, more experienced than Bigfoot in the ways of the wilderness, but Shadrach was ill tempered, with a tendency to growl and snarl if approached when he wasn't in the mood for conversation. He didn't like to talk and had no interest in sharing his information with men who lacked his experience. He might help, if the mood struck him, or he might just ride away.

Bigfoot Wallace, on the other hand, loved to talk. He was a gifted explainer—once when a little drunk he had spent an hour lecturing Call and Gus on three sets of horse tracks they had come across. He told them everything he knew about the tracks—why he knew they were Mexican horses, how heavy the riders were, when the tracks had been made, and what, in his judgment, the condition of the animals was who had made the tracks. The two of them had gone off and located another set of tracks; they tried to apply a few of the things Bigfoot had taught them, but with poor success. About all they knew about their set of tracks was that they were horse tracks—as to the weight or nationality or general health of the men riding their horses, they could only speculate. In fact, they were so green when it came to tracking, that they couldn't even be sure *anyone* was riding the horses. They might merely have been horses grazing along. Of course, they both did know that the horses were unshod, but that was as far as their training took them.

"Maybe he's killed a wild pig," Gus said. "We could eat it." Bigfoot's horse was still quite a distance away—there was as yet no sign of the tall man himself.

"I'd rather he killed a fat doe, myself," Rip Green said. "I'd a bunch rather eat some tender venison than that old tough pig meat."

"Them corn cakes don't stick to the ribs," Gus said. "Melly's pretty, though."

"Yes, you were ready to run off with her, I noticed," Matilda said. Even though it had been dark, Gus's response to the young woman had not escaped her attention.

"Maybe that cyclone caught Bigfoot," Long Bill said. "That may just be his nag. He may have got blown away."

"Not likely," Gus said. "I imagine he got down in a buffalo wallow, like we did."

"There might not have been no buffalo wallow handy," Johnny Carthage said. "That twister might have caught Bigfoot out on the flat."

The relief everybody in the troop had felt at the thought that they would soon have a reliable guide to lead them over the prairies to Austin went away, to be replaced by dread. The experience beyond the Pecos had left its mark on all of them—even in the comparatively settled country between San Antonio and Austin, the Comanche and Kiowa lurked, running off horses and occasionally even beeves. The plain ahead of them, where they saw Bigfoot's horse, was wide and empty—the last thicket that might provide cover was behind them, back near the smashed cabin. The sight of Bigfoot Wallace would have made every man feel a good deal more confident of reaching Austin alive.

"Dern, it's just his horse," Rip Green said. "I bet that storm spooked his sorrel, like it did our nags. Bigfoot's probably on foot, looking for his horse right now."

They loped on across the wide prairie, which wasn't as flat as it looked. It rolled a little, and dipped. When they were a hundred yards from the sorrel horse they looked down into a little dip and saw the man they had been talking about: Bigfoot Wallace. He was kneeling by two blackened wagons, digging in the dirt with a large bowie knife.

"Now what's he doing digging, out on the prairie?" Long Bill asked. "Do you think he's digging for onions, or spuds of some kind?"

Bigfoot stopped digging when he saw the group approaching. They all waved, even though they were a hundred yards away. Bigfoot didn't wave. He watched a minute, and then returned to his digging.

Call was a little ahead of the troop—there was a smell in the air that Call had never smelled before, a burned smell with a sweetness in it like cooked meat sometimes had when the meat was fresh. When old Jesus roasted a baby lamb in its skin it sometimes smelled like what they were smelling then.

Then, abruptly, Call saw what Bigfoot was doing—he stopped his horse, causing Gus, who was just behind him, to ride into him.

"Whoa, what is it?" Gus asked, confused for a moment.

"Bigfoot ain't digging onions," Call said.

"What is he digging, then?" Long Bill asked—he was too near-sighted to see clearly what young Call saw.

"He's digging a grave," Call said.

3.

THE RANGER TROOP APPROACHED, but too slowly to suit Bigfoot Wallace. He had already cut the blackened corpses of the two mule skinners loose from the wagon wheels where they had been tied. Though he had smelled burned human flesh before, he didn't like to smell it, and he was anxious to get the burying over with in case the Indians who had burned the two men chose to come back and try him.

"Are you men praying? If you ain't, get down and help me," he said impatiently.

"Oh Lord, look!" Rip Green said. He barely was off his horse before he began to puke. Gus didn't dare look, really—he threw the briefest glance at the two blackened corpses and turned his eyes away. Even so, his stomach rose—he rode off a few steps, hoping to get the smell out of his nostrils before he had to dismount and puke like Rip.

Call got down and immediately began to help Bigfoot. He tried not to look at the two corpses but could not help seeing that their teeth were bared in the agony in which they died. There were ashes in front of the wagon wheels they had been tied to. A twist of smoke still rose in front of the fires.

Call did have a good knife. Old Jesus had forged it for him, sharpened it carefully, and bound the handle with tight rawhide. Call dug hard—it was the only way he could keep his mind off what had happened to the two men. One of the burned wagons was still smouldering. It was only then, when he glanced up, that he noticed that the prairie around the wagon was white: the two mule skinners had been hauling flour, and the Indians had ripped up the sacks and scattered the flour on the grass.

"Lordy, these boys weren't lucky," Long Bill observed philosophically, walking around the scene of the torture.

"Nope, and they weren't prepared, either," Bigfoot said. "I guess that old shotgun was the only weapon they had with them." He nodded toward the shotgun, which had been broken in two on a large rock that stuck up from the ground.

"I wouldn't set off with a load of flour and nothing to defend myself with except a fowling piece—not in this country," Blackie Slidell remarked.

"There's empty sacks in that other wagon that ain't too burned," Bigfoot said. "Go get a few, Gus, and roll these men in them. We need to move out. I make it about nine Indians that cooked these men, and one of them was Buffalo Hump."

"Did you see him?" Johnny Carthage asked, turning white. All the Rangers touched their weapons, to make sure they were still there.

"No, but he's still riding that painted pony he rode that day he killed Josh and Zeke," Bigfoot said. "I studied his track, in case I ever had to fight him again, and his track is all around these wagons."

"Oh, Lord—I was afraid it was him," Rip Green said. He was white and shaky.

Johnny Carthage knew a little cobbling. He had been offered a job making shoes in San Antonio. Looking at the two burned wagoneers, their bodies blackened and swollen, their teeth bared in terrible grimaces, he wondered why he hadn't had the good sense to take the job. Cobbling down by the San Antonio River had a lot to recommend it. It wasn't exciting, but neither would it expose you to the risk of being caught on the open prairie, roped to a wagon wheel, and burned to death. Of course, he could go back and take the job—the old cobbler liked him—but he was already a long ride out of San Antonio, and would run the very risk he wanted to avoid if he tried to go back alone.

"I wish there was more timber on this road," Blackie Slidell said. "I don't know if we could whip nine of those rascals if they came charging and we had nothing to hide behind."

"Nine's about the right size for a raiding party," Bigfoot observed. He had about finished his digging. The grave wasn't deep enough, but it would have to do.

"Why?" Call asked.

"Why what?" Bigfoot replied. The youngster was a good digger, and besides, he was steady. Of all the troop, he was the least affected by the sight of charred bodies. Of course, Long Bill wasn't shaking or puking, but Long Bill was notorious for his bad eyesight. He probably hadn't come close enough to take a good look.

"Why is nine a good size?" Call asked, as Gus handed him an armful of sacks. He spread one layer of sacking over each man, and then rolled the bodies over and tucked another layer of sacking over their backsides. It was curious how stiff bodies got—the dead men's limbs were as stiff as wood.

"Nine's about right," Bigfoot said, impressed that young Call was eager to learn, even while performing an unpleasant task. "Nine men who know the country can slip between the settlements without being noticed. They can watch the settlers and figure out which farms to attack. If there's a family with four or five big strapping boys who look like they can shoot, they'll leave it and go on to one where there's mostly womenfolk."

Matilda Roberts stood looking at the corpses as Call and Gus finished covering them with sacking. She recognized one of the men; his name was Eli, and he had come to her more than once.

"That nearest one is Eli Baker," she said. "He worked in the flour mill. I know him by his ear."

"What about his ear?" Bigfoot asked.

"Look at it, before you rake the dirt over him," Matilda said. "He got half his ear cut off when he was a boy—the bottom half. That's Eli Baker for sure. We ought to try to get word to his family. I believe he had several young 'uns."

[108]

"And a wife?" Bigfoot asked.

"Well, he didn't have the young 'uns himself," Matilda said. "I ain't seen him in a year or two, but I know he's Eli Baker."

When the corpses were covered, everyone stood around awkwardly for a minute. The wide prairie was empty, though the tall grass sang from the breeze. The sun shone brilliantly. Bigfoot took the stock of the broken shotgun and tamped the dirt solidly over the grave of the two wagoneers.

"If anybody knows a good scripture, let them say it," Bigfoot said. "We need to skedaddle. I'd rather not have to race no Comanches today—my horse is lame."

"There's that scripture about the green pastures," Long Bill recalled. "It's about the Lord being a shepherd."

"So say it then, Bill," Bigfoot said. He caught his horse and waited impatiently to mount.

Long Bill was silent.

"Well, there's the green pastures," he said. "That's all I can recall. It's been awhile since I had any dealings with scriptures."

"Can anyone say it?" Bigfoot asked.

"Leadeth me beside the still waters," Matilda said. "I think that's the one Bill's talking about."

"Well, this is a green pasture, at least," Bigfoot said. "It'll be greener, if it keeps raining."

"I wonder why people want to say scriptures when they've buried somebody?" Call reflected to Gus as they were trotting on toward Austin. "They're dead—they can't hear no holy talk."

Gus had the scared feeling inside again. The Indian who had nearly brought him down with a lance was somewhere around. He might be tracking them, or watching them, even then. He might be anywhere, with his warriors. They were approaching a little copse of live-oak trees thick enough to conceal a party of Comanches. What if Buffalo Hump and his warriors suddenly burst out, yelling their terrible war cries? Would he be able to shoot straight? Would he have the guts to fire a bullet through his eyeball if the battle went against them? Would he end up burned, swollen, and stiff, like the two men they had just buried? Those were the important questions, when you were out on the prairie where the wild men lived. Why people said scriptures over the dead was not an issue he could concentrate his mind on, not when he had the scared feeling in his stomach. Even if he could have had the pork chop his mouth had been watering for the night before, he had no confidence that he could have kept it down.

"It's the custom," he said, finally. "People get to thinking of heaven, when people die."

Call didn't answer. He was wondering what the mule skinners were thinking and feeling when the Comanches tied them to the wagon wheels and began to build fires under them. Were they thinking of angels, or just wishing they could be dead?

"As soon as we get to Austin, I want to buy a better gun," he said. "I mean to practice, too. If we're going on this expedition, we need to learn to shoot."

Toward evening, the sky darkened again toward the southwest. Once again the sky turned coal black, with only a thin line of light at the horizon. The rolls of thunder were so loud that the Rangers had to give up conversation.

"It might be another cyclone," Blackie yelled. "We need to look for a gully or a ditch."

This time, though, no twisting snake cloud formed, though a violent thunderstorm slashed at them for some fifteen minutes, drenching them all. They expected a wet, cold night but by good fortune came upon a big live-oak tree that lightning had just struck. The tree had been split right in two. Part of the tree was still blazing, when the rain began to diminish. It made a good hot fire and enabled everybody to strip off and dry their clothes. Matilda, far from shy, stripped off first—Call was reluctant to take all his clothes off in her presence, but Gus wasn't. He didn't have a cent, but hoped the sight of him would incline Matilda to be friendly, or a little more than friendly, later in the evening—a hope that was disappointed. Bigfoot had Buffalo Hump on his mind: there was a time for sport, and a time to keep a close watch. None of the Rangers slept much —but the blazing fire was some comfort. By midnight, when it was Call's turn to watch, the sky was cloudless and the stars shone bright.

4.

CALEB COBB AND HIS sour captain, Billy Falconer, enlisted the six Rangers for the expedition against New Mexico immediately. The Rangers simply walked up to the hotel where the enlistments were being handled, and the matter was done.

Billy Falconer was a dark little snipe of a man, with quick eyes, but Caleb Cobb was large; to Call he appeared slow. He stood a good six foot five inches, and had long, flowing blond hair. On the table in front of him, when he cast his lazy gaze over the men who hoped to go with him on the expedition, were two Walker Colt pistols, the latest thing in weaponry. Call would have liked one of the Walkers—at least he would have liked to hold one and heft it, though of course he knew that such fine guns were far beyond his means.

"There's no wages, this is volunteer soldiering," Caleb Cobb pointed out at once. "All we furnish is ammunition and grub."

"When possible, we expect you to rustle your own grub, at that," Captain Falconer said.

Caleb Cobb had a deep voice—he kept a deck of cards in his hand, and shuffled them endlessly.

"This is a freeman's army—only we won't call it an army," Caleb said.

"I wouldn't call it an army anyway, if these fellows outside the hotel are specimens of the soldiers," Bigfoot said.

Caleb Cobb smiled, or half smiled. Billy Falconer's eyes darted everywhere, whereas Caleb scarcely opened his. He leaned back in a big chair and watched the proceedings as if half asleep.

"Mainly we're a trading expedition, Mr. Wallace," Caleb Cobb said after a moment. "St. Louis has had the Santa Fe business long enough. Some of us down here in the Texas Republic think we ought to go up there and capture a bunch of it for ourselves."

"That crowd outside is mostly bankers and barbers," Bigfoot said. "If they want to trade, that's fine, but what are we going to do for fighting men if the Mexicans decide they don't like our looks?"

"That ain't your worry, that's ours," Captain Falconer snapped.

"It's mine if I'm taking my scalp over in that direction," Bigfoot said.

"Why, we'll gather up some fighters, here and there," Caleb said. "Captain Billy Falconer's such a firebrand I expect he could handle the Mexican army all by himself."

"If he's such a scrapper then let him go handle Buffalo Hump," Bigfoot suggested. "He and his boys cooked two mule skinners yesterday, not thirty miles from this hotel."

"Why, the ugly rascal," Falconer said, grabbing one of the Walker Colts. "I'll get up a party and go after him right now. You boys can come if you're game."

"Whoa, now, Billy," Caleb Cobb said. "You can go chase violent Comanches if you want to, but you ain't taking one of my new pistols. That humpback man might get the best of you, and then I'd be out a gun."

"Oh—I thought one of these was mine," Falconer said. He put the gun back on the table with a sheepish look.

"It ain't," Cobb said, sitting up a little straighter. Then he looked at Bigfoot again, and let his sleepy eyes drift over the troop. Call didn't like the man's manner—he considered it insolent. But he was conscious that he and Gus were the youngest men in the troop—it was not his place to speak.

"When are we leaving, then?" Bigfoot asked.

"Day after tomorrow, if General Lloyd gets here," Caleb said. "The roads down Houston way are said to be muddy—they're generally muddy. I guess the General may be stuck."

"General Lloyd?" Bigfoot asked, a little surprised. "I scouted for the man a few years back. Why are we taking a general, if this is a trading expedition?"

"It never hurts to have a general in tow, especially if you're dealing with Mexicans," Cobb said. "They like to deal with the jefe, in my experience. If they get ructious we can hang a few medals on Phil Lloyd and send him in to parley with the governor of Santa Fe —it might spare us some hostilities."

"I'd rather avoid hostilities, if we can," Caleb added, shuffling his cards.

"I'd rather avoid them myself—we'll be outnumbered fifty to one," Bigfoot commented. "The reason General Lloyd ain't here is because he got drunk and got lost. The man was dead drunk the whole time I scouted for him, and he got lost every time he stepped out of his tent to piss. He couldn't find Mexico if you pointed him south and gave him a year, and what's more, he can't ride."

Caleb Cobb chuckled. "Well, he can ride in a wagon, and if he can't we'll tie him in," he said.

"Our mounts are a little on the feeble side," Long Bill put in. "What do we do about horses?"

"You look like seasoned men," Caleb said. "The Republic of Texas will furnish you a horse apiece—Billy, sign them some chits. Half the men in Austin are horse traders—I expect you can find good mounts."

"What about guns? Mine's a poor weapon," Call asked. "I would like to replace it if possible, before we leave."

"Guns are your lookout," Captain Falconer snapped. "If you're Rangers I guess you're drawing Rangers' pay. You can buy your own guns."

"No, I think some new guns would be a sound investment, Billy," Caleb said. "I expect the Mexicans will welcome us with open arms and probably cook a few goats and lay us out a feast. But folks are unpredictable. If the Mexicans get fractious it would be good if we're well armed, so we can shoot the damn bastards. Tell the quartermaster to help these gentlemen arm themselves proper."

[113]

"So what's our route, Colonel?" Bigfoot inquired.

"You're too full of questions—we ain't figured out the route," Falconer snapped. "We ain't got all day to stand around talking, either."

Caleb Cobb merely smiled.

Captain Falconer briskly wrote them out some chits for horses—good with any trader in Austin, he claimed—and then marched them over to a man named Brognoli, who was in charge of stores and armaments. Brognoli was in the process of buying livestock when they found him. Twenty beeves had been driven in—they were ambling around the town square, which, at that time, was a maelstrom of activity. A wagon master was hammering together a new wagon, several saddle makers were making repairs on saddles the volunteers had brought in, and a dentist was pulling a man's tooth right in the middle of it all. The man yowled, but the dentist persisted and brought out a tooth with a long red root.

"I'll be damned if I'd let a man stick pliers in my mouth and pull out my teeth," Gus said, as they walked through the crowd. Horses, mules, sheep, pigs, and chickens crowded the square. Call had never been in the midst of so much activity before—he felt a little hemmed in. There was so much to see that it was more than a little confusing. So engrossed was the quartermaster Brognoli in purchasing livestock that it was half an hour before he could attend to their request for guns. When he did get time for them, he proved to be a friendly man.

"Muskets are what we've got—I've not been issued pistols," he said. "The muskets will do for buffalo, or Indians, either."

He took them into a storeroom behind a large general store—cases of muskets were stacked on top of one another. While Call and the others were hefting various rifles and looking at ammunition pouches, Gus happened to peek into the store itself—there was a girl standing there by a counter who was so lovely that Gus immediately forgot all about cap-and-ball muskets, ammunition pouches, and everything else. The girl seemed to work in the store—she was helping an old lady try on a sunbonnet. The girl was slim; she had the liveliest expression—also, she was alert. Gus had merely glanced at her, supposing that she was too busy to notice, but she caught his glance and looked at him so directly that it unnerved him. He would have retreated back to the muskets had she not immediately smiled at him in a quick, friendly way.

Emboldened by that smile, Gus abandoned his comrades and walked into the store. It was a big, high-ceilinged store filled with every kind of goods, from hammers and nails to fine headwear—he couldn't resist trying on a new grey hat with a sweeping brim, though he knew he couldn't afford it. He could hear the old lady chattering on—she was in no hurry to choose her sunbonnet. Twice Gus decided the young woman was so busy with the old harpy that he could risk another glance or two, but both times he risked it, the girl caught the glance, as if it were a ball he had tossed her. She didn't allow his glances to distract her from her work, but she didn't fail to notice them, either.

Gus proceeded to examine a case full of knives; he had always had a strong fondness for knives. Some of the ones in the case would have excited him a lot on any other day—they had gleaming blades, with handles of ivory or horn; but compared to the pretty girl selling sunbonnets, knives were of little interest.

When the old lady finally chose her sunbonnet and paid for it, Gus was trying to work up his nerve to say good morning to the girl, but before he had it worked up there was another interruption: a brusque little man in a black frock coat bustled in, and went straight to the cigars.

"Morning, Miss Forsythe," the fellow said. "I'm here for my cigar."

"Here it is, Dr. Morris," the girl said. "We've already got it wrapped up. My father tended to it personally."

"Yes, but he attended to it too well," the little doctor said, quickly tearing the wrapping off the little package the girl handed him. He extracted a long cigar and pulled it slowly under his nose.

"Never buy a cigar without smelling it," he advised the girl—then he tipped his hat and walked out, the cigar jutting out of his mouth.

"I guess that was good advice," the young woman said, strolling over to Gus. "But I won't take it."

"Well, why wouldn't you?" Gus asked, amazed that the young woman had simply walked over and addressed him.

"Because I don't fancy cigars," the girl said, with a smile.

Then she thrust the wadded-up paper from the doctor's package into his hand.

"Here, dispose of this, sir," she said, with a fetching smile.

"Do what?" Gus asked, paralyzed with anxiety lest he do something wrong and scare the girl away—though, he had to admit, she didn't look easily scared.

"Dispose of this paper—I can see that you're tall, but I don't know if you're useful," the girl said. "I'm Clara. Who are you?"

"Augustus McCrae," Gus said. Though he rarely used his full name, he felt that on this occasion it would be proper.

"Augustus—did you hear that? He's a Roman like you, Mr. Brognoli," Clara said, addressing the quartermaster, who had stepped into the store for the moment to give her chits for the muskets.

"I don't think so, Miss Forsythe," Brognoli said, tipping his cap to the girl. "I think he's just a young rascal from Tennessee.

"You better get your musket—you'll need it where you're going," he added, looking at Gus. "What's that in your hand? You ain't been stealing from Miss Forsythe, have you?"

"Oh no—it's just some wrapping I asked him to dispose of," Clara said. "I like to find out quick if a man's useful or not. So far he ain't disposed of it. I guess that means he's a laggard."

"Oh, this—I aim to keep it forever," Gus said, flushed with embarrassment. Brognoli had already turned and disappeared—he was alone with Clara Forsythe, who was watching him out of two keen eyes.

"Keep it forever, that scrap!" Clara said. "Why would you do such a foolish thing as that, Mr. McCrae? You have important soldiering to do—I expect you'll need both hands."

"I'll keep it because you gave it to me," Gus said.

Clara stopped smiling and looked at him calmly. The speech didn't seem to surprise her, though it greatly surprised Gus. He had not meant to say anything of the sort. But such a feeling had risen in him, because of Clara Forsythe, that he couldn't move his limbs or control his speech.

"Here, don't you want to pick a gun?" Call asked, sticking his head in the store for a moment. He saw Gus standing by a girl and supposed he was trying to buy something he couldn't afford and didn't need—whereas he did need a gun.

"You pick one for me—I expect it will do," Gus said, determined not to leave Miss Forsythe's presence until he absolutely had to.

[116]

"We're going to buy horses—don't you want to pick your own mount?" Call asked, a little puzzled by his friend's behaviour.

He looked again at the young shop girl and saw that she was unusually pretty—perhaps that explained it. Still, they were about to set off on a long, dangerous expedition—choosing the right gun and the right mount could mean life or death, once they were out on the prairies. If he was that taken with the shop girl, he could come back later and chatter—though, for once, Gus wasn't chattering. He was just standing there, as if planted to the floor, holding some scraps of paper in his hand. It was unusual behaviour. Call stepped into the store, thinking his friend might be sick. He tipped his straw hat to the pretty shop girl as he approached.

"Hello, are you a Roman too, sir?" Clara asked, with a smile.

Call was stumped—he didn't understand the question. The young woman's look was so direct that it startled him. What did it mean, to be a Roman, and why had she asked?

"No, this is Woodrow Call, he's a plain Texan," Gus said. "I don't know how that fellow knew I was from Tennessee."

In fact, Brognoli's comment had irked him—what right had a quartermaster to be speculating with Miss Forsythe about where he was from?

"Why, Mr. Brognoli's a traveled man," Clara said. "He's been telling me about Europe. I mean to go there someday, and see the sights."

"If it's farther off than Santa Fe I doubt I'll have time to go," Call said. He found that he didn't feel awkward talking to the shop girl —she was so friendly that talking was easy, even though he had no idea where Europe was or what sights might be there for a young lady to see.

Call was impatient, though—they had to outfit themselves for a great expedition, and they only had a day to do it. He glanced around the big store and saw that it contained goods of every description, many of which would probably be useful on their expedition—but their chits only covered guns and horses. It was pointless to waste time looking around a big store, when they had no money to spend at all. Yet Gus seemed reluctant to move.

"I'll be along, Woodrow—I'll be along," Gus said. "Just grab me a musket as you leave."

[117]

"Why, I believe I've smitten Mr. McCrae," Clara said, with a laugh. "I doubt I could smite you, though, Mr. Call—not unless I had a club."

With no more said, she turned and began to unpack a large box of dry goods.

Call turned and left, a little puzzled by the shop girl's remark. Why would she want to smite him with a club? She seemed a friendly girl, though the meaning of her remark was hard to puzzle out.

Clara whistled a tune as she unpacked the big box of dry goods. She glanced up after a bit and saw that Augustus McCrae, the young Tennessean, was still standing exactly where he had been when she last addressed him.

"Hey you, go along," she said. "Your friend Mr. Call is waiting."

"No, he ain't waiting," Gus said. "He left with the boys."

"Are you really a Texas Ranger?" Clara asked. "I've not met too many Texas Rangers. My father says they're rascals, mostly. Are you a rascal, Mr. McCrae?"

Gus hardly knew how to respond to such a barrage of questions.

"I may have done a rascally thing or two," Gus said. Since Clara was so frank, he decided honesty might be the best policy. She was smiling when she looked at him, which was puzzling.

"Here, since you're still around, put this cotton over on that bench," she said. "It's got mussed up, somewhere along the way. I expect we'll have to wash it before we can sell it. Folks around here won't pay money for cotton goods that look mussed."

Gus took the swatch of cotton cloth and put it where she had told him to. An old man in a brown coat came in while he was doing it. The old man had on a grey hat and had a patch over one eye. He looked a little surprised to see a stranger carrying his dry goods around.

"Hi, Pa, this is Mr. Augustus McCrae of Tennessee," Clara said merrily. "He's a Texas Ranger but he seems to have time to spare, so I put him right to work."

"I see," Mr. Forsythe said. He shook Gus's hand and looked at Clara, his daughter, with great fondness.

"She's brash, ain't she?" he said to Gus. "You don't need to wait for an opinion, if Clara's around. She'll get you an opinion before you can catch your breath."

Clara was still unpacking goods, whistling as she worked. She had her sleeves rolled up, exposing her pretty wrists.

"Well, I must go look at them horses," Gus said. "Many thanks for the visit."

"Was it a visit?" Clara said, giving him one of her direct glances.

"Seemed like one," Gus said. He felt the remark was inadequate, but couldn't think of another.

"That door ain't locked. You can come back and pitch in with the unpacking, Mr. McCrae, if you have time," Clara said.

Old man Forsythe chuckled.

"If he doesn't have it, he'll make it," he said, putting his arm around his daughter's shoulder for a moment.

Gus tipped his hat to both of them and walked out the front door, the scraps of wrapping paper still in his hand. Once out of Clara's sight he carefully folded the brown paper and put it in his breast pocket.

Although he had left the general store and was back amid the throng of peddlers and merchants, all hoping to profit from the coming expedition, in his mind Gus still stood by the big box of dry goods, waiting for Clara Forsythe to hand him another swatch of cloth. Call, who was standing with Long Bill and Blackie Slidell not twenty yards away, had to yell at him three times to get his attention.

"Here, I hope you're pleased with this musket," Call said, when Gus finally strolled over. "It's new and it's got a good heft. I don't know what we'll do about pistols. Mr. Brognoli says they're costly."

"I don't want to go," Gus said flatly. "I wonder if that girl's pa would hire me to work in that store?"

"What?" Call said, shocked. "You don't want to go on the expedition?"

"No, I'd rather marry that girl," Gus said.

Long Bill and Blackie Slidell thought it was the funniest joke of the year. They laughed so hard that the dentist, who was about to pull another tooth out of another customer, stopped his work for a moment in amazement.

Call, however, was embarrassed for his friend. The expedition to Santa Fe was a serious matter. They were Rangers—they had to defend the Republic. Yet Gus had just walked into a store to select a musket, spotted a girl with a frank manner, and now wanted to quit rangering.

"Marry her—you ain't got a cent," Call said. "Anyway, why would she have you? You ain't known her ten minutes."

"Ten minutes is enough," Gus said. "I want to marry her, and I aim to."

"He's a cutter, ain't he?" Long Bill commented. "Meets a girl and the next thing you know, he's off to hunt a preacher."

"Well, you heard me," Gus said. "I aim to marry her, and that's that."

"No, now you can't, that's desertion," Blackie pointed out. "You signed your mark this morning, right in front of Caleb Cobb. I expect he'd hang you on the spot if you tried to quit."

The remark had a sobering effect. Gus had totally forgotten signing his mark and putting himself under military command. He had forgotten most of his life prior to meeting Clara. The fact that he could be executed for changing his mind had never occurred to him.

"Why, that marking don't amount to much," Gus said. He didn't want to be hanged, but he also didn't want to leave Austin, now that he had found the woman he intended to marry.

"You need to visit the whorehouse, it will clear your head," Long Bill said. "My head's cloudy, too. I say we all go, once we've picked our horses."

"I don't want no whore," Call said—but in fact, once they picked their horses and bought a slicker apiece, they all went down by the river, where several whores were working out of a shanty. There were six stalls, with blankets hung between them. Gus chose a Mexican girl, and did his business quickly—once he was done, even as he was buckling his pants, he still thought of Clara Forsythe and her pretty wrists.

Call chose a young white woman named Maggie, who took his coins and accepted him in silence. She had grey eyes—she seemed to be sad. The look in her eye, as he was pulling his pants up, made him a little uneasy—it was a sorrowful look. He felt he ought to say something, perhaps try to talk to the girl a little, but he didn't know how to talk to her, or even why he felt he should.

"Thank you, good-bye," he said, finally.

Maggie didn't smile. She stood at the back of the stall, by the quilt she slept on and worked on, waiting for the next Ranger to come in.

Johnny Carthage was waiting when Call came out. He had a policy of not buying Mexican women, the reason being that a Mexican whore had stabbed out his eye while trying to rob him.

"Well, what's your opinion? Is she lively?" Johnny asked, as Call came out.

"I have no opinion," Call said, still troubled by the sorrow in Maggie's eyes.

5.

Gus McCrae moped all afternoon, and would do no work. Call, who had become an expert farrier, took it upon himself to shoe the Rangers' new horses. He didn't want one of them coming up lame, not on such a long, risky trip. Shadrach showed up while he was working—he was dusty and grizzled. When asked where he had been, Shadrach said he had been west, hunting cougars.

"Dern, when I hunt I want something that's better eating than a cougar," Bigfoot informed him.

"I just take the liver," Shadrach said.

"Cougar liver?" Bigfoot asked in amazement. "I've heard the Comanches eat the liver out of cougars, but Comanches eat pole-cats, too. I ain't yet et a polecat, and I hope I never have to eat the liver out of a mountain cat."

"It's medicine," Shadrach said. "Good medicine. I'm likely to see some cougars, going across the plains."

"Oh—I guess you've started thinking like an Indian, Shad," Big-foot said.

"The better to fight 'em," Shadrach said. He went over and dipped his head in a big water trough to get some of the dust out of his long, shaggy hair.

Gus finally agreed to help a little with the horseshoeing, but his mind wasn't on his work. If Call asked for a rasp, Gus would likely hand him an awl, or even a nail. Twice he wandered off to visit the general store, but Clara was off on errands. Mr. Forsythe was pleasant to him, but vague about when his daughter might return.

"I can't predict her," he said. "She's like the wind. Sometimes she's quiet, and sometimes she's not."

Annoyed at the girl—why couldn't she stay where he could find her?—Gus took the best alternative left to him, which was to get drunk. He bought a jug of liquor from a Mexican peddler and sat under a shed and drank it, while Call finished the horseshoeing. While he was working, a buggy drove by—an old man wearing a military coat was asleep in it. The old man had a red face, and was snoring so loudly they could hear him even after the buggy had passed.

"Well, that's Phil Lloyd, the damned sot," Bigfoot said. "He's a general, but he ain't a good one. I doubt we could get enough barrels of whiskey in a wagon to keep Phil Lloyd happy all the way to Santa Fe, unless we lope along quick."

Call decided the military was peculiar—why make a general out of an old man who couldn't even find his way around? He tried to interest Gus in the question, but Gus could not be bothered by such business.

"She wasn't there," he said several times, referring to Clara. "I went back twice to visit—she said I might—but she wasn't there either time."

"I expect she'll be there in the morning," Call said. "You can trot by and say adios. They say we're leaving tomorrow."

"You may be leaving, I ain't," Gus replied. "I ain't leaving tomorrow, or any other time."

Call knew his friend was too drunk to make sense—he didn't press him.

"Let's walk down by the river, I feel restless," Gus said a little later. "That store's closed by now—there's no chance to visit until tomorrow."

Call was happy to walk with him. It was a starry night, and the

[123]

Rangers had just made a good meal off some tamales Blackie Slidell had purchased from a Mexican woman. A little walk would be pleasant. He took his new musket, in case they encountered trouble. The Comanches had been known to come right into Austin and take children, or even young women. It wouldn't hurt to be armed.

They walked a good distance on the bluffs over above the Colorado River—they could see a light out in the water. Somebody was out in a boat.

"Fishing, I expect," Call said.

Gus was still fairly drunk.

"What kind of fool would fish at night? The fish wouldn't be able to see the bait," Gus said. Then, between one step and the next, he suddenly plunged into space. He was so drunk he wasn't frightened; sometimes when very drunk he passed out—it felt a little like falling. He assumed, for a moment, that he must be in the process of passing out. The lantern light on the water was spinning, which went with being drunk, too.

He felt himself turn over, which was also a feeling he got when he was drunk; then he saw the river again, but it seemed to him that it was above him. He began to realize that he *was* falling, through a night so dark that he couldn't see anything. He couldn't even remember what he had been doing before he fell.

"A fish don't need to see, it can smell," Call said, just before noting, to his shock, that he was talking to nobody. Gus McCrae, at his elbow only the moment before, had disappeared. Call's first thought was that an Indian had snatched Gus, though he didn't see how, since he and Gus had only been a step apart. But Buffalo Hump had taken Josh Corn, and he hadn't been far away, either.

Call whirled around, almost going off the bluff himself. He couldn't see the edge, but he could see the river in the starlight. The river was a good distance down—he realized then that Gus must have fallen. He didn't know what to do—probably it was too late to do anything. Gus might already be dead or dying. Call knew he had to get down to him, but he didn't know how to go about it without falling himself. He had no rope, and it was so dark he feared to try and climb down.

Then he remembered that during the day he had seen an old man with a fishing pole making his way down a kind of trail. There was a way down, but he would need a light of some kind if he was going to find it.

Call began to run back toward town, staying well clear of the bluff; he was hoping to encounter someone with a light. But it was as if suddenly he were back on the long plain beyond the Pecos: he saw not a soul until he had run all the way back to where the Rangers were camped. When he got there he discovered that the only Ranger who wasn't dead drunk was gimpy Johnny Carthage, the slowest man in camp. Blackie Slidell and Rip Green were so drunk they couldn't even remember who Gus McCrae was. Johnny Carthage was willing, at least; he and Call found a lantern, and made their way back to the river. In time, they found a place where they could scramble down the cliff.

The problem then was that Call could not tell how far down the bluff they had walked before Gus fell. With the help of the lantern, though, he could see that the bluff wasn't high enough for a fall to be fatal, unless Gus had been unlucky and broken his neck or his back.

Johnny Carthage was fairly stalwart while they were on the bluff. But once down by the river, with help far away, his fear of Indians grew to such proportions that he flinched at every shadow.

"Indians can swim," he announced, looking out at the dark water.

"Who can?" Call asked. He wanted to call out to Gus, but of course if there were Indians near, the calling would give them away. He was afraid Johnny might panic, if the risks increased much.

"Indians," Johnny said. "That big one with the hump could be right out there in the water."

"Why would he be out there, this time of night?" Call asked. Mainly he was trying to distract Johnny from his fear by asking sensible questions.

"Well, he might," Johnny said. He had a great urge to shoot his gun, although he couldn't see a thing to shoot at. He just had the feeling that if he shot his gun, he might feel a little less scared.

To Call's shock and surprise, Johnny suddenly shot his gun. Call assumed it meant he had seen Indians—perhaps Buffalo Hump *was* in the river. Johnny Carthage was ten years older than he was, and more experienced—he might have spotted an Indian in the water somehow.

"Did you hit him?" Call asked.

"Hit who?" Johnny said.

"The Indian you shot at," Call said.

Johnny was so scared he had already forgotten his own shot. He remembered wanting to shoot—he felt it would make him less nervous—but he had no memory of actually firing the gun.

Gus McCrae couldn't get the stars above him to come into focus. He was lying on his back, a terrible pain in his left ankle, wondering if he was drunk or dead. Surely if he was dead, his ankle wouldn't hurt so badly. But then, he wasn't sure—perhaps the dead could still feel. He couldn't be sure of anything, except that his left ankle hurt. He could hear the lap of water against the shore, which probably meant that he was still alive. He wasn't wet, either—that was good. One of the things he disliked most about rangering was that it very often left him unprotected from the elements. On the first march to the Pecos, he had been drenched several times—once, crossing some insignificant little creek, his boots had filled with water. When he took them off to empty them, he noticed several of the older Rangers laughing, but it wasn't until he tried to put his boots back on that he realized what they were laughing at. He *couldn't* get his boots back on—his feet, which had just come out of those very boots, wouldn't go back in. They didn't go back in for almost two days, until the boots had thoroughly dried. Gus remembered the incident mainly because his ankle hurt so—he knew he could never force his foot into a boot, not with his ankle hurting so badly. He would just have to go bootless on that foot for awhile, until his ankle mended.

While he was thinking about the difficulties that arose when you got wet, a gun went off nearby. Gus's thought was that it was an Indian—he tried to roll under a bush, but there were no bushes on the river shore. Even though he disliked being wet, he didn't dislike it as much as he disliked the thought of being taken by an Indian. He started to roll into the water, thinking that he could swim out far enough that the Indians couldn't find him, when he heard nearby the voices of Johnny Carthage and Woodrow Call, talking about the very subject he had just been thinking about: Indians.

"Here, boys—it's me!" he cried out. "Come fast—I'm right by the bluff."

A moment later Call and Johnny found him, to his great relief.

"I was afraid it was that big one," he said, when they came with the lantern. "He could poke that big lance right through me, if he came upon me laying down."

Though glad to have found Gus alive, Call was still not sure exactly what the situation was. Neither was Johnny. The fact that the latter had fired his gun confused them both. Though not quite dead drunk, Johnny was actually less sober than Call had supposed him to be back at the camp. He had seemed sober in comparison with Blackie and Rip, but now whatever he had drunk seemed to have suddenly caught up with him. He couldn't remember whether he had fired his gun because he had seen an Indian, or whether he had just shot to be shooting—it could even be that the gun had gone off entirely by accident.

Call was exasperated. He had never known a man to be so vague about his own behaviour.

"You shot the gun," he reminded Johnny, for the third time. "What did you shoot it at—an Indian?"

"Matilda et that big turtle," Johnny said—he was growing rapidly less in command of his faculties. All he could remember of his earlier life was that Matilda Roberts had cooked a snapping turtle in a Ranger camp on the Rio Grande.

"That wasn't tonight, Johnny," Call insisted. "That was a long time back, and I don't know what it's got to do with tonight. You didn't shoot at a snapping turtle, did you?"

Johnny Carthage was silent, perplexed. Call couldn't help but be annoyed. They were in a life-or-death situation—why couldn't the man remember what he shot at?

"What did you shoot at *tonight?*" he asked again.

Gus was feeling more and more convinced that he was alive and well—except, of course, for a damaged ankle.

"I hope my ankle ain't broke—it hurts," he said. "You might as well let up on Johnny, though. He ain't got no idea why he shot his gun."

"I'd have to be hungry to eat a dern turtle," Johnny Carthage said. It was his final comment of the evening. To Call's intense annoyance he lapsed into a stupor, and was soon as prostrate as Gus.

"Now I've got two of you down," Call said. "This is a damn nuisance."

Gus was too relieved to be alive, to worry very much about his friend's distemper.

"I wonder if that girl will be in the store tomorrow?" he asked, out loud. "I sure would like to see that girl again, although my ankle's bad."

"Go see her, then," Call said brusquely. "Maybe she'll sell you a crutch."

6.

WHEN CALL HELPED GUS hobble back to camp—Johnny Carthage was no help, having passed out drunk near where Gus had fallen—Bigfoot happened to be there, drinking with Long Bill and Rip Green. After a certain amount of poking and prodding, during which Gus let out a yelp or two, Bigfoot pronounced his ankle sprained but not broken. Gus's mood sank—he was afraid it meant that he would not be allowed to go on the expedition.

"But you wasn't going anyway, you were aiming to stay and marry that girl," Call reminded him.

"No—I aim to go," Gus said. "If I could collect a little of that silver we could live rich, if I do marry her."

In fact he was torn. He had a powerful desire to marry Clara; but at the same time, the thought of watching his companions ride off on their great adventure made him moody and sad.

"You reckon Colonel Cobb would leave me, because of this ankle?" he asked.

"Why no, there's plenty of wagons you could ride in—a sprain's usually better in a week," Bigfoot said. "I guess they could put you in that buggy with old Phil Lloyd, unless they mean to transport him in a cart."

"Ride with a general?" Gus asked. "I wouldn't know what to say to a general."

"You won't have to say a word to Phil Lloyd, he'll be too drunk to talk," Bigfoot assured him.

The next morning, the sprained ankle was so swollen Gus couldn't put even a fraction of his weight on it. The matter chagrined him deeply—he had hoped to be at the general store at opening time, in order to help Miss Forsythe with her unpacking. Yet even standing up was painful—needles of pain shot through his ankle.

"I expect they have liniment in that store," Call told him. "I guess I could walk up there and buy you some liniment."

"Oh, you would!" Gus said, agitated at the thought that Call would get to see Clara before he did. "I suppose you'll want to help her unpack dry goods, too."

"What?" Call said, puzzled by Gus's annoyance. "Why would I want to help her unpack? I don't work in that store."

"Bear grease is best for sprains," Long Bill informed him.

"Well, do we have any?" Gus asked, eager to head off Call's trip to the general store.

"Why no—I don't keep any," Long Bill said. "Maybe we can scrape a little up, next time we kill a bear."

"I seen a bear once, eating a horse," Gus remembered. "I didn't kill him, though."

Call grew tired of the aimless conversation and walked on up to the store. The girl was there, quick as ever. She wasn't unpacking dry goods, though. She was stacking pennies on a counter, whistling while she did it.

"Be quiet, don't interrupt me," she said, throwing Call a merry glance. "I'll have to do this all over if I lose my count."

Call waited patiently until she had finished tallying up the pennies —she wrote the total on a little slip of paper.

"So it's you and not Mr. McCrae," she said when she was finished. "I rather expected Mr. McCrae. I guess he ain't as smitten as I thought."

"Oh, he's mighty smitten," Call assured her. "He meant to be here early, but he fell and hurt his ankle."

[130]

"Just like a man—is it broke?" Clara asked. "I expect he done it dancing with a señorita. He looks to me like he's the kind of Texas Ranger who visits the señoritas."

"No, he fell off a bluff," Call said. "I was with him at the time. He's got a bad sprain and thought some liniment might help."

"It might if I rubbed it on myself," Clara said.

Call was plain embarrassed. He had never heard of a woman rubbing liniment on a man's foot. It seemed improper to him, although he recognized that standards might be different in Austin.

"If I could buy some and take it to him, I expect he could just rub it on himself," Call said.

"I see you know nothing of medicine, sir," Clara said, thinking she had never met such a pompous young fool as Mr. Woodrow Call.

"Well, can I buy some?" Call asked. He found it tiring to do so much talking, particularly since the girl's manner was so brash and her attitude so confusing.

"Yes, here—we have the best liniment of any establishment in town," Clara said. "My father uses this one—I believe it's made from roots."

She handed Call a big jar of liniment, charging him twenty cents. Call was dismayed at the price—he hadn't supposed liniment would cost more than a dime.

"Tell Mr. McCrae I consider it very careless of him, to go falling off a bluff without my permission," Clara said, as she was wrapping the jar of liniment in brown paper. "He might have been useful to me today, if he hadn't been so careless."

"He had no notion that he was so close to the edge, Miss," Call said, thinking that he ought to try and defend his friend.

"No excuses, tell him I'm very put out," Clara demanded. "Once I smite a man, I expect more cautious behaviour."

When Call reported the conversation to Gus, Gus blamed it all on him.

"I suppose you informed her that I was drunk—you aim to marry her yourself, I expect," Gus said, in a temper.

Call was astonished by his friend's irrationality.

"I don't even know the woman's name," he told his friend.

"Pshaw, it don't take long to learn a name," Gus said. "You mean to marry her, don't you?"

"You must have broke your brain, when you took that fall," Call said. "I don't intend to marry nobody. I'm off to Santa Fe."

"Well, I am too—I wish I'd never let you go up to that store," Gus said. He was tormented by the thought that Clara Forsythe might have taken a liking to Call. She might have decided she preferred his friend, a thought so tormenting that he got up and tried to hobble to the store. But he could put no weight on the wounded ankle at all—it meant hopping on one leg, and he soon realized that he couldn't hop that far. Even if he had, what would Clara think of a man who came hopping in on one leg?

He was forced to lie in camp all day, sulking, while the other Rangers went about their business. Long Bill Coleman grew careless with the jug of whiskey he had procured the night before. While he was trying to repair a cracked stirrup, Gus crawled over to Bill's little stack of bedding, uncorked the jug, and drank a good portion of it. Then he crawled back to his own spot, drunk.

Brognoli, the quartermaster, showed up about that time, looking for men to load the ammunition wagons. Call and Rip Green were recruited. Gus was fearful Brognoli would remove him from the troop once he found out about the ankle, but Brognoli scarcely gave him a glance.

"You'll be running buffalo in a few days, Mr. McCrae," Brognoli said. "I'll warn you though: be careful of your parts, once we're traveling. Colonel Cobb won't tolerate stragglers. If you can't make the pull, he'll leave you, and you'll have to come back as best you can."

Gus managed to sneak several more pulls on Long Bill's jug, and was deeply drunk when he woke from a light snooze to see a girl coming toward the camp. To his horror, he realized it was Clara Forsythe. It was a calamity—not only was he drunk and too crippled to attend himself, he was also filthy from having accidentally rolled into a mud puddle during the night.

He looked about to see if there was a wagon he could hide under, but there was no wagon. Johnny Carthage was snoring, his head on his saddle, and no one else was in camp at all.

"There you are—I had hoped you would show up early and help me unpack those heavy dry goods," Clara said. "I see you're unreliable—I might have suspected it."

She was smiling as she chided him, but Gus was so sensitive to the fact that he was drunk and filthy that he hardly knew what to do.

"Let's see your foot," Clara said, kneeling down beside him.

Gus was startled. Although Call had informed him that Clara intended to rub liniment on his foot herself, Gus had given the report no credit. It was some lie Call had thought up, to make him feel worse than he felt. No fine girl of the class of Miss Forsythe would be likely to want to rub liniment on his filthy ankle.

"What?" he asked—he was so drunk that he could hardly stammer. He wished now that he had not been such a fool as to drain Long Bill's jug—but then, how could he possibly have expected a visit from Miss Forsythe? Only whores prowled around in the rough Ranger camps, and Clara was clearly not a whore.

"I said, let's see your foot," Clara said. "Did the fall deafen you, too?"

"No, I can hear," Gus said. "What would you want with my foot?" he asked.

"I need to know if I think you're going to recover, Mr. McCrae," Clara said, with a challenging smile. "If you do recover, I might have plans for you, but if you're a goner, then I won't waste my time."

"What kind of plans?" Gus asked.

"Well, there's a lot of unpacking that needs to get done around the store," Clara said. "You could be my assistant, if you behave."

Gus surrendered the wounded foot, which was bare, and none too clean. Clara touched it gently, cupping Gus's heel in one hand.

"The thing is, I'm a Ranger," Gus reminded her. "I signed up for the expedition to Santa Fe. If I try to back out now, the Colonel might call it desertion and have me hung."

"Fiddle," Clara said, feeling the swollen ankle. She lowered his foot to the ground, noticed the jar of liniment sitting on a rock nearby, and removed the top.

"Well, they *can* hang you for desertion, if they take a notion to," Gus said.

"I know that, shut up," Clara said, scooping a bit of liniment into her hand. She began to massage it into the swollen ankle, a dab at a time.

[133]

"My pa thinks this expedition is all foolery," Clara went on. "He says you'll all starve, once you get out on the plains. He says you'll be back in a month. I guess I can wait a month."

"I hope so," Gus said. "I wouldn't want no one else to get the job."

Clara looked at him, but said nothing. She continued to dab liniment on his ankle and gently rub it in.

"That liniment stinks," Gus informed her. "It smells like sheep-dip."

"I thought I told you to shut up," Clara reminded him. "If you weren't crippled we could have a picnic, couldn't we?"

Gus decided to ignore the comment—he *was* crippled, and wasn't quite sure what a picnic was, anyway. He thought it was something that had to do with churchgoing, but he wasn't a churchgoer and didn't want to embarrass himself by revealing his ignorance.

"What if we're out two months?" he asked. "You wouldn't give that job to nobody else, would you?"

Clara considered for a moment—she was smiling, but not at him, exactly. She seemed to be smiling mostly to herself.

"Well, there are other applicants," she admitted.

"Yes, that damn Woodrow Call, I imagine," Gus said. "I never told him to go up there and buy this liniment. He just did it himself."

"Oh no, not Corporal Call," Clara said at once. "I don't think I fancy Corporal Call as an unpacker. He's a little too solemn for my taste. I expect he would be too slow to make a fool of himself."

"That's right, he ain't foolish," Gus said. He thought it was rather a peculiar standard Clara was suggesting, but he was not about to argue with her.

"I like men who are apt to make fools of themselves immediately," Clara said. "Like yourself, Mr. McCrae. Why, you don't hesitate a second when it comes to making a fool of yourself."

Gus decided not to comment. He had never encountered anyone as puzzling as the young woman kneeling in front of him, with his foot almost on her lap. She didn't seem to give a fig for the fact that his foot was dirty, and he himself none too clean.

"Are you drunk, sir?" she asked bluntly. "I think I smell whiskey on your breath."

"Well, Long Bill had a little whiskey," Gus admitted. "I took it for medicine."

Clara didn't dignify that lie with a look, or a retort.

"What were you thinking of when you walked off that cliff, Mr. McCrae?" Clara asked. "Do you remember?"

In fact, Gus didn't remember. The main thing he remembered about the whole previous day was standing near Clara in the general store, watching her unpack dry goods. He remembered her graceful wrists, and how dust motes stirred in a shaft of sunlight from the big front window. He remembered thinking that Clara was the most beautiful woman he had ever encountered, and that he wanted to be with her—beyond being with her, he could conceive of no plans; he had no memory of falling off the cliff at all, and no notion of what he and Woodrow Call might have been discussing. He remembered a gunshot and Call and Johnny finding him at the base of the bluff. But what had gone on before, or been said up on the path, he couldn't recall.

"I guess I was worrying about Indians," he said, since Clara was still looking at him in a manner that suggested she wanted an answer.

"Shucks, I thought you might have been thinking of me," Clara said. "I had the notion I'd smitten you, but I guess I was wrong. I haven't smitten Corporal Call, that's for sure."

"He ain't a corporal, he's just a Ranger," Gus said, annoyed that she was still talking about Call. He didn't trust the man, not where Clara was concerned, at least.

"Why, that's better, perhaps I have smitten you."

She closed the jar of liniment, eased his foot to the ground, and stood up.

"It does smell a little like sheep-dip—that's accurate," she said. "What do you gentlemen use to wash with around this camp?"

"Nothing, nobody washes," Gus admitted. "Sometimes we wash in a creek, if we're traveling, but otherwise we just stay dirty."

Clara picked up a shirt someone had thrown down, and carefully wiped her fingers on it.

"I hope the owner won't mind a little sheep-dip on his shirt," she said.

"That's Call's extra shirt, he won't mind," Gus assured her.

"Oh, Corporal Call—where is he, by the way?" Clara asked.

"He ain't a corporal, I told you that," Gus said. He found her use of the term very irritating; that she felt the need to refer to Call at all was more than a little annoying.

"Nonetheless I intend to call him Corporal Call, and it's not one bit of your business what I call him," Clara said pertly. "I'm free to choose names for my admirers, I suppose."

Gus was so annoyed that he didn't know what to say. He sulked for a bit, thinking that if Call were there, he'd give him a punching, sore ankle or no sore ankle.

"Well, good-bye, Mr. McCrae," Clara said. "I hope your ankle improves. If you're still in camp tomorrow, I'll come back and give it another treatment. I don't want a crippled assistant, not with all the unpacking there is to do."

To his surprise, she reached down and gave him a handshake—her fingers smelled of the liniment she had just rubbed on him.

"We're supposed to pull out tomorrow—I hope we don't, though," Gus said.

"You know where the store is," Clara said. "I certainly expect a visit, before you depart."

She started to leave, and then turned and looked at him again.

"Give my respects to Corporal Call," she said. "It's a pity he's not more of a fool."

"If he's a corporal, I ought to be a corporal too," Gus said, bitterly annoyed by the girl's manner.

"Corporal McCrae—no, that don't sound right," Clara said. "Corporal Call—somehow that has a solid ring."

Then, with a wave, she walked off.

When Call came back to camp in the evening, sweaty from having loaded ammunition all day, he found Gus drunk and boiling. He was so mad his face turned red, and a big vein popped out on his nose.

"She calls you a corporal, you rascal!" Gus said in a furious voice. "I told you to stay clear of that store—if you don't, when I get well, I'll give you a whipping you'll never forget."

Call was taken completely by surprise, and Long Bill, Rip Green, and a new recruit named Jimmy Tweed, a tall boy from Arkansas, were all startled by Gus's belligerence. Jimmy Tweed had not yet met Gus, and was shocked to find him so quarrelsome.

Call didn't know what reply to make, and so said nothing. He had known that sometimes people took fevers and went out of their heads; he supposed that was what was the matter with Gus. He walked closer, to see if his friend was delirious, and was rewarded for his concern with a hard kick in the shin. Gus, though in a prone position, had still managed to get off the kick.

"Why, he's unruly, ain't he?" Jimmy Tweed said. "I expect if he wasn't crippled we'd have to chain him down."

"I don't know you, stay out of it!" Gus warned. "I'd do worse than kick him, if I could."

"I expect it's fever," Call said, at a loss to explain Gus's behaviour any other way.

Before the dispute could proceed any further, Bigfoot came loping up on a big grey horse he had just procured.

"Buffalo Hump struck a farm off toward Bastrop," he said. "An old man got away and spread the news. We're getting up a troop, to go after the Indians. You're all invited, except Gus and Johnny. Hurry up. We need to ride while the trail's fresh."

"Why ain't I invited?" Johnny Carthage asked. He had just limped into camp.

"Because you got to do the packing," Bigfoot said. "The expedition's leaving early. I doubt we'll be back. You got to get all this gear together and pack Gus into a cart or a wagon or something. We'll meet you on the trail—if we survive."

"This is a passel of stuff for one fellow to pack," Johnny observed bleakly. "Gus won't be no help, either—he's poorly."

"Not poorly enough—he just kicked my leg half off," Call said. The more he thought about the incident, the more aggrieved he felt. All he had done all day was load ammunition—why did he have to be kicked because of some joke a girl made?

Shadrach came trotting up, his long rifle across his saddle. He didn't say anything, but it was clear that he was impatient.

"Let's go, boys—Buffalo Hump will be halfway to the Brazos by now," Bigfoot said.

Call had been assigned a new mount that day. As yet he had barely touched him, but in a minute he was in the saddle. The little horse, a bay, jumped straight up, nearly throwing him; after that one jump, he didn't buck again. Call only had time to grab his rifle and ammunition pouch. Shadrach had already left. Long Bill, Rip

Green, and Jimmy Tweed were scrambling to get mounted. Bigfoot was the only calm man in camp. He reached down without dismounting and grabbed a piece of bacon someone had brought in, stuffing it quickly into his saddlebag.

"It's a passel of stuff to pack up," Johnny Carthage said again, looking at the litter of blankets, cook pots, and miscellaneous gear scattered around him.

"Oh, hush your yapping," Bigfoot said.

Blackie Slidell came racing up—he had had his shirt off, helping to load a wagon, and was so fearful of being left that he had put it back on, wrong side out, as he rode.

Call looked down at Gus—he was still prone, but not so angry.

"I have no idea what you're riled about," he said. "I guess I'll see you up the trail."

"Good-bye," Gus said, suddenly sorry for his angry behaviour. Before he could say more, Bigfoot wheeled his horse and loped off after Shadrach; the Rangers, still assembling themselves, followed as closely as they could.

Gus felt a sudden longing to be with them, though he knew it was impossible. Tears came to his eyes, as he watched his companions lope away. It would be lonely with no one but the cranky Johnny Carthage to talk to all night.

In a minute or two, though, he felt better. His ankle still felt full of needles, but Clara Forsythe had said she would come and rub more liniment on his sore ankle, if the expedition didn't depart too early. All he had to do was get through the night, and he would see her again.

What made him feel even better was that this time he would have Clara all to himself. Call was gone. The thought cheered him so that within ten minutes he was pestering Johnny to go buy them a fresh jug of whiskey from the Mexican peddler.

"I can't be getting too drunk, I got all this packing to do," Johnny protested, but Gus shrugged his protest off.

"You just buy the whiskey," he instructed. "I'll do the getting drunk."

7.

A STORM BLEW UP during the night, with slashing rain and wind and thunder. Shadrach and Bigfoot paid the weather no attention—they set a fast pace, and didn't stop. In the dark, Call grew fearful of falling behind and being lost. They cut through several clumps of live oak and scrub—he was afraid he and his little bay would fight themselves out of a thicket, only to find themselves alone. He stayed as close to the rump of the horse in front of him as he could. He didn't want to get lost on his first Indian chase. The party consisted of fifteen men, many of whom he didn't know. Call would have thought it would be easy to keep fifteen riders in sight, but he hadn't counted on the difficulties posed by rain and darkness. At times, he couldn't see his own horse's head—he had to proceed on sense, like a night-hunting animal.

It was a relief, when the smoky, foggy dawn came, to see that he was still with the troop. All the men were soaked, streams of water running from their hats or their hair. There was no stopping for breakfast. Shadrach peeled off, and ranged to the north of the troop. He was lost to sight for an hour or more, but when they came to the burned-out farm he was there, examining tracks.

At first, Call saw no victims—he supposed the family had escaped. The cabin had been burned; though a few of the logs still smouldered. The area around the cabin was a litter, most of it muddy now. There were clothes and kitchen goods, broken chairs, a muddy Bible, a few bottles. The corn-shuck mattresses had been ripped open, and the corn shucks scattered in the mud.

Bigfoot dismounted, and stepped inside the shell of the cabin for a moment—then he stepped out.

"Where are they?" he asked Shadrach, who looked up briefly and pointed to the nearby cornfield.

"Call, gather up them wet sheets," Bigfoot said. Several muddy sheets were amid the litter.

"Why?" Call asked, puzzled.

"To wrap them in—why else?" Bigfoot said, swinging back on his horse.

The woman lay between two corn rows, six arrows in her chest, her belly ripped up. The man had been hacked down near a little rock fence—when they ripped his scalp off, a long tear of skin had come loose with the scalp, running down the man's back. A boy of about ten had three arrows in him, and had had his head smashed in with a large rock. A younger boy, six or seven maybe, had a big wound in his back.

"Lanced him," Bigfoot said. "I thought there was a young girl here."

"They took her," Shadrach informed him. "They took the mule, too. I expect that's what she's riding."

Call felt trembly, but he didn't throw up. He noticed Bigfoot and Shadrach watching him, from the edge of the cornfield. Though they had all expected carnage, most of them had not been prepared for the swollen, ripped-open bodies—the smashed head, the torn stomach.

"Roll them in the sheets, best you can," Bigfoot told him. "When you get to the woman, just break them arrows off. They're in too deep to pull out."

Shadrach walked over and squatted by the dead woman for a moment—he seemed to be studying the arrows. Then he tugged gently at an arrow in the center of the woman's breastbone.

"This one's gone clean through, into the ground," he said. "This is Buffalo Hump's arrow."

"How do you know that?" Call asked.

Shadrach showed him the feathers at the end of the arrow.

"Them's from a prairie chicken," he said. "He always feathers his arrows with prairie chicken. He stood over her and shot that arrow clean through her breastbone."

Bigfoot came over and looked at the arrow, too. The woman's body didn't budge. It was as if it were nailed to the ground. It was a small, skinny arrow, the shaft a little bent. Call tried to imagine the force it would take to send a thin piece of wood through a woman's body and into the dirt. Several of the new men came over and stood in silence near the body of the woman. One or two of them glanced at the body briefly, then walked away. Several of them gripped their weapons so hard their knuckles were white. Call remembered that it had been that way beyond the Pecos—men squeezing their guns so hard their knuckles turned white. They were scared: they had ridden out of Austin into a world where the rules were not white rules, where torture and mutilation awaited the weak and the unwary, the slow, the young.

Bigfoot rode off with Shadrach to study the trail, leaving Call to wrap the four bodies in the muddy sheets. From the center of the cornfield the little cabin, now just a shell, its logs still smouldering, seemed small and sad to Call. The little family had built it, with much labor, in the clearing, sheltered in it, worked and planted their crops. Then, in an hour or less, it was all destroyed: four of them dead, one girl captured, the cabin burnt. Even the milk cow was dead, shot full of arrows. The cow was bloated now, its legs sticking up in the air.

Call did his best with the bodies, but when it came to the woman, he had to ask Blackie Slidell for help. Blackie had to take her feet and Call her arms before they could pull her free, so deep was Buffalo Hump's arrow in the ground. Call had butchered several goats and a sheep or two, when he worked for Jesus—the woman he was trying to wrap in a wet, mouldy sheet had been butchered, just like a sheep.

"Lord, I hope we can whip 'em if we catch up to them," Blackie said, in a shaky voice. "I don't want one of them devils catching me."

Long Bill came over and helped Call with the graves. "I'll help—I'd rather be working than thinking," he said.

They scooped out four shallow graves, rolled the bodies in them, and covered them with rocks from the little rock fence the family had been building.

"They won't need no fence now," Rip Green observed. "All that work, and now they're dead."

Before they had quite finished the burying, Bigfoot and Shadrach came loping back. Bigfoot had the body of a dead girl across his horse.

"Here's the last one—bury her," Bigfoot said, easing the body down to Call. "The mule went lame a few miles from here. I guess they didn't have no horse to spare for this girl. They brained her and shot the mule."

A little later, as the troop was riding north, they passed the dead mule. A big piece had been cut out of its haunch.

"Shadrach done that," Bigfoot said. "He says the game's poorly this year, and it was a fat mule."

They rode north all day, into a broken country of limestone hills. It rained intermittently, the clouds low. In the distance, some of the clouds rested on the low hills, like caps. Now and again Shadrach or Bigfoot rode off in one direction or another, but never for long. In the afternoon, they stopped and cooked the mule meat. Shadrach cut the haunch into little strips and gave each man one, to cook as preferred. Call stuck his on a stick and held it over the fire until it was black. He had never planned to eat mule and didn't expect to like the taste, but to his surprise the meat was succulent—it tasted fine.

"When will we catch 'em?" he asked Bigfoot at one point. They had not seen a trace of the Comanches—yet for all he knew, they were close, in one of the rocky valleys between the hills. Several times, as they rode north, he kept his eyes to the ground, trying to make out the track that the troop was following. But all he saw was the ground. He would have liked to know what clues the two scouts picked up to guide the chase, but no one offered to inform him. He was reluctant to ask—it made him seem too ignorant. But in fact he *was* ignorant, and not happy about it. At least Shadrach had taught him how to identify Buffalo Hump's arrow—he thought he could recognize the feathers again, if he saw them. That was the only piece of instruction to come his way, though.

When he asked Bigfoot when he thought they would catch up with the Comanches, Bigfoot looked thoughtful for a moment.

"We won't catch them," he said.

Call was puzzled. If the Rangers weren't going to catch the enemy, why were they pursuing them at all?

Bigfoot's manner did not invite more questions. He had been eager, back on the Rio Grande, to talk about the finer points of suicide, but when it came to their pursuit of the Comanche raiding party, he was not forthcoming. Call rode on in silence for a few miles, and then tried again.

"If we ain't going to catch them, why are we chasing them?" he asked.

"Oh, I just meant we can't outrun them," Bigfoot said. "They can travel faster than we can. But we might catch 'em anyway."

"How?" Call asked, confused.

"There's only one way to catch an Indian, which is to wait for him to stop," Bigfoot said. "Once they get across the Brazos they'll feel a little safer. They might stop."

"And then we'll kill them?" Call said—he thought he understood now.

"Then we'll try," Bigfoot said.

8.

To Gus's DISMAY, THE order to move out of Austin came at three in the morning. Captain Falconer rode through the camps on a snorting, prancing horse, telling the men to get their gear.

"Colonel Cobb's ready," he informed them. "No lingering. We'll be leaving town at dawn."

"Dern, it's the middle of the night," Johnny Carthage said. Though he had been provided with two mules and a heavy cart, he had as yet totally neglected his instructions in regard to packing. Instead, he and Gus had got drunk. Nothing was packed, and it was raining and pitch dark.

Gus's preparations for the grand expedition to Santa Fe consisted in dragging himself, his guns, and a blanket into the heavy cart. Then he huddled in the cart, so drunk that he was not much bothered by the fact that Johnny Carthage was pitching every object he could get his hands on in on top of him. The cooking pots, the extra saddlery, blankets and guns, ropes and boxes of medicines, were all heaped in the cart, with little care taken as to placement.

"Why do we have to leave in the middle of the night?" Gus asked, several times—but Johnny Carthage was muttering and coughing; he made no reply. He had an old lantern, and was searching all around the large area of the camp, well aware that he would be blamed if he left anything behind. But with only one eye and a gimpy leg, and with Gus too crippled and too drunk to help, gathering up the belongings of the whole troop on a dark, rainy night was chancy work.

At some point well before dawn, Quartermaster Brognoli made a tour of the area, to see that the fifteen or twenty different groups of free-ranging adventurers, many of them merchants or would-be merchants, were making adequate progress toward departure. Gus stuck his head out from under a dripping blanket long enough to talk to him a minute.

"Why leave when it's dark?" he asked. "Why not wait for sunup?"

Brognoli had taken a liking to the tall boy from Tennessee. He was green but friendly, and he moved quick. Years of trying to get soldiers on the move had given Brognoli a distaste for slow people.

"Colonel Cobb don't care for light nor dark," he informed Gus. "He don't care for the time of day or the month or the year. When he decides to go, we go."

"But three in the morning's an odd time to start an expedition," Gus pointed out.

"No, it's regular enough," Brognoli said. "If we start pushing out about three the stragglers will clear Austin by six or seven. Colonel Cobb left an hour ago. We're going to stop at Bushy Creek for breakfast, so we better get moving. If we ain't there when the Colonel expects us, there won't be no breakfast."

The mules were hitched, and the cart with all the Rangers' possessions in it was moving through the center of Austin when Gus McCrae suddenly remembered Clara Forsythe. More than thirty wagons, small herds of sheep and beef cattle, and over a hundred horsemen of all ages and degrees of ability were jostling for position in the crowded streets. Some of the mule skinners had lanterns, but most didn't. There were several collisions and much cursing. Once or twice, guns were fired. Occasional lightning lit the western sky— the faint grey of a cloudy dawn was just visible to the east.

The reason Gus remembered Clara was that the little cart, driven by a wet, tired, apprehensive Johnny Carthage, happened to pass right in front of the general store. Gus suddenly recalled that the pretty young woman he had such a desire to marry had been meaning to come and rub liniment on his wounded ankle sometime during the day that was just dawning. He had been drinking for quite a few hours—most of the hours since he fell off the bluff, in fact—and had reached such a depth of drunkness that he had temporarily forgotten the most important fact of all: Clara, his future wife.

"Stop, I got to see her!" he told Johnny, who was urging the mules through a sizable patch of mud, while at the same time trying to avoid colliding with the wagon containing the comatose General Lloyd. He knew it was General Lloyd's wagon because a kind of small tent had been erected in it so the General could be protected from the elements while he drank and snoozed.

"What?" Johnny Carthage asked.

"Stop, goddamn you—stop!" Gus demanded. "I've got business in the general store."

"But it ain't open," Johnny protested. "If I stop now we'll never get out of this mud."

"Stop or I'll strangle you, damn you!" Gus said. It was not a threat he had ever made before, but he was so desperate to see Clara that he felt he could carry it out. Johnny Carthage didn't hear it, though —one of the mules began to bray, just at that moment, and a rooster that had managed to get in General Lloyd's wagon was crowing loudly, too.

The mud was thick—the cart was barely inching forward anyway, so Gus decided to just flop out of it. In his eagerness to get to Clara he forgot about his sore ankle, though only until the foot attached to it hit the ground. The pain that surged through him was so intense that he tried to flop forward, back into the cart, but the cart lurched ahead just as he did it, and he went facedown into the slick mud. The patch of mud was deep, too—Gus was up to his elbows in it, trying to struggle up onto his one good foot, when he thought he heard a peal of girlish laughter somewhere above him.

"Look, Pa, it's Mr. McCrae—come to propose to me, I expect," Clara said.

Gus looked up to see a white figure, standing at a window above the street. Although he knew he was muddy, his heart lifted at the thought that at least he had not missed Clara. It was her. She was laughing at him, but what did that matter? He looked up, wishing the sun would come out so he could see her better. But he knew it was her, from the sound of her voice and the fact that she was at a window above the store. The thought of her father seeing him in such a state was embarrassing—but in fact, there was no sign of the old man. Perhaps she was just joshing him—she did seem to love to josh.

"Ain't you coming down?" he asked. "I've still got this sore foot."

"Shucks, what kind of a Romeo would fall off a bluff and hurt his foot just when it's time to propose to Juliet?" Clara asked. "You're supposed to sing me a song or two and then climb up here and beg me to marry you."

"What?" Gus asked. He had no idea what the woman was talking about. Why would he try to climb up the side of the general store when all she would have to do was come down the stairs? He had seen the stairs himself, when he was in the store helping her unpack.

"What, you ain't read Shakespeare—what was wrong with your schooling?" Clara asked.

Gus's head had cleared a little. He had been so drunk that his vision swam when he got to his feet—or foot. He still held his sore ankle just above the mud. Now that he was upright he remembered that his sisters had been great admirers of the writer Shakespeare, though exactly what had occurred between Romeo and Juliet he could not remember.

"I can't climb—won't you come down?" he said. Why would Clara think a man standing on one foot in a mud puddle could climb a wall, and why was she going on about Shakespeare when he was about to leave on a long expedition? He felt very nearly exasperated—besides that, he couldn't stand on one foot forever.

"Well, I guess I might come down, though it is early," Clara said. "We generally don't welcome customers this early."

"I ain't a customer—I want to marry you, but I've got to leave," he said. "Won't you come? Johnny won't wait much longer."

In fact, Johnny was having a hard time waiting at all. The expedition was flowing in full force through the streets of Austin; there was the creak of harness, and the swish of wagon wheels. Johnny had tried to edge to the side, but there wasn't much space—a fat mule skinner cursed him for the delay he had caused already.

[147]

"Won't you come?—I have to go," Gus said. "We're hurrying to meet Colonel Cobb—he don't like to wait."

Clara didn't answer, but she disappeared from the window, and a moment later, opened the door of the general store. She had wrapped a robe around her and came right down the steps of the store, barefoot, into the muck of the street.

"Goodness, you'll get muddy," Gus said—he had not supposed she would be so reckless as to walk barefoot into the mud.

Clara ignored the remark—young Mr. McCrae was muddy to the elbows and to the knees. She could tell that he was drunk—but he had not forgotten to call on her. Men were not perfect, she knew; even her father, kindly as he was, flew into a temper at least once a month, usually while doing the accounts.

"I don't see Corporal Call—what's become of him?" she asked.

"Oh now . . . you would ask," Gus complained. "He's off chasing Indians. He ain't no corporal, either—I've told you that."

"Well, in my fancy he is," Clara retorted. "Don't you be brash with me."

"I don't want him anywhere in your damn fancy!" Gus said. "For all we know he's dead and scalped, by now."

Then he realized that he didn't want that, either. Annoying as Call was, he was still a Ranger and a friend. Clara's quick tongue had provoked him—she *would* mention Call, even in the street at dawn, with the expedition leaving.

"Now, don't be uncharitable to your friend," Clara chided. "As I told you before, he would never do for me—too solemn! You ain't solemn, at least—you might do, once you've acquired a little polish and can remember who Romeo is and what he's supposed to do."

"I ain't got the time—will you marry me once I get back?" he asked.

"Why, I don't know," Clara said. "How should I know who'll walk into my store, while you're out wandering on the plains? I might meet a gentleman who could recite Shakespeare to me for hours— or even Milton."

"That ain't the point—I love you," Gus said. "I won't be happy a minute, unless I know you'll marry me once I get back."

"I'm afraid I can't say for sure, not right this minute," Clara said. "But I will kiss you—would that help?"

Gus was so startled he couldn't answer. Before he could move

[148]

she came closer, put her hands on his muddy arms, reached up her face, and kissed him. He wanted to hug her tight, but didn't—he felt he was all mud. But Gus kissed back, for all he was worth. It was only for a second. Then Clara, smiling, scampered back to the porch of the general store, her feet and ankles black with mud.

"Good-bye, Mr. McCrae, don't get scalped if you can help it," she said. "I'll struggle on with my unpacking as best I can, while you travel the prairies."

Gus was too choked with feeling to answer. He merely looked at her. Johnny Carthage was yelling at him, threatening to leave him. Gus began to hobble toward the cart, still looking at Clara. The sun had peeked through the clouds. Clara waved, smiling. In waving back, Gus almost slipped. He would have gone down again in the mud, had not a strong hand caught his arm. Matilda Jane Roberts, the Great Western, plodding by on Tom, her large grey, saw his plight just in time and caught his arm.

"Here, hold the saddle strings—just hold them and hop, I'll get you to Johnny," she said.

Gus did as he was told. He looked back, anxiously, wondering what the young woman who had just kissed him would think, seeing a whore help him out, so soon after their kiss.

But the porch of the general store was empty—Clara Forsythe had gone inside.

9.

When the troop of Rangers reached the Brazos River, the wide brown stream was in flood. The churning water came streaming down from the north, through the cut in the low hills where the Rangers struck the river.

The hills across the river were thick with post oak and elm. Call remembered how completely the Comanches had managed to hide themselves on the open plain. Finding them in thickets such as those across the river would be impossible.

Long Bill looked apprehensive, when he saw that the Brazos was in flood.

"If half of us don't get drowned going over, we'll get drowned coming back," he observed. "I can't swim no long distance. About ten yards is my limit."

"Hang on to your horse, then," Bigfoot advised. "Slide off and grab his tail. Don't lose your holt of it, either. A horse will paw you down if he can see you in the water."

Call's little bay was trembling at the sight of the water. Shadrach had ridden straight into the river and was already halfway across. He clung to his saddle strings with one hand, and kept the long rifle above the flood with the other. Bigfoot took the water next; his big bay swam easily. The rest of the Rangers lingered, apprehension in their eyes.

"This is a mighty wide river," Blackie Slidell said. "Damn the Comanches! They *would* beat us across."

Call thumped the little grey's sides with his rifle, trying to get him to jump in. It was time to go—he wanted to go. The horse made a great leap into the water and went under briefly, Call with him. But once in, the little horse swam strongly. Call managed to catch his tail—holding the rifle up was tiring. When, now and then, he caught a glimpse of the far shore, it seemed so far away that he didn't know if a horse could swim that far. Curls of reddish water kept breaking over his head. In only a minute or two, he lost sight of all the other Rangers. He might have been in the river alone, for all he could tell. But he was in it: there was nothing to do but cling to the horse's tail and try to keep from drowning.

When Call was halfway across, he caught a glimpse of something coming toward him, on the reddish, foaming flood. It seemed to be a horse, floating on its side. Just at that time he went under—when his head broke the surface again he saw that it was actually a dead mule, all bloated up, floating right down at him. The little bay horse was swimming as hard as he could—it looked, for a moment, as if the dead mule was going to surge right into them. Call thought his best bet might be to poke the mule aside with his rifle barrel; and he twisted a little and brought the rifle into position, meaning to shove the mule away. Just as he twisted he saw two eyes that weren't dead and weren't mule's eyes, staring at him from between the stiff legs of the dead mule. The mule and the Indian boy floating down with him were only five feet away when Call fired. The boy had just raised his hand, with a knife in it, when the bullet took him in the throat. Then the mule and the body of the dying boy crashed into Call, carrying him under and loosening his grip on the bay gelding's tail. Call went under, entangled with the corpse of the Comanche boy he had just killed. The red current rolled them over and over—all Call knew was that he mustn't lose his musket. He clung to the gun even though he knew he might be drowning. He was so confused for a moment that he didn't know the difference between up and down. It seemed to him he was getting deeper into the water; it was all just a red murk, with sticks and bits of bushes floating in it, but then he felt himself being lifted and was able to draw his breath.

The clouds had broken, while Call was struggling under water— the sunlight when he broke the surface, bright sunlight on the foam-flecked water, with the deep blue sky above, was the most welcome sight he had ever seen.

"Don't try to swim, just let me drag you," a voice said. "I believe I can get you to the shallows if you'll just keep still, but if you struggle we'll likely both go under."

Call was able to determine that his rescuer was the tall boy from Arkansas, Jimmy Tweed. Unlike the rest of the Rangers, Jimmy had declined to dismount and cross the river holding on to his horse's tail. He was still in the saddle, which was mostly submerged. But his horse was a stout black mare, and she kept swimming, even though not much more than her nose and her ears were above the stream.

Jimmy Tweed had reached into the river and grabbed Call's shirt collar, which he gripped tightly. Call managed to get a hand into the black mare's mane, after which he felt a little more secure.

"Watch out for dead mules—there's apt to be Comanches with 'em," Call informed him. Jimmy Tweed seemed as calm as if he were sitting in church.

"I seen you shoot that one," Jimmy said. "Hit him in the neck. I'd say it was a fine shot, being as you was in the water and about to drown."

Just then something hit the water, not far from Call's shoulder, with a sound like spitting. They were not far from the east bank, then—Call looked and saw puffs of smoke from a stand of trees just above the river.

"They're shooting!" he said—another bullet had sliced the water nearby. "You oughtn't to be sitting up so tall in the saddle—you make too good a target."

"I guess I'd rather be shot than drownt," Jimmy Tweed said. "If there's one thing I've never liked it's getting water up my nose."

In another moment, Call felt his feet touch bottom. The water was still up to his chin, but he felt a little more confident and told Jimmy that he could let go his grip. Just as Jimmy let go, Call saw a

Ranger fall. One of the new men had just made it to shore and was wading through the mud when a bullet knocked him backwards.

"Why, that be Bert," Jimmy Tweed said, in mild surprise. "He sure didn't pick much of a place to land."

"We can't land here, they'll shoot us like squirrels," Call said. "Slide off now, and turn the horse."

"I expect Bert is dead," Jimmy said calmly—the fact was confirmed a moment later when two Comanches ran down the muddy riverbank and quickly took his scalp.

Call managed to point the black horse downstream—he was able to feel his way behind him, clinging to saddle strings and then to the horse's tail, until he had the black horse between him and the riverbank. With only a bit of his head showing, he didn't figure a Comanche marksman would be very likely to hit him. Jimmy Tweed, though, flatly refused to slide off into the water.

"Nope, I prefer to risk it in the saddle," he said, though he did consent to lean low over the black horse's neck.

They heard fire from the near bank and saw that Shadrach, Bigfoot, and Blackie Slidell had made it across and taken cover behind a jumble of driftwood. Call looked up and saw what looked like a muskrat in the water, not far from where the Rangers were forting up. On closer inspection the muskrat turned out to be the fur cap procured by Long Bill Coleman before he left San Antonio. Long Bill was underneath the cap. He was walking slowly out of the river, though the water was still up to his Adam's apple. There was no sign of the horse he had tried to cross the Brazos River on.

By the time Call and Jimmy Tweed struggled out of the water and took cover behind the driftwood, the firing had stopped. Bigfoot had walked downstream a few yards, in order to pull a body out of the water. Call supposed a Ranger had been shot but was surprised to see that the body Bigfoot pulled out of the Brazos was the Comanche boy he himself had shot. Several more Rangers began to struggle out of the flood, some of them clinging to the bridle reins or tails of their mounts. Others were without horses, having lost hold of their mounts during the swim.

"Well, you got him," Bigfoot said, looking at Call. "I forgot to tell you to look out for dead animals—Comanches will use them for floats."

Call was surprised at how young the boy looked. He could have been no more than twelve.

"You're lucky your gun fired," Shadrach said. "Them old muskets will usually just snap on you, once they get wet."

Call didn't say anything. He knew he had been lucky—another second and the dead boy would have had a knife in him. He could remember the boy's eyes, staring at him from between the legs of the dead mule.

He didn't want to look at the corpse, though—he turned to walk away and noticed that both Shadrach and Bigfoot were looking at him curiously. Call stopped, puzzled—their looks suggested that he had neglected something.

"Ain't you going to scalp him?" Bigfoot asked. "You killed him. It's your scalp."

Call was startled. It had never occurred to him to scalp the Comanche boy. He was a young boy. Although he was glad that he had escaped death himself, he felt no pride in the act he had just committed—the boy had been daring, in his view, to float down a swollen river, armed only with a knife, clinging to a dead mule in hopes of surprising and killing an armed Ranger. The reward for his bravery had been a bullet wound that nearly tore his head off. He would never ride the prairies again, or raid farms. Although he had had to kill him, Call thought the boy's bravery deserved better than what it had got him. There would be no time to bury the boy, anyway—the thought of cutting his hair off did not appeal.

"No, I don't want to scalp him," Call said.

"He would have scalped you, if he could have," Bigfoot said.

"I don't doubt it," Call said. "Scalping's the Indian way. It ain't my way."

"It'll be your way when you're a year or two older, boy—if you survive," Shadrach said. Then he casually knelt by the Comanche boy and took his scalp. When he finished, he pulled the boy well back into the current and let him float away.

"I should have buried him—I killed him," Call said.

"No, you don't bury Indians," Bigfoot informed him. "They gather up their own dead, when they can. I guess Shad wants to make them work at it, this time."

Shadrach had just turned and started back toward the shore, when they heard a scream from far down the river.

"Oh Lord, it's Rip—he went downstream too far," Long Bill said. "I believe he's bogged."

"Puny horse," Bigfoot commented, raising his rifle. Rip's horse seemed to be bogged, some twenty yards out into the stream. Five Comanches, screaming their wild cries, raced out of the scrub oak toward the river. Bigfoot shot and so did Shadrach, but the range was long and both missed. Just then a rain squall passed over them, making it hard to see well enough to shoot accurately at such distances. Rip screamed again and flailed at his horse, but his horse was too weak from his long swim to pull out of the thick river mud. The first Comanche had already splashed into the edge of the river. Call had reloaded his musket—he took careful aim and thought he hit the first Comanche, but the hit was not solid enough to slow the man. They saw Rip raise his rifle and fire point-blank at the first Comanche, but the gun misfired and in a second the Indians swarmed over him. His final scream was cut short. Before Call could get off another shot, Rip Green was hacked to death and scalped. His body was soon floating down the same river as that of the Indian boy.

Several Rangers shot at the Indians who killed Rip, but none of the shots had any effect. Bigfoot and Shadrach, concluding that the range was hopeless, didn't shoot.

"It don't pay to be a poor judge of horseflesh, not in this country," Bigfoot observed. "He ought never to have tried the river on that nag, not with the river running this high."

"What could he do? He couldn't just sit over there and watch," Call said. Rip Green had gone into the water just as he did—it was just Rip's bad luck to float downstream, out of the range of help.

"Well, he could have let the horse go and swum out, like me," Long Bill said. "I reckon I'm a better swimmer than I thought I was. My pony gave out when we was right in the middle, but here I am."

"If you don't hunker down you won't need to swim no more rivers—you'll be floating down this one, dead," Bigfoot said. Bullets began to hit the water all around them—the Rangers were forced to huddle together in the shelter of a small patch of driftwood. No men were hit, though—probably the driving rain threw off the Comanche marksmen. Call watched the trees above them as closely as he could, but he was unable to glimpse a single Indian—just puffs of smoke from their guns. The shots were coming from a semicircle of woods above them.

"There's too many of them, Shad," Bigfoot concluded. "They had a party waiting, I expect."

Call tried to get a sense of how many Indians they faced by counting the shots—but he knew the method wasn't accurate. After all, the Indians were hidden. They could move around at will, shooting from one part of the woods and then another.

When the Rangers counted heads they discovered that they were down to eleven men, four less than they had started across the river with. Rip was dead, and so was the man named Bert—the whereabouts of the other two could not be ascertained.

"Probably drowned—I nearly did," Long Bill said.

"No, probably deserted," Shadrach said. "One is that fellow from Cincinnati. I don't think he had much stomach."

All that could be remembered about the other missing man was that he had ridden a roan horse. No roan horses were visible among the horses, though Long Bill's horse and two others were also unaccounted for.

Call supposed the Comanches would charge any minute. He kept his gun as dry as he could and got ready to shoot accurately, when the charge came. Once again he found himself questioning the competence of the Rangers—here they were, huddled behind a few trees, four men and three horses short of what they had started out with, facing a Comanche force that had so far been invisible, commanding the woods above them. Behind them was the churning, flooding Brazos River. Their retreat would be watery, if they had to make one. Only those whose horses were good swimmers would have much of a chance.

But the day passed with no charge. From time to time the skies cleared and the sun shone; then clouds would pour over the western hills, and squalls would wet them once again, just when they had begun to hope of being dry. Shadrach and Bigfoot had long since decided that a retreat back across the river was their best chance—Shadrach thought there might be as many as thirty warriors opposing them, more than they could reasonably hope to whip.

A retreat in daylight, though, would be suicidal. The minute the Comanches saw them turn into the river, they would swarm down the shore like hornets and pick them off.

"We'll wait," Bigfoot said. "That's the hard part of Indian fighting. Waiting. You never know what those red boys are doing. They may be up there cooking a coon or a possum, or they may be sneaking up. Try not to let your eyes get tired. It's when your eyes get tired that your scalp's in the worst danger."

Call didn't know how you were supposed to avoid the danger of tired eyes, when the Comanches were so clever at hiding. Who would think to look for an Indian boy between the legs of a floating mule?

The day passed very slowly. Though several Rangers speculated that the river would soon begin to fall, it didn't. Clouds continued to roll through—Call thought the muddy flood looked higher, not lower. He was dreading the crossing—it had been bad in daylight, and would be even worse in darkness. He was not the only one worrying, either. Long Bill, despite his successful swim that morning, was once again doubtful that he could survive in the water if he had to navigate more than ten yards.

While the dusk gathered and the tops of the hills darkened, the Rangers debated whether it was better to hold the horse's mane or the horse's tail, the saddle strings, a stirrup, or even a saddle horn. Call didn't enter the debate—his concern was to keep his musket in firing order—but he thought that if he clung to a stirrup he might be better able to keep his gun across the saddle, where it ought to stay fairly dry.

In the midst of the talk, with Shadrach and Bigfoot squatting at the edge of the driftwood, watching the woods, a man standing just beside Call—he was one of the new men—suddenly jerked, lurched forward, and fell facedown in the water, an arrow right between his shoulders. Call brought his gun up and whirled to face the darkening water. He saw a floating log, and just above it, for a second, the curve of a great wet hump; it might have been a huge fish diving, but Call knew it was Buffalo Hump behind the log. He fired immediately, and a chip of wood flew off the log; then several of the Rangers fired, but to no avail. The current swept the log downstream into the deep dusk, and there was no more sign of the Comanche chief.

Longen, the man who had fallen, was not yet dead—he was jerking and flapping in the water, like a fish that had been speared but not killed.

Bigfoot, annoyed to have been slipped up on so easily, waded several steps into the river, as if he meant to swim after the log and engage the Comanche, but Shadrach yelled at him to come back.

"Come back here," he said. "Don't be trying no ignorant fighting."

Bigfoot hesitated a minute—he wanted to go—but the floating log was barely visible, in the dusk. If he tried to swim for it, Buffalo Hump might slip into the shallows and fill him with arrows while he swam. He knew it was folly to try it, but his fighting blood was up—it was all he could do to check himself; but he did check himself. Crouching low, he waded back to the little group of Rangers by the stand of driftwood.

"Dern, I hate to let him come at us like that," he said. "The goddamn devil! He took Josh and took Zeke and now he's taken this tall fellow here."

All the Rangers stood around uneasily as the tall man named Longen continued to jerk and flop. They pulled him up on the muddy, darkening shore, but no one had any remedy for the fact that the man had an arrow lodged in his backbone. He flopped and jerked, but made no sound at all. Shadrach made one attempt to pull the arrow out, but couldn't budge it.

"I guess we could tie him on a horse," Bigfoot speculated. "Maybe if we can get him across the river he'll live till we can get him to a doc."

"No, let him die," Shadrach said. "His lights are nearly out."

A moment later the man named Longen—no one could remember his first name—ceased to flop. Shadrach felt his neck, and pronounced him dead.

"Get his possibles, boys," Shadrach said, addressing Call.

Call had no idea what the old mountain man was talking about. What were possibles?

"He means empty his pockets—take his gun and his ammunition," Bigfoot informed him. "Don't leave a thing on him that might help the red boys. They don't need no help—they got five of us with no assistance, it looks like."

The last light faded soon after that. Now and again the clouds would break, bringing a glimpse of faint stars, or a thin moon. Call got every item of use off the dead man: his guns, his bullets, tobacco, a knife, a few coins. The knife was a good one—Call meant to keep it for Gus, who had no knife, and had long envied him the one old Jesus had made him.

"It's dark enough—I expect it's time to swim," Bigfoot said.

"Dern it, I hope there ain't no red boys out there, floating around on logs or dead mules," Long Bill said. "My eyesight's poorly, in this kind of weather."

Call wedged Longen's gun beneath his girth, and led the little bay back into the river. The horse had more confidence crossing back. He took the water easily and swam well. Bigfoot and Shadrach were ahead. Jimmy Tweed, true to his convictions, refused to leave the saddle. Long Bill and Blackie Slidell were right behind Call. Blackie Slidell's horse proved to be a frantic swimmer. He swam past Call, so close that Call's bay was pushed off course and floundered for a moment. Call was irritated, but it was so dark he couldn't even see Blackie. When he opened his mouth to say something he got water in it and nearly choked. He tried to keep an eye out for floating logs or floating mules, but it was so dark he couldn't see upriver at all. He concentrated on keeping his musket securely across his saddle. When his feet finally touched bottom and he and the little bay struggled out of the water, a lucky feeling came over him. The river hadn't killed him, and neither had the Comanches. He was tired, and supposed they would be stopping, but he was wrong. Shadrach and Bigfoot led them through the hills all night, toward the big encampment on Bushy Creek.

10.

AN HOUR AFTER HE arrived in the big camp, to his surprise and embarrassment, Woodrow Call was made a corporal in the Texas Rangers. The Ranger troop rode in, five men short, and Bigfoot made a hasty report to Colonel Cobb, who sat outside his tent, smoking a big cigar and scratching the head of a large Irish dog who accompanied him everywhere. The dog was old. His long tongue lolled out, and he panted loudly.

"Yep, this youngster killed his first Comanche," Bigfoot said. "The Comanche was floating down the Brazos holding on to a dead mule. Young Call shot him point-blank."

Caleb Cobb let his sleepy eyes shift to Call for a moment; then he looked back at the Irish dog.

"That's alert behaviour, Mr. Call," he said. "I'll make you a corporal on the spot—we ain't got many corporals in this troop, and I expect we'll need a few."

"I say it's hasty, it could have been luck," Captain Falconer said, annoyed. He thought young Call far too green for such distinction.

The Captain was wearing a black coat, and his mood seemed as dark as his garment. He was sharpening a knife on a large whetstone.

Caleb Cobb smiled.

"Now, Billy," he said, "let me decide on the promotions. If a Comanche was to swim up on you, in the middle of a big river, underneath a dead mule, you might be scalped before you noticed the mule."

"I have always been wary of dead animals when I cross rivers," Captain Falconer said, stiffly. It was clear that he did not appreciate the Colonel's remark.

"Would you go grind that knife out of my hearing?" Caleb asked. "It's hard to think with you grinding that knife, and I need to think."

Without a word, Falconer got up and walked away from the tent.

"Billy's too well educated," Caleb Cobb remarked. "He thinks he knows something. How many Comanches did the rest of you kill?"

"None," Bigfoot admitted. "We might have winged one or two, but I doubt it. They was in good cover."

The Colonel did not change expression, but the tone of his voice got lower.

"You lost five men and this cub's the only one of you who was able to kill an Indian?" he asked.

"The weather was goddamn dim," Bigfoot reminded him.

"It was just as dim for Buffalo Hump and his warriors," Caleb said. "I won't be sending out any more punishment squads, if this is the best we can do. I can't afford to lose five men to get one Indian. From now on we'll let them come to us. Maybe if we bunch up and look like an army we can get across the plains and still have a few men left to fight the Mexicans with, if we have to fight them."

"Colonel, we didn't have good horses," Bigfoot said. "A few of us did, but the rest were poorly mounted. It cost three men their lives."

"What happened to the other two—I thought you lost five," Caleb asked. The big Irish dog had yellow eyes—Call had heard it said that the dog could run down deer, hamstring them, and rip out their throats. Certainly the dog was big enough—he was waist high to Bigfoot, and Bigfoot was not short.

"The other two weren't lucky," Bigfoot said. "I don't know for sure that one of them is dead—but there's no sign of him, so I suspect it."

"If poor horseflesh is the reason you lost a third of your troop, go complain to the quartermaster," the Colonel said. "I ain't the wrangler. I will admit there's a lot of puny horses in this part of Texas."

"Thank you for the promotion," Call said, though he didn't know what it meant, to be a corporal. Probably there were increased duties—he meant to ask Brognoli, when he saw him next. But curiosity got the better of him, and he asked Bigfoot first.

"It just means you make a dollar more a month," Bigfoot said. "Life's just as dangerous, whether you're a corporal or a private."

"With a whole extra dollar you can buy more liquor and more whores," Bigfoot added. "At least you can if you don't let Gus McCrae cheat you out of your money."

The company, in all its muddle and variety, was unlimbering itself for the day's advance. Wagons and oxcarts were snaking through the rocky hills and bumping through the little scrubby valleys. Several of the more indolent merchants were already showing the effects of prairie travel—the dentist who had decided to emigrate to Santa Fe in hopes of doing a lucrative business with the Mexican grandees had tripped over his own baggage and fallen headfirst into a prickly-pear patch. A sandy-haired fellow with a pair of blacksmith's pinchers was pulling prickly-pear thorns out of the dentist's face and neck when Call strode by. The dentist groaned, but the groans, on the whole, were milder than the howls of his patients.

When Call located Gus McCrae and Johnny Carthage he was happy to see that Gus was his feisty self again, his ankle much improved. He was just hobbling back from visiting a young whore named Ginny—Caleb Cobb had permitted a few inexpensive women to travel with the company as far as the Brazos, after which, they had been informed, they would have to return to Austin, the expectation being that enough of the merchants would have given up by that point that the whores would have ample transport. Whether the Great Western would be an exception to this rule was a subject of much debate among the men, many of whom were reluctant to commit themselves to long-distance journeying without the availability of at least one accomplished whore.

"I wouldn't call Matilda accomplished," Johnny Carthage argued. "Half the time she ain't even friendly. A woman that catches snapping turtles for breakfast is a woman to avoid, if you ask me."

He was uncomfortably aware that he had only been partially successful at avoiding Matilda himself—in general, though, he preferred younger and smaller women, Mexican if possible.

Gus had picked up a spade somewhere and was using it intermittently as a crutch. His injured ankle would bear his weight for short distances, but occasionally, he was forced to give it a rest.

Gus had taken to wearing both his pistols in his belt, as if he expected attack at any moment.

"Howdy, did you get wet?" he asked, very glad to see Woodrow Call. Although Woodrow was contrary, he was the best friend Gus had. The thought that he might be killed, and not reappear at all, had given Gus two uneasy nights. Buffalo Hump had risen in his dreams, holding bloody scalps.

"I came near to drowning in the Brazos River, but I didn't lose my gun," Call said. He was especially proud of the fact that he hadn't lost his gun, though no one else seemed to consider it much of an accomplishment.

"The river was up," he added. "Most of the Comanches got away."

"Did you see that big one?" Gus asked.

"I seen his hump," Call said. "He floated down behind a log and put an arrow in a man standing right by me—split his backbone."

The sun had broken through the last of the clouds—bright sunlight gleamed on the wet grass in the valleys and on the hills.

"I wish I could have gone—we would have killed several if we'd worked together," Gus said.

Long Bill Coleman walked up about that time, in a joshing mood.

"Have you saluted him yet?" he asked Gus, to Call's deep embarrassment.

"Why would I salute him, he's my pard," Gus said.

"He may be your pard but he's a corporal now—he killed a red boy and the Colonel promoted him," Long Bill said.

Gus could not have been more taken aback if Call had come back

[163]

scalpless. The very thing that Clara teased him about had actually happened. Woodrow *was* Corporal Call now. No doubt Clara would hurry to court him, once they all got back.

"So that's the news, is it?" Gus said, feeling slightly weak all of a sudden. He had not forgotten Clara and her kiss. Young Ginny had been pleasant, but Clara's kiss was of another realm.

"Yes, he done it just now," Call admitted, well aware that his friend would be at least a little discommoded by the news.

"You kilt one—what was it like?" Gus asked, trying to act normal and not reveal his acute discomfort at the fact of his friend's sudden success.

"He was almost on me—I shot just in time," Call said. "As soon as your ankle heals proper I expect we'll have another engagement. Once you kill a Comanche the Colonel will promote you, too, and we can be corporals together."

He wanted to do what he could to lighten the blow to his friend.

"If I don't, then one will kill me and that will be the end of things," Gus said, still feeling weak. "I just hope I don't get scalped while I'm alive, like Ezekiel done."

"Why, you won't get killed," Call said, alarmed at his friend's sudden despondency. Gus possessed plenty of fight, but somehow that willful girl in the general store had deprived him of it. All he could think about was that girl—it was not good. You couldn't be thinking about girls in general stores, when you were out in Indian country and needed to be alert.

With Call's help, Gus at least managed to get saddled and mounted on the shorter of the two horses that had been assigned him. The two young Rangers rode side by side all day, at a lazy pace, while the wagons and oxcarts toiled up the low hills and across the valleys. Call told the story of the chase, and the fight by the river, but he couldn't tell that his friend was particularly interested.

He held his tongue, though. At least Gus was in the saddle. Once they got across the Brazos, farther from the girl, he might eventually forget her and enjoy the rangering more.

In the afternoon of the third day they glimpsed a fold of the Brazos, curving between two hills, to the west. The falling sun brightened the brown water. To the east they couldn't see the river at all, but gradually the Rangers at the head of the expedition, who included Gus and Call, heard a sound they couldn't identify. It was akin to the sound a cow might make, splashing through a river, only multiplied thousands of times, as if someone were churning the river with a giant churn.

Captain Falconer was at the very front of the troop, on his pacing black. When he heard the sound like water churning, he drew rein. Just as he did the Colonel's big Irish dog shot past him, braying. His ears were laid back—in a second he was out of sight in the scrubby valley, but not out of earshot.

"It's buf," Shadrach said, pulling his rifle from its long sheath.

Just then, two riders came racing from the east. One of the rider's horses almost jumped the Irish dog, which was racing in sight again. Then it raced away, braying loudly.

"Bes-Das has seen 'em," Shadrach said.

Bes-Das was a Pawnee scout—he ranged so far ahead that many of the Rangers had scarcely seen him. The other rider was Alchise, a Mexican who was thought to be half Apache. Both were highly excited by what they had seen behind the eastern hills. Colonel Cobb came galloping up to meet the two scouts; soon the three wheeled their horses and went flying after the dog. The horses threw up their heads and snorted. The excitement that had taken the troop when they thought they were racing to kill mountain goats seized them again—soon forty riders were flying after the Colonel, the Irish dog, and the two scouts.

As the horses fled down the hill, Gus clung tightly to his saddle horn. He could put a little weight on his wounded ankle, but not enough to secure a stirrup when racing downhill over such rocky terrain at such a pace. He knew that if he fell and injured himself further he would be sent home to Austin—all hope of securing promotion and matching his friend Call would be lost.

The sight they saw when they topped the next hill and drew rein with the troop was one neither Call nor Gus would ever forget. Neither of them, until that moment, had ever seen a buffalo, though on the march to the Pecos they had seen the bones of several, and the skulls of one or two. There below them, where the Brazos cut a wide valley, was a column of buffalo that seemed to Gus and Call to be at least a mile wide. To the south, approaching the river, there seemed to be an endless herd of buffalo moving through the hills and valleys. Thousands had already crossed the river and were plodding on to the north, through a little pass in the hills. So thick were the buffalo bunched, as they crossed the river, that it would have been possible to use them as a bridge.

"Look at them!" Gus said. "Look at them buffalo! How many are there, do you reckon?"

"I could never reckon no number that high," Call admitted. "It's more than I could count if I counted for a year."

"This is the southern herd," Captain Falconer commented—even he was too awed by the sight of the thousands of buffalo, browner than the brown water, to condescend to the young Rangers. "I expect it's at least a million. They say it takes two days to ride past the herd, even if you trot."

Bes-Das came trotting back to where Captain Falconer sat. He said something Call couldn't hear, and pointed, not at the buffalo, but at a ridge across the valley some two miles away.

"It's him!" Gus said with a gasp, grabbing his pistol. "It's Buffalo Hump. He's got three scalps on his lance."

Call looked and saw a party of Indians on the far ridge, eight in all. He could see Buffalo Hump's spotted pony and tell that the man was large, but he could not see scalps on his lance. He felt a little envious of his friend's eyesight, which was clearly keener than his.

"Are those the bucks that whipped you?" Caleb Cobb asked, loping up to Bigfoot.

Bes-Das, a short man with greasy hair and broken teeth, began to talk to the Colonel in Pawnee. Cobb listened and shook his head.

"No, we'd have to ford this damn buffalo herd to go after them," he said. "I doubt many of these boys could resist shooting buffalo instead of Comanches. By the time we got to the Indians we'd be out of ammunition and we'd probably get slaughtered. Anyway, I doubt they'd sit there and wait for us to arrive, slow as we are."

"Can't we shoot some buffalo, Colonel?" Falconer asked. "We'd have meat for awhile."

"No, wait till we cross this river," Caleb said. "Half these wagons will probably sink, anyway—if we load them with buffalo roasts we'll just end up feeding buffalo roasts to the turtles."

Call was surprised at the Indians. Why did they just sit there, with a force more than one hundred strong advancing toward them? The scalps on the lance were probably those of Rip Green, Longen, and the man called Bert. Did the red men think so little of the whites' fighting ability that they didn't feel they had to retreat, even when outnumbered by a huge margin?

Slowly, more and more of the riders and wagoneers came up to the ridge and sat watching the buffalo herd. A few of the young men wanted to charge down and start killing buffalo, but Colonel Cobb issued a sharp command and they all stayed where they were.

Shadrach and Bigfoot stood apart, talking to the scouts Bes-Das and Alchise. They were watching the Comanches, who sat on the opposite hill as the great brown herd surged across the Brazos. Below them the Irish dog was barking and leaping at the buffalo, but the buffalo paid him no attention. Now and then he could see the dog nip at the heels of a straggling cow, but the cow would merely kick at him or make a short feint before trotting on with the herd.

"It's way too many buffalo for old Jeb," Caleb said, smiling at the sight of his dog's frustration. "One at a time he can get their attention, but right now they don't think no more of him than a gnat."

Then he pulled a spyglass out of his saddlebag and put it to his eye. He studied the Comanches for awhile, and something that he saw gave him a start.

"Kicking Wolf is there," he said, turning to Falconer as if he were delivering an important piece of news. Call remembered that he had heard the name before—someone, Bigfoot maybe, had suspected that it was Kicking Wolf who had shot the Major's runaway horse, on the first march west.

"Sorry, I ain't heard the name," Captain Falconer said. Though watchful of the Indians, he was more interested in the buffalo, a species of game he had never killed, though hunting was his passion. Now as many as a million animals were right in front of him, but the Colonel had ordered him to hold off until they crossed the river. In his baggage he had a fine sporting rifle, made by Holland and Holland in London—it was all he could do to keep from racing back to his baggage wagon to get it.

"Buffalo Hump is the killer, Kicking Wolf is the thief," the Colonel said. "He's the best horse thief on the plains. He'll have every horse and mule we've got before we cross the Red River, unless we watch close."

He paused and extracted a cigar from his shirt pocket, as he studied the situation.

"If I had to choose who I'd have to harass me I might pick Buffalo Hump," the Colonel said. "If I couldn't whip him, he'd just kill me. It might be bloody, but it would be final. If I went up against Kicking Wolf, the first time I took a nap I'd be afoot.

"There's places off north of here where I'd rather be dead than be afoot," he added. "Ever drunk horse piss?"

He looked at Call and Gus, when he asked the question.

"No sir," Gus said. "I never have and I don't plan to, either."

"I drunk it once—I was traveling with Zeb Pike," the Colonel said. "We kept a horse alive just so we could drink its piss. I was so goddamn thirsty it tasted like peach nectar. When we finally came to water we ate the horse."

To Call's embarrassment his horse stretched itself and began to piss, just as the Colonel spoke. The yellow stream that splashed on the ground didn't smell much like peach nectar, though.

"What will we do about our red neighbors, Billy?" Caleb asked. "Here we are and there they are, with a lot of goddamn buffalo in between."

"Why sir, I expect they'll leave," Falconer said. "I can pursue them, if you prefer."

"No, I don't want you to pursue them," the Colonel said. "My thinking was different. It's almost time to make camp and prepare the grub. Maybe we ought to trot over and invite them to dinner."

"Sir?" Captain Falconer said, not sure that he had heard the Colonel correctly.

"Invite them to dinner—I'd enjoy it," the Colonel said. "A little parley might not hurt."

"Well, but who would ask them?" Captain Falconer asked.

"How about Corporal Call and his *compañero*?" the Colonel said. "It would give the Corporal a chance to live up to his promotion. Just tear up a sheet and wrap it around a rifle barrel. Comanches respect the white flag, I guess. Send Bes-Das with them, to make the introductions. I expect they know Bes-Das."

Gus felt his legs begin to quiver, as they had that day near the western mountains, when he stood near the patch of ground soaked with Josh Corn's blood. The Colonel had looked right at him, when he gave the duty of Call and his *compañero*.

Captain Falconer had gone back to the wagons to find a sheet. The Indians were still sitting on the opposite hill. The long ridge where the Rangers sat soon filled up with men—the whole expedition arranged itself along the ridge to watch the great spectacle below. There was no end to the column of buffalo, either north or south. They moved toward the river and curled out of it like the body of a great snake whose head and tail were hidden. Among the crowd of Rangers, merchants, blacksmiths, whores, and adventurers Call suddenly noticed John Kirker, the scalp hunter who had left them on the Rio Grande. His large colleague, Glanton, was not with him. Kirker had a rifle across the cantle of his saddle—while everyone else watched the buffalo, he watched the Indians.

"You mean we're supposed to just ride over and talk to them?" Gus asked. It was a shock to him to realize that he had been ordered to approach the Comanches. He felt that he had been foolish to hop out of the sick wagon so soon. He should have nursed his sore ankle another week at least, but some of the Rangers had been chiding him for malingering and he had started traveling horseback sooner than he should have.

"That's what Colonel Cobb said," Call answered. "I don't know how we're going to get through them buffalo, though. They're thick."

"I don't want to go through them," Gus said. "I don't want to go. Buffalo Hump stuck a lance in me once, he might poke it clear through me this time."

"No, we'll be under a flag of truce," Call reminded him. "He won't bother you."

"He ain't holding up no white sheet," Gus said. "Why would a white sheet matter to a Comanche?"

"If you're scared you should just go on back and marry that girl," Call said. "Unpack dry goods all your life. I aim to stay with rangering and be a captain myself, someday."

"I aim to be a captain too, unless it means drinking horse piss," Gus said. "I don't intend to get caught in no place so dry that I'd need to drink horse piss."

"Well, you might—the Colonel did," Call said. "That damn Kirker is here—did you notice?"

"He slipped in while you were off on the chase," Gus said. "I understand he's a friend of Colonel Cobb."

[169]

"I deplore traveling with a man who hunts scalps," Call said. "I don't know why the Colonel would be his pard."

"Comanche Indians hunt scalps," Gus pointed out.

"No, they take them in war," Call said. "Kirker hunts them for money. I think Bes-Das is ready. Let's go."

11.

WATCHED BY THE WHOLE expedition, Call and Gus followed Bes-
Das down the ridge toward the buffalo herd. Bigfoot came behind.
No one had ordered Bigfoot to come, or not to come—he joined
the parley because he wanted a closer look at the Comanches than
he had been able to get during the rainy day on the Brazos. Bes-
Das held his rifle high, the white sheet fluttering in the wind.

Across the valley, the eight Comanches waited. They had become
as still as statues. The only movement was the fluttering of the three
scalps on Buffalo Hump's lance.

As the four horses approached the great moving mass of buffalo,
they began to show some anxiety. Their nostrils flared and they
tried to turn back—it was with difficulty that Call kept his little bay
in check. Gus was having trouble too, made worse by the fact of his
sore ankle. Bes-Das, the broken-toothed Pawnee, whacked his
mount with a rifle twice and the horse settled down. Bigfoot kept a
tight rein on his grey mount—the smell of the thousands of animals

affected men and horses alike; the dust they raised was as thick as any sandstorm.

"We'll never get through them—they're too thick," Gus said. "They'll trample us for sure."

"Go quick," Bes-Das said, turning his horse parallel to the herd. "Go with the buffalo."

As Call and Gus kept close, the Pawnee slipped into the buffalo herd, moving in only a few feet and letting the horse turn in the same direction as the herd was going. Moving steadily over, giving ground and turning toward the river if there was no room between animals, Bes-Das was soon halfway across the herd.

"That's the way, just keep a strong rein and ease on through," Bigfoot said. Soon he was in the thick of the herd—Bes-Das was almost to the other side.

"Go on, you're next," Call said to Gus.

"I ain't next, you go," Gus said. "I'll be right behind you."

"Nope," Call said. "I'm the corporal and I'm telling you to go. If I leave you behind you might claim your ankle's hurt and get shot for desertion."

"Why, hell . . . you don't trust your own partner," Gus said, so irritated that he immediately kicked his horse and slipped into the buffalo. In fact he *had* thought of finding an excuse to wait; he didn't want to ride into the herd, and even more, he didn't want to ride up to Buffalo Hump's war party. But he was not going to let Woodrow Call slight his courage, either. He had always supposed he had as much guts as the next man; but his nerves had been somewhat affected by the bloody events of the first march, and were still not under perfect control. He felt sure, though, that he could match Woodrow Call ability for ability, and beat him at most contests. He could see farther, for one thing, though being in the middle of a buffalo herd didn't give him much opportunity to test his vision. All he could see was the brown animals all around him. None of them seemed too interested in him or his horse, and he soon found that he could use the Bes-Das technique as well as Bigfoot or the Pawnee scout. Once he let his horse step too close to the horns of a young bull, but the horse turned just in time. In ten minutes he was almost across the herd—Bes-Das and Bigfoot were there waiting. He didn't know where Woodrow Call was—slipping through the buffalo required all his attention. He was only twenty yards from being free of the herd when suddenly buffalo all around him began to swerve and jump. Gus's horse jumped too, almost unseating him. All the buffalo on the far side of the herd were lowering their heads and acting as if they wanted to butt. Gus was thrown over the saddle horn, onto the horse's neck, but just managed to hang on and regain his seat. He saw Bes-Das and Bigfoot laughing and felt rather annoyed—what was so funny about his nearly getting thrown and trampled?

He spurred through the last few animals and turned to see what had caused the commotion—all he could see was a large badger, snapping at a buffalo cow. The badger was so angry he had foam on his mouth—the buffalo were giving ground, too. Woodrow Call's horse was pitching with him, agitated by the snorting buffalo cow that was faced off with the badger. Woodrow hung on and made it through.

"Why would anything as big as a buffalo shy at a badger?" Gus asked, when he rode up to Bigfoot. "A buffalo could kick a badger halfway to China."

"That badger bluffed 'em," Bigfoot said. "He's so mad he's got 'em convinced he's as big as they are, and twice as mean."

"I wonder if *they're* mad?" Call said, looking at the Comanches, who sat without moving on the hill above them.

"If they are we'd be easy pickings," Bigfoot said. "We'd never get back through them buffalo quick enough to get away, and the troop couldn't get through quick enough to save us, either."

Call looked up at the Indians and back across the valley, at the body of the expedition. He wished Bigfoot had not made the last comment. The buffalo herd they had just slipped through was like a moving wall, separating them from the safety of the troop. All the Comanches would have to do would be to trot down the hill and kill them with lances or arrows. The thought made him feel wavy, and without strength.

Neither Bigfoot nor Bes-Das seemed concerned, though. They walked their horses slowly toward the hill, Bes-Das holding up the rifle with the white sheet on it. Call and Gus fell in behind.

"What if they don't pay no attention to the sheet?" Call asked. He wanted to know what the procedure would be, if they had to fight.

[173]

"If they come for us put as many bullets into the big one as you can," Bigfoot said. "Always kill the biggest bull first—then kill the littlest."

"Why the littlest?" Gus asked.

"Because the littlest is apt to be the meanest, like the badger," Bigfoot said. "That one standing off to the right is Kicking Wolf— he's the littlest and the meanest. You don't want to let your horse graze off nowhere, with Kicking Wolf around. He's so slick he can steal a horse with a man sitting on it."

"He's stumpy, ain't he?" Gus said.

"Kicking Wolf always rides to the outside," Bigfoot said. "Buffalo Hump is the hammer, but Kicking Wolf is the nail. He don't like to be in a crowd. He's the best shot with a rifle in the whole Comanche nation. If they go out and they've only got one rifle between them, they give it to him. Buffalo Hump's old-fashioned. He still prefers the bow."

With the Pawnee scout, Bes-Das, slightly in the lead, the party moved slowly up the hill toward the waiting Indians. Call glanced at the short, stumpy Indian on the right edge of the group and saw that he was the only Indian armed with a rifle. All the rest carried bows or lances. When they were halfway up the hill Buffalo Hump touched his mount with his heels and came down to meet them. When he was still some fifty yards away Call looked at Gus, to see if he was firm. To his surprise Gus looked nonchalant, as if he were merely riding out for a little sport with his pals.

"Here he comes, I hope he's friendly," Gus said. "I never expected to have to go and palaver with him, not after he stuck me with that lance."

"Shut up—Bes-Das will do the palavering," Bigfoot instructed. "You young boys keep your damn traps shut. It don't take much to rub a Comanche the wrong way."

As Buffalo Hump approached, holding his spotted pony to a slow walk, Call felt the air change. The Comanche's body shone with grease; a necklace made of claws hung on his bare chest. Call looked at Gus, to see if he felt the change, and Gus nodded. They had entered the air of the wild men—even the smell of the Indian horses was different.

Bes-Das stopped, waiting. Buffalo Hump came on until the nose of his spotted pony was only a few feet from the nose of the Pawnee's black mare. Then Buffalo Hump lifted his lance and pointed first at Gus, and then at Call. Though he sat erect on his horse, the great hump was visible, rising from between his shoulders behind his neck. When he spoke his voice was so wild and angry that it was all Call could do to keep from grabbing his gun. Call met the man's eyes for a moment—the Comanche's eyes were like stone. Buffalo Hump lowered his lance, glanced at Bigfoot dismissively for a second, and then waited for Bes-Das to speak. Bigfoot seemed not to interest him. Bigfoot returned the favor by looking pointedly up the hill, at Kicking Wolf.

Bes-Das spoke briefly, in Comanche. Buffalo Hump raised his arm and the other Comanches trotted down the hill, to join him. He turned and spoke to his warriors for several minutes. Kicking Wolf grunted something and rode away, back to his position at the side.

"I hope he ain't getting ready to shoot," Gus said.

"I told you to keep your goddamn mouth shut," Bigfoot said. "We'll get out of this with our hair if you'll just keep quiet."

Bes-Das listened to Buffalo Hump, who made a long speech in his thick, angry voice. Call decided then that he would do what he could to learn the Comanche language. It seemed foolish to parley with wild red men if you did not know what was being said in the discussion. He could be talking of ways to kill them, for all he knew.

When Buffalo Hump finished, Bes-Das said a few words and immediately turned his horse and began to walk him back toward the buffalo herd. Bigfoot waited a moment, as if absent-mindedly, and then turned his horse, too. Call and Gus fell in behind. Call felt so much danger in the air that it took all his self-control not to look back. A lance like the one that had pierced Gus's hip could be singing toward them. He glanced at Gus and saw that his friend seemed perfectly firm—something had happened to toughen his attitude since they left the camp and slipped through the buffalo herd.

The recrossing of the herd went quickly—they had learned the edging technique on the first crossing and were soon almost through. Once the buffalo herd was between them and the Indians, Call felt free to look back. The air had changed again—they were in the air of safety, not the air where the quick death was.

[175]

"I guess you grew your backbone again," Call said, noting that Gus looked so cheerful that he was almost whistling.

"Yes, I ain't scared of him now," Gus said. "Clara wouldn't want no coward. I kept my mind on her. We'll be married once we get back to Austin."

Indeed, he felt cheered by the encounter. He had looked Buffalo Hump in the eye and lived—it made him feel lucky again. He was curious, though, about one aspect of the parley.

"I wonder why he pointed that lance at us, when he first rode up?" Gus asked.

Bes-Das turned briefly, and laughed his broken-toothed laugh.

"He said you both belong to him," he told them. "He says he will take you when he is ready—but not today. He is coming to eat supper with the Colonel, and he will bring his wives."

"Why do we belong to him and not you and Bigfoot?" Gus asked.

"You cheated his lance," Bes-Das told him. "He says his lance is hungry for your liver."

"It can just stay hungry," Gus said boldly, though the threat did make his stomach feel wavy for a moment.

"Why me, then?" Call asked. "I didn't cheat his damn lance."

Bes-Das laughed again.

"No, with you it's different," he said, smiling at Call.

"Why would it be different?" Call asked, wishing he could have understood the Indian's talk.

"Different because you killed his son," the Pawnee said.

12.

CALL WAS MORE SOBERED than Gus by the news Bes-Das had delivered. He had killed the war chief's son. Buffalo Hump might forget that he had missed Gus with his lance, but he would not forget the loss of a son. As long as the humpbacked Comanche was alive, Call knew he would have an enemy. Anytime he traveled in Comanche country, his life would depend on keeping alert.

He was silent as they rode back to camp, thinking of all the years of vigilance ahead.

Gus McCrae, though, was in high spirits. Now that he had survived, he was glad he had gone to the parley. Not only had he threaded his way through the great buffalo herd, he had faced the Comanche killer at close range and ridden away unharmed. Now he was safely back with the big troop. Buffalo Hump could threaten all he wanted to—his lance would have to go hungry. Once Clara Forsythe heard what he had done she would know she had kissed a brave man, a Ranger on whom her affections would not be wasted.

It wouldn't be long before the news reached her, either—several of the merchants and most of the whores would soon be going back. In a town as small as Austin the news that he had been selected for a dangerous mission would soon reach the young lady in the general store.

There was a crowd around Caleb Cobb when they rode up to report. The big Irish dog was back—it sat panting at Caleb's feet, its long tongue hanging out. John Kirker was there, sitting on a stump, his big scalping knife at his belt. Shadrach stood to one side, looking disgruntled. He had not liked the order forbidding him to shoot buffalo until they were across the Brazos. When he looked at Caleb Cobb, he glowered his displeasure.

Matilda Roberts stood with him. Lately, the old mountain man and the large whore seemed to have formed an attachment. Often, when Shadrach was out scouting, the two would be seen riding together. At night they sometimes sat together, around a little campfire of their own. No one had heard them exchange a word, and yet they were together, united in their silence. Some of the younger men had become afraid to approach Matilda—they didn't want to risk stirring the old mountain man's wrath. He was said to be terrible in his angers, though no one there could actually remember an occasion when Shadrach had lost his temper.

"Well, are we to have guests for supper?" Caleb Cobb asked. "Does the chief prefer to eat with a fork or with a scalping knife?"

"He will come in one hour," Bes-Das said. "He wants to eat quick. He will leave the camp at sundown. He will bring three wives with him but no braves."

"Well, that's rare," Caleb said. "Does he have any other requests, this chief?"

"Yes," Bes-Das said. "He wants you to give him a rifle."

Caleb chuckled. "A rifle to kill us with," he said. "I sure hope he likes the cooking, when he tastes it—if he don't find it tasty he might scalp Sam."

Black Sam had become Caleb Cobb's personal cook. The Colonel was so partial to rabbit that Sam had stuffed a cage of fat rabbits into one of the supply wagons. The Colonel didn't like large game— Sam trapped quail for him, and kept him fed with small, succulent bunnies.

"Well, if he's coming so soon, the chef will have to hurry," Caleb said. "Falconer, you like to shoot. Lope down and kill a couple of buffalo calves. Take the liver and sweetmeats and leave the rest. Call and McCrae will escort you—their horses are already used to the bufs."

Falconer started for the wagon, to get his fine gun, but the Colonel stopped him with an impatient wave.

"You don't need that damn English gun just to shoot two calves," he said. "Shoot 'em with your pistol, or let Corporal Call do it."

Call was disconcerted, as they rode down to the herd, to see John Kirker following, only a few yards to the rear. Call rode on for a bit and then decided he couldn't tolerate the man's presence. He nodded at Gus, and the two of them turned to face the scalp hunter.

"You weren't told to come," Call informed Kirker. "I'd prefer it if you'd go back."

"I don't work for no army and I won't be told what to do by no one," Kirker said. "Caleb Cobb can pretend he's a colonel if he wants to. He don't tell me what to do and neither do you, you damn pups."

"You weren't told to come," Call repeated. He was trying to be calm, though he felt his anger rising.

"There's Indians around buffalo," Kirker said. "They crawl in with them and shoot from under their bellies. I got business to tend to—I don't care if that murdering humpback is coming to eat. Get out of my way."

"Tell him, Captain," Call said, turning to Falconer, but Falconer ignored the request.

"Last time you rode with us you scalped some Mexicans," Gus remarked.

Kirker brought the rifle up and looked at them coolly, his thin lip twisted in a kind of sneer.

"I despise young fools," he said. "If you don't like my trade have at me and do it now. I might get a scalp before sundown if I'm active."

Kirker spoke with the same insolence with which he had confronted Bigfoot and Shadrach, back on the Rio Grande.

Gus found the man's insolence intolerable. To Call's surprise, he yanked one of the big pistols out of his belt and whacked Kirker right across the forehead with it. The lick made a dull sound—a mule kicking a post made such a sound. Kirker was knocked backward, off his horse. He lay still for a moment, curled on the ground, but his eyes were open.

Call leapt down and took Kirker's pistol, as the man struggled to his feet. Kirker reached for his big knife, but before he could pull it Call clubbed his arm with his musket—then he clubbed him twice more.

"Whoa, Woodrow," Gus said, alarmed by the look in Call's eye and the savage force of his clubbing. He himself had been angry enough to knock Kirker off his horse with a pistol, but the one hard lick satisfied him. The man's forehead was split open—he was streaming blood. It was enough, at least, to teach him respect. But Woodrow Call had no interest in respect. He was swinging to kill.

"He's a friend of the Colonel's—we don't need to kill him," Gus said, leaping down, as did black Sam, who had come along to select the cuts. Call swung a third time, at the man's Adam's apple—only the fact that Sam grabbed at the barrel and partially broke the force of the swing saved Kirker—even so the man went down again, rolling and clawing at his throat, trying to get air through his windpipe. Gus and Sam together managed to hold Call and keep him from smashing the man's head with the musket.

Falconer, who didn't like the scalp hunter either, turned for a moment, to look at the fallen man.

"Disarm him," he said. "He's got guns in his boots. If we leave him anything to shoot he'll try to kill us all, once he gets his wind."

Call was remembering the filthy, fly-bitten scalps, hanging from the man's saddle; he also remembered Bigfoot's contention that some of them were the scalps of Mexican children.

"Don't be beating nobody to death—not here," Sam said. "Colonel Cobb, he'll hang you. He hangs folks all the time."

With difficulty, Call made himself mount and ride on to the herd. When they left, Kirker was on his knees, spitting blood.

"You yanked that pistol quick," Falconer said, to Gus. "I think I'll make you my corporal. You could make a fine *pistolero*."

"Thank you, the fellow was rude," Gus said. "Do you think the Colonel will let me be a corporal?"

Though he didn't much like Falconer, the man's words filled him with relief. He felt he had caught up with Call again, in terms of rank. He also felt that he was staunch again, and could fight when a fight was required. The weak feeling that had troubled him since his first glimpse of Buffalo Hump wasn't there anymore—or at least, not there steadily. He might die, but at least he could fight first, and not simply pass his days shaking at the expectation of slaughter.

They rode on to the herd, quickly shot two fat calves, and took their livers and sweetmeats, as instructed. Sam was deft at the cutting. He had brought a sack to put the meat on, and knotted it deftly once he was finished.

"I'll kill some big meat tomorrow," Falconer said, as they rode back toward camp. "Once we get across the river the Colonel won't mind."

"These buffalo be gone tomorrow," Sam said.

"Gone—what do you mean—there's thousands of them," Falconer said, in surprise.

"They be gone tomorrow," Sam said—he did not elaborate.

When they passed the spot where the fight with Kirker had occurred there was no trace of the man, though the grass was spotted with blood from his broken forehead.

"I hope I broke his damn arm, at least," Call said.

Nobody else said anything for a bit. They rode up to the troop in silence, Sam carefully holding his sack of meat.

"Sam knows where to cut into a buffalo calf," Gus remarked. "You might give us lessons, next time we have an opportunity. I could slide around on one for an hour and not know when I had come to the liver."

"Just watch me, next time," Sam said. "Buffalo liver tastes mighty good."

13.

GENERAL PHIL LLOYD, IN his youth one of the heroes of the Battle of New Orleans, was so impressed by the news that Buffalo Hump was coming to supper that he made his manservant, Peedee, scratch around amid his gear until he found a clean coat. It was wrinkled, true, but it wasn't spotted and stained with tobacco juice, or beef juice, or any of the other substances General Lloyd was apt to dribble on himself in the course of a day's libations.

"I might be getting dressed up for nothing," he informed Caleb Cobb. "There's a hundred men, at least, right here in this camp, who would like to shoot that rascal's lights out. Why would he come?"

"Oh, he'll come, Phil," Caleb Cobb said. "He wants to show off his wives."

Looking around the camp, Call decided that he agreed with the General. Most of the Rangers, and not a few of the merchants and common travelers, had lost friends or family members to the Comanches; some of the lost ones had died by Buffalo Hump's own hand. There were mutterings and curses as the time for his arrival approached. Several of the more radical characters were for hanging Caleb Cobb—he ought never to have issued the invitation, many Rangers felt. Sam had to hurry his cooking, but when the smell of the sizzling liver wafted through the camp it added to the general discontent. Why should a killer get to dine on such delicacies, while most of them were making do with tough beef?

"He'll come," Gus said. "It would take more than this crowd to scare him away."

Like Call, he had begun to doubt the competence of the military leadership. General Lloyd, who had been drunk the whole trip and unconscious for most of it, had his servant pin more than a dozen medals on the front of his blue coat.

"He must have won them medals for drinking, he don't do nothing else," Gus observed.

While the liver was sizzling and the sweetbreads simmering in a small pot with some onions and a little wild barley Sam had managed to locate, Caleb Cobb, noting the mood of surliness among the men, told Falconer to round up the malcontents and assemble them. Falconer liked nothing better than ordering men to do things they didn't want to do—he had a little black quirt that he popped against his leg; he circled the camp, popping the quirt against his leg and forcing the men to stroll over to Caleb Cobb's tent.

Cobb was large; he enjoyed imposing himself. When the men were assembled he stretched himself and pointed toward the hill to the east. Four horses were moving across the ridge—Buffalo Hump was coming with his wives.

"Here he comes, right on time," Caleb said. "I'll make a short speech. He's a murdering devil but I invited him to supper and I won't have no guest of mine interfered with."

"Does that mean we ain't to spit while he's in camp?" Shadrach asked. He had no great respect for Caleb Cobb, who, in his view, was just a pirate who had decided to come ashore. Cobb had caught several Mexican ships, so it was said, and had made off with the gold and silver, and the women. That was the rumour in the Galveston waters, anyway. Shadrach suspected that the main reason for the Texas–Santa Fe expedition was that Cobb wanted to get the gold and silver at its source. None of that gave Cobb license to instruct him in behaviour, and Shadrach wanted him to know it.

"You can spit, but not in his direction," Caleb said. He was well aware that the mountain man didn't like him.

"Why are you having him, Colonel, if he's such a killer?" the dentist, Elihu Carson, asked. He had heard that the Comanches sometimes removed the jawbones of their captives with the teeth intact; as a professional he would have liked to question Buffalo Hump about the technique involved, but he knew that at such an important parley he was unlikely to get the chance.

"Curiosity," Caleb replied. "I've never met him, and I'd like to. If you want to know the mettle of your opponent, it don't hurt to look him in the eye. Besides, he knows the country—he might loan us a scout."

"He won't loan you no scout, he'll kill the ones we got," Bigfoot said.

"Mr. Wallace, it won't hurt to try," Caleb said. "I brought you all here to make a simple point: Buffalo Hump's my guest at dinner. I will promptly hang any ill-tempered son of a bitch who interferes with him."

The men stared back at him, unawed and unpersuaded.

"If we kill him, the Comanche and the Kiowa will rise up and wipe out every damn farm between the Brazos and the Nueces," Caleb said. "We have to cross his country to reach Santa Fe, and we don't know much about it. If it turns out that we have to fight him, we'll fight him, but right now I'd like to see some manners in this camp."

The men were silent, watching the horses approach. They gave ground a few steps, so that the Comanches could ride up to Caleb's tent, but their mood was dark. While not eager to be hanged, they all knew that hanging was gentle compared to what would happen to them if Buffalo Hump caught them. Those who had lost sons in the Comanche wars, or had daughters stolen, thought that a hanging would be a cheap price to pay for the opportunity to put a bullet in the big war chief. Yet they held back—bound, if uneasily, by the rules their commander had laid down.

Buffalo Hump still had the three scalps tied to his lance when he rode into camp. He had on leggins but no shirt—he had coated his face and body with red clay and had painted yellow lines across his cheeks and forehead. The three women riding behind him were all young and plump. If frightened at riding into the white man's camp, they didn't show it. They rode a short distance behind Buffalo Hump, and kept their eyes on the ground.

Call thought it remarkably bold of the war chief to ride into such a camp alone. Gus agreed. He tried to imagine himself riding into a Comanche camp with no one beside him but a whore or two, but remembering the tortures Bigfoot had described, he thought he would decline the invitation, if one ever came.

"He ain't afraid of us—and every man in camp wants to kill him," Call said. "He don't think much of Rangers, I guess."

When Buffalo Hump dismounted, his wives did, too—they quickly spread a robe for him outside the Colonel's tent. Caleb Cobb offered tobacco. One of the wives took it and gave it to Buffalo Hump, who smelled it briefly and gave it back. Call knew the man had to be powerful just to carry his own hump, a mass of gristle as broad as his back—it rose as high as his ears.

Yet, Buffalo Hump wasn't stooped. He didn't so much as glance at the massed Rangers, but he did take note of Caleb Cobb's Irish dog, who was watching him alertly. The dog wasn't growling, but his hair bristled.

"Tell him he's welcome and put in some guff about what a great chief he is," Caleb instructed Bes-Das.

Bes-Das turned to Buffalo Hump and spoke five or six words. Buffalo Hump was watching the dog; he didn't answer.

"That was too short a compliment," Caleb said. "Tell him he's stronger than the buffalo and wiser than the bear. Tell him his name is enough to freeze Mexican blood. We need some wind here —they expect it."

Bes-Das tried again, but Buffalo Hump didn't appear to pay his words the slightest attention. He gestured toward the food, which Sam had waiting, but he made no gesture at all toward Caleb Cobb. Two of the plump young women took wooden bowls and went over to Sam, who ladled up his sweetbreads and filled the other bowl with large slices of liver. Gus thought the red clay and the yellow paint made the Comanche look even more terrible. Call watched closely, wondering why the air itself seemed to change when a wild Indian came around. He decided it was because no one but the Indian knew the rules that determined actions—if there were rules.

For a moment it seemed that Buffalo Hump was simply going to eat his food standing up, ignoring Caleb Cobb. Caleb himself was worried—with all his men watching, it would only do to let himself be insulted up to a point. But after he had sniffed the dishes, Buffalo Hump gestured again to the young women, who took two more bowls and filled them; these they brought to Caleb.

Buffalo Hump looked at Caleb for the first time, lifting the bowls. Then he took a place on the robe and handed the bowls to his young wives, who then began to take turns feeding him with their fingers.

"If I could find a woman to hand-feed me sweetbreads, I expect I'd get married too," Caleb said. "Tell that to the rascal."

At the word "rascal," Buffalo Hump lifted his head slightly. It occurred to Caleb too late that perhaps the Comanche had picked up few words of English—after all, he had taken many captives who spoke it.

Bes-Das spoke at length, in Comanche, but if his words made any impression on the chief, Buffalo Hump didn't show it. His young wives continued to feed him buffalo liver and sweetbread stew. The camp had become completely silent. The men who had been cursing Buffalo Hump merely stood looking at him. Several who had proposed to risk hanging by attempting to kill him offered no threat. Call and Gus stood stock-still, watching, while Buffalo Hump ate. Caleb Cobb took a bite or two of liver himself, but seemed to have lost his usual vigorous appetite.

Buffalo Hump paid little attention to the company, at least until he noticed Matilda Roberts, standing with Shadrach. Once he noticed, he gave Matilda a long look; then he turned to Bes-Das and spoke what seemed like a long speech. Bes-Das glanced at Matilda and shook his head, but Buffalo Hump repeated what he had said.

"Taken a fancy to Matty, has he?" Caleb asked.

"Yes, he wants her for a wife," Bes-Das said. "He has seen her before. He calls her Turtle Catching Woman."

"First he wants a rifle and now he wants a wife," Caleb said. "What is it they call Shadrach, in Comanche?"

"They call him Tail-Of-The-Bear," Bes-Das said.

"Tell the great chief that Matilda is the wife of Tail-Of-The-Bear," Caleb said. "She ain't available for marriage unless she gets divorced."

Bes-Das spoke to Buffalo Hump, who seemed amused by what

was said. He replied at length, in a tone of derision; the reply made Bes-Das rather uncomfortable, Call thought.

"Well, what's the report?" Caleb asked, impatiently.

"He says Tail-Of-The-Bear is too old for such a large woman," Bes-Das said. "He says he will give him a young horse, in exchange."

Neither Matilda nor Shadrach moved, or changed expression.

"Tell him we can't accept—it is not our custom to trade people for horses," Caleb said. "Falconer, go get your fancy rifle."

Captain Falconer was startled.

"What for?" he asked.

Ignoring this exchange, Buffalo Hump suddenly spoke again. This time he spoke at more length, looking at Shadrach as he talked. When he stopped he reached for the pot that had the sweetbread stew in it, and drained it.

"What was that last?" Caleb said. "It had a hostile kind of sound."

"He says he will take the scalp of Tail-Of-The-Bear if he crosses the Canadian River," Bes-Das said. "Then he will take the woman and keep the horse."

"Go get the rifle, Billy—supper's about over," Caleb said, though in a mild tone.

"Why, it's my rifle?" Captain Falconer said.

"Go get it, Billy—we need a good present and it's the only gun in camp fine enough to offer the chief," Caleb said. "Hurry. I'll buy you one just as good as soon as we get to Santa Fe."

Captain Falconer balked. The Holland and Holland sporting rifle was the finest thing he owned. He had ordered it special, from London, and had waited two years for it to come. The case he kept it in was made of cherry wood. One of his reasons for signing on with the expedition was an eagerness to try his rifle on the game of the prairies—buffalo, elk, antelope, maybe even a grizzly bear. The rifle had cost him six months' wages—he intended to treasure it throughout his life. The thought of having to hand it over to a murdering savage with yellow paint on his face was more than he could tolerate, and he said so.

"I won't give it up," he said bluntly. "Give the man a musket. It's more than he deserves."

"I'll decide what he deserves, Captain," Caleb Cobb said. He had been sitting, but he rose; when he did, Buffalo Hump rose, too.

"I won't do it, Colonel—I'll resign first," Captain Falconer said.

In a motion no one saw clearly, Caleb Cobb drew his pistol and fired point-blank at Captain Falconer. The bullet took him in the forehead, directly above his nose.

"You're resigned, Captain," Caleb said. He walked over to the baggage wagon containing the officer's baggage and came back with the cherry wood case containing the dead man's Holland and Holland rifle. The body of Billy Falconer lay not two feet from the edge of Buffalo Hump's robe. Neither the war chief nor his women gave any sign that they had noticed the killing.

Caleb Cobb opened the gun case and handed it to Buffalo Hump. The rifle was disassembled, its barrel in one velvet groove, the stock and trigger in another. Caleb set the case down, lifted the two parts out, and quickly fitted them together. Then he handed the gun to Buffalo Hump, who hefted it once and then, without another word, took the rifle and walked over to his horse. He mounted and gestured to his wives to bring the blanket and the cherry wood case. He didn't thank Caleb, but he looked once more at Matilda, and bent a moment, to speak to Shadrach.

"If I don't take yours first," Shadrach said, quietly.

Then Buffalo Hump rode off, followed by his wives. The sun was just setting.

The strange silence that had seized the troop continued, even though the Comanches were soon well out of hearing.

Captain Falconer's wound scarcely bled—only a thin line of blood curled down his ear.

"Bury this skunk, I won't have mutiny," Caleb said. He glanced at the troop, to see if anyone was disposed to challenge his action. The men all stood around like statues, all except Sam. He was expected to do the burying, as well as the cooking. He picked up a spade.

"You can have that pacing black—I intend to make you a scout," Caleb said, to Call.

"Sir, Captain Falconer made me a corporal," Gus McCrae said. He knew it was bold to speak, so soon after a captain of the Rangers had been executed for mutiny, but the fact was, he had been awarded the rank and he meant to have it. He had been made a corporal legally, he believed, and he wanted Clara Forsythe to know that Woodrow Call was not the only one to earn a quick promotion.

Caleb Cobb was a little surprised, but more amused. The young

Tennessee boy had gumption, at least, to insist on his promotion at such a time.

"Well, let's have your report—what did you do to earn this honor?" Caleb asked.

"I whacked John Kirker on the head with my pistol," Gus said. "He followed us when he wasn't told to, and he wouldn't go back when we asked."

"You whacked Johnny?" Caleb asked, in surprise. "How hard did you whack him?"

"He knocked him off his horse and split his forehead open," Bigfoot said. "I seen it. Kirker was mean spoken—I had a notion to whack him myself."

"Scalp hunters are apt to be a little short on manners," Caleb said. "John Kirker's the sort of fellow who will kill you for picking your teeth, if you happen to do it at a time when he ain't in the mood to see no teeth picked. If you laid him out, then Falconer was wrong just to make you a corporal—he ought to have made you a general."

He paused, and smiled.

"However, since I didn't witness the action and don't know all the circumstances, I'll just let the rank of corporal stand. What became of Kirker after you whacked him?"

"We don't know," Call said. "He left."

Caleb nodded. "If I were you I'd watch my flank for a few days, Corporal McCrae," he said. "John Kirker ain't one to forget a whacking."

Then he turned, and went into his tent.

Soon the company found its legs and drifted back to normal pursuits: cooking, drinking, standing guard, making fires. Call and Gus, feeling a kinship with Sam because they were all from San Antonio, took shovels and picks and helped him dig Falconer's grave.

General Phil Lloyd stood by Caleb Cobb's tent, feeling forgotten. Falconer, too, was well on his way to being forgotten, though he had only been dead ten minutes. The difference was that Falconer was actually dead, whereas General Lloyd merely felt he might as well be. He had put on his cleanest blue coat, in preparation for Buffalo Hump's visit. He had even had Peedee, his man, hang all his twelve medals on it. Once he had had as many as eighteen medals—he was pretty sure the correct figure was eighteen—but six of them had been lost, in various drunken outings, in various muddy towns.

Still, twelve medals was no small number of medals; it was an even dozen, in fact. An even dozen medals was a solid number, yet out on the Brazos, with the sky getting cloudy and a gloomy dusk coming on, a dozen medals seemed to count for nothing. Buffalo Hump hadn't even glanced at him, or his medals, though in his experience, red Indians were usually attracted to military decorations.

Not only that: Caleb Cobb had not bothered to introduce him; nor had he asked him to sit. The buffalo liver had smelled mighty appetizing, but Caleb Cobb hadn't offered him any.

The two young Rangers, Corporal Call and Corporal McCrae, came over and rolled Captain Falconer's body onto a wagon sheet. General Lloyd walked over and watched them tie the body into its rough shroud. He had once been the hero of the Battle of New Orleans—Andrew Jackson had made a speech about him. It seemed to him that the two youngsters, just getting their start in military life, might appreciate his history. They might want to hear how it had been, fighting the British—far different, certainly, from fighting savages such as Buffalo Hump. They might want to look at his medals and ask him what this one was for, or what exploit that one celebrated.

"It will be fine to be in Santa Fe—that high air is too good for your lungs," he said, to put the young men at ease.

"Yes sir," Gus said. He was wondering whether a salute was necessary, with darkness nearly on them.

Before Call could speak—he had only been planning to say something simple, as Gus had—General Lloyd decided he didn't want to be around a corpse wrapped in a wagon sheet. He couldn't get a bad notion out of his head, the notion being that he was really the one who was dead and wrapped in a wagon sheet.

The notion disturbed General Lloyd so much that he turned and stumbled away, to look for his wagon, his servant Peedee, and his bottle. He thought he might send Peedee after a whore.

In New Orleans, in the old days, there had been winsome and willing Creole girls—his hope was that there might be something of the sort in Santa Fe. Santa Fe was high, he knew that much; high air was thought to be good for women's complexions. In Santa Fe he might find a young beauty to marry him; if he could, then it wouldn't matter so much about lost medals, or the fact no one took much notice of him at parleys.

At present, though, they had only advanced to the Brazos and the only women around were rough camp whores. He thought he might send Peedee to look for one, though. It might help him sleep.

Gus and Call were trying to keep their minds off Falconer's abrupt execution. Neither of them had supposed that the military life involved such extreme risks. They were so disturbed by what they had seen that they were having an awkward time getting Falconer's body wrapped in its rough shroud; neither of them had had much training at burials. When Gus saw General Lloyd stumble away, he grew apprehensive. If the penalty for failing to give a fine rifle to an Indian was instant death, what might the penalty be for failing to salute a general?

"We didn't salute him. What if he has us hung?" Gus asked. He was troubled by the thought that he might have made a serious breach of military etiquette only a few minutes after having been promoted to corporal.

Call was still trying to puzzle out the logic of Falconer's execution. Caleb Cobb had brooked almost no argument. Without warning, he had merely yanked out his pistol and shot the Captain dead. Of course, Falconer had balked at an order, but he was a captain. He could hardly have suspected that his refusal to hand over his prized rifle would mean instant execution. If Caleb had put it to him that he viewed the matter as serious—that it meant life or death—no doubt Captain Falconer would have given up the gun. But Caleb hadn't given a chance to argue. Call would have thought there would have to be some kind of trial, before a captain in the Rangers could be executed. He meant to ask Bigfoot about the matter the next time he saw him.

"I think we could have saluted," Gus said again. With darkness coming, and a dead man to bury, the omission of the salute loomed large in his mind.

"Hush about it," Call said. "I don't even know how to salute. Help me tie this end of the wagon sheet. He's going to slip out if you don't."

14.

RAIN BEGAN AT MIDNIGHT and continued until dawn and then on through the day. Call and Gus crawled under one of the wagons, hoping for a little sleep, but the water soon puddled around them and they slept little. Gus kept remembering the puzzled look on Falconer's face, when Caleb Cobb raised his gun to kill him. He mentioned it to Call so often that Call finally told him to shut up about it.

"I guess he *was* puzzled," he said. "We were all puzzled. You don't expect to see a man shot down like that, just to please an Indian."

"I doubt Bigfoot was puzzled," Gus said. "It takes a lot to puzzle Bigfoot."

Call was glad when it became their turn to stand guard. Standing guard beat trying to sleep in a puddle.

By midmorning the Brazos was impassable—the rains fell for three days, and then the river only fell enough for a general crossing to be feasible after three more days, by which time morale in the expeditionary party had sunk very low.

In the wake of Falconer's death, men began to remember other tales they had heard, or thought they had heard, about Caleb Cobb's violent behaviour as a commander. Long Bill Coleman recalled that someone had told him Caleb had once hanged six men at sea, in his pirating days. The men's crime, as Long Bill remembered it, was to get into the grog and turn up drunk.

"I heard it was four," Blackie Slidell said.

"Well, that's still a passel of men to hang because they were drunk," Long Bill argued.

During the day, hunting parties scoured the south bank of the Brazos, sure that some of the thousands of buffalo they had seen must still be on the south side of the river; their hopes were disappointed. Not a single buffalo could be located, nor were deer or wild pigs easy to find. Caleb ordered the killing of three beeves— but the meat was stringy, and the men's discontent increased.

"We could have been eating buffalo liver every night," Johnny Carthage complained. "I've heard the hump is good, too."

"No, the hump is fatty," Bigfoot said. "I generally take the liver and the tongue."

That was the first Gus McCrae had heard about people eating tongue.

"Tongue?" he said. "I won't be eating no tongues—I don't care if they do come from a buffalo."

"I'll take yours, then," Bigfoot said. "Buffalo tongue beats polecat by a long shot, although polecat ain't bad if you salt it heavy."

"What happens in an army if the colonel goes crazy?" Call asked. It seemed to him that Caleb Cobb might be insane. His own promotion, for doing nothing more than defending himself from sure death, had been a whimsy on Caleb's part—as much a whimsy as Falconer's execution. During the long rainy nights, huddled around campfires, their pants soaked, the men speculated and speculated about Caleb Cobb's surprising action.

"He had to make a show for Buffalo Hump," Bigfoot contended. "He wanted him to know he had sand. Once an Indian thinks you don't have sand, he don't show no mercy."

"That one don't show no mercy, sand or not," Long Bill said. "Zeke Moody had plenty of sand, and so did Josh."

"Maybe Falconer tried to steal his girl, or beat him at cards or something," Blackie suggested. "Caleb might have had a grudge."

Call couldn't see that it mattered why—not now. In his view, the killing had not been done properly, but he was young and he didn't voice his opinion. Captain Falconer had been an officer. If there were charges against him he should have been informed of them, at least. But the only message he got was the bullet that killed him. Probably Caleb Cobb would have been just as quick to kill any man who happened to be standing there at that time. Probably Bigfoot was right: Caleb had just wanted to show Buffalo Hump that a colonel in the Rangers could be as cruel as any warchief, dealing out death as he chose.

Call resolved to do his duties as best he could, but he meant to avoid Caleb Cobb whenever possible. He thought the man was insane, though Gus disagreed.

"Killing somebody don't mean you're insane," he argued.

"I think he's insane, you can think what you like," Call told him. "It was Falconer made you a corporal, remember. The Colonel might decide he don't like you, for no better reason than that."

Gus thought the matter over, and decided there could be some truth in it. Yet, unlike Call, he was drawn to Caleb Cobb. It interested him that a pirate had got to be commander of an army. Whenever he happened to be around the Colonel, he listened carefully.

On the sixth day, the Colonel decided to cross the river, though it was still dangerously high. Every night his forces diminished—men slipped off, back toward Austin. They decided they had no stomach for prairie travel, and they left. Caleb didn't have them pursued—half the troop had no idea why they were bound for Santa Fe, anyway; most of them would have been useless in a fight and a burden, had supplies run low, as they were likely to do, on the high plains. Yet, by the sixth day, discontent was so rife that he decided to ford the river despite the risk. Another day or two of waiting and the whole Texas–Santa Fe expedition might simply melt into the Brazos mud. In retrospect, he regretted not letting the men chase the buffalo—it would have given them some sporting exploits to talk about around the campfires. His reasoning in holding them back had been sound, but the weather confounded his reason, as it was apt to.

Both Bes-Das and Alchise were against the crossing. The Brazos was still too high. Shadrach was against it, and Bigfoot too, although Bigfoot agreed with the Colonel that if they didn't cross soon the expedition would quietly disband. All the scouts remembered the fate of Captain Falconer, though. They offered little advice, knowing that the wrong piece of advice might get them shot.

Gus had not been along for the earlier river crossing, but he had crossed the Mississippi and had no fear of the Brazos.

"Why, this is just a creek," he said. "I could swim it on my back."

"I couldn't," Call told him. "I swum it twice and it was all I could do, even with a horse pulling me."

There was no agreement as to the swimming capacity of sheep, so the twenty sheep were tied and tossed in the sturdiest of the wagons. Then, for no reason that anyone could determine, the wagon with the sheep in it capsized in midstream, drowning the driver—he got a foot tangled in the harness—two of the horses, and all twenty sheep. Three of the beeves wandered into quicksand on the south bank—they were mired so deep that Caleb ordered them shot. Sam waded in mud to his thighs, with his butcher knife, to take what meat he could from the three muddy carcasses. Six merchants and four whores decided the Brazos was their limit, and turned back for the settlements. Brognoli was the only man to swim the river without a horse. It was rumoured that Brognoli could swim five miles or more, though there was no body of water large enough to allow the claim to be tested. Caleb Cobb crossed in a canoe he had brought along in one of the wagons for that purpose. The wagon they had been hauling the canoe in was hit by some heavy driftwood; it broke up just shy of the north bank. Only four wagons survived the crossing, but they were the ones containing the ammunition and supplies. The expeditionary force, though a little leaner, was still mostly intact. The four wagons had all they could haul as it was, but Caleb Cobb proceeded to hoist his canoe on top of the largest wagon, despite his scouts' insistence that he wouldn't need it.

"Colonel, most of the rivers between here and the Arkansas is just creeks," Bigfoot said. "That canoe's wider than some of them. You could turn it upside down and use it as a bridge."

"Fine, that's better than traveling wet," Caleb said. "I despise traveling wet."

The fourth day north of the Brazos the post oak and elm petered out, and the troop began to move across an open, rolling prairie. There were still plenty of trees along the many creeks, so the troop didn't lack for firewood, but the traveling was easier, and the men's mood improved. Little seeping springs dotted the prairie, producing water that was clearer and more tasteful than that of the muddy Brazos. Deer were plentiful though small, but the men could scarcely raise an interest in venison. They expected to come on the great buffalo herd any day. They had all smelled the buffalo liver Sam had cooked for the Comanches, and were determined to try it for themselves.

Call and Gus had been made scouts, assigned to range ahead with Bes-Das and Alchise. Bigfoot the Colonel kept close at hand—though he valued Bigfoot's advice, he mainly wanted him handy because he was amused by his conversation. Shadrach had taken a cough, and roamed little. He rode beside Matilda Roberts, his long rifle always across his saddle.

They crossed the Trinity River on a sunny day with no loss of life other than one brown dog, a mongrel who had hung around the camp since the troop's departure. Sam liked the little dog and fed him scraps. The dog was swimming by a big bay gelding, when the horse panicked and pawed the dog down. Sam was gloomy that night, so gloomy that he failed to salt the beans.

The stars were very bright over the prairie, so bright that Call had trouble sleeping. The only Indians they had seen were a small, destitute band of Kickapoos, who seemed to be living off roots and prairie dogs. When asked if the buffalo herd were near, they shook their heads and looked blank.

"No buffalo," one old man said.

None of the men could figure out what had become of the buffalo —hundreds of thousands of them had crossed the Brazos less than a week before, and yet they had not seen one buffalo, or even a track. Call asked Bigfoot about it, and Bigfoot shrugged.

"When we got across the river, we turned west," he said. "I reckon them buffalo turned east."

Even so, the men rode out every day, expecting to see the herd. At night they talked of buffalo, anticipating how good the meat would taste when they finally made their kills. In Austin, they had talked of women, or of notable card games they had been in; on the prairie, they talked of meat. Sam promised to instruct them all in buffalo anatomy—show them where the liver was, and how best to extract the tongue. After weeks in the trees, the breadth and silence of the prairie unnerved some of the men.

"Dern, I can't get cozy out here," Johnny Carthage observed. "There's nothing to stop the damn wind."

"Why would you want to stop it—just let it blow," Gus said. "It's just air that's on the move."

"It rings in my ears, though," Johnny said. "I'd rather bunk up behind a bush."

"I wonder how far it is, across this prairie?" Jimmy Tweed asked.

"Well, it's far," Blackie Slidell said. "They say you can walk all the way to Canada on it."

"I have no interest in hearing about Canada," Jimmy Tweed said. "I'd rather locate Santa Fe and get me a shave."

There was a whole group of men just come from Missouri, especially to join the expedition. They were a sour lot, in Gus's view, seldom exchanging more than a word or two with the Texans, and not many among themselves. They camped a little apart, and were led by a short, red-bearded man named Dakluskie. Gus tried to make friends with one or two of the Missourians, meaning to draw them into a card game, but they rebuffed him. The only one he developed a liking for was a boy named Tommy Spencer, no more than fourteen years old. Dakluskie was his uncle and had brought him along to do camp chores. Tommy Spencer thought Texas Rangers were all fine fellows. When he could, he sneaked over to sit at the campfire with them, listening to them yarn. He had a martial spirit, and carried an old pistol that was his pride.

"I wish I was from Texas," he told Gus. "There ain't no fighting much left, back in Missouri."

The second day north of the Trinity, Gus and Call had ridden out with Bes-Das to scout for easy fords across the many creeks, when they came over a ridge and saw a running buffalo coming right toward them. The buffalo was a cow, and had been running awhile—her tongue hung out, and her gait was unsteady. Some thirty yards behind her an Indian was in pursuit, with a second Indian still farther back. The buffalo and her two pursuers appeared so suddenly that no one thought to shoot either the beast or the Comanches. The first Indian had a lance in his hand, the second one a bow. They rode right by Call, not thirty yards away, but seemed not to notice him at all, so focused were they on the buffalo they wanted to kill.

Bes-Das looked amused—he flashed a crooked-toothed smile, and turned his mount to lope back and watch the chase. Gus and Call turned, too—the encampment was only one or two miles back: the Comanches were chasing the exhausted buffalo right toward a hundred Texans and a few Missourians.

It was a warm, pretty morning. Most of the men were feeling lazy, hoping the Colonel would content himself with a short march for the day. They were lying on their saddles or saddle blankets, playing cards, discoursing about this and that, when suddenly the buffalo and the two Comanches ran right into camp, with Bes-Das, Call, and Gus loping along slightly to the rear. The spectacle was so strange and so unexpected that several of the men decided they must be dreaming. They lay or stood where they were, amazed. Caleb Cobb had just stepped out of his tent and stood dumbfounded, as a buffalo and two Comanches ran right in front of him, scarcely twenty feet away. The Irish dog had gone hunting, and missed the scene. Neither of the Comanches seemed to notice that they were right in the middle of a Ranger encampment, so intent were they on not letting their tired prey escape. They had passed almost through camp, from north to south, when a shot rang out and the buffalo cow fell dead, turning a somersault as she fell. Old Shadrach, shooting across his saddle, had fired the shot.

When the buffalo fell, the two Comanches stopped and simply sat on their horses, both of which were quivering with fatigue. The skinny warriors had a glazed look; they were too exhausted to get down and cut up the meat they had wanted so badly. Around the encampment, Rangers began to stand up and look to their guns. The Comanches came to with a start and flailed their horses before anyone could fire.

"Hell, shoot 'em—shoot 'em!" Shadrach yelled. His ammunition was over by Matilda's saddle—he could not get it and reload in time to shoot the Comanches himself.

The Rangers got off a few shots, but by then, the Comanches had made it into a little copse of post oak; the bullets only clipped leaves.

"Well, this is a record, I guess," Caleb said. "Two red Indians rode all the way through camp, chasing a tired buffalo, and nobody shot 'em."

"It's worse than that," Call said. "We rode along with them for two miles, and didn't shoot 'em."

"They were after the buffalo," Gus said. "They didn't even notice us."

"No, they were too hungry, I expect," Bigfoot said. He had witnessed the event with solemn amazement. It seemed to him the Indians must have been taking some kind of powders, to miss the fact that they were riding through a Ranger camp.

"Yes, I expect so," Caleb said. "They wanted that buffalo bad."

"Should we go get them, sir?" Long Bill asked. "Their horses are about worn out."

"No, let them go, maybe they'll starve," Caleb said. "If I send a troop after them, they'll just kill half of it and steal themselves fresh horses."

Shadrach was annoyed all day because no one had shot the Comanches.

"Bes-Das should have shot them, he seen them first," he said. "Bigfoot must have been drunk, else he would have shot 'em."

Shadrach had begun to repeat himself—it worried Matilda Roberts.

"You say the same things, over and over, Shad," she told him, but Shadrach went right on repeating himself. Over and over he told her the story of how he saved himself in a terrible blizzard on the Platte: he killed a large buffalo cow, cut her open, and crawled inside; the cow's body stayed warm long enough to keep him alive.

Matilda didn't want to think of Shadrach inside a buffalo cow. Sam butchered the one the two Comanches had chased into camp; he made blood sausage of the buffalo blood, but Matilda didn't eat any. Shad's story was too much on her mind.

That night, lying with the old man as he smoked his long pipe, Matilda held his rough hand. The plains scared her—she wanted to be close to Shadrach. Since crossing the Brazos, she had begun to realize that she was tired of being a whore. She was tired of having to walk off in the bushes with her quilt because some Ranger had a momentary lust. Besides, there were no bushes anymore. Whoring on the prairies meant going over a hill or a ridge, and there could always be a Comanche over the hill or the ridge.

Besides, she had come to have such a fondness for Shadrach that she had no interest in going with other men, and in fact didn't like it. Shad's joints ached at times, from too many blizzards on the Platte and too many nights sleeping wet. He groaned and moaned in his sleep. Matilda knew he needed her warmth, to ease his joints.

Shadrach had become so stiff that he could not reach down to pull his boots on and pull them off. Matilda faithfully pulled them off for him. No woman had been so kind before, and it touched him. He had begun to get surly when a Ranger with an interest in being a customer approached Matilda now.

"Would you ever get hitched, Shad?" Matilda asked, the night after the buffalo ran through camp.

"It would depend on the gal," Shadrach said.

"What if I was the gal?" Matilda asked. It was a bold question, but she needed to know.

Shadrach smiled. He knew of Matilda's fondness for him, and was flattered by it. After all, he was old and woolly, and the camp was full of young scamps, some of them barely old enough to have hair on their balls.

"You—what would you want with me?" he asked, to tease her. "I'm an old berry. My pod's about dry."

"I'd get hitched with you anyway, Shad," Matilda said.

Shadrach had been married once, to a Cree beauty on the Red River of the north. She had been killed in a raid by the Sioux, some forty years back. All he remembered about her was that she made the tastiest pemmican on the Northern plains.

"Why, Matty, I thought you had the notion to go to California," Shadrach said. "I've not got that much traveling in me, I don't expect. I've done been west to the Gila and that's far enough west for me."

"They'll have a train to California someday," Matilda said. "I'll wait, and we'll take the train. Until then I guess New Mexico will do, if it ain't too sandy."

"I'd get hitched with you—sure," Shadrach said. "Maybe we'll run into a preacher, somewhere up the trail."

"If we don't, we could ask the Colonel to hitch us," Matilda said.

A little later, when the old man was sleeping, Matilda got up and sneaked two extra blankets out of the baggage wagon. The dews had been exceptionally heavy at night. She didn't want her husband-to-be getting wet on the dewy ground.

Black Sam saw her take the blankets. He used a chunk of firewood for a pillow, himself. Sometimes, when the fire burned low, he would turn over and burn his pillow.

"I need those blankets, Sam—don't tell," Matilda said. She was fond of Sam too, though in a different way.

"I won't, Miss Matty," Sam said.

15.

In two weeks the beeves were gone, and the troop was living on mush. The expedition had pointed to the northwest, and came to a long stretch of rough, bald country that led upward to a long escarpment. Though the escarpment was still fifty miles away, they could see it.

"What's up there?" Gus asked Bigfoot.

"Comanches," Bigfoot said. "Them and the Kiowa."

The tall boy, Jimmy Tweed, had begun to bunk with Call and Gus. Jimmy and Gus were soon joshing each other and trying to outdo each other in pranks or card tricks. They would have tried to beat each other at whoring, but all the whores except Matilda had turned back at the Brazos, and Matilda had retired. So desperate was the situation that a youth from Navasota named John Baca was caught having congress with his mare. The troop laughed about it for days; Johnny Baca blushed every time anyone looked at him. But many of the men, in the privacy of their thoughts, wondered if Johnny Baca had not made a sensible move. Brognoli, the quartermaster, merely shrugged tolerantly at the notion of a boy having congress with a mare.

"Why not?" he asked. "The mare don't care."

"She may not care, but I'll be damned if I'll go with a horse," Gus said.

"Besides, I don't own a mare," he added, a little later.

The complete disappearance of the great buffalo herd continued to puzzle everyone. Call, Gus, and Bes-Das scouted as much as thirty miles ahead, and yet not an animal could be found.

"No wonder them Comanches run that one cow right into camp," Gus said on the third evening, when they sat down to a supper of mush. "It was that or starve, I guess."

"It's a big prairie," Bigfoot reminded him. "Those buffalo could be three or four hundred miles north, by now."

Not long before they spotted the escarpment they came upon a stream that Bes-Das thought was the Red, the river they counted on to take them west to New Mexico. Bes-Das was the scout who was supposed to be most familiar with the Comanche country— everyone felt relieved when they struck the river. It seemed they were practically to New Mexico. The water was bad, though—not as bad as the Pecos, in Call's view, but bad enough that most of the troop was soon bothered with cramps and retchings. The area proved to be unusually snaky, too. The low, shaley hills were so flush with snakes that Call could sometimes hear three or four rattling at the same time.

Before they had been on the river half a day, Elihu Carson, the dentist, walked off to squat awhile, in the grip of a series of cramps, and had the bad luck to get bitten in the ass by a rattlesnake. Several men testified that they had heard the snake rattle, but Elihu Carson was a little deaf—he didn't hear the warning.

"I think you're cursed, Carson," the Colonel said, when informed of the accident. "First you trip on your suitcase and get stickers in your face, and now you have fangs in your ass."

"Sir, everything is sharp in this part of the country," the dentist said.

Most of the men expected Carson to die of snakebite, and those he had extracted teeth from hoped that he would. But Elihu Carson confounded them. He showed only brief ill effects—four hours after the bite, he was pulling one of young Tommy Spencer's teeth.

The boy from Missouri had let a horse kick him right in the face, and had two broken front teeth to show for his carelessness.

Later that day, the mules pulling the main supply wagon spooked at a cougar that bounded out of a little clump of bushes right in front of them. Gus and several others blazed away at the cougar, but the cat got clean away. The mules fled down a gully, pulling the heavy wagon: it struck a rock, turned completely over in the air, and burst apart. One of the wheels came off its axle and rolled on down the gully out of sight. Caleb Cobb's canoe, which had been on top of the load, smashed to bits. One mule broke its leg and had to be shot.

While Brognoli and several other Rangers were standing around the wreck, debating whether there was any hope of repairing the big wagon, Alchise, the half-breed scout, pointed to the north. All Call saw was an advancing cloud of dust—the troop took cover and prepared for battle, but the source of the dust turned out to be a herd of horses, about twenty in number, being driven by two white men and a Negro. One of the white men, a bulky fellow with a thick brown beard, was leading another horse, with two little girls on it. The little girls were about five or six; both were blond. They were a good deal scratched up, and looked scared. Neither of them spoke at all, though Sam and Brognoli tried to coax them down, and offered them biscuits. The three men looked as if they had been dipped in dust. They had clearly ridden fast and hard.

"Howdy, I'm Charlie Goodnight," the large man said. "This is Bill and this is Bose."

"Get down and take some coffee," Caleb offered. "We've just had a wreck. My canoe is ruined and I don't know what else."

"No, we can't pause," Charles Goodnight said. "These girls were stolen two weeks ago, from down by Weatherford. Their parents will have no peace of mind until I return them."

"They also ran off these horses," the man said. "We had to race to catch up with the rascals."

"At least you succeeded," Caleb said. "Comanches took 'em?"

"Yes, Kicking Wolf, he's a clever thief," Goodnight said. "What are you doing taking wagons across the baldies?"

"Why, ain't you heard of us, Mr. Goodnight?" Caleb asked. By this time the whole troop had gathered around the travelers. "I'm

Colonel Cobb. We're the Texas–Santa Fe expedition, heading out towards New Mexico."

"Why?" Goodnight asked bluntly. Call thought the man's manner short to the point of rudeness. He wasn't insolent, though—just blunt.

"Well, we mean to annex it," Caleb said. "We may have to hang a few Mexicans in the process, but I expect we'll soon whip 'em back."

"No, they'll hang you—if you get there," Goodnight said.

"Why wouldn't we get there, sir?" Caleb asked, a little stung by the man's brusque attitude.

"I doubt you know the way—that's one reason," Goodnight said. "There ain't water enough between here and Santa Fe to keep this many horses alive. That's two reasons."

He rose in his saddle and pointed toward the escarpment, a thin line in the distance, with white clouds floating over it.

"That's the caprock," he said. "Once you're on top of it there's nothing."

"Well, there has to be something," Caleb said. "There's grass, at least."

"Yes sir, lots of grass," Goodnight said. "I've rarely met the man who can live on grass, though, and I've rarely seen the horse that could travel five hundred miles without water."

Caleb Cobb was stunned by the comment.

"Five hundred miles—are you sure?" he asked. "We thought it would be another hundred, at most."

"That's what I said to begin with," Goodnight said. "You don't know where you're going."

He turned and glanced at the three remaining wagons. The mules were exhausted from pulling the heavy wagons in and out of gullies —and Call could see that there seemed to be no end of gullies stretching west. Goodnight shook his head, and glanced back at the little girls, to see that they were all right.

"We would appreciate some biscuits," he said. "These children ain't eaten nothing but a few bites of rabbit, in the last day."

"Give them what they need," Caleb said. "Give them the biscuits and some bacon too."

He looked back at the escarpment, clearly disturbed by Good-night's news.

"I guess you don't think much of our wagons, do you?" he asked.

"Them wagons would do fine to go to market in," Goodnight said. "But you ain't going to market. You'll never get 'em up the hill. You'll have to take what you can carry and hope you find game."

"Why, dammit, I was told there was a passage along the Red River," Caleb said. "I was hoping we'd come to it tomorrow."

Goodnight looked at him oddly, as if he were listening to a child.

"If you suppose you're on the Red, then you're worse lost than I thought," Goodnight said. "This ain't the Red, it's the Big Wichita. The Red is a far piece ahead yet—I took back these horses just shy of the Red. You might make the Prairie Dog Fork of the Brazos, if you don't jump no more cougars and lose no more mules."

"You're a wonder, sir—how did you know about the cougar?" Caleb asked.

"Tracks," Goodnight said. "I ain't blind. I've never met the mule yet that could tolerate cougars."

Then he noticed Shadrach, standing by Matilda—Bigfoot was nearby.

"Why, Shad—are you a hundred yet?" he asked. "Hello, Miss Roberts."

He tipped his hat, as did the cowboy named Bill and the Negro named Bose.

"I'm crowding it, Charlie," Shadrach said.

"Hello, Wallace—why would you want to walk all the way to New Mexico to get hung?" Goodnight asked Bigfoot. "Ain't there enough hang ropes in Texas for you?"

"I ain't planning on no hanging, Charlie," Bigfoot said. "I expect to fill my pockets with gold and silver and go back to Texas and buy a ranch."

Goodnight nodded. "Oh, that's it, is it?" he said. "You're all out for booty, I guess. You've heard there are big chunks of gold and silver lying in the streets, I expect."

"Well, we've heard minerals were plentiful," Caleb said. Less and less did he like this blunt fellow, Charlie Goodnight—yet the man's news, unwelcome as it was, was valuable, considering their situation. It was mortifying to be the leader of an expedition and discover that you were not even on the right river.

"There are minerals aplenty—in the governor's vault," Goodnight said. "He might open it for you and ask you to help yourselves, but I doubt it. That ain't the way of governors—not the ones I've met."

There was silence throughout the troop. Goodnight was not particularly likable, but few of the men could doubt that he knew what he was talking about. If he said they were putting themselves in danger of starvation only to run the risk of being hanged upon arrival, it well might be true.

"It's a marvel that you rode off and got your horses back, Mr. Goodnight," Caleb said. "We've not had much luck pursuing the red boys. If there's a special method you use I'd appreciate it if you'd tell us what it is—it could be that we'll lose stock, and we can't afford to."

"No, you can't, you'll have to eat most of these horses, I expect," Goodnight said.

He looked at the solemn group of men, some of them with hopes still high for adventure and booty in New Mexico. Not for the first time, he was impressed by the folly of men.

"How'd you get 'em back, sir?" Caleb asked again.

"Well, they were my horses," Goodnight said. "I'll be damned if I'll give up twenty horses to Kicking Wolf, not without a chase.

"Pardon me for cussing, Miss Roberts," he said, again tipping his hat.

"The only way to get horses back from Indians is to outrun them —it's why I try to stay well mounted," he went on. "We caught them near the Red. There were four warriors and these children. We killed two warriors, but Kicking Wolf and his brother got away."

Sam handed him a little packet of biscuits, and some meat.

"Thank you," Goodnight said. "These young ladies have been too scared to eat. But they ain't hurt—I expect they'll get hungry one of these days."

"They're pretty girls—I hope they eat," Sam said. "I have a little jelly saved—plum jelly. Maybe it will tempt them."

He handed Goodnight a small jar of jelly—Goodnight looked at it and put it in his saddlebag.

"If it don't tempt the young ladies it will sure tempt me," he said. Then he looked again at Caleb Cobb.

"If you make the Red and any of them wagons still have the wheels on them, stick to the river and follow it west. There's a place called the Narrows, where you might get through."

"Angosturas," Alchise said, nodding.

"Yes, that's what the Mexicans call it," Goodnight said. "I call it the Narrows."

Then he tipped his hat to Matilda a third time.

"Let's go, Bose," he said.

Soon the cloud of dust from the twenty horses was floating over the gullies to the south.

"Charlie Goodnight's salty," Bigfoot observed.

"I agree," Caleb said.

16.

CALEB COBB RODE ALONE most of that day, accompanied only by his Irish dog. If he was disturbed to discover that he was not on the river he thought he was on, he didn't express it. Nonetheless, the troop was uneasy. There was little talk. Each man rode along, alone with his thoughts. Gus tried once or twice to discuss the situation with Call, but Call didn't answer. He was trying to push down the feeling that the whole expedition was foolish. They didn't even know which river they were on, and their commander's estimation of the distance they had to travel was off by hundreds of miles. They had already lost several men and most of their wagons; they had killed and eaten the last of their beeves. If there was any game in the area, no one could spot it.

"I despise poor planning," he said.

Gus, though, was feeling frisky. He could not stay in low spirits long, not when the day was fine and the country glorious.

"Why, you can see a hundred miles, if you stand up in your stirrups," he said. "I prefer it to the trees, myself.

"For one thing, Indians can hide in the trees," he added.

"They hid pretty well out beyond the Pecos, and there wasn't no trees out there," Call reminded him. "There could be a hundred of them watching us right now and you'll never see them."

"Oh, shut up, you always think the worst," Gus said, annoyed by his friend's pessimistic nature. All he wanted to do was enjoy a fine afternoon on the prairies. He did not want to have to consider that there might be a hundred Indians in hiding in the next gully, or any gully. All he wanted was to enjoy the gallop out to New Mexico—it took the pleasure out of adventure to always be worrying, as his friend did.

Call was not the only one in the company who was worried, though. That night Bes-Das and Alchise disappeared, taking six horses.

"I guess they didn't want to be shot down like Falconer was," Bigfoot said. "Caleb's too quick to flare. It ain't good leading to be shooting down people we might need."

"I don't guess we're any worse off than we were," Long Bill pointed out. "Those two were lost anyway. That fellow Goodnight is about the only man who knows his way around, out in these parts."

Two more wagons were lost between the Prairie Dog Fork of the Brazos and the wide pans of the Red River. Caleb put all the ammunition in the one wagon and told the men to keep only such gear as they could carry on their horses. That night they ate cat-fish—the river was low and some of the fish were trapped in shallow ponds. The men sharpened willow sticks into crude spears. More than fifty sizable fish were taken, cooked, and devoured, and yet the men went to bed unsatisfied.

"Eating fish is like eating air," Jimmy Tweed observed. "It goes in but it don't fill you up."

Once they passed through the Narrows the great plain spread west before them. Though they had been on the prairie for weeks, none of them were prepared for the way the sky and the earth seemed to widen, once they rose onto the Llano Estacado. After a day or two on the llano the meaning of distance seemed changed. The great plain, silent and endless, became the world. In relation to the plain, they felt like ants. The smaller world of towns and creeks and clumps of forest seemed difficult to remember. At night on the llano, with the sky a star-strewn plain of darkness overhead, Gus tried to keep Clara in mind, but the thought that he had fallen in love with a girl, in a dusty little general store in Austin, had come to seem far away and insubstantial, like the dust motes that had floated down the sunbeams in the store. The girl and the store had been for the day—the great plain was forever.

The whole troop was dismayed by the stretch of empty land ahead. If the Indians fell upon them when they were on the llano, what chance could they have?

Bigfoot had been made chief of scouts. He took Gus and Call with him when he rode out every day. Gus he took mainly for his eyesight. It was generally acknowledged that Gus could see farther and more accurately than anyone in the troop. Call he took for his steadiness; Call didn't flinch from trouble.

On their third day on the plain, they saw that there was a difference in the horizon ahead. None of them, though, could puzzle the difference out. The clouds seemed closer to the surface of the ground. Gus was the first to note something strange: not far ahead, a hawk had dived at a rabbit or a quail, and yet the hawk didn't swoop on its prey and lift it. The hawk kept going, as if it had dived into a hole.

Ten minutes later they came to the lip of the Palo Duro Canyon, and the mystery was explained. The hawk hadn't dived into a hole; it had dived into the canyon, which looked to be several miles across, and so many miles long that they couldn't see the western end of it. Hundreds of feet below them buffalo were feeding in long grass.

"Hurrah, we found the bufs," Gus said. "Let's climb down and shoot some—maybe the Colonel will promote us."

"He won't, because you'll break your neck going down, and even if you don't you'll never get back up, not carrying no buffalo meat," Bigfoot said.

"I've heard about this canyon," he said, a little later. "I just had no idea we were close by."

He sent Call racing back to inform the company—he and Gus stayed, to explore the canyon wall and see if there was a way down. The sight of the grazing buffalo reminded him that he was hungry

[211]

for meat—mush and Red River catfish didn't fill you like buffalo ribs.

While loping southeast toward the camp they had just left not long before, Call's horse suddenly jumped sideways, so violently that Call lost his seat and was thrown high and hard. He managed to hang on to his bridle rein, but he landed on his head and shoulders so hard that his vision blurred for a moment. As it cleared he saw something white, nearby. In a moment, he realized that the white thing that had spooked his horse was the body of a man. At first he thought it might be one of the Rangers, out for a ride or a hunt. The man had been shot, scalped, stripped, and mutilated. Someone had hacked into his chest cavity and taken out his vitals. Call looked closely at the face, which was the face of a stranger. He didn't think it belonged to anyone in the troop. The man had not a stitch of clothes on. There was no way to identify him. Call felt his neck, which was cold.

Even so, his killer or killers might be close by. Call drew his pistol, just in case, and mounted cautiously. Just as he did he saw movement out of the corner of his eye: three Comanches and their horses seemed to rise up, out of the bare earth, only a hundred yards away. Call spurred his horse, and bent low as she raced. He knew his only chance was to run. To his relief, Buffalo Hump was not one of his pursuers. The troop was probably not more than five miles back, and he was on Betsy, a fleet sorrel mare. Betsy was one of the fastest horses in camp, and her wind was excellent. Yet before he had been running a minute, Call realized that the Comanches were gaining. Their horses were no faster than Betsy, but they knew the land better—it was the same thing he had felt west of the Pecos. They took advantage of every roll and dip. The lead warrior had a bow and arrow, and he was closing. To his left Call spotted something he had seen on the way up: a large prairie-dog town. Without hesitation he pointed Betsy toward it. It was a risk—the mare might step in one of the holes, in which case it would all be over, but it was a risk for the Comanches, too. Maybe they would slow down —he himself had no intention of slowing. If luck was with him he might race through the town and gain a few yards. He had to try it.

At the approach of the racing mare, prairie dogs throughout the town whistled and darted into their holes. Betsy kicked up dust from the edge of more than one hole, but she wove through the town without slowing. Even so, Call didn't gain much. The Comanches, too, avoided the holes. Just as he cleared the prairie-dog town, Call felt something nudge his arm and looked down to see an arrow sticking in his left arm, just above the elbow. He had not felt the arrow go in, and had no time to pay attention to it. He spurred Betsy, urging her to even more speed, and seemed, for the space of a mile, to gain a little on the Indians. No more arrows flew. Yet when he dared glance back, he saw that he wasn't gaining. The Comanches were racing abreast, and they were still almost within arrow range.

Call turned and fired his pistol at them once, but the shot had no effect. Now he was racing along the edge of a little bluff some fifteen feet high—ahead, the bluff gradually sloped off, but Call couldn't wait for the slope. He put Betsy over the edge; she just managed to keep her feet when she hit, and he just managed to keep his seat. At once he heard a buzzing. Betsy began to jump and dance. Call looked around, and saw rattlesnakes everywhere. He had jumped to the edge of a den. It seemed to him that at least a hundred snakes surrounded him—they had been sunning themselves on the rocky slope: the abrupt arrival of a horse and rider startled them. Now they were buzzing in chorus. A shot came from above, but it zinged off a rock. Call put spurs to Betsy again—he couldn't worry about the snakes—he would be dead anyway, if he didn't run.

Seeing the snakes, the Comanches chose to lose ground and not risk the jump. But they were racing along a short decline and would soon be trying to overtake him. When he ran over the next ridge Call saw the troop—there they were, but they still seemed miles away, and the Comanches had returned to the pursuit. They were a hundred yards back, but he knew they would close with him before he could make the troop, unless he was very lucky. They had fanned out now. Two were trying to flank him on his right, while the third was directly behind him. Betsy was running flat out: so far her wind had held. Call debated the wisdom of shooting off his pistol, in the hope that someone in the troop would hear it and rush to his aid. It was a point of tactics he had not thought out in advance. If he fired, he would soon have an empty pistol.

He kept the pistol ready, but didn't fire. He thought he could kill one Indian, anyway, if there was a close fight. Perhaps he would wound another. If the third man got him, at least he would have made a strong struggle.

Then he heard rifle shots from just ahead of him, where two or three trees bordered a little stream. A doe came bounding through the trees, so close that Betsy almost collided with it. Call skirted the spring and saw Long Bill Coleman ahead—he had been chasing the doe. He had shot once and was just reloading. He was startled to see Call, but even more startled to see the Comanches. Although the odds had altered, the Comanches were still coming.

"Oh, boy, where's that damn Blackie when we need him?" Long Bill said, wheeling his horse. "He rode out with me but he thought the doe was too puny to bother about."

An arrow dropped between them, and then two gunshots came from behind, one of which nicked Call's hat brim. They raced on, hoping someone in the troop would hear the shooting and respond—it was awhile before they realized the Comanches were no longer chasing them. When they pulled up and looked back, they saw that the three Comanches, having missed the scalps, had taken the small doe instead. One of them had just slung the carcass onto his horse.

"Oh boy, I'm winded," Long Bill said. "I was just trying to kill a little meat. I sure wasn't looking for no Indian fight."

Call remembered that Gus and Bigfoot were alone, at the lip of the great canyon. The three men who chased them might have been part of a larger party. With so many buffalo grazing in the canyon, it was likely more Indians were about.

Caleb Cobb was enjoying a long cigar when Call raced up: he seemed more interested in Betsy than in the news.

"I come close to choosing that little mare for myself," he said. "I expect it's lucky for you that I didn't. I think Mr. Bigfoot Wallace made a good point when he said it's horseflesh that usually makes the difference in Indian fighting."

"Colonel, there's hundreds of buffalo down in that canyon," Call said. "There might be more Indians, too."

"All right, we're off to the rescue," Caleb said. "We'll take about ten men. Me and Jeb will come too. It's a fine morning for a fracas."

Call had forgotten to mention the dead man. He had had only a moment to look at him, before the Comanches attacked. When he told the Colonel about it, the Colonel shrugged.

"Likely just a traveler who took the long route," he said. "Traveling alone in this part of the country is generally foolhardy."

"I wouldn't do it for seventy dollars," Long Bill observed.

Shadrach had been napping when Call arrived. The change in the old mountain man surprised everyone: from being independent, stern, and a little frightening, even when he was in a good temper, he had become aged. Though Call had always known that Shadrach was old, he had not thought of him that way until they crossed the Brazos; now, though, it was impossible to think of him any other way. He had once wandered off alone for days; now, when he left camp to hunt, he was always back in a few hours. He sometimes dozed, even when on horseback. Unless directly addressed, he spoke only to Matilda.

The news that they were near the Palo Duro Canyon seemed to take years off Shadrach, though—at once he was mounted, his long rifle out of its scabbard.

"I've heard of it all my life, now I aim to see it," Shadrach said.

Then he turned to Matilda.

"If it's safe, then I'll come and get you, Matty," he said, before loping off.

Sam took a hasty look at Call's arrow wound, broke off the arrow shaft and cut the arrow free. Call was impatient—he didn't regard the wound as serious: he wanted to be off. But Sam made him wait while he dressed the wound correctly, and the Colonel, though mounted, waited with no show of impatience.

"I want Corporal Call to be well doctored," he said. "We can't afford to have him sick."

Call led them to the dead man, whom Shadrach recognized.

"It's Roy Char—he was a mining man," Shadrach said.

"I don't know what there could be to mine, out in this country," Caleb said.

"Roy was after that old gold," Shadrach said.

"What old gold?" Caleb asked. "If there's a bunch of old gold around here we ought to find it and forget about New Mexico."

"Some big Spaniard came marching through here in the old times," Shadrach said. "They say he found a town that was made of gold. I guess Roy figured some of it might still be around here, somewhere."

"Oh, Señor Coronado, you mean," Caleb said. "He didn't find

no city of gold—all he found was a lot of poor Indians. Your friend Mr. Char lost his life for nothing. The gold ain't here."

The canyon was there, though. They buried Roy Char hastily, and rode along the rim of the canyon until they found Gus and Bigfoot, hiding in a small declivity behind some thorny bushes. Both had their rifles at the ready.

"What took you all day?" Gus asked—he was badly annoyed by the fact that he had had to cower behind a bush for an hour, while he waited for Call to bring up the troop.

"I got an arrow in my arm, but it wasn't as bad as what happened to a man we just buried," Call said.

"You could be burying us—and you would have if we hadn't been quick to hide," Bigfoot told them. "There's fifty or sixty Indians down below us—I wish you'd brought the whole troop."

"Well, we can fetch the troop," Caleb said. "I doubt those Indians can ride up this cliff and scalp us all."

"No, but it's their canyon," Bigfoot reminded him. "They might know a trail."

Caleb walked out on a little promontory, and looked down. He saw a good number of Indians, butchering buffalo. Six buffalo were down, at least.

"If they know a trail I hope they show it to us," Caleb said, coming back. "We'd ride down and harvest a few of them buffalo ourselves."

"There could be a thousand Indians around here," Bigfoot said. "I ain't putting myself in no place where I have to climb to get away from Indians. They might be better climbers than I am."

"You're right, but I hate to pass up the meat," Caleb said.

Nonetheless, they did pass it up. The troop was brought forward and proceeded west, along the edge of the canyon. They were never out of sight of buffalo—or Indians. Quartermaster Brognoli, who believed in numbers—so many boots, so many rifles, so many sacks of flour—counted over three hundred tribesmen in the canyon, most of them engaged in cutting up buffalo. Call and Gus both kept looking into the canyon—the distance was so vast that it drew the eye. Both strained their eyes to see if they could spot Buffalo Hump, but they didn't see him.

"He's there, though," Gus said. "I feel him."

"You can't feel an Indian who's miles away," Call said.

[216]

"I can," Gus affirmed, without explanation.

"He could be five hundred miles from here—there are thousands of Indians," Call reminded him.

"I can feel him," Gus insisted. "I get hot under the ribs when he's around. Don't you ever get hot under the ribs?"

"Not unless I've eaten putrid beef," Call said. Twice on the trip he had eaten putrid beef, and his system had revolted.

The night was moonless, which worried Caleb Cobb somewhat and worried Bigfoot more. The horses were kept within a corral of ropes, and guard was changed every hour. Caleb called the men together in the evening, and made a little speech.

"We've come too far to go back," he said. "We're bound for Santa Fe. But the Indians know we're here, and they're clever horse thieves. We have to watch close. We won't get across this long prairie if we lose our horses—the red boys will tag after us and pick us off like chickens."

Despite the speech and the intensified guard, the remuda was twenty horses short when dawn came. None of the guards had nodded or closed an eye, either. Caleb Cobb was fit to be tied.

"How could they get off with twenty horses and not one of us hear them?" he asked. Brognoli kept walking around the horse herd, counting and recounting. For awhile he was sure the count was wrong—it wasn't easy to count horses when they were bunched together. He counted and recounted until Caleb lost his temper and ordered him to stop.

"The damn horses are gone!" he said. "They're forty miles away by now, most likely. You can't count them because they're gone!"

"I expect it was Kicking Wolf," Bigfoot said. "He could steal horses out of a store."

"If I could catch the rascal I'd tie him to a horse's tail and let the horse kick him to death," Caleb said. "Since his name is Kicking Wolf it would be appropriate if the son of a bitch got kicked to death."

With the night's theft, the horse situation became critical. Three men were totally without mounts, and no man had more than one horse. To make matters worse, Tom, Matilda's big grey, was one of the horses that had been stolen. She was now afoot. Matilda cried all morning. She had a fondness for Tom. The sight of Matilda crying unnerved the whole camp. Since taking up with Shadrach

Matilda had raged less—everyone noted her mildness. But watching such a large woman cry was a trial to the spirit. It fretted Shadrach so that he grew restless and rode out of camp, over Matilda's protests.

"Now he'll go off and get killed," Matilda said.

"Well, if you hush up that crying, maybe he'll come back," Long Bill said. He was one of the men who was afoot, and as a result, was in a sour mood. The prospect of walking to Santa Fe, across such a huge plain, did not appeal to him—but the thought of walking back to Austin didn't appeal to him, either. He had seen what had just happened to the mining man, Roy Char. He was determined to stay with the troop, even if it meant blisters on his feet.

Call and Gus had both been on guard, in the darkest part of the night. Call felt shamed by the thought that he had not been keen enough to prevent the theft.

"Why, I wasn't sleepy a bit," Gus said. "It couldn't have happened on our watch. I can hear a rat move, when I'm that wide awake."

"You might could hear a rat, but you didn't hear the Indians and you didn't hear the horses leaving, either," Call told him.

That night Call, Bigfoot, and a number of other guards periodically put their ear to the ground to listen. All they heard was the tramp of their own horses in the rope corral. In addition to the rope, most of the horses had been hobbled, so they couldn't bolt. Call and Gus had the watch just before sunrise. They moved in circles around the herd, meeting every five minutes. Call was certain no Indians were there. It was only when dawn came that he had a moment of uncertainty. He saw the beginnings of the sunrise—the light was yellow as flame. But the yellow light was in the west, and dawn didn't come from the west.

A second later Bigfoot saw it too, and yelled loud enough to wake the whole camp.

"That ain't the sunrise, boys!" he yelled.

Just as he said it, Call saw movement to the north. Two Indians had sneaked in and slipped the hobbles on several horses. Call threw off a shot, but it was still very dark—he could no longer see anything to the north.

"Damn it all, they got away again," he said. "I don't know how many horses they got away with, this time."

"Don't matter now, we've got to head back to that last creek," Bigfoot said.

"Why?" Call asked, startled.

Bigfoot merely pointed west, where the whole horizon was yellow.

"That ain't sunrise," he said, in a jerky voice. "That's fire."

17.

THE TROOP HAD NO sooner turned to head back south toward the little creek Bigfoot mentioned when they saw the same yellow glow on the prairie south of them. The flames to the west were already noticeably closer. Bigfoot wheeled his mount, and rode up to Caleb.

"They set it," he said. "The Comanches. They waited till the wind was right. Now we have the canyon at our backs and prairie fires on two sides."

"Three," Caleb said, pointing west, where there was another fierce glow.

The whole troop immediately discerned the nature of their peril. Call looked at Gus, who tried to appear nonchalant.

"We'll have to burn or we'll have to jump," Call said. "I hate the thought of burning most, I guess."

Gus looked into the depths of the canyon—he was only twenty feet from its edge. The prairie now was a great ring of burning grass. Though he sat calmly on his horse, waiting for Bigfoot and the

Colonel to decide what to do, inside he felt the same deep churning that he had felt beyond the Pecos. The Indians were superior to them in their planning. They would always lay some clever trap.

"Ride, boys," Bigfoot said. "Let's try the west—it's our best chance."

Soon the whole troop was fleeing, more than twenty of the men mounted double for lack of horses. Shadrach took Matilda on behind him—he rode right along the canyon edge, looking for a way down.

"I believe we could climb down afoot," he told Caleb. "If we can get a little ways down, we won't burn. There's nothing to burn, on those cliffs."

Caleb stopped a minute, to appraise the fire. The ring had now been closed. With every surge of wind the fire seemed to leap toward them, fifty yards at a leap. The prairie grass was tall—flames shot twenty and thirty feet in the air.

"The damn fiends," Caleb said. "Maybe we can start a backfire, and get it stopped. I've heard that can be done."

"No time, and the wind's wrong," Bigfoot said. "I think Shad's right. We're going to have to climb a ways down."

Caleb hesitated. It might be the only good strategy, but it meant abandoning their mounts. There was no trail a horse could go down. They might survive the fire, but then what? They would be on the bald prairie—no horses, no supplies, no water. How long would it take the Comanches to pick them off?

The troop huddled around Bigfoot and their commander. All eyes were turned toward the fire, and all eyes were anxious. The flames were advancing almost at loping speed. They were only three hundred yards away. The men could hear the dry grass crackle as it took flame. When the wind surged there was a roar, as the flames were sucked into the sky.

Call felt bitter that their commander had had no more forethought than to bring them to such an exposed place. Nothing about the expedition had been well planned. Of course, no one would have imagined that the Indians could steal horses at will, from such a tight guard. But now they were caught: he imagined Buffalo Hump, somewhere on the other side of the flames, his lance in his hand, waiting to come in and take some scalps.

[221]

Caleb Cobb waited until the flames were one hundred yards away to make his decision. He waited, hoping to spot a break in the flames, something they might race through. But there was no break in the flames—the Indians who set the fire had done an expert job. The ring of flames grew tighter every minute. General Lloyd, drunk as usual, was shivering and shaking, although the heat from the great fire was already close enough to be felt.

"We're done for now—we'll cook," he said.

"No, but we will have to climb down this damn cliff," Caleb said, turning his horse toward the canyon's edge. No sooner had he turned than he heard a gunshot—General Phil Lloyd had taken out his revolver and shot himself in the head. His body hung halfway off his horse, one foot caught in a stirrup.

The horses were beginning to be hard to restrain, jumping and pitching, their nostrils flaring. Two or three men were thrown— one horse raced straight into the flames.

"Let's go boys—keep your guns and get over the edge, as best you can," Caleb yelled.

To Gus's relief the canyon walls were not as sheer as they had first looked. There were drop-offs of a hundred feet and more, but there were also humps and ledges, and inclines not too steep to negotiate. The Irish dog went down at a run, his tail straight in the air. Before the men had scrambled thirty feet down there was another tragedy: the horses were in panic now—some raced into the flames, but others raced straight off into the canyon. Some hit ledges, but most rolled once or twice and fell into the void. One of the leaping horses fell straight down now on Dakluskie, the leader of the Missourians. Several of the Rangers saw the horse falling, but Dakluskie didn't. He was crushed before he could look up. The horse kept rolling, taking Dakluskie with it. General Lloyd's horse made the longest leap of all—he flew over the group and fell out of sight, General Lloyd's body still dangling from the stirrup.

"Oh God, look there!" Gus said, pointing across the canyon. "Look at them—where are they going?"

Not all of the men could afford to look—some of them clung to small bushes, or balanced on narrow ledges in terror. Over them the fire roared right to the edge of the canyon; the heat made all of them sweat, although they were cold with fear.

Call looked, though, and so did Caleb Cobb. At first Call thought it was goats, creeping along the face of the cliff across the canyon. Just as he looked, a ledge crumbled under Black Sam—Call saw a startled look on Sam's face, as he fell. He did not cry out.

"My God, look at them!" Caleb said.

Across the canyon, on a trail so narrow that they had to proceed single file, a party of fifty Comanches were moving west. It seemed from across the great distance that the Comanches were walking on air.

In the lead was Buffalo Hump, with the lance Gus had imagined in his fear.

"Look at them!" Bigfoot said. "Are they flying?"

"No, it's a trail," Shadrach told him. He was on a tiny ledge of rock, with Matilda. He shushed her like a child, hoping to keep her from making a foolish movement.

"What if the fire don't stop?" Matilda asked, looking upward. She had always been scared of fire; now she could not stop trembling. She expected flames to curl over the edge of the canyon and come down and burn her shirt. She had such a horror of her clothes being on fire that she began to take her shirt off.

"What . . . stop that!" Shadrach said, one eye on Matilda and the other eye on the Comanches.

"No, I have to get this shirt off, I don't want to burn up in it," Matilda said, and she half undressed on the small ledge.

Call could look up and see flames at the canyon's edge, but he knew Matilda's fear was unfounded. Ash from the burning prairie floated down on them, but the fire was not going to curl over. He kept watching the Indians across the Palo Duro. It did seem that their horses were walking delicately, on the air itself.

"Can you see a trail—you've got those keen eyes?" Call asked Gus.

Gus himself had to squint—smoke was floating over the canyon now, from the fire. But when he looked close he could see that the Indians weren't flying. Buffalo Hump was picking his way slowly, a step at a time, along a small trail.

"He ain't flying, there's a trail," he said. "But if any man could fly I expect it would be that rascal. It felt like he was flying that night he chased me."

"I don't care if they're flying or walking," Caleb said—he was clinging to a small bush. "I'd be happier if they were going in the other direction—it looks like they're flanking us."

Just then the dentist, Elihu Carson, lost his balance and began to roll downward.

"Grab his foot!" Call yelled to Long Bill, who was nearest the falling man. Long Bill grabbed but missed by an inch or less. His own situation was so precarious that he did not dare lean farther. The dentist bounced off a boulder and flew out of sight, screeching loudly as he vanished.

"We'll have to take care, now, and not get no toothaches," Bigfoot said, his eyes still on the file of Indians across the canyon, who seemed to be walking on air.

18.

When the Rangers crawled back out of the canyon, the prairie was black and smouldering, as far as anyone could see. Here and there a little bush, a cactus or a pack rat's den still showed a trace of flame. Several dead horses were in sight; the gear the men had dumped smouldered like the rats' dens. Young Tommy Spencer was sobbing loudly. Dakluskie had been his only relative. Black Sam was gone, and the dentist—Brognoli had been kicked in the neck by a falling horse, and sat glassy eyed. His head was set at an odd angle; from time to time his head seemed to jerk, backward and forward, quickly. He couldn't speak, though whether from fear or injury no one yet knew.

Much of the extra ammunition had exploded. This surprised everyone, because no one could remember having heard an explosion. By hasty count more than twenty men were missing, fallen unobserved. In view of the fact that at least fifty Indians were to the west of them, not to mention the armies of Santa Fe, the loss of the ammunition was a grave problem. Various of the men commented apprehensively on this fact, but Bigfoot Wallace merely smiled.

"I ain't worried about bullets, yet," he said. "We're afoot, and there ain't many water holes. We'll probably starve before we can find anybody to shoot."

Caleb Cobb's Irish dog, Jeb, had gone so far down the cliff that he could not get back up. He was crouched more than a hundred feet below on a small ledge, in danger of falling off down a sheer cliff at any moment.

"I've either got to shoot him or rescue him," Caleb said. "Any volunteers for a dog rescue?"

The troop was silent—the thought of going over the edge again, just to rescue a dog that no one but Caleb liked, did not appeal.

"I'll make the man a sergeant who'll rescue my damn dog," Caleb said.

"I'll do it," Gus said, at once. He was thinking of Clara Forsythe when he said it. The dog's dilemma had presented him with a golden opportunity to get ahead of Call. Once ahead, in the race for rank, he meant to stay ahead. Clara would probably hurry to kiss him, if he came back from the trip a sergeant. Corporal Call wouldn't loom so large—not then.

Call was startled by his friend's foolish offer. There was no footing around the dog at all—just a tiny ledge. There was not a bush or a tree within twenty feet of the dog—there was nothing to hold on to. Besides that, the dog was big.

"Gus, don't do it," Call said. "You'll go on over, like the dentist."

But Gus was in a reckless mood, emboldened by the thought of how proud Clara would be of him, when he returned a sergeant. It was a steep stretch between him and the dog, but he had been over the edge of the canyon once and had survived. No doubt he could survive again.

"Somebody tie a rope to me," he said. "That'll be safe enough—unless all the ropes burnt up."

Call and Long Bill quickly poked through the smouldering baggage, using their rifle barrels to turn the hot rags and smoking blankets. They found three horsehide ropes that, though charred, were not burnt through. Call inspected them carefully, inch by inch, to see if there were any weak spots in the rawhide. He found none.

"I still think it's foolish," he said, as he carefully tied the ropes together. Even with all three ropes knotted into one, it still looked short to him. Every time he looked over the edge of the canyon the dog seemed farther away. The dog had brayed himself out. He lay flat on the ledge now, his head on his paws. His tail stuck over the chasm.

Six Rangers, Call at the front, held the end of the rope and lowered Gus slowly over the canyon rim. In places there were bushes he could hold on to. Caleb Cobb stood at the edge of the canyon, supervising the operation.

"The point about heights is that you don't want to look down, Corporal," he said. "Just look at the dirt in front of you."

Gus took the advice. He studiously kept his eyes on the cliff wall, reaching down carefully, a foot at a time. Though he didn't look down, he did look up, and immediately felt a serious flutter in his stomach. The rim above him seemed halfway to the sky. He could not even see the men who were holding the rope. He knew they were trustworthy men, but it would have reassured him to see them.

Suddenly he remembered the Comanches, the ones who had seemed to walk on air. What if they crossed the canyon and attacked? The men would drop him for sure—they'd have to.

"Lower me faster," he said. "I'm anxious to get back."

When Gus was within fifteen yards of the dog, the dog began to whine and scratch. He knew Gus was coming to rescue him—but the rope didn't quite reach, and the stretch between the dog and Gus was stony and steep. Gus began to feel fear rising. If the men lost their hold, or if he slipped trying to grab the dog, he would fall hundreds of feet and be dead. He wanted the promotion, and he wanted Clara's love—yet his fear rose and swallowed the feelings that had caused him to volunteer.

A moment later, he came to the last foothold and saw that he was beaten: the rope was just too short.

"Colonel, can't you call him?" Gus yelled—"I can't go no lower —maybe he can come up a ways."

Caleb Cobb gave a holler, and the dog began to scramble up.

"Ho, Jeb! Ho, Jeb!" Caleb yelled.

The dog made a frantic effort to scramble back up the cliff. He lunged upward just enough that Gus could grab its thick collar. But the weight of the dog was an immediate shock—the dog weighed as much as small man. When Gus tried to lift the dog by its collar,

Call was almost dragged over the edge—Bigfoot caught his belt, or he might have slipped off.

The weight of the dog cost Gus his narrow foothold. He swung free, into space, holding the dog's collar with one hand. Then, to his horror, he began to swivel. The rope was tied to his belt—the weight of the dog caused him to turn in the air. In a moment his head was pointed down and his legs were waving above him.

"Pull, pull!" he yelled. When he opened his eyes, the world swirled. One moment he would be facing the cliff, the next he would be looking into space. Once, when he twisted, two buzzards flew right by him, so close he felt the beat of their wings in the air.

Then, in a moment, the dog dropped, gone so quickly that he didn't even bark. Gus still had the collar in his hand—the dog's skinny head had slipped out. Gus twisted and twisted, as the men pulled him up. He lost consciousness; when he came to he was flat on his back, looking up at the great sky. Call and Bigfoot and Long Bill stood over him—the dog's collar was still tightly gripped in his hand. He reached up and handed it to Caleb Cobb, who took it, scowling.

"No promotion, Corporal," Caleb said. "I wanted the dog, not the collar."

Then he walked away.

"Just be glad you're back on solid earth," Bigfoot said.

"I'm glad, all right—real glad," Gus said.

19.

THE BURNED PRAIRIE RINGED the canyon for five miles—the Rangers had to huddle where they were all day, lest the burnt grass damage their boots.

"Some of our horses might have made it out," Gus said. "I doubt they all burnt."

"Buffalo Hump will have taken the ones that lived," Bigfoot said. "We've got to depend on our own feet now. I'm lucky I got big ones."

"I ain't got big ones," Johnny Carthage said, apprehensively. "I ain't even got but one leg that's like it ought to be. How far is it we got to walk before we find the Mexicans?"

No one answered his question, because no one knew.

"I expect it's a far piece yet," Long Bill said. "Long enough that we'll get dern thirsty unless we find a creek."

Most of the men squatted or sat, looking at the blackened plain. In the space of a morning they had been put in serious peril. The thought of water was on every man's mind. Even with horses it had sometimes been hard to find water-holes. On foot they might stumble for days, or until they dropped, looking for water. Caleb Cobb was still very angry over the loss of his dog. He sat on the edge of the canyon, his legs dangling, saying nothing to nobody. The men were afraid to approach him, and yet they all knew that a decision had to be made soon. They couldn't just sit where they were, with no food and almost no water—some of the men had canteens, but many didn't. Many had relied on leather pouches, which had burnt or burst in the fire.

Finally, after three hours, Caleb stood up.

"Well, we're no worse off than old Coronado," he said, and started walking west. The men followed slowly, afraid of scorching themselves. The plain was dotted with wands of smoke, drifting upward from smouldering plants. Call was not far behind Caleb—he saw Caleb reach down and pick up a charred jackrabbit that had been crisped coming out of its hole. Caleb pulled a patch of burned skin off the rabbit and ate a few bites of rabbit meat, as he walked.

Looking back, he noticed that Call was startled.

"We're going to have to eat anything we can scratch up now, Corporal," he said. "You better be looking for a rabbit yourself."

Not ten minutes later, Call saw another dead rabbit. He picked it up by its leg and carried it with him—he did not feel hungry enough to eat a scorched rabbit; not yet. Gus, still weak from his scare, saw him pick it up.

"What's the jackrabbit for?" he asked.

"It's to eat," Call said. "The Colonel ate one. He says we have to eat anything we can find, now. It's a long way to where we can get grub."

"I mean to find something better than a damn rabbit," Gus said. "I might find a deer or an antelope, if I look hard."

"You better take what you can get!" Bigfoot advised. "I'm looking for a burnt polecat, myself. Polecat meat is tastier than rabbit."

A little later he came upon five dead horses; evidently they had run into a wall of fire and died together. Call's little bay was one of them—remembering how the horse had towed him across the Brazos made him sad; even sadder was the fact that the charred ground ended only a hundred yards from where the horses lay. A little more speed, or a shift in the wind, and they might have made it through.

"Why are we walking off from this meat?" Shadrach asked. He wore moccasins—the passage through the hot plains had been an ordeal for him. Matilda Roberts half carried him, as it was. But Shadrach had kept his head—most of the men were so shocked by the loss of the horses and the terrible peril of the fire that they merely trudged along, heads down, unable to think ahead.

Caleb Cobb wheeled, and pulled out his big knife.

"You're right," he said. "We got horse meat, and it's already cooked. That's good, since we lost our cook."

He looked at the weary troop and smiled.

"It's every man for himself now, boys," he said. "Carve off what you can carry, and let's proceed."

Call carved off a sizable chunk of haunch—not from his bay, but from another horse. Gus whittled a little on a gelding's rump, but it was clear his heart was not in the enterprise.

"You better do what the Colonel said," Call said. "You'll be begging for mine, in a day or two."

"I don't expect I will," Gus said. "I've still got my mind on a deer."

"What makes you think you could hit a deer, if you saw one?" Call asked. "It's open out here. A deer could see you before you got anywhere near gunshot range."

"You worry too much," Gus said. At the moment, meat was not what was on his mind. Caleb Cobb's treachery in denying him the promotion was what was on his mind. He had gone over the edge of the canyon and taken the risk. Suppose his belt had slipped off, like the dog's collar? He would be dead, and all for a dog's sake. It was poor commanding, in Gus's view. He had been the only man who volunteered—he ought to have been promoted on that score alone. He had been proud to be a corporal, for awhile, but now it seemed a petty title, considering the hardship that was involved.

While he was thinking of the hardship, an awful thought occurred to him. They were now on the open plain, walking through waist-high grass. The canyon was already several miles behind them.

But where the Comanches were, no one knew. The Indians could be drawing a circle around them, even as they walked. If they fired the grass again, there would be no canyon to hide them. They had no horses, and even horses had not been able to outrun the fire.

"What if they set another fire, Woodrow?" Gus asked. "We'd be fried like that jackrabbit you're carrying."

Call walked on. What Gus had just said was obviously true. If the Indians fired the grass again they would all be killed. That was such a plain fact that he didn't see any need to talk about it. Gus would do better to be thinking about grub, or water-holes, it seemed to him.

"Don't it even worry you?" Gus asked.

"You think too much," Call said. "You think about the wrong things, too. I thought you wanted to be a Ranger, until you met that girl. Now I guess you'd rather be in the dry goods business."

Gus was irritated by his friend's curious way of thinking.

"I wasn't thinking about no girl," he informed Call. "I was thinking about being burned up."

"Rangering means you can die any day," Call pointed out. "If you don't want to risk it, you ought to quit."

Just as he said it an antelope bounded up out of the tall grass, right in front of them. Gus had been carrying his rifle over one shoulder, barrel forward, stock back. By the time he got his gun to his shoulder, the antelope was an astonishing distance away. Gus shot, but the antelope kept running. Call raised his gun, only to find that Gus was right between him and the fleeing animal. By the time he stepped to the side and took aim the antelope was so far away that he didn't shoot. Shadrach, who had seen the whole thing, was annoyed.

"You didn't need to shoot it, you could have hit it over the head with your gun," he said.

"Well, it moved quick," Gus said, lamely. Who would expect an antelope to move slow? The whole troop was looking at him, as if it was entirely his fault that a tasty beast had escaped.

The incident brought Bigfoot to life, though—and Shadrach, too. The old man had entrusted his rifle to Matilda, but he got it back.

"That little buck was just half grown," Bigfoot said. "I doubt it will run more than a mile. Maybe if we ease along we can kill it yet."

"Maybe," Shadrach said. "Let's go."

The two scouts left together—Caleb Cobb had been walking so far ahead that he was unaware of the incident until he decided it was time to make a dry camp for the night. He had heard the shot and supposed someone had surprised some game. When he got back and discovered that both his scouts were gone in pursuit of an antelope, he was not pleased.

"Both of them went, after one little buck?" he asked. "Now, that was foolish, particularly when we got all this good horse meat to nibble on."

Night fell and deepened, the sunset dying slowly along the wide western horizon. Matilda Roberts was pacing nervously. She blamed herself for not having tried harder to discourage Shadrach from going after the antelope. Bigfoot was younger—he could have tracked the antelope alone.

By midnight the whole camp had given up on the scouts. Matilda could not stop sobbing. Memory of Indians was on everybody's mind. The two men could be enduring fierce tortures even then. Gus thought of the missed shot, time after time. If he only hadn't had his rifle over his shoulder, he could have hit the antelope. But all his remembering didn't help. The antelope was gone, and so were the scouts.

"Maybe they just camped and went to sleep," Long Bill suggested. "It's hard enough to find your way on this dern plain in the daylight. How could anyone do it at night?"

"Shadrach ain't never been lost, night or day," Matilda said. "He can find his way anywhere. He'd be here, if he wasn't dead."

Then she broke down again.

"He's dead—he's dead, I know it," she said. "That goddamn hump man got him."

"If he wasn't dead, I'd shoot him, or Wallace one," Caleb said. "I lost my dog and both my scouts in the same day. Why it would take two scouts to track one antelope buck is a conundrum."

"Say that again—a what?" Long Bill asked. Brognoli sat beside him, his head still jerking, his look still glassy eyed. In the moments when his head stopped jerking, it was twisted at an odd angle on his neck.

"A conundrum," Caleb repeated. "I visited Harvard College once and happened to learn the word."

"What does it mean, sir?" Call asked.

"I believe it's Latin," Gus said. One of his sisters had given him a Latin lesson, in the afternoon once, and he was anxious to impress Caleb Cobb with his mental powers—perhaps he'd make sergeant yet.

"Oh, are you a scholar, Mr. McCrae?" Caleb asked.

"No, but I still believe it's Latin—I've had lessons," Gus said. The lessons part was a lie. After one lesson of thirty minutes duration he had given up the Latin language forever.

"Well, I heard it in Boston, and Boston ain't very Latin," Caleb said. "Conundrum is a thing you can't figure out. What I can't figure out is why two scouts would go after one antelope."

"Two's better than one, out here," Long Bill said. "I wouldn't want to go walking off without somebody with me who knew the way back."

"If Shad ain't dead, he's left," Matilda said. "He was talking about leaving anyway."

"Left to do what?" Caleb asked. "We're on the Staked Plains. All there is to do is wander."

"Left, just left," Matilda said. "I guess he didn't want to take me with him."

Then Matilda broke down. She sobbed deeply for awhile, and then her sobs turned to howls. Her whole body shook and she howled and howled, as if she were trying to howl up her guts. In the emptiness of the prairies the howls seemed to hover in the air. They made the men uneasy—it was as if a great she-wolf were howling, only the she-wolf was in their midst. No one could understand it. Shadrach had gone off to kill an antelope buck, and Matilda was howling—a woman abandoned.

Many of the men shifted a little, wishing the woman would just be quiet. She was a whore. No one had asked her to form an attachment to old Shadrach anyway. He was a mountain man—mountain men were born to wander.

Several men had been hoping Matilda would become a whore again—they had a long walk ahead, and a little coupling would at least be a diversion. But hearing her howl, the same men, Long Bill among them, began to have second thoughts. The woman was howling like a beast, and a frightening beast at that. Coupling with her would be risky. Besides, old Shadrach might not be gone. He might return at an inconvenient time and take offense.

Caleb Cobb was unaffected by Matilda's howling. He was eating a piece of horse meat—he glanced at Matilda from time to time. It amused him that the troop had become so uneasy, just because a woman was crying. Love, with all its mystery, had arrived in their midst, and they didn't like it. A whore had fallen in love with an old man of the mountains. It wasn't supposed to happen, but it had.

The men were unnerved by it—such a thing was unnecessary, even unnatural. Even the Comanches, in a way, worried them less. Comanches did what they were expected to, which was kill whites. It might mean war to the death, but at least there was no uncertainty about what to expect. But here was a woman howling like a she-wolf—what sense did that make?

"Love's a terrible price to pay for company, ain't it, Matty?" Caleb said. "I won't pay it, myself. I'd rather do without the company."

One by one, the exhausted men fell asleep. Gus wanted to play cards; there was rarely a night when the urge for cardplaying didn't come over him. But the men ignored him. They didn't want to play cards when they had nothing to play for, and were thirsty anyway. It was pointless to play cards when Buffalo Hump and his warriors might be about to hurl down on them, and Johnny Carthage said as much.

"Well, they ain't here now, why can't we play a few hands?" Gus asked, annoyed that his friends were such sleepyheads.

The men didn't even answer. They just ignored him. For awhile, once Matty's howls subsided, the only sound in camp was the sound of shuffling cards—Gus shuffled and shuffled the deck, to keep his hands busy.

Call took the guard—he went away from camp a little ways to stand it. He preferred to be apart at night, to think over the day's action—if there was action. It might be that he would command a troop someday. He wanted to learn; and yet he had no teachers. He was on his second expedition as a Ranger and nothing on either expedition had been well planned. In all their encounters with the Indians, the Indians had outplanned them and outfought them, by such a margin that it was partly luck that any of them survived.

Call couldn't understand it. Caleb Cobb had spoken of Harvard College, and Major Chevallie had been at West Point—Call knew little about Harvard College, but he did know that West Point was where generals and colonels were trained. If these men had such good schooling, why didn't they plan better? It was worrisome. Now they were out in the middle of a big plain, and no one seemed to know much about where they were going or how to survive until they got there. No one knew how to find water reliably, or what plants they could eat, if they had to eat plants. It was fine to rely on game, if there was game, but what if there wasn't? Even old Jesus,

[235]

the Mexican blacksmith in San Antonio, knew more about plants than any one of the Rangers—though maybe not more than Sam had known.

It was obviously wrong to allow only one or two men in a troop to be keepers of all the knowledge that the troop needed for survival. Sam had known how to doctor, but he had fallen over a cliff and no one had bothered to get instructions from him about how to treat various wounds. Call had been made a little uneasy by Matilda's howling, but he was not as affected by it as most of the other men. Probably she would stop crying when she wore out; probably she would get up and be herself again, the next day. Call liked Matilda: she had been helpful to him on more than one occasion. The fact that she had fastened on Shadrach to love was a matter beyond his scope. People could love whom they pleased, he supposed. That was excusable—what wasn't excusable, in his view, was setting off on a long, dangerous expedition without adequate preparation. He resolved that if he ever got to lead Rangers, he would see that each man under his command received clear training and sound instruction, so they would have a chance to survive, if the commander was lost.

Call enjoyed his guard time. Now that there were no horses to steal, the Indians would not need to come around, unless it was to murder them. He could see no reason for them to risk a direct attack. The Rangers had no water and little food. It was hundreds of miles to where they were going, and no one knew the way. The Comanches didn't need to put themselves at risk, just to destroy the Rangers; the country would do the job for them.

He liked sitting apart from the camp, listening to the night sounds from the prairie. Coyotes howled, and other coyotes answered them. Occasionally, he would hear the scratchings of small animals. Hunting birds, hawks or owls, passed overhead. Sometimes Call wished that he could be an Indian for a few days, or at least find a friendly Indian who could train him in their skills. The Comanches, on two nights, had stolen thirty horses from a well-guarded place. He would have liked to go along with the horse thieves on such a raid, to see how they did it. He wanted to know how they could creep into a horse herd without disturbing it. He wanted to know how they could take the horses out without being seen, or heard.

He knew, though, that no Indian was likely to come along and offer to instruct him; he would just have to watch and learn. It annoyed him that Gus McCrae had so little interest in the skills needed for rangering. All Gus thought of was whores, cards, and the girl in the general store in Austin. If Gus had been carrying his rifle correctly, he could have killed the buck antelope and the troop would not have lost its scouts.

Just before dawn, with the night peaceful, Call relaxed and dozed for a minute. Though it seemed only minutes that he dozed, his awakening was rude. Someone yanked his head back by the hair, and drew a finger across his throat.

"They say you don't feel the knife that cuts your throat," Bigfoot said. "If I had been a Comanche, you'd be dead."

Call was badly embarrassed. He had been caught asleep. It was only just beginning to be light. He saw Shadrach, a little distance behind Bigfoot. The old man was leading three horses.

"Yep, we found three nags," Bigfoot said. "I guess they were lucky and found a thin patch of fire."

"We thought you were dead," Call told them. "Matty was upset about Shad."

"Shad's fine—he wants to go look for more horses," Bigfoot said. "Three nags won't carry this troop to New Mexico."

Caleb Cobb gave the returning scouts a stony welcome. A rattlesnake had crawled across him during the night and disturbed his sleep. His temper was foul, and he didn't bother to conceal the fact.

"Nobody told you to go chasing antelope," he said. "But since you went, where's the meat? If I still had chains I'd put them on you."

The carcass of the little antelope was slung across one of the recaptured horses. Shadrach pulled it off, and pitched it at Caleb's feet. He was angry, but Bigfoot Wallace was angrier. Few of the men had seen Bigfoot's temper rise, but those who had knew to lean far back from it. His face had grown red and his eyes menacing, as he stood before Caleb Cobb.

"You wouldn't put no damn chains on me, I guess," he said. "I won't be chained—not by you and not by any man.

"You ain't no colonel!" he added. "You're nothing but a land pirate. They run you off the seas, so now you're out here trying to pirate Santa Fe. I've took my last orders from you, Mr. Cobb, and Shadrach feels the same."

Caleb calmly stood up and drew his big knife. "Let's fight," he said. "We'll see how hard you are to chain once I cut your goddamn throat."

In an instant, Bigfoot's knife was out; he was ready to start slashing at Caleb Cobb, but before the fight started old Shadrach slipped between them. He grabbed two pistols from Gus, and pointed one at each combatant.

"No cutting," he said. The pistols were pointed at each man's chest. Shadrach's action was so unexpected that it chilled the fury in Caleb and Bigfoot.

"You goddamn fools!" Shadrach said. "We need every man we can get—I'll do the killing, if there's killing to be done."

Caleb and Bigfoot lowered their knives—both looked a little sheepish, but the menace was not entirely gone.

"We best save up to fight the Comanches," Shadrach said, handing Gus back his guns.

"All right," Caleb said. "But I don't tolerate mutiny. I still give the orders, Wallace."

"Give better ones, then," Bigfoot said. "I wouldn't waste a fart on your damn orders."

Most of the Rangers were black to the waist, from tramping through five miles of sooty grass. They had used up all the water in their canteens and were already feeling thirsty, although it was early morning and still cool. Bigfoot and Shadrach had seen no water while tracking the antelope. Old Shadrach's beard had red smudges on it. He had cut the little antelope's throat and drunk some of its blood.

"I wonder who gets to ride the horses?" Gus asked. "I guess we ought to let Johnny ride one—he's so gimpy he can't keep up."

Indeed, the walk across the hot grass had been an ordeal for Johnny Carthage. In the course of the march he had fallen almost an hour behind the troop. He knew that he would have been easy prey for a Comanche. He struggled so, to keep up, that he exhausted himself and simply lay down and went sound asleep once he finally struggled to the outskirts of camp. Call had heard his wheezy snores as he stood guard.

"There's probably more horses that didn't get scorched," Gus said.

Call didn't answer. One or two more horses would not solve their problems. The sun had come up, lighting the plain far to the west and north. On the farthest edge little white clouds lined the horizon. The plain was absolutely empty. Call saw no animals, no birds, no trees, no river courses, no Indians—nothing.

"Who do you think would have won, if Caleb and Bigfoot had fought?" Gus asked.

"Shadrach would have won," Call said. "He would have killed them both."

"That wasn't what I meant," Gus said, but Call had turned away. Long Bill was cooking the antelope, and the meat smelled good. He wanted a slice, before the meat was all gone. One little antelope wouldn't go far, not with so many hungry men.

"Carry your gun right today," Call told Gus, when the march started. "We might see another antelope, and we can't afford another miss."

"I won't miss, next time," Gus said.

20.

THE NEXT DAY THEY found four more horses. Two had serious burns, but two were healthy. Caleb killed the two burned horses, and dried their meat. In the afternoon they found a tiny, muddy depression on the plain, with a little scummy water in it. The depression was full of frogs and tadpoles—though the water was greenish, the Rangers drank it anyway. Some of the men immediately vomited it back up. They were thirsty, and yet could not keep the water down.

The next morning, Caleb decided to divide the troop.

"Corporal Call and Corporal McCrae can go with you, Wallace," Caleb said. "Take three horses and try to reach the settlements. Ride night and day, but rest your mounts every three hours. Look for a village called Anton Chico. You ought to strike it first."

"Who gets the other horses?" Long Bill asked.

"I'll take one, and Shadrach can take the other," Caleb said. "We'll travel parallel to one another, as best we can. Some of us ought to strike water."

"What if we don't?" Johnny asked.

"I guess we can pray," Caleb replied. "God might send a rainstorm."

Neither Call nor Gus had expected to be separated from the troop. Both had become good friends with Jimmy Tweed, who had managed to keep a lively attitude, despite all that had happened. When Long Bill and Blackie Slidell sang at night, Jimmy would always join in. Tommy Spencer, the youngster from Missouri, sat and listened. Johnny Carthage bemoaned the fact that he had no way to get drunk. He suffered from fearsome nightmares, and liked to dull himself with liquor before they began. The boys were a group within the larger group, and it was hard to leave them. Gus was wishing Matilda would come with their party—sometimes she mothered him, when he was feeling sorry for himself. He didn't see why old Shadrach should get all the mothering.

"If you're captured by the Mexicans, keep quiet," Caleb said, as they were leaving.

"Keep quiet about what?" Bigfoot asked.

"Don't tell them our numbers," Caleb said. "Let them think there's a thousand of us out here."

Bigfoot looked around at the blackened, exhausted men, many of them already so thirsty that their tongues were thick in their mouths.

"I ain't gonna be bragging about no mighty army," Bigfoot said. "Half of you may be dead before we find anybody to report to."

He rode a few steps west, and then turned his horse.

"Getting captured may be the only way any of you will stay alive," he said. "If I could get you captured, I'd do it right now."

Then he turned, and loped off to the northwest. Gus and Call waved at Long Bill and the others, and loped after him. As they rode, the space ahead of them seemed to get wider and emptier. Gus looked back after a few minutes of riding for one last look at the troop, and found that it had vanished. The big plain had engulfed them. Though it looked level, there were many shallow dips and gentle rolls. Gus made sure he kept up. He didn't want to lag and get lost. The sky was so deep and so vast that it took away his sense of direction. Even when he was looking directly at the sun, he had no confidence that he really knew which way he was going.

They rode six hours without seeing a moving object, other than the waving grass, and one or two jackrabbits. Call had a sense of trespass, as he rode. He felt that he was in a country that wasn't his. He didn't know where Texas stopped and New Mexico began, but it wasn't the Texans or the New Mexicans whose country he was riding through: it was the Comanches he trespassed on. Watching them move across the face of the canyon, on a trail so narrow that he couldn't see it, had shown him again that the Comanches were the masters of their country to a degree no Ranger could ever be. Not one horse or one Comanche had fallen, or even stumbled, as they walked across the cliff face—the Rangers had been on foot and had plenty of handholds when they went over the edge, and yet several had fallen to their deaths. The Indians could do things white men couldn't do.

He mentioned as much to Bigfoot, who shrugged.

"We'll be beyond them, pretty soon," he said. "We'll be moving into the Apache country—we may be in it already. They ain't no better, but they don't have so many horses, so they're slower. Most Apaches are foot Indians."

"Oh well, I expect I could outrun them, then," Gus said. "I could if I see them before they stab me or something. I've always been fleet."

"You *won't* see them before they stab you, though," Bigfoot said. "The Apaches hide better than the Comanches—and that's saying something. An Apache could hide under a cow turd, if that's all there was."

A minute or two later, they saw a dot on the horizon. The dot didn't seem to be moving. Bigfoot thought it might be a wagon. Call couldn't see it at all, and grew annoyed with his own eyes. Why wouldn't they look as far as other men's eyes?

Gus, whose eyesight was the pride of the troop, ruled out the possibility that the dot was a wagon. When he looked hard, the dot seemed to dance in his vision. At times it became two or three dots, but it never became a wagon.

"No, if it was a wagon there'd be mules or horses," Gus said. "Or there'd be people. But there ain't no mules or horses, and I don't see the people."

"It could just be a lump of dirt," Bigfoot said. "I've heard that out in New Mexico you'll find piles of dirt sticking up. I expect that's one of them."

But when they were a mile or two closer, Gus saw the dot move. A lump of dirt might stick up, but it shouldn't move. He galloped ahead, anxious to be the one to identify whatever they were seeing, and he did identify it: it was a solitary buffalo bull.

"Well, there's meat, let's kill it," Bigfoot said, pulling his rifle.

Almost as he said it, the buffalo saw them coming and began a lumbering retreat. It seemed to be moving so slowly that Call was confident they would come up on it in a minute or two, but again appearances deceived him. The buffalo looked slow, but the horses they were riding were no faster. They had had thin grazing, and were gaunt and tired. Even at a dead run, they scarcely gained on the buffalo. They had to run the animal almost three miles to close within rifle range, and then it was a long rifle range. At thirty yards they all began to fire, and to reload and fire again, and yet again. But the buffalo didn't fall, stop, or even stagger. It just kept running at the same lumbering pace, on and on over the empty plain.

Three times the Rangers closed with the buffalo, whipping their tired horses to within twenty feet of it. They emptied their rifles at almost point-blank range several times, and they didn't miss. Gus could see the tufts of brown hair fly off when the heavy bullets hit. Yet the buffalo didn't fall, or even flinch. It just kept running, at the same steady pace.

"Boys, we better stop," Bigfoot said, after the third charge. "We're running our horses to death for nothing. That buffalo's got fifteen bullets in him, and he ain't even slowed down."

"Why won't the goddamn animal fall?" Gus said, highly upset. He was angered by the perversity of the lone buffalo. By every law of the hunt, it should have fallen. Fifteen bullets ought to be enough to kill anything—even an elephant, even a whale. The buffalo wasn't very large. It ought to fall, and yet, perversely, it wouldn't. It seemed to him that everything in Texas was that way. Indians popped out of bare ground, or from the sides of hills, disguised as mountain goats. Snakes crawled in people's bedrolls, and thorns in the brush country were as poisonous as snakebites, once they got in you. It was all an aggravation, in his view. Back in Tennessee, beast and man were much better behaved.

But they weren't in Tennessee. They were on an empty plain, chasing a slow brown animal that should long since have been dead. Determined to kill it once and for all, Gus spurred his tired horse into a frantic burst of speed, and ran right up beside the buffalo. He fired, with his rifle barrel no more than a foot from the buffalo's heaving ribs, and yet the animal ran on. Gus drew rein—his horse was staggering—and fired again; the buffalo kept running.

"Whoa, now, whoa!" Bigfoot cautioned. "We better give up—else we'll kill all our horses."

Call tried a long shot, and thought he hit the buffalo right where its heart should be, but the buffalo merely lost a step or two and then resumed its heavy run.

"I expect it's a witch buf," Bigfoot said, dismounting to rest his tired horse.

"A what?" Gus asked. He had never heard of a witch buf.

"I expect the hump man put a spell on it," Bigfoot said. "It's got twenty-five bullets in it now—maybe thirty. If it wasn't a witch buf, we'd be eating its liver already.

"Indians can make spells," he added. "They're a lot better at it than white folks. Buffalo Hump is a war chief, but he's got some powerful medicine men in the tribe. I expect he sent this buffalo out here to make us use up all our ammunition."

"Why, how would he do that?" Gus asked, startled by the concept.

"Praying and dancing," Bigfoot said. "That's how they do it."

"I don't believe it," Call said. "We just ain't hit it good."

"Hit it good, we shot it thirty times," Gus said.

"That don't mean we hit it good," Call said.

Just as he said it, Gus's horse collapsed. He sank to the ground and rolled his eyes, his limbs trembling.

"Get him up! Get him up!" Bigfoot instructed. "Get him up! If we don't, he'll die."

Gus began to jerk on the bridle rein, but the horse merely let him pull its head up.

Call grabbed its tail, and Bigfoot began to kick it and yell at it, but it did no good. The horse made no effort to regain its feet, and the three of them together could not lift it. When they tried, expending all their strength, the horse's legs splayed out beneath it—the moment they loosened their hold, the horse fell heavily.

"Let it go, it ain't gonna live," Bigfoot said. "We should have reined up sooner. We'll be lucky if we all three don't die."

The buffalo had run on for another five hundred yards or so, and stopped. It had not fallen, but at least it had stopped. Gus felt a fury building; now, thanks to the aggravating buffalo, his horse was dying. He would have to walk to Santa Fe.

"I'll kill it if I have to beat it to death," he said, grabbing his rifle and his bullet pouch.

"If it's a witch buf, you won't kill it—it will kill you," Bigfoot said. "Best thing to do with a witch buffalo is leave it alone."

"He don't listen when he's mad," Call said. He unstrapped Gus's bedroll from the dying horse, and brought it with him. Gus was striding on ahead, determined to walk straight up to the wounded buffalo and blow its brains out. He didn't believe an Indian could pray and dance and keep a buffalo from dying. Bigfoot could believe such foolery if he wanted to.

Yet, when he approached the buffalo, the animal turned and snorted. It lowered its head and pawed the ground. There was a bloody froth running out of its nose, but otherwise there was no evidence that the thirty bullets had weakened it seriously. It not only wasn't dead, it was showing fight.

Gus knelt and carefully put a bullet right where he thought the buffalo's heart would be. He was only twenty yards away. He couldn't miss from such a distance. He fired again, a little higher, but with the same lack of result.

"Leave it be—we've wasted enough ammunition," Bigfoot said. "We need to save some of it for the Mexicans."

"At this rate we'll never see a Mexican," Call remarked.

He was losing his belief in their ability to find their way across the plain. It was too vast, and they had no map. Bigfoot admitted that he really didn't know where the New Mexican settlements were, or how far ahead they might be.

Before Call could say more, Gus threw his rifle down and pulled his knife.

"It's a weak gun—the bullets must not be going in far enough," Gus said. "I'll kill the goddamn thing with this knife, if that's all that will do it."

When he rushed the buffalo and began to stab it in the side, the beast made no attempt to run or fight. It merely stood there, its head down, blowing the bloody froth out of its nostrils.

"By God, he's going to finish it, let's help him," Bigfoot said, drawing his own knife. Soon he had joined Gus, and was stabbing at the buffalo's throat. Call thought their behaviour was crazy. There were only three of them; they couldn't eat that much of the buffalo even if they killed it. But for Bigfoot and Gus, the animal had become a kind of test. The two men could think of nothing but killing the one animal. Unless they could kill it, they wouldn't be able to go on. The settlements would never be reached unless they could kill the buffalo.

Call drew his knife and approached the animal from the other side. It had a short, thick neck, but he knew the big vein had to be somewhere in it; if he could cut the big vein the buffalo would eventually die, no matter how much praying and dancing the Comanches had done over it.

He stabbed and drew blood and so did Gus and Bigfoot—they stabbed until their arms were tired of lifting their knives, until they were all three covered with blood. Finally, red and panting from their efforts, they all three gave up. They stood a foot from the buffalo, completely exhausted, unable to kill it.

As a last effort, Call drew his pistol, stuck it against the buffalo's head just below the ear, and fired. The buffalo took one step forward and sank to its knees. All three men stepped back, thinking the animal would roll over, but it didn't. Its head sank and it died, still on its knees.

"If only there was a creek—I'd like to wash," Gus said. He had never liked the smell of blood and was shocked to find himself covered with it, in a place where there was no possibility of washing.

They all sank down on the prairie grass and rested, too tired to cut up their trophy.

"How do Indians ever kill them?" Call asked, looking at the buffalo. It seemed to be merely resting, its head on its knees.

"Why, with arrows—how else?" Bigfoot asked.

Call said nothing, but once again he felt a sense of trespass. It had taken three men, with rifles, pistols, and knives, an hour to kill one beast; yet, Indians did it with arrows alone—he had watched them kill several on the floor of the Palo Duro Canyon.

"All buffalo ain't this hard," Bigfoot assured them. "I've never seen one this hard."

"Dern, I wish I could wash," Gus said.

21.

BIGFOOT WALLACE TOOK ONLY the buffalo's tongue and liver. The tongue he put in his saddlebag, after sprinkling it with salt; the liver he sliced and ate raw, first dripping a drop or two of fluid from the buffalo's gallbladder on the slices of meat.

"A little gall makes it tasty," he said, offering the meat to Call and Gus.

Call ate three or four bites, Gus only one, which he soon quickly spat out.

"Can't we cook it?" he asked. "I'm hungry, but not hungry enough to digest raw meat."

"You'll be that hungry tomorrow, unless we're lucky," Bigfoot said.

"I'd just rather cook it," Gus said, again—it was clear from Bigfoot's manner that he regarded the request as absurdly fastidious.

"I guess if you want to burn your clothes you might get fire enough to singe a slice or two," Bigfoot said—he gestured toward the empty plain around them. Nowhere within the reach of their eyes was there a plant, a bush, a tree that would yield even a stick of firewood. The plain was not entirely level, but it *was* entirely bare.

"What a goddamn place this is," Gus said. "A man has to tote his own firewood, or else make do with raw meat."

"No, there's buffalo chips, if you want to hunt for them," Bigfoot said. "I've cooked many a liver over buffalo chips, but there ain't many buffalo out this way. I don't feel like walking ten miles to gather enough chips to keep you happy."

As they rode away from the dead buffalo, they saw two wolves trotting toward it. The wolves were a long way away, but the fact that there were two living creatures in sight on the plain was reassuring, particularly to Gus. He had been more comfortable in a troop of Rangers than he was with only Call and Bigfoot for company. They were just three human dots on the encircling plain.

Bigfoot watched the wolves with interest. Wolves had to have water, just as did men and women. The wolves didn't look lank, either—there must be water within a few miles, if only they knew which way to ride.

"Wolves and coyotes ain't far from being dogs," he observed. "You'll always get coyotes hanging around a camp—they like people —or at least they like to eat our leavings. The Colonel ought to catch him a coyote pup or two and raise them to hunt for him. It'd take the place of that big dog you dropped."

Call thought they were all likely to die of starvation. It was gallant of Bigfoot to speculate about the Colonel and his pets when they were in such a desperate situation. The Colonel was in the same situation, only worse—he had the whole troop to think of; he ought to be worrying about keeping the men from starving, not on replacing his big Irish dog.

They rode all night; they had no water at all. They didn't ride fast, but they rode steadily. When dawn flamed up, along the great horizon to the east, they stopped to rest. Bigfoot offered the two of them slices of buffalo tongue. Call ate several bites, but Gus declined, in favor of horse meat.

"I can't reconcile myself to eating a tongue," he said. "My ma would not approve. She raised me to be careful about what foods I stuff in my mouth."

Call wondered briefly what his own mother had been like—he had only one cloudy memory of her, sitting on the seat of a wagon;

in fact, he was not even sure that the woman he remembered had been his mother. The woman might have been his aunt—in any case, his mother had given him no instruction in the matter of food.

During the day's long, slow ride, the pangs of hunger were soon rendered insignificant beside the pangs of thirst. They had had no water for a day and a half. Bigfoot told them that if they found no water by the next morning, they would have to kill a horse and drink what was in its bladder. He instructed them to cut small strips of leather from their saddle strings and chew on them, to produce saliva flow. It was a stratagem that worked for awhile. As they chewed the leather, they felt less thirsty. But the trick had a limit. By evening, their saliva had long since dried up. Their tongues were so swollen it had become hard to close their lips. One of the worst elements of the agony of thirst was the thought of all the water they had wasted during the days of rain and times of plenty.

"I'd give three months wages to be crossing the Brazos right now," Gus said. "I expect I could drink about half of it."

"Would you give up the gal in the general store for a drink?" Bigfoot asked. "Now that's the test."

He winked at Call when he said it.

"I could drink half a river," Gus repeated. He thought the question about Clara impertinent under the circumstances, and did not intend to answer it. If he starved to death he intended, at least, to spend his last thoughts on Clara.

The next morning, the sorrel horse that Gus and Call had both been riding refused to move. The sorrel's eyes were wide and strange, and he did not respond either to blows or to commands.

"No use to kick him or yell at him, he's done for," Bigfoot said, walking up to the horse. Before Gus or Call could so much as blink, he drew his pistol and shot the horse. The sorrel dropped, and before he had stopped twitching Bigfoot had his knife out, working to remove the bladder. He worked carefully, so as not to nick it, and soon lifted it out, a pale sac with a little liquid in it.

"I won't drink that," Gus said, at once. The mere sight of the pale, slimy bladder caused his stomach to feel uneasy.

"It's the only liquid we got," Bigfoot reminded him. "We'll all die if we don't drink it."

He lifted up the bladder carefully, and drank from it as he would from a wineskin. Call took it next, hesitating a moment before putting it to his mouth. He knew he wouldn't survive another waterless day. His swollen tongue was raw, from scraping against his teeth. Quickly he shut his eyes, and swallowed a few mouthfuls. The urine had more smell than taste. Once he judged he had had his share, he handed the bladder to Gus.

Gus took it, but, after a moment, shook his head.

"You have to drink it," Call told him. "Just drink three swallows —that might be enough to save you. If you die I can't bury you— I'm too weak."

Gus shook his head again. Then, abruptly, his need for moisture overcame his revulsion, and he drank three swallows. He did not want to be left unburied on such a prairie. The coyotes and buzzards would be along, not to mention badgers and other varmints. Thinking about it proved worse than doing it. Soon they went on, Bigfoot astride the one remaining horse.

That afternoon they came to a tiny water-hole, so small that Bigfoot could have stepped across it, or could have had there not been a dead mule in the puddle. They all recognized the mule, too. Black Sam had had an affection for it—in the early days of the expedition, he had sometimes fed it carrots. It had been stolen by the Comanches, the night of the first raid.

"Why, that's John," Gus said. "Wasn't that what Black Sam called him?"

John had two arrows in him—both were feathered with prairie-chicken feathers, the arrows of Buffalo Hump.

"He led it here and killed it," Bigfoot said. "He didn't want us to drink this muddy water."

"He didn't want us to drink at all," Call said, looking at the arrows.

"I'll drink this water anyway," Gus said, but Bigfoot held him back.

"Don't," he said. "That horse piss was clean, compared to this water. Let's go."

That night, they had no appetite—even a bite was more than any of them could choke down. Gus pulled out some rancid horse meat, looked at it, and threw it away, an action Bigfoot was quick to criticize.

"Go pick it up," he said. "It might rain tonight—I've been smelling moisture and my smeller don't often fail me. If we could get a little liquid in us, that horse meat might taste mighty good."

About midnight they heard thunder, and began to see flashes of lightning, far to the west. Gus was immediately joyful—he saw the drought had broken. Call was more careful. It wasn't raining, and the thunder was miles away. It might rain somewhere on the plain —but would it rain where they were? And would any water pool up, so they could drink it?

"Boys, we're saved," Bigfoot said, watching the distant lightning.

"I may be saved, but I'm still thirsty," Gus said. "I can't drink rain that's raining miles away."

"It's coming our direction, boys," Bigfoot said—he was wildly excited. Privately, he had given the three of them up for lost, though he hadn't said as much to the young Rangers.

"If the rain don't come to us, I'll go to the rain," Call said.

Soon they could smell the rain. It began to cool the hot air. They were so thirsty it was all they could do to keep from racing to meet the storm, although they had nothing to race on except one tired horse and their feet.

Bigfoot had been right: the rain came. The only thing they had to catch it in was their hats—the hats weren't fully watertight, but they caught enough rainwater to allow the starving men to quench their thirst.

"Just wet your lips, don't gulp it—you'll get sick if you do," Bigfoot said.

The lightning began to come closer. Soon it was striking within a hundred yards of where they were huddled; then fifty yards. Call had never been much afraid of lightning, but as bolt after bolt split the sky he began to wonder if he was too exposed.

"Let's get under the saddle," Gus said. Lightning spooked him. He had heard that a lightning bolt had split a man in two and cooked both parts before the body even fell to the ground. He did not want to get split in two, or cooked either. But he was not sure how to avoid it, out on the bare plain. He sat very still, hoping the lightning would move on and not scorch anybody.

Then a bolt seemed to hit almost right on Bigfoot. He wasn't hit, but he screamed anyway—screamed, and clasped his hands over his eyes.

"Oh, Lord," he yelled, into the darkness. "I looked at it from too close. It burnt my eyes, and now I'm blind.

"Oh Lord, blind, my eyes are scorched," Bigfoot screamed. Call and Gus waited for another lightning bolt to show them Bigfoot. When it came, they just glimpsed it—he was wandering on the prairie, holding both hands over his eyes. Again, as darkness came back, he screamed like an animal.

"Keep your eyes shut—don't look at the lightning," Call said. "Bigfoot's blind—that's trouble enough."

"Maybe he won't be blind too long," Gus said. With their scout blinded, what chance did they have of finding their way to some-place in New Mexico where there were people? He thoroughly regretted his impulsive decision to leave with the expedition. Why hadn't he just stayed with Clara Forsythe and worked in the general store?

Bigfoot screamed again—he was getting farther and farther away. Dark as it was, once the storm passed, they would have no way to follow him, except by his screams. Call thought of yelling at him, to tell him to sit down and wait for them, but if the man's eyes were scorched, he wouldn't listen.

"At least it's washing this dern blood off me," Gus said. Having to wear clothes encrusted with buffalo blood had been a heavy ordeal.

For a few minutes, the lightning seemed to grow even more intense. Call and Gus sat still, with their eyes tight shut, waiting for the storm to diminish. Some flashes were so strong and so close that the brightness shone through their clamped eyelids, like a lantern through a thin cloth.

Even after the storm moved east and the lightning and thunder diminished, Call and Gus didn't move for awhile. The sound had been as heavy as the lightning had been bright. Call felt stunned—he knew he ought to be looking for Bigfoot, but he wasn't quick to move.

"I wonder where the horse went?" Gus asked. "He was right here when all this started, but now I don't see him."

"Of course you don't see him; it's dark," Call reminded him. "I expect we can locate him in the morning. We'll need him for Bigfoot, if he's still blind."

Call yelled three or four times, hoping to get a sense of Bigfoot's position, but the scout didn't answer.

"You try, you've got a louder voice," Call said. Gus's ability to make himself heard over any din was well known among the Rangers.

But Gus's loudest yell brought the same result: silence.

"Can you die from getting your eyes scorched?" Gus asked.

The same thought had occurred to Call. The lightning storm had been beyond anything in his experience. The shocks of thunder and lightning had seemed to shake the earth. Once or twice, he thought his heart might stop, just from the shock of the storm. What if it had happened to Bigfoot? He might be lying dead, somewhere on the plain.

"I hope he ain't dead," Gus said. "If he's dead, we're in a pickle."

"He could have just kept walking," Call said. "We know the settlements are north and west. If we keep going, we're bound to find the Mexicans sometime."

"They'll probably just shoot us," Gus said.

"Why would they, if it's just the two of us?" Call asked. "We ain't an army. We're nearly out of bullets anyway."

"They shot a bunch of Texans during the war," Gus recalled. "Just lined them up and shot them. I heard they made them dig their own graves."

"I wish we could just go back to Austin," he added. "Why can't we? The Colonel don't even know where we are. He's probably given up and gone back himself, by now."

"We've only got one horse and a few bullets," Call reminded him. "We'd never make it back across this plain."

Gus realized that what Call said was true. He wished Bigfoot was there—not much fazed Bigfoot. He missed the big scout.

"Maybe Bigfoot ain't dead," he said.

"I hope he ain't," Call said.

22.

Bigfoot wasn't dead. As the storm was playing out, he lay down and pressed his face into the grass, to protect his eyes. The grass was wet—its coolness on his eyelids was some relief. While cooling his eyelids, he went to sleep. In the night he rolled over—the first sunlight on his eyelids brought a searing pain.

Gus and Call were sleeping when they heard loud moans. Bigfoot had wandered about a half a mile from them before lying down.

When they approached him he had his head down, his eyes pressed against his arms.

"It's like snow blindness, only worse," he told them. "I been snow blind—it'll go away, in time. Maybe this will, too."

"I expect it will," Call said. Bigfoot was so sensitive to light that he had to keep his eyes completely covered.

"You need to make me blinders," Bigfoot said. "Blinders—and the thicker the better. Then put me on the horse."

Until that moment Call and Gus had both forgotten the horse, which was nowhere in sight.

"I don't see that horse," Gus said. "We might have lost him."

"One of you go find him," Bigfoot said. "Otherwise you'll have to lead me."

"You go find him," Call said, to Gus. "I'll stay with Bigfoot."

"What if I find the horse and can't find you two?" Gus asked. The plain was featureless. He knew it to be full of dips and rolls, but once he got a certain distance away, one dip and roll was much like another. He might not be able to find his way back to Call and Bigfoot.

"I'll go, then," Call said. "You stay."

"He won't be far," Bigfoot said. "He was too tired to run far."

That assessment proved correct. Call found the horse only about a mile away, grazing. Call had been painstakingly trying to keep his directions—he didn't want to lose his companions—and was relieved when he saw the horse so close.

By the time he got back, Gus had made Bigfoot a blindfold out of an old shirt. It took some adjusting—the slightest ray of light on his eyelids made Bigfoot moan. They ate the last of their horse meat, and drank often during the day's march from the puddles here and there on the prairie. Toward the end of the day, Call shot a goose, floating alone in one such small puddle.

"A goose that's by itself is probably sick," Bigfoot said, but they ate the goose anyway. They came to a creek with a few bushes and some small trees around it and were able to make a fire. The smell of the cooking goose made them all so hungry they could not sit still—they wanted to rip the goose off its spit before it was ready, and yet they also had a great desire to eat cooked food. Bigfoot, who couldn't see but could certainly smell, asked Gus and Call several times if the bird was almost ready. It was still half raw when they ate it, and yet, to all of them, it tasted better than any bird they had ever eaten. Bigfoot even cracked the bones, to get at the marrow.

"It's mountain man's butter," he said. "Once you get a taste for it you don't see why people bother to churn. It's better just to crack a bone."

"Yeah, but you might not have a bone," Gus said. "The bone might still be in the animal."

Bigfoot kept his eyes tightly bandaged, but he no longer moaned so much.

"What will you do if you're blind from now on, Big?" Gus asked.

Call felt curious about the same thing, but did not feel it was appropriate to ask. Bigfoot Wallace had roamed the wilderness all his life; his survival had often depended on keenness of eye. A blind man would not last long, in the wilderness. Bigfoot could scout no more —he would have to leave off scouting the troops. It would be a sad change, if it happened.

"Oh, I expect I'll get over being scorched," Bigfoot said.

Gus said no more, but the question still hung in the air.

Bigfoot reflected for several minutes, before commenting further.

"If I'm blind, it will be good-bye to the prairies," he said. "I expect I'd have to move to town and run a whorehouse."

"Why a whorehouse?" Gus asked.

"Well, I couldn't see the merchandise, but I could feel it," Bigfoot said. "Feel it and smell it and poke it."

"I been in whorehouses when I was too drunk to see much, anyway," he added. "You don't have to look to enjoy whores."

"Speaking of whores, I wonder what they're like in Santa Fe?" Gus asked. Eating the goose had raised his spirits considerably. He felt sure that the worst was over. He had even argued to Call that the reason the goose had been so easy to shoot was that it was a tame goose that had run off from a nearby farm.

"No, it was a sick goose," Call insisted. "There wouldn't be a farm around here. It's too dry."

Despite his friend's skepticism, Gus had begun to look forward to the delights of Santa Fe, one of which would undoubtedly be whores.

"You can't afford no whore, even if we get there alive," Bigfoot reminded him.

"I guess I could get a job, until the Colonel shows up," Gus said. "Then we can rob the Mexicans and have plenty of money."

"I don't know if the Colonel will make it," Bigfoot said. "I expect he'll starve, or else turn back."

That night, their horse was stolen. They were such a pitiful trio that no one had thought to stand guard. Eating the goose had put them all in a relaxed mood. The horse, in any case, was a poor one. It had never recovered fully from the wild chase after the buffalo. Its wind was broken; it plodded slowly along, carrying Bigfoot. Still, it had been their only mount—their only resource in more ways than one. They all knew that they might need to eat it, if they didn't make the settlements soon now. The goose had been a stroke of luck—there might not be another.

Call had hobbled the horse, to make sure it didn't graze so far that he would have to risk getting lost by going to look for it in the morning. They called the horse Moonlight, because of his light coat. Before Call slept he heard Moonlight grazing, not far away. It was a reassuring sound; but then he slept. When he woke, the hobbles had been cut and there was no sign of Moonlight. The three of them were alone on the prairie.

"We'll track 'em, they probably ain't far," Bigfoot said, before he remembered that he was blind. His eyes were paining him less, but he still didn't dare remove his blinders.

"If he was close enough to steal Moonlight, he could have killed me," Call said. The stealth Indians possessed continued to surprise him. He was a light sleeper; the least thing woke him. But the horse thief had repeatedly come within a few steps of him, yet he had had no inkling that anyone was near.

"Dern, it's a pity you boys don't know how to track," Bigfoot said. "I expect it was Kicking Wolf. That old hump man wouldn't follow us this far, not for one horse. Kicking Wolf is more persistent."

"Too damn persistent," Gus said. He was affronted. Time and again, the red man had bested them.

"All they've done is beat us," he added. "It's time we beat them at something."

"Well, we can beat them at starving to death," Bigfoot said. "I don't know much else we can beat them at."

"Why didn't they kill us?" Call asked.

"I doubt there was more than one of them—I expect it was just Kicking Wolf," Bigfoot said. "Stealing horses is quiet work, but killing men ain't. He might have woke one of us up and one of us might have got him."

"It's a long way to come for one damn horse," Gus commented. He still stung, from the embarrassment of being so easily robbed.

"Kicking Wolf is horse crazy, like you're whore crazy. You'd go anywhere for a whore, and he'd go anywhere for a horse."

"I don't know if I'd go halfway across a damn desert, for a whore," Gus said. "I sure wouldn't for a worn-out horse like Moonlight. Kicking Wolf is crazier than me."

Bigfoot looked amused. "There's no law saying an Indian can't be crazier than a white man," he said.

All that day, and for the next two, Call and Gus took turns leading Bigfoot. It was tiring work. Bigfoot had a long stride, longer even than Gus's—the two of them had almost to trot, to keep ahead of him. Then, too, the prairie was full of cracks and little gullies. They had to be alert to keep him on level ground—it annoyed him to stumble. It stormed again the second night, though with less lightning. Water puddled here and there; they were not thirsty, but once they finished the last few bites of horse meat, they had no food. Call was afraid to roam too far to hunt, for fear of losing Gus and Bigfoot. In any case they saw no game, except a solitary antelope. The antelope was in sight for several hours—Gus thought it was only about three miles away, but Call thought it might be farther. In the thin air, distances were hard to judge.

Bigfoot considered it peculiar that the antelope stayed in sight so long. Not to be able to use his own eyes was frustrating.

"If I could just have one look, I could give an opinion," he said. "It might not even be an antelope—remember them mountain goats that turned into Comanches?"

Reminded, Gus and Call gave the distant animal their best scrutiny. Gus was of the opinion that the animal might be a Comanche, but Call was convinced it was just a plain antelope.

"Go stalk it, then," Bigfoot said. "We'll sit down and wait. A little antelope rump would be mighty tasty."

"Let Gus stalk it," Call said. "He's got better eyes. I'll wait with you."

Gus didn't relish the assignment. If the antelope turned out to be a Comanche, he would be in trouble. He was hungry, though, and so were the others.

"Don't shoot until you've got a close shot," Bigfoot said. "If you can't hit the heart, shoot for the shoulder. That'll slow him down enough that we can catch him."

Gus stalked the antelope for three hours. The last three hundred yards, he edged on his belly. The antelope lifted its head from time to time, but mostly kept grazing. Gus got closer and closer—he remembered that he had missed the first antelope, at almost point-blank range. He wanted to get very close—it would do his pride good to bring home some meat, and his belly would appreciate it, too.

He got to within two hundred yards, but decided to edge a little closer. He thought he might hit it at one hundred and fifty yards. He kept his head down, so as not to show the animal his face. Bigfoot had informed him that prairie animals were particularly alarmed by white faces. Indians could get close enough to kill them because their faces weren't white. He kept his hat low, and his face low, too. When he judged he was within about the right distance, he risked a peek and to his dismay saw no antelope. He looked—then stood up and looked—but the antelope was gone. Gus ran toward where it had been standing, thinking the animal would have lain down—then he glimpsed it running, far to the north, farther than it had been when they first noticed it. Following it would be pointless; for a moment, stumbling around after the antelope, he felt a panic take him. He could not be sure which direction he had come from. He might not even be able to find Bigfoot and Call. Then he remembered a rock that stuck up a little from the ground. He had passed it in his crawl. He walked in a half circle until he saw the rock and was soon back on the right course.

Even so, he was disgusted when he got back to his companions.

"I wasted all that time," he said. "He took off and ran. Let's just hurry up and get to New Mexico."

"Oh, we're in New Mexico," Bigfoot said. "We just ain't in the right part of it, yet. My eyes are improving, at least. Pretty soon I won't have to be led."

Bigfoot's eyes did improve, even as their bellies grew emptier. On the third day after the storm, he was able to take his blinders off in the late afternoon. Soon afterward, he found a small patch of wild onions and dug out enough for them to have a few each to nibble. It wasn't much, but it was something.

The next morning, waking early, Gus saw the mountains. At first, he thought the shapes far to the north might be clouds—storm clouds. Once the sun was well up, he saw that the shapes were mountains. Call saw them, too. Bigfoot still had to be careful of his eyes in full light—he wanted to look, but had to give up.

"If it's the mountains, then we're saved, boys," he said. "There's got to be people between here and the hills."

They walked all day, though, without food—the mountains seemed none the less distant.

"What if we ain't saved?" Gus whispered to Call. "I'm hungry enough to eat tongue, or bugs, or anything I can catch. Them mountains could be fifty miles away, for all we know. I ain't gonna last no fifty miles—not unless I get food."

"I guess you'll last if you have to," Call told him. "Bigfoot says we'll come to villages before we get to the hills. Maybe it will only be twenty miles—or thirty."

"I could eat my belt," Gus said. He actually cut a small slice off his belt and ate it, or at least chewed it and swallowed it. The result didn't please him, though. The little slice of leather did nothing to relieve his hunger pangs.

They walked steadily all day, toward the high mountains. They ignored their stomachs as best they could—but there were moments when Call thought Gus might be right. They might starve before they reached the villages. Bigfoot had taken a fever somehow—most of the day he stumbled along, delirious; he seemed to think he was talking to James Bowie, the gallant fighter who had died at the Alamo.

"We ain't him, we're just us," Gus told him several times, but Bigfoot kept on talking to James Bowie.

Toward the evening of that day, as the shadows from the mountains stretched across the plain, Gus thought he saw something encouraging—a thin column of smoke, rising into the shadows. He looked again, and again he saw smoke.

"It's from a chimney," he said. "There's a house with a chimney up there somewhere."

Gus saw the smoke, too, and Bigfoot claimed he smelled it.

"That's wood smoke, all right," he said. "I reckon it's piñon. They use piñon for fires, out here in New Mexico."

They hurried for three miles and still weren't to the village. Just as they were about to get discouraged again, they came over a little rise in the ground and saw forty or fifty sheep, grazing on the plain ahead. A dog began to bark—two sheepherders, just making their campfire, looked up and saw them. The sheepherders were unarmed and took fright at the sight of the three Rangers.

"I expect they think we're devils," Bigfoot said, as the two sheepherders hurried off toward a village, a mile or two away. The sheep they left in care of the two large dogs, both of whom were barking and snarling at the Texans.

"They didn't need to run—I'm just glad to be here," Gus said. In fact, he was so moved by the sight of the distant houses that he felt he might weep. Crossing the prairie he had often wondered if he would ever see a house again, or sleep in one, or ever be among people again at all. The empty spaces had given him a longing for normal things—women cooking, children chasing one another, blacksmiths shoeing horses, men drinking in bars. Several times on the journey, he had thought such things were lost forever—that he would never get across the plain to sit at a woman's table again. But now he had.

Call was glad to come to the village, too. He had been hearing about New Mexico for months, and yet, until they spotted the sheepherders, had not seen a single Mexican. He had begun to doubt that there were towns in New Mexico at all.

"I wouldn't mind stopping and cooking one of them sheep right now," Bigfoot said. "I guess that wouldn't be friendly, though. Maybe they'll cook one for us, once they see we ain't devils."

"They may think we're devils, even if we're friendly," Gus said. "I could use a barbering, and so could the rest of you."

Call knew he was right. They were filthy and shaggy. They had only their guns and the clothes they had on. And they were afoot. Who but devils would emerge from the great plain afoot?

They gave the sheep a wide berth—the big dogs acted as if they might charge at the slightest provocation; none of them felt in the mood for a dogfight.

"I have always wondered why people keep dogs," Bigfoot said. "Now, the Indians, they eat puppies, and a puppy might be tasty. But a big dog is only a step from being a wolf, and it's foolish to get too close to wolves."

The village consisted of about twenty houses, all of them made of brown adobe. Long before the three of them arrived, the whole village had gathered to watch their approach. The men, the women, and the children stood in one group, clearly apprehensive. One or two of the men had old guns.

"By God, I guess Caleb *could* conquer this state, if he gets here," Bigfoot said. "They don't even have a gun apiece, and I doubt they know how to shoot, anyway."

"Don't be talking of conquering them," Gus said. The mention of mutton had made him realize how hungry he was. He didn't want to lose his chance for a good meal because of any foolish talk about military matters. Let the conquering wait until they had eaten their fill.

"Wave at them, let them know we're friendly," Bigfoot said. "They don't look hostile, but there might be a show-off who wants to impress a gal. That's usually what starts a fight, in situations like this."

They walked into the village slowly, giving evident signs that their intentions were friendly. Some of the little children hid their faces in their mothers' skirts. Most of the women kept their faces down—only a few bold little girls stared at the strangers. The men stood still as statues.

"This is when I wish I was better at the Spanish lingo," Bigfoot said. "I know some words, but I can't seem to get my tongue around them right."

"Just name off some grub," Gus advised. "Frijoles or tortillas or *cabrito* or something. I'm mostly interested in getting a meal and getting it soon."

They walked on, smiling at the assembled people, until they were at the center of the little village, near the common well. A bucket of water had just been brought up—Bigfoot looked around and smiled, before asking if they might drink.

"*Agua?*" he asked. He addressed the question to an old man standing near the well. The old man looked embarrassed—he didn't raise his eyes.

"Certainly—you may drink your fill—it's a very long walk from Texas," a forceful voice said, from behind them.

They turned to see ten muskets pointed at them. A little group of militia had been hiding behind one of the adobe houses. The man who spoke stood somewhat to the side. He wore a military cap, and had a thin mustache.

"What's this? We just want a drink," Bigfoot said. He looked chagrined. Once again, they had been easily ambushed.

"You can have the drink, but I must ask you to lay down your arms, first," the large man said, firmly.

"Who are you?" Bigfoot asked. "We just walked in. We're friendly. Why point a bunch of guns at us?"

"I am Captain Salazar," the man said. "Lay down your weapons, and you will come to no harm."

Bigfoot hesitated a moment—so did Gus and Call. Although ten rifles were pointed at them, at a distance of no more than thirty feet, they didn't want to lay down their arms.

There was dead silence in the village for several moments, while the Rangers considered the order. Captain Salazar waited—he was smiling, but it was not a friendly smile. The soldiers had their rifles ready to fire.

"Now, this is a fine welcome," Bigfoot said, hoping to get the man into a conversation. If they talked a minute, he might ease off.

"Señor, it is not a welcome," Captain Salazar said. "It is an arrest. Please lay down your arms."

Bigfoot saw it was hopeless.

"If that's your opinion, I guess it wins the day," he said. He laid down his guns.

After a moment, Call and Gus did the same. A soldier ran over and took the weapons.

"Help yourselves to the water," Captain Salazar said.

23.

"IF THAT'S THE SHOW, we might as well drink, at least," Bigfoot said. There were two stone dippers in the water bucket. He filled one, and offered the other to Gus. Call waited until they drank. The ten soldiers had not lowered their muskets. Though he was thirsty, he found it unpleasant to drink with guns pointed at him. While Gus and Bigfoot drank, he inspected the Mexican militia. They were a mixed lot—several were boys not older than twelve or thirteen, but two were old men who looked to be seventy, at least. None of them had the appearance of being formidable fighters—any three Rangers could have scattered them easily, had it not been for the awkward fact that they had the drop. Also, Captain Salazar knew his job and his men. Call knew they would have fired together, had he given the order.

"I am surprised you chose to make such a long walk, Señores," Captain Salazar said. "Very few people have walked across the llano. You may be the first, in which case you deserve congratulations."

He gestured to a blacksmith, who stood in front of one of the little shacks. The blacksmith had an anvil and a pile of chains.

"Put the leg irons on them," he said.

"Leg irons," Gus said. "I thought you said we deserve congratulations. Leg irons ain't my notion of congratulations."

"Which of us gets what he deserves in life?" Salazar said, smiling his unfriendly smile again. "I deserve to be a general but am only a captain, sent to this wretched village to catch invaders."

"Shoot them if they resist," he added, turning to the militia.

Call looked at Bigfoot, who was standing calmly by the well. He had mastered his anger and looked as calm as if he had been listening to a sermon.

"Do we have to do it?" Call asked. "I hate like hell to be chained."

"No, you don't have to do it," Bigfoot said. "But it's be chained or be shot. I'll be chained myself. I've been chained before. It ain't a permanent condition, like being dead."

"Your commander is wise," Salazar said. "I would rather feed you than shoot you, but I will shoot you if you don't obey."

"I'll go first, I've had more experience with chaining," Bigfoot said. He walked over, smiled at the blacksmith, and put one of his big feet on the anvil.

"Hammer careful," he said. "I'd hate it if you smashed my toes."

The blacksmith was a young man. He was very, very careful in his work and soon had leg irons on Bigfoot.

Captain Salazar came over and gave the irons a close inspection. It was obvious to Call that the man had made himself feared in the village. Though Bigfoot was calm during the chaining, the young blacksmith wasn't.

"These are important prisoners," Salazar said. "You must do your work well. If one of them escapes while they are in this village, I will hang you."

Call felt a rage building in him, as the young blacksmith tightened the iron around his ankle. He regretted laying down his gun. He felt it would have been better to die fighting than to submit to the indignity of chains.

None of the people in the village so much as moved during the whole procedure. The sheepherders did not go back to their sheep. Two old men with hoes stood where they were. The women of the village, many of whom were plump, kept their eyes downcast—yet once or twice, Call thought he saw looks of sympathy in the eyes of the women. One girl not more than twelve looked at him several times. She didn't dare smile, but she looked. She was a pretty thing, but the sight of a pretty girl could not distract him from the fact that the young blacksmith had just hammered an iron band around his leg.

"I guess this town ain't got no jail," Gus said, to Captain Salazar. "If it had one, I guess you'd just stick us in it."

"No, it is a poor village," Salazar said. "If it had a jail I would put you in it for tonight. But the leg irons are for your march."

"What march? We're just about marched out."

"Don't worry—we don't start until tomorrow," Captain Salazar said. "The women will give you lots of *posole* and you will have all night to rest."

"Oh, then we're off to Santa Fe?" Bigfoot asked. "At least we'll get to see the town."

"No, you are off to El Paso," Salazar said. "El Paso is in the south. You will never see Santa Fe, I am afraid."

"Well, that's a pity—I've heard it's a fine town," Bigfoot said. He was being very friendly—too friendly, Call thought. He didn't intend to be at all friendly to the man—it was clear to him that Salazar would kill them all in an instant if it suited his whim.

Gus amused himself, during his chaining, by looking over the women of the village. Several seemed disposed to be sympathetic, though none would raise their eyes for more than a second. Two or three of them resumed their cooking, which they did outdoors in round ovens. They were cooking corn tortillas. The smell was a torment to one as hungry as he was, but he tried not to show it.

Salazar turned to the militia, and pointed to a small adobe house.

"Put them in there," he said. "Lock the door and four of you stand watch—these are dangerous men. If you let them get away, I will tie your hang ropes with my own hand."

The little house they were shoved into had a door so low that Gus and Bigfoot had to bend almost to their knees to get through it. It was a single room with a mud floor and a small window with bars in it. There was nothing in the room—no pitcher, no bed, nothing. Neither Gus nor Bigfoot could stand erect. Call could, but when he did his hat touched the ceiling.

"They're a small people, ain't they?" Bigfoot said, settling himself in a corner. "I expect we could whip a passel of them, if we hadn't walked into a dern ambush."

"Salazar ain't timid," Call remarked. "He's got all these people scared."

"Well, all he talks about is hanging people," Gus said. He settled in another corner. They had been allowed a jug of well water; Gus remembered that *posole* had been mentioned, but two hours passed and no people arrived. The four guards were standing right outside the little window. They had lowered their muskets and were talking to three girls from the village. One of the girls was the pretty one Call had noticed while he was being chained. Though she chatted with the soldiers, the girl kept looking toward the hut where they were being held.

Gus, too starved to worry about being shot or hanged, finally lost his temper and yelled at the guards.

"We're Texas Rangers, we need to be fed!" he yelled. "Your own captain said to give us *posole*, so go get it."

"They don't know what you're talking about," Bigfoot pointed out. "They don't know the English language."

"They know what *posole* is," Gus declared. "That's not English, that's Mexican."

One of the soldiers went to a house not far away, and said something to an old woman. Soon, the old woman and another came and handed in three hot bowls of *posole*. When the Rangers emptied them, which they quickly did, the old women brought second helpings.

"See, it don't hurt to ask, even if you're in jail," Gus said. "They ain't allowed to just let prisoners starve."

"How do you know their rules—you ain't Mexican," Call said.

24.

THOUGH GUS AND BIGFOOT had been in jail often, Call had never been locked up before—much less locked up and shackled. He found both experiences humiliating. More and more, he regretted laying down his arms. None of the Mexicans looked like good shots. The range was close, of course, but the more he thought over their surrender, the more he wished he had fought.

"I expect we'd have got at least half of them," he said.

"It don't matter if you got nine out of ten, if the tenth one killed you," Gus pointed out. "That was good *posole*. This ain't the worst jail I've ever been in. They don't feed you nothing half that good in the San Antonio jail."

"It'll take more than them ten Mexicans to round up Caleb Cobb," Bigfoot said. "I expect he'll show Captain Salazar a trick or two, if the boys ain't too starved to fight when the fight starts."

"This is just a mud building," Call said. "I imagine we could dig out, if we tried."

"Dig out and go where?" Gus asked. "We nearly starved getting this far. Besides, we're chained."

"I know enough blacksmithing to get these chains off in two minutes," Call reminded him. "I think we ought to try and escape. Somebody needs to warn the boys."

"I ain't going—let Caleb fight his own fights," Bigfoot said. "Those old women seem friendly. I'm tired from that long walk. I say we lay around here and eat soup for a day or two before we do anything frisky."

"There's a pretty girl or two in this village," Gus said. "Some of them might take pity on us and let us out."

"No, Salazar's got 'em buffaloed," Bigfoot said. A minute later, he fell asleep and snored loudly.

Call still smarted from the humiliation of being caught so easily. They had escaped some very skillful Indians, only to be captured by a motley crew of Mexicans with rusty muskets. He was annoyed with himself, because he had been resolved to practice careful planning and avoid traps, yet he had let the fatigue of their journey wear him down. Anyone ought to have known there might be soldiers in the town—yet, once again, he had failed in alertness.

"So far we've been a disgrace in every encounter," he told Gus, but Gus was not in the mood for gloomy military critiques.

"Well, but we ain't dead," Gus said. "We still have time to learn. I guess this ain't the part of New Mexico that's filled with gold and silver."

"I told you not to expect gold and silver," Call said.

Soon Gus, too, fell asleep, but Call couldn't. He stood by the little window most of the night, looking out. There was a high moon over the prairies. Now and then, the sheepdogs barked when a coyote came too close to the flock. The soldiers who were guarding them, all of them just boys, were playing cards by the light of a little oil lantern. They didn't look capable of killing anyone, unless by accident.

Toward morning the old woman came back, bringing them coffee. Call saw the pretty girl come out of a little hut with her water jar and go toward the well. Although he was in no position to say much to her, he had the urge to exchange a good morning, at least. He regretted that he didn't know more Spanish, though, of course, working for old Jesus, he had picked up a phrase or two. As the sun rose, he could see how small the village was—just a few low houses on the edge of the great wide plain.

Bigfoot woke and drank his coffee, but Gus McCrae slept on, stretched comfortably across half the length of the floor.

"I guess he'd sleep like that if they were about to hang him," Call said.

"Well, if they were about to hang him, he might as well snooze," Bigfoot said. "He could go from one nap right into the old nap you don't wake up from."

When the sun was well up the old woman came back, bringing them hot tortillas. The smell woke Gus; he sat up, looking half asleep, but he ate as if he were wide awake.

A little later, Captain Salazar rode along the one street, mounted on a fine black horse. His militia seemed to have increased during the night—some twenty-five soldiers stood at attention, awaiting his order.

Salazar rode over to their little window, and bent in the saddle to look in.

"Good morning, Señores," he said. "I hope you are all refreshed. We have a long way to travel."

"Well, we're getting a late start," Bigfoot said. "The sun's been up an hour. What's the delay?"

"You will see—I had to conduct a trial," Salazar said. "They're bringing the scoundrel now—as soon as we shoot him we'll be on our way."

"I ain't in the mood to see nobody shot. I think I'll just snooze some more," Gus said when Salazar passed on up the street. "I wonder what the fellow did."

Before Gus could stretch out, six soldiers came; one unlocked the door to their little prison. Again, Gus and Bigfoot had to bend nearly double to get out. Once in the street, Call saw that the whole town had turned out for the event that was about to take place. Salazar had ridden up to a little church and was waiting impatiently, now and then popping his quirt against his leg. The church was not much larger than some of the houses, but it had a little bell on top and its walls had been whitewashed. Four soldiers came out, dragging a blindfolded man.

"Why, it's Bes—I wonder how they caught him?" Bigfoot said, recognizing the Pawnee scout.

Indeed, it was Bes-Das: barefoot, blindfolded, and with blood on his shirt.

"The skunks, they've been beating on him," Gus said.

"He's a skunk himself—he deserted us," Call reminded them—and yet he, too, felt sorry for the man. The whole village fell silent as he was hustled across the little plaza and placed in front of the white wall of the church. Bes-Das limped as he walked to the wall.

Salazar rode over to his militia and pointed six times, at six of the young soldiers. An old priest, barefoot like the prisoner, came out of the little church and watched—he did not approach the prisoner. The six soldiers lined up in front of Bes-Das and leveled their muskets. Gus felt his stomach quiver—he did not want to see Bes-Das shot down, but he could not seem to turn his face away. Salazar motioned to the firing squad, and all the soldiers fired—one shot came a moment later than the others. Bes-Das slammed back against the church, and then fell forward on his face. Salazar rode over, drew his pistol, and handed it to one of the young soldiers, who quickly stepped across the body and fired one shot into Bes-Das's head.

"I think that was a wasted bullet," Bigfoot said. "I think old Bes was dead."

Salazar reached down for his pistol, looking over at Bigfoot as he took it.

"Men have survived six bullets before," he remarked. "The pistol was to make sure."

"What did he do?" Call asked, looking at the body of the scout. Some of the young soldiers on the firing squad had not liked their task—one or two were trembling.

"He was a thief," Salazar said. "All Indians are thieves. This one stole a ring from the governor's wife."

He reached into the pocket of his blue tunic and pulled out a large silver ring.

"This ring," he said.

The ring he had was large, with a green stone of some kind set in it. Salazar rode over to where the Texans stood and showed them the ring, one by one.

"The finest silver," he said. "Silver from our own mines, the ones you Texans hope to steal from us. This is why you made your long walk, isn't it—to steal our silver and gold?"

"Captain, we ain't miners," Bigfoot said. "We come for the scenery, mostly—and for the adventure."

"Oh," Salazar said. "Of course the scenery is free. We have no objection to your looking at it, if you do it with respect. As for the adventure . . ."

He stopped, and looked over his shoulder at the body of the man he had just executed. Two old men were digging a grave behind the church.

"As you see, some adventures end badly," he went on. "This man paid his debt. Now we must hurry to meet your friends."

The little militia assembled itself and followed Salazar southwest, onto the plain but in the direction of the line of mountains. The three Texans marched at the rear, guarded by two soldiers on mules. Three soldiers flanked them on either side.

As they passed out of town the two old men were carrying Bes-Das, the crooked-toothed Pawnee, toward the little grave behind the whitewashed church.

"He got killed for a ring," Call observed.

"It looked like pure silver, to me," Gus said. "I guess he just thought he'd grab it and go."

"He didn't go fast enough, then," Bigfoot said. "I wonder what happened to that Apache boy he left with. If he's loose around here somewhere I'd like to know. Apaches are slick when it comes to escapes."

"They don't mean for us to escape," Call said, looking at the three armed soldiers who were marching one on each side of them. Salazar, riding at the head of the little column, frequently turned his horse and sometimes rode all the way back and walked his mount behind the prisoners for a few steps, to remind them of his vigilance.

"They don't mean for us to, but they could get fooled," Bigfoot said.

"That ring was pure silver," Gus said. "I told you there was silver out here."

"You didn't mention the firing squad, though," Call said.

25.

BEFORE THE RANGERS HAD walked a mile they had learned to their vexation the difficulties of walking while chained. The irons soon chafed their ankles raw—they were forced to tear off pieces of their shirts to wrap their ankles with, as some protection from the rough iron.

"Dern, I'll be scraped to the bone before we get ten miles," Gus said. "They ought to unchain us during the march—they could always hammer the chains back on at night."

The scraping, though, was only a part of the vexation. The chains dragged on the ground and caught on small protuberances—rocks, cactus, small bushes. Call, though the shortest man, had been given the longest chain. He found that he could hitch his chain to his belt and proceed at a normal stride, but that was not the case with Gus McCrae or Bigfoot Wallace, both of whom had to adjust their long strides to the length of the chains. Both men soon grew so annoyed at having to hobble mile after mile that they conceived a murderous hatred for Captain Salazar and for all Mexicans.

"Let's throttle these two boys back here and grab the mules and go for it," Gus suggested, more than once. The plain stretched before them, empty for fifty miles at least.

"There's two mules and three of us," Call pointed out. "They're small mules, too. Before we could get out of rifle range, they'd shoot us fifty times."

Bigfoot was as annoyed with the irons as Gus, but when he looked the situation over, he decided Call was right.

"Maybe that Apache boy will show up some night and help us slip off," he said.

Call thought that Gus's hope that Alchise would show up and free them a far-fetched one, at best. Alchise had never been particularly friendly. That very night, though, he fell into a shivery sleep and dreamed that one-eyed Johnny Carthage, the slowest member of the troop, slipped into camp and helped him ride off on Salazar's black horse. The dream was so powerful that he awoke at four in the morning with his teeth chattering and could not at first convince himself that he was where he was, instead of on the black horse, speeding away. They had been given no *posole* that evening, just a few scraps of tortillas and a handful of hard corn. They had no blankets either; a frost crept down from the mountains and edged out onto the plain. Many of the Mexican soldiers were as tired and cold as the three prisoners. They huddled around small campfires, some dozing, some simply trying to keep warm. Several were barefooted, and few had any footgear except sandals. By morning, there were groans throughout the camp as men tried to hobble around on their cold feet. The Texans found to their surprise that they were better off than all but a few of their captors. Though their clothes were frayed and ragged, they were still warmer than what the Mexicans wore.

"Why, we won't have to whip this army," Bigfoot said. "Half of them will freeze before the fight starts, and the other half will be too sleepy to load their guns."

Captain Salazar was the only member of the company to have a portable shelter with him. He owned a fine tent, made of canvas. A large mule carried it for him from camp to camp, and two soldiers were assigned to set it up at the end of each day. Besides the tent, there were a cot and several brightly colored blankets, to keep the Captain warm. In the morning Salazar came out, wrapped in one of the blankets, and sat before a substantial fire that one of his soldiers tended. Salazar also had a personal cook, an old man named Manuel, who brewed his coffee and brought it to him in a large tin cup. Two nanny goats trailed the troop, in order to provide milk for the Captain's coffee.

"He could offer us some of that coffee," Gus said. "If I could get a few drops of something warm inside me, I might not be so cold."

Bigfoot Wallace appeared not to be affected by the chill.

"You boys have lived too south a life," he said. "Your blood gets thin, when you're living south. This ain't cold. If we're still in these parts in a month or two you'll see some weather that makes this seem like summer."

Gus McCrae received that information with a grim expression. The morning had been so cold that he had found himself almost unable to urinate, a difficulty he had not experienced before.

"Hell, it's so cold it took me ten minutes to piss," he said. "I won't be here two months from now, if you think it'll be colder than this, not unless I have a buffalo hide to wrap up in or a big whore to sleep with."

Mention of a big whore reminded them all of Matilda—it set them all to wondering about the fate of their companions, somewhere out on the long plain to the south.

"I wonder if they're all still alive?" Gus said. "What if the hump man came after them with two hundred warriors? Every one of them might be dead, for all we know—these Mexicans can march us to China and we won't find them, if that's the case."

"He wouldn't have needed two hundred warriors," Call said.

"Oh, they're there somewhere," Bigfoot said. "The Mexicans have had reports, I expect. They wouldn't march these barefoot boys around the prairie unless they thought there was somebody to fight, somewhere."

Captain Salazar waited until midmorning before setting the company in motion. Many of the men were so tired from the cold night that they merely stumbled along. Captain Salazar rode ahead, on his fine black gelding.

In the middle of the afternoon, a curl of dark clouds appeared over the mountains to the north. An hour before darkness, snow began to fall, blown on a cold north wind. Call had never seen snow to any extent—just a dusting now and then, in midwinter. Though it was not yet the end of October, snow was soon falling heavily, the white flakes swirling silently out of the dark sky. In half an hour, the whole plain was white.

"It'll be a bad night for these barefoot boys," Bigfoot said. "They ain't dressed for such weather."

"We ain't, either," Gus said. He was appalled at the uncomfortable state he found himself in. The irons were like ice bands around his ankles—soon he was having to drag his chains through the slushy snow.

Captain Salazar had formed the habit of dropping back every hour or so, to exchange a few words with his captives. He had enveloped himself in a warm poncho, and seemed to enjoy the sudden storm.

"This snow will refresh us for battle," he said.

"I guess it might refresh the soldiers it don't freeze," Bigfoot said.

"My men are hardy, Señor," Salazar said. "They won't freeze."

That night, at least, there was coffee for all the men, including the prisoners. Gus kept his hands cupped around his coffee cup as long as he could, for the warmth—he had always had trouble keeping his hands warm in chilly weather. The meal, again, was tortillas and hard corn. The snow swirled thickly in the dusk. Call and Gus and Bigfoot were sitting close together around a little fire when they suddenly heard a high terrified squealing from Captain Salazar's horse. The nanny goats, tethered nearby, began to bleat frantically. The mules began to bray—they were tame mules and had not been hobbled. Soon they were racing away into the darkness. Captain Salazar began to fire his pistol at something Call couldn't see. Then, a moment later, he saw a great shape lope into the center of the camp. Men were grabbing muskets and firing, but the great shape came on.

"Is it a buffalo?" Gus asked—then he saw the shape rear on its hind legs, something no buffalo would be likely to do.

"That ain't no buf, that's a grizzly," Bigfoot said, springing to his feet. "Here's our chance, boys—let's go, while he's got 'em scattered."

The great brown bear was angry—Call could see the flash of his teeth in the light of the many campfires. The bear came right into the center of the camp, roaring. Mexican soldiers fled in every direction; they left their food and their guns, their only thought escape. The bear roared again, and turned toward Captain Salazar's tent—old Manuel had just served him a nice rib of venison in the snug tent. Salazar fired several times, but the bear seemed not to notice. Salazar fled, his gun empty. Old Manuel stepped out of the tent right into the path of the charging bear, who swiped the old man aside with a big paw and went right into the tent.

"Grab a gun and see if you can find a hammer, so we can knock these irons off," Bigfoot said. "Hurry, we need to move while the bear's eating the Captain's supper."

Call and Gus found guns aplenty—each took two muskets and grabbed some bullet pouches. While Call was looking for a hammer, the bear came ripping through the side of Salazar's tent. The black horse was twisting wildly at the end of the rawhide rope it had been tethered with. As the Texans watched, the bear swiped at the horse, as it had at Manuel. The black gelding fell as if shot, the grizzly on top of it.

"Let's go, while it eats that horse," Bigfoot said. He had a pistol and a rifle.

"I didn't know a bear could knock down a horse," Gus said. "I'm glad to be leaving, myself."

"A bear can knock down anything," Bigfoot said. "It could knock down an elephant if it met one—it et the Captain's supper and now it's carrying off his horse."

As they watched, the great bear sank its teeth into the neck of the dead gelding, lifted it, and moved with it into the darkness. It dragged the horse over the top of the old cook, Manuel, as it moved away from the camp that was no longer a camp, just a few sputtering campfires with gear piled around them. Not a single Mexican was visible as the Texans left.

"That bear done us a fine turn," Bigfoot said. "They'd have marched us till our feet came off, if he hadn't come along and scared this little army away."

Call was remembering how easily the bear had lifted the horse and moved away with it. The black gelding had been heavy, too, yet the bear had made off with it as easily as a coyote would make off with a kitten.

The snow continued to fall—once they got behind the circle of firelight, it was very dark.

"The bear went toward the hills," Bigfoot said. "Let's leave the hills—maybe we can catch one or two of them mules, in the morning."

Gus reached down to adjust his leg iron, and for a second had the fear that he had lost his companions.

"Hold on, boys, don't leave me," he said.

"By God, this is a thick night if I ever saw one," Bigfoot said. "We'd better hold on to one another's belts, or we'll all be traveling single, pretty soon."

They huddled together, took their belts off, and strung them out —Bigfoot in the lead; Call at the rear.

"We don't even know which way we're walking," Call said. "We could be walking right back to Santa Fe. They'll just catch us again, if we're not careful."

"I know which way I'm walking," Bigfoot said. "I'm walking dead away from a mad grizzly bear."

"He won't be so bad, once he eats that horse," Gus said.

"It's just one horse—he might not be satisfied," Bigfoot said. "He might want a Tennessean or two, for dessert. I say we keep plodding —we can worry about the Mexicans tomorrow."

"That suits me," Call said.

26.

THE THREE RANGERS WALKED through the snow all night, clinging to one another's belts. All of them thought of the bear. It had killed a large horse with one swipe of its paw. Call remembered the flash of its teeth as it whirled toward Salazar's tent. Gus remembered seeing several men shoot at the bear—he didn't suppose they had missed, at such short range, and yet the bear had given not the slightest indication that it felt the bullets.

"I hope we're going away from it," Gus said, several times. "I hope we ain't going toward it."

"It won't matter which way we're going, if it wants us," Bigfoot informed him. "Bears can track you by smell. If it wanted us it could be ten feet behind us, right now. They move quiet, unless they're mad, like that one was. I had a friend got killed by a bear out by Fort Worth—I found his remains myself, although I didn't find the bear."

Having delivered himself of that piece of information, Bigfoot said no more.

"Well, what about it?" Gus asked, exasperated. "If you found him, what's the story?"

"Oh, you're talking about Willy, my friend that got kilt by the bear?" Bigfoot said. "It was on the Trinity River—I figured it out from the tracks. Willy was sitting there fishing, and the bear walked up behind him so quiet Willy never even had a notion a bear was anywhere around—that's how quiet they are, when they're stalking you."

"So . . . tell us . . . was he torn up bad?" Call asked. He too was annoyed with Bigfoot's habit of starting stories and failing to finish them.

"Yes, he was mostly et—the bear even et his belt buckle," Bigfoot said. "He had a double eagle made into a belt buckle. I always admired that belt buckle and was planning to take it, since Willy was dead anyway and didn't have no kinfolks that I knew of. But the dern bear ate it, along with most of Willy."

"Maybe he fancied the taste of the belt," Gus suggested. The notion that a bear could be ten feet behind him, stalking them, was a notion he couldn't manage to get comfortable with. He turned around to look so many times, as they walked, that by morning his neck was sore from all the twisting. The night was so dark he couldn't have seen the bear even if it had been close enough to bite him—but he couldn't get Bigfoot's story off his mind, and couldn't keep himself from looking around.

The dawn was soupy and cold—the snow turned to a heavy drizzle, and the plains were foggy. They had nothing to eat and had had no luck pounding their chains off with the few rocks they could find. The rocks broke, but the chains held. Exasperated beyond restraint, Bigfoot Wallace tried to shoot his chain off, only to have the musket ball ricochet off the chain and pass through the lower part of his leg.

"Missed the bone, or I'd be done for," Bigfoot remarked grimly, examining the wound he had foolishly given himself.

Gus had been about to try and shoot his chain in two, but changed his mind when he saw what happened to Bigfoot.

"We ought to stop and wait for clearer weather—we could be headed for Canada, I guess," Bigfoot said. "There's bad Indians up in Canada—the Sioux, they call themselves. I don't want to go marching in that direction."

Nonetheless, they didn't stop. Memory of captivity was fresh, and kept them moving. The need to stay warm was also a factor—they had nothing to eat, and no fire to sit by. Waiting would only have meant getting colder.

The fog gradually thinned—by noon, they could see the tops of the mountains again. In midafternoon the sky cleared and the Rangers saw to their relief that they had been moving south, as they had hoped. They were far out on the plain, not a tree or shrub in sight.

"I hope that bear don't spot us," Gus said.

Though the fog and drizzle had been depressing, at least they had given them a little sense of protection; now they felt exposed—Indians on the one side, a grizzly bear on the other.

"I see somebody," Bigfoot said, pointing to two dots on the prairie, west, toward the mountains. "Maybe it's trappers. If it is, we're in luck."

"Trappers always have grub," he added.

The two dots, however, turned out to be two of the Mexican soldiers—two young boys, not more than fifteen, who had happened to flee the bear in the same directions the Texans had taken —they were cold, hungry, and lost. Neither of them were armed. When they saw the Texans marching up, well armed, they both held up their hands, expecting to be killed on the spot.

"What do we do, boys?" Bigfoot asked. "Shoot 'em or take 'em with us?"

"We don't need to shoot them," Call said. "They can't hurt us. I expect they should just go home."

The two boys were named Juan and José. One of them, Call remembered, had tended the nanny goats that supplied Captain Salazar his milk.

"You're going in the wrong direction, boys," Bigfoot told them. He pointed north, toward the village they had started from.

"Vamoose," he said. "We ain't got time for conversation."

The two boys, though, refused to leave them. When the Rangers started south, they followed, though at a respectful distance.

"I expect they're afraid of that bear," Bigfoot said. "I don't blame 'em much. The bear's in that direction."

Call didn't think the bear was following them—after all, it had a horse to eat, and an old man as well—but he admitted that it was hard to get the bear off his mind. He had supposed there could be nothing more fearsome in the West than the Comanches, but the great grizzly was a force even more formidable than Buffalo Hump. Even Buffalo Hump couldn't kill a horse just by hitting it. He remembered how many times they had shot and stabbed the stubborn buffalo, before they got it to die. Yet, the grizzly was far stronger than the buffalo. What kind of gun would it take to kill a grizzly? He knew that men had killed bears, even grizzly bears, but having seen the bear scatter the militia, and reduce even Salazar to terror, he wondered what it would take to bring the beast down.

In any case, it was another reason to stay alert. If a bear could sneak up on a man, as it had on Bigfoot's friend Willy, it behooved them to be watchful.

Walking near dusk, they surprised six prairie chickens and managed to run them down. The heavy birds could only fly a little distance. The Rangers, with the help of the starving Mexican boys, managed to catch all of them. They crossed a little creek, just at dark, with a few trees around it, enough to enable them to have a good fire. They let Juan and José eat with them, and sleep near the fire—the boys just had thin clothes.

"That was luck," Bigfoot said, as they finished the last of the birds. "Caleb can't be too far, unless they've all been massacred. If we walk hard enough we ought to locate them tomorrow."

Call thought that was probably only hopeful thinking. So far, nothing Bigfoot or any of the others had predicted had happened the way it was supposed to. The plain was a vast ocean of grass— Caleb could be anywhere on it. Even a troop of men could be easily lost in such a space.

This time, though, the scout's prediction was accurate. All day they walked steadily south on the sunlit plain. Toward evening, they saw smoke in the distance, rising into the deepening blue of the sky. Like the smoke from the chimneys of the village where they had been captured, the smoke was farther away than it looked. It grew full dark as they walked toward it—now and then, from a roll of the prairie, they could see the flicker of the campfires.

"But they might not be our campfires," Call pointed out. "They could be Mexican campfires."

They stumbled on, the Mexican boys following apprehensively. Another hour passed before the fires were really close. No horses neighed, as they approached the fires. Gus began to feel fearful. He decided Call was right—it was probably Mexicans sitting around the fires, not Texans.

"We could just squat and wait for morning," he whispered. "Then we can see who it is—if it's Indians, we'd still have a chance to get away."

"Shut up, they can hear you," Call said.

"I was whispering," Gus told him.

"Well, you whisper loud enough to wake the dead," Call said.

"Hold on—who's there?" a voice said, and at once relief swept over the Rangers, for the voice that challenged them was none other than Long Bill Coleman's.

"Billy, it's us—don't shoot!" Bigfoot called.

There was silence for a moment, as Long Bill absorbed what he had heard.

"Boys, is that you?" he asked.

"It's us, Bill," Gus said, so relieved he couldn't wait to speak.

"Why, that sounds like Gus McCrae," Bill Coleman said.

"It's us, Bill—it's us," Gus said, again.

Long Bill Coleman peered into the darkness as hard as he could, but he couldn't see a thing. Despite the fact that the voices had sounded as if they were the voices of Bigfoot Wallace and Gus McCrae, he remained apprehensive. It was an odd time of night for folks to be showing up. He had heard somewhere that Indians could do perfect imitations of white men's voices, much as they could imitate birdcalls and coyote howls.

He wanted to believe that the voices he was hearing were the voices of his friends—it was just that all the stories of Comanches imitating white men's voices weighed in his mind.

"If it's you, who's with you, then?" he called out, wondering if he was inviting a scalping. He cocked his gun, just to be on the safe side.

"Gus and Call and two prisoners," Bigfoot said. "Don't you know us?"

Just at that moment Long Bill caught a glimpse of Bigfoot, and realized he had been too suspicious.

"Nerves, I'm jumpy," Long Bill said. "Come on in, boys."

"It's just us, Bill," Gus said, to reassure the man that no ambush was imminent. "It's just us. We're back."

27.

THE ARRIVAL OF THE three Rangers, in leg irons, trailed by two shivering Mexican boys, aroused the whole camp. The blacksmith soon had the chains knocked off. There were some who favored chaining José and Juan, but Bigfoot wouldn't hear of it. The sight of so many Texans, all armed to the teeth, set both boys to quaking as if their last hour had come, and it would have come had some of the harsher spirits had their way. None were quite thirsty enough for Mexican blood to buck Bigfoot, though.

"Those boys don't want to fight," Bigfoot said. "They're too starved to fight, and so are we. What's to eat?"

Caleb Cobb looked rueful.

"I'd like to lay out a banquet for you and the corporals, Mr. Wallace," Caleb said. "I'm sure you deserve one, for making your way back to us under hazardous conditions."

"Hazardous is right, a damn bear nearly killed us all," Gus piped up.

"If one of you had had the foresight to shoot the bear, then we could lay out a banquet," Caleb said. "As it is, we can't. We ran out of food yesterday. We don't have a goddamn thing to eat."

"Nothing?" Gus asked, surprised.

"Not unless you can eat firewood," Long Bill said. "We're all hungry."

Quartermaster Brognoli sat by one of the fires. His condition had not improved. He still looked glassy eyed, and his head still shook.

"Hell, we would have done better to stay prisoners," Bigfoot said. "At least the Mexicans fed us corn. We even had soup when we were still in that little town."

"We're close to the mountains—there'll be deer, I expect," Caleb said. "With a little luck we'll all have meat tomorrow."

Call noticed at once that the company didn't seem as large as it had been when they left it, less than a week earlier. He missed a number of faces, though, in many cases, the faces were not those to which he could put a name. There just didn't seem to be as many men as there had been when they left. Jimmy Tweed was still there, tall and gangly, and Johnny Carthage, and Shadrach and Matilda, huddled around a fire to themselves. But the troop seemed diminished, and Bigfoot said as much to Caleb Cobb.

"Yes, several fools headed off on their own," Caleb admitted. "I expect they're all dead by now, from one cause or another. I didn't have enough ammunition to shoot them all, so I let them go. We're down to forty men."

"Forty-three, now that you men are back," he added, a moment later.

"Forty-three, that's all?" Bigfoot asked. "You had nearly two hundred when we left Austin."

"The damn Missouri boys left first—I expect they'll all starve," Long Bill Coleman said. "Then a bunch went back to try and strike a river. I wouldn't be surprised if they starve, too."

"I don't care who starves and who don't," Bigfoot said. "The Mexicans are bringing a thousand men against us. Salazar told me that. Even if they're mostly boys, like Juan and José, we'll have to shoot mighty good to whip a thousand men."

Caleb Cobb looked undisturbed.

"I expect the figure's high," he said. "I'll worry about a thousand Mexicans when I see them."

"The man who took us prisoner said a general was coming," Call said—Salazar had dropped the remark while they were on the march.

"Well, there's generals and generals," Caleb said. "Maybe their general will be a drunk, like old Phil Lloyd."

"Caleb, there's too many of them," Bigfoot said. "They're raising the whole country against us. If you don't have enough bullets to shoot a few deserters, how are we going to whip a thousand men?"

"You damn scouts are too pessimistic," Caleb said. "Let's go to sleep. Maybe we can wipe out a battalion and steal their ammunition."

He walked off and settled himself by his own campfire, leaving the men apprehensive. Seeing the leg irons on the three Rangers had put the camp in a dour mood.

"We ought to turn back," Johnny Carthage said. "I can barely walk as it is. If they catch me and put me in leg irons I'll be lucky to keep up."

"This is like it was the first time we went out," Call said. "Nobody knows what to do. We're worse off than we were with Major Chevallie. We've got no food and no bullets, either. We can't whip the Mexicans and we can't get home, either. We'll starve if we turn back, and they'll catch us all, if we don't."

Gus had no rejoinder. The fact that there was no food in camp had left him in soggy spirits. All during the long, cold walk, through the snow and drizzle, he consoled himself with the prospect of hardy eating once they got back to their companions. Maybe someone would have killed a buffalo—he had visions of fat buffalo ribs, dripping over a fire.

But there were no buffalo ribs—there was not even corn mush. He had eaten nothing since the prairie chickens—he felt he might become too weak to move, if he didn't get food soon.

"At least the Mexicans fed us," he said, echoing Bigfoot's remark. "I'd rather be taken prisoner than starve to death."

Caleb Cobb's indifference to their plight annoyed Call. The man had led them so far out on the plain that they couldn't get back—and yet the company was so weakened and so badly supplied that they couldn't expect to defeat a Mexican army, either. He wondered if he would live long enough to serve under a military leader who really knew what he was doing. So far, he had not found one who could survive the country itself, much less one who could beat the country *and* the enemy. Buffalo Hump, with only nine men, had nearly destroyed Major Chevallie's command, and now Caleb Cobb's force of two hundred men had dwindled to forty before it even got to its destination.

There was nothing to do but keep the campfires going and wait for morning. They made a fire not far from where Shadrach lay with Matilda. The old man was coughing constantly. Matilda came over briefly, to welcome them back. She looked dispirited, though.

"This bad weather's bad for Shad," she said. "I'm afraid if it don't dry up he'll die. I do my best to keep him warm, but he's getting worse, despite me."

Indeed, the old mountain man coughed all night—long, heaving coughs. Gus finally got warm enough to stretch out and sleep, but Call was awake all night. He didn't leave the fire and walk, as he often did, but he didn't sleep, either. Both the Mexican boys came and sat with him. They were fearful of all Texans, except the three they knew.

Finally, just as grey light was edging across the long plain, Call slept a little, but the sleep produced a nightmare in which the great bear and Buffalo Hump both attacked the troop. Men were falling and running, and he had become separated from his weapons and could not defend himself. He saw arrows going into Long Bill Coleman; the great bear had knocked Gus down and was snarling over him. Call wanted to attack the bear, but he had nothing but his hands. Then he saw Buffalo Hump catch Bigfoot and slash at his head with a knife. Bigfoot's head came off, and the huge Comanche held it up and cried a terrible war cry.

"Wake up . . . Woodrow . . . you've skeert the camp!" Matilda said, shaking him out of his dream. Juan and José were staring at him as if he had gone mad. Gus still slept, but men from the other campfires were rousing themselves and looking at Call, who felt deeply embarrassed by the scrutiny.

"I didn't mean to scare folks," he said, his hands shaking. "I was just dreaming about that bear."

28.

THE TROOP, HUNGRY, COLD, and discouraged, had marched only five miles when they topped a rise and saw the Mexican army camped on the plain before them. The encampment seemed to cover the whole plain; it stretched far back toward the mountains.

Bigfoot saw the camp first and motioned for the troop to hold up, but the signal came too late. Two Indian scouts on fast horses were already speeding back toward the Mexican camp.

Caleb Cobb was the only man on horseback. He rode to the crest of the ridge and surveyed the encampment, silently.

"I told you they'd raise the whole country," Bigfoot said.

"Shut up, I'm counting," Caleb said. He had his spyglass out and was looking the Mexicans over—if he was alarmed he didn't show it.

Bigfoot, though, immediately saw something he didn't like.

"Colonel, they have cavalry," he said. "I'd make it at least a hundred horses."

"More than a hundred," Caleb said, without removing his spyglass from his eye. "That's what I'm counting. I make it a hundred and fifty horses."

Then he took the spyglass out of his eye and looked around at the men. He was astride the only horse.

"That beats us by one hundred and forty-nine horses, I guess," he said.

"Hell, they've even got a cannon," Bigfoot said. "They drug a cannon all this way, thinking we was an army."

"We *are* an army, Mr. Wallace," Caleb said. "We're just a small army. It looks like we're up against superior numbers."

"Not all armies can fight," Shadrach said. "Maybe they're an army of boys, like these two here. We're an army of men."

Call and Gus stood looking at the assembled Mexicans, wondering what would happen.

"I guess we need a herd of bears," Call said. "Ten or twelve big bears could probably scatter them like that one bear scattered that first bunch."

Long Bill Coleman began to look around for cover—only there was no cover, only rolling prairie. Shadrach was still coughing, but he had his long rifle in his hand and seemed invigorated by the prospect of battle. Matilda had even acquired a rifle from someone —she planted herself by Shadrach.

The troop stood together, and watched the two scouts race toward the Mexican camp.

"Them scouts were Mescalero Apache," Bigfoot said. "Those hills are their country. The Mexicans must have paid them big, because Apaches don't usually work for Mexicans."

The arrival of the Texans, in plain view on the ridge, put the whole Mexican encampment into a ferment of activity. The cavalrymen raced to saddle their mounts, many of which were skittish and resistant. Everywhere men were loading guns and making ready for war. In the center of the encampment was a huge white tent.

"I expect that's where the general sleeps," Caleb said. "I regret losing my canoe."

"Why?" Bigfoot asked. "We're on dry land."

"I know, but if I had my canoe I'd hurry back with it to the nearest river, and I'd paddle down whatever stream it was until

I came to the Arkansas, and then I'd paddle down the Arkansas until I came to the Mississippi, and then I'd paddle right on down Old Miss until I struck New Orleans."

He stopped and smiled at Brognoli, who stared back, glassy eyed.

"Once I got to New Orleans I'd stop and buy me a whore," Caleb went on. "Once I had my fill of whores I'd go back to the pirate life, on the good old gulf, and rob all the ships leaving Mexico. That would be the easy way to get the Spanish silver. They ship most of it to Spain, anyway. It would sure beat traipsing across these goddamn plains."

"I think we should count the ammunition, Colonel," Bigfoot said. "We don't have any to waste."

Caleb ignored this sensible suggestion.

He sat on his horse, watching the flurry of preparations in the Mexican camp.

"The truth is, I ain't felt the same about this enterprise since Corporal McCrae let my dog, Jeb, fall to his death," Caleb said. "I think I'll just ride over and have a parley with this army. Do we still have the flag?"

They had brought along the flag of the Republic of Texas, but no one had seen it in awhile.

"Why would you need a flag?" Bigfoot asked.

"Well, we brought the damn rag, why not use it?" Caleb said. "It might impress that general, if there is a general."

The flag was finally located, in Johnny Carthage's kit. At some point he had become the keeper of the flag, but life had been so strenuous that he had forgotten the fact.

Caleb tied the flag to his rifle barrel, and prepared to leave. The troop was apprehensive, not sure what his intentions were. Half of the men were disposed to run, though running across the prairies on foot, with their stomachs empty, offered a poor prospect, considering that the Mexicans, by Caleb's count, had one hundred and fifty cavalrymen.

At the last minute, Caleb looked at Call and nodded.

"Come with me, Corporal—I need attendants," he said. "You too, McCrae. Let's march over there and test this general's manners. If he's got any, he'll ask us to breakfast."

"If he does, snatch us some bacon," Long Bill Coleman said. "I sure would like to have a nice bite of bacon."

"Can we take our guns?" Gus asked. He did not want to go among so many Mexicans without his guns.

"You're my escort—take your guns," Caleb said. "An escort's supposed to march in front. I wish we had a drummer, but we don't. Let's get going."

Gus and Call started marching straight for the Mexican camp. Caleb paused long enough to light a cigar—he had carefully preserved and rationed his cigars—before coming along behind them.

"Good Lord, look at them," Gus said, pointing toward the Mexican camp. "We ought to have brought the whole troop as an escort."

"I don't think they'll shoot us—this is a parley," Call said, though he wasn't fully confident on that score. Across the plain the whole Mexican army stood in battle readiness, waiting for them. The one hundred and fifty cavalrymen were mounted—the infantry, hundreds strong, had been assembled in lines by several captains and lieutenants, who rode back and forth yelling instructions. There were men standing by the cannon. An imposing man in a white uniform stood outside the tent, surrounded by aides.

For once, the law of distance that seemed to govern their travels on the prairies was reversed. Instead of the Mexican army being farther away than it seemed—half a day away would have been fine with Gus—it proved to be closer than it seemed. In no time, Call and Gus were looking right down into the barrel of the cannon—or so it seemed. The first line of soldiers was only a hundred yards away.

"They won't kill us," Call said. "It wouldn't be worth their while. There's only three of us, and look at them. They'd be behaving like cowards if they took advantage of us."

"But maybe they *are* cowards," Gus suggested. "If they shoot off that cannon it will blow us to bits."

Now and then they looked back at their commander, Caleb Cobb —he seemed undisturbed, keeping his horse to a walk and smoking his long cigar.

"Just ignore the army," he told them. "Head right for that tent. The only person we need to talk to is the jefe."

The young Rangers did as instructed, passing between the lines of infantry and the massed cavalry. Both of them looked straight ahead, trying to ignore the fact that hundreds of men around them were all primed to kill them.

On the ridge behind them, Matilda Roberts gave way to a fit of crying.

"They're lost—they're just boys," she said. "They're lost—they'll kill them for sure."

"Now, Matty—it's just a parley," Bigfoot said, but Matilda would not be comforted. Her worries overcame her. She put her face in her hands and sobbed.

Gus was disconcerted, as they approached the General's tent, to see Captain Salazar standing amid the Mexican officers.

"I was hoping the bear got him," Gus said.

"Well, the bear didn't," Call said.

Seven officers stood around the General, a heavy man with much gold braid on his uniform. He had a curling mustache and held a silver flask in his hand, from which he drank occasionally. Several of the officers surrounding him had sabres strapped to their legs— they looked at the young Rangers sternly, as they continued toward the tent. The only one, in fact, who seemed well disposed toward them was Captain Salazar himself. He stepped forward to greet them, and actually saluted.

"Congratulations, gentlemen," he said. "You escaped the bear. Ordinarily, of course, I would shoot you for escaping, but no one could be blamed for running from a grizzly bear. That bear killed my horse and my cook. I have another horse, but I miss the cook."

"I guess you soldiers are acquainted," Caleb said. He dismounted and handed his reins to a Mexican orderly, who took them with a look of surprise.

"Yes, we traveled together, Colonel," Captain Salazar said. "Unfortunately our travels were interrupted, as you may have heard."

"Oh, the bear, yes," Caleb said. "You're Captain Salazar?"

"At your service," the Captain said, saluting again. "Allow me to introduce you to General Dimasio."

The large General did not salute—he nodded casually, and gestured toward his tent.

"We hope you will join us for coffee," Salazar said, to Caleb. "It is fortunate that we found one another so quickly. General Dimasio does not like to travel on the llano. The fact that you came to greet us will save him much trouble."

"Why, that's lucky, then," Caleb said. Without a word to Gus or Call, he bent and went into the tent.

As soon as Caleb Cobb disappeared into the General's tent, the two Mexican soldiers closed the flaps and stood in front of it, muskets held across their chests. Call and Gus were alone amid hundreds of enemy soldiers, most of whom clearly registered hostility. No guns were pointed at them, and no sabres drawn, but the moment was awkward. Across the plain, on the neighboring ridge, the little knot of Rangers stood watching. To Call's mind, they looked forlorn. The Mexicans mostly wore clean uniforms; cooking pots simmered on many campfires. The army they were in the midst of was well equipped and well trained, a far cry from the frightened village militia they had encountered in Anton Chico.

"Well, here we are," Gus said. He found the silence uncomfortable.

"Yes, for now," Captain Salazar said. He was the only Mexican whose manner was friendly.

"Would you like breakfast?" he asked. "As you can see, we have plenty to eat. We even have eggs."

Gus was about to accept, happily—he felt he could eat thirty or forty eggs, if he were offered that many—but Call immediately rejected Salazar's offer.

"No sir, much obliged," Call said. "We've et."

"In that case, at least let me offer you coffee," Salazar said.

"I'll have some coffee, thanks," Gus said at once, fearing that his friend would decline even that.

Salazar motioned to an orderly, who soon brought each of them coffee in small cups.

"Why did you say we et?—you know we ain't et since we killed those prairie chickens," Gus said. "You could have let them feed us —they've got plenty."

"Our men ain't got plenty," Call reminded him, glancing toward the little group on the distant ridge. "I won't sit down and stuff myself with these enemies when our men are about ready to eat their belts."

"It ain't our fault they didn't get to be escorts," Gus said. "Escorting's hard work—here we are with a thousand men ready to kill us. Maybe they will kill us. If I have to die I'd just as soon do it with something in my stomach."

"No," Call said. "Just shut up and wait. Maybe Colonel Cobb will buy food for the troop and then we can all eat."

Caleb Cobb was in the General's tent for over an hour. Not a sound came through the canvas. Gus and Call had nothing to do but wait. Captain Salazar soon went off to attend to some duty, leaving the two of them standing there amid their foes. The cups of coffee had been tiny; no one else offered them anything.

While they stood and waited, though, the Mexican cavalry divided itself into two groups, and moved out. One wing went south of the group of Rangers; the other wing flanked the Rangers to the north.

Then the massed infantry began the same maneuver. Several hundred men marched north of the Rangers—another several hundred marched south. The Rangers stood as they were, watching these developments helplessly.

"I wish our boys would take cover—only where's the cover to take?" Gus asked. "Pretty soon they'll be surrounded."

"You're right about the cover," Call said. "There ain't none to take."

"I wish the Colonel would come out—I'd like to know he's still alive," Gus said. The fact that no sound had come from the General's tent had begun to worry him.

"I expect he's alive—we'd have heard it if they shot him," Call said.

"Well, they might have cut his throat," Gus said. "Mexicans are handy with knives."

He had scarcely said it before the flaps of the tent opened and Caleb Cobb stepped out, wearing the same pleasant expression he had worn when he went in.

"Corporal McCrae, did they feed you?" he asked.

"They offered," Gus said. "Corporal Call declined."

"Oh, why's that? I had an excellent breakfast myself. The eggs were real tasty."

"I won't eat with skunks when my friends are starving," Call said.

"I see—that's the noble point of view," Caleb said. "I'm better at the selfish point of view, myself. You'll seldom see me neglect my own belly. My friends' bellies are their lookout."

"I'd just as soon leave," Call said. "I've been stared at long enough by people I'd just as soon shoot."

"That's brash, under the circumstances," Caleb said. "You can't go, though."

"Why not?" Call asked.

"Because I just surrendered," Caleb said. "I've a promise that if we lay down our arms not a man will be killed. I've done laid down mine—handed them to the General's orderly."

Gus was startled, Call angry. It was infuriating to have their own leader simply walk into a fancy tent with a fat general and surrender, without giving any of his men a chance to have their say.

"I expect to keep my weapons, unless I'm killed," Call said, in a tight voice.

"You can't keep them, Corporal—you have to give them up," Caleb said, with a menacing glance. "When I give an order I expect to have it obeyed. You're a young man. I won't have you dying over this foolishness."

"I'd rather die right now, fighting, than to be put in irons again," Call said. "I won't be put in irons."

"Why, no—there'll be no fetters this time," Caleb said. "This is a peaceable surrender the General and I have worked out. Nobody on either side needs to get hurt. As soon as the boys over there on the ridge have given up their weapons, we can all sit down and have breakfast like friends."

"You mean we can just go home, as long as we ain't armed?" Gus asked.

"No, not home—not right away," Caleb said. "You'll all be visiting Mexico, for a spell."

"We'll be prisoners, you mean?" Call asked. "You mean we've marched all this way just to be prisoners?"

Caleb Cobb turned to one of the Mexican officers, and said a few words in Spanish. The officer, a young skinny fellow, looked startled, but he immediately took his sidearm and handed it to Caleb, who leveled it at Call.

"Corporal, if you're determined to be dead I'll oblige you myself," he said. "I shot Captain Falconer for disobedience and I'll shoot you for the same reason."

He cocked the pistol.

"Woodrow, give up your guns," Gus said, putting a hand on Call's arm. He could see that his friend was tight as a spring. He had never intervened in Woodrow Call's conflicts before, but he felt that if he didn't try this time, his only true friend would be shot before his eyes. Caleb Cobb was not a man to make idle threats.

Call shook off Gus's hand. He was ready to leap at Caleb, even if it meant his death.

Gus quickly stepped between the two men, handing over his pistol and rifle as he did. The nearest Mexican officer took them.

"Give it up, Woodrow," he repeated.

"Corporal McCrae, you're more sensible than your pal," Caleb said. "Corporal Call ain't sensible, but if he'll take your advice and hand over them weapons, we'll all get out of this without loss of life."

Call saw, with bitter anger, that his situation was hopeless. Even if he sprang at Caleb and knocked the pistol aside, a hundred Mexicans would shoot him before he could flee.

"I despise you for a coward," he said to Caleb; but he handed over his guns.

Caleb shrugged, and turned to Captain Salazar, who had come out of the tent in time to witness the little standoff.

"Captain, would you oblige me and put this man under heavy guard until he cools off?" Caleb asked. "He's too brash for his own damn good."

"Certainly, Colonel," Salazar said. "I'll assign six men."

Caleb looked at Call again—the young Ranger was quivering, and the look in his eyes was a look of hatred.

"Assign ten, Captain," Caleb said. "Six men might could handle him, if he decides to break out. But this is the man who shot Buffalo Hump's son—he'll fight, if he sees any room."

"I don't care if you do call yourself colonel," Call said. "You had no right to surrender us."

Caleb Cobb ignored him—he gave the skinny young officer the sidearm he had just borrowed.

"*Gracias*," he said. "Corporal McCrae, I want you to walk back over to that ridge where the troop is and tell them to give up their guns. Tell them they won't be hurt, and tell them they'll be fed as soon as they surrender."

"I'll go, Colonel, but they may not like the news," Gus said.

Caleb gestured toward the Mexican army, which had quickly surrounded the little group on the ridge. The infantry had formed a tight ring, with the cavalry massed in two lines outside it.

"We're not having an Alamo or a Goliad, not here," Caleb said.

"Colonel Travis was a fool, though a brave fool. At least he had a church to fight in—we don't even have a tree to hide behind. This little war is over."

"Go along—tell them that," he added. "The sooner you go, the sooner they'll get breakfast."

"Woodrow, hold steady," Gus said, before leaving. "It won't help nobody for you to get killed."

Caleb Cobb went back into the General's tent. Nearby, three soldiers were hitching a team of sorrel mares to a fine buggy with a canvas canopy over it.

Gus gave Call's arm a squeeze, and started walking back toward the ridge where the troop waited. He had assumed a few Mexicans would go along to keep an eye on him, but none did. He walked out of the Mexican camp alone, through the blowing grass.

A group of ten soldiers, led by Captain Salazar, surrounded Call and marched him about a hundred yards from the General's tent.

"Sit, Corporal—rest yourself," Salazar said. "You have a very long walk ahead. Perhaps now that this foolish invasion is over, you would care to eat."

Call shook his head—he was still very angry.

"I'll eat when my friends can eat," he said. "What's this about a long walk? Colonel Cobb just said we'd be going to Mexico—ain't we in Mexico?"

"New Mexico, yes," Salazar said. "But there is another Mexico, and that is where you are going—to the City of Mexico, in fact."

"That's where the trial will be held," he went on. "Or it will be, if any of you survive the long march."

"How far is the City of Mexico?" Call asked.

"I don't know, Señor," Salazar admitted. "I have never had the pleasure of going there."

"Well, is it a hundred miles?" Call asked. "That's a long enough walk if we're just going to be shot at the end of it."

Salazar looked at him in surprise.

"I see you know little geography," he said. "The City of Mexico is more than a thousand miles away. It may be two thousand—as I said, I have never been there. But it is a long walk."

"Hell, that's too far," Call said. "I don't care to walk my feet off, just to get someplace where I'll be put up against a wall and

[299]

shot. I've done walked a far piece, getting here from Texas. I don't care to walk another thousand miles, and the boys won't care to, either."

"You may not care to, but you will go," Salazar said. "You will go, and you will be tried properly. We are not barbarians—we do not condemn men without a fair trial."

Call accepted another cup of coffee, but he didn't eat, nor did he encourage any more conversations with Captain Salazar, or anyone. Across the plain, he could see Gus walking—he had not even reached the company yet, to inform them of Caleb's treachery. Call wished he could be walking with him, so he could encourage the Rangers to fight, even if to the death. It would be better to die than to submit to captivity again. But Gus was gone, and he was guarded too closely to attempt to follow. He was being watched, not only by the ten soldiers who had been assigned to him but by most of the soldiers still in camp. In the darkness he would have tried it, but the clouds were thinning; it was bright daylight. Patches of sunlight struck the prairie through the thinning clouds. Gus was walking in a patch of light, toward the ridge.

As Call sat surrounded, trying to control his bitter anger, General Dimasio came out of the white tent, with Caleb Cobb just behind him. The two men, accompanied by the General's orderlies, walked to the fancy buggy and got in. Call had supposed the General was about to leave—why else hitch the buggy?—but he was shocked when Caleb got in the buggy with the General. The General was drinking liquor, not from a flask but from a heavy glass jar, as they waited for the soldier who was to drive the buggy. Caleb had no jar, but as Call watched, he extracted another cigar from his shirt pocket and carefully readied it for lighting. The soldier who was to drive the team hopped up in his seat, and the buggy swung around to the west. Eight cavalrymen fell in behind it.

As the General and his guest started out of camp, the General stopped the buggy for a moment, in order to say something to Captain Salazar. Call was sitting only a few yards from where the buggy stopped. The sight of Caleb, his own commander, sitting at ease with the Mexican general, caused his anger to rise even higher. Call got to his feet, watching. Captain Salazar sent a soldier running back to the tent—the General had forgotten his fur lap robe. In a moment the soldier came out of the tent with it, being careful to keep the end of the robe from dragging on the wet ground. The robe was almost as heavy as the soldier who was carrying it.

Before anyone could stop him, Call stepped closer to the buggy.

"Where are you running to?" he asked Caleb.

There was such anger in his voice that the ten soldiers who were guarding him all flinched. Caleb Cobb himself looked surprised and annoyed—he had already consigned Call to the past, and did not appreciate being approached so boldly.

"Why, to Santa Fe, Corporal," Caleb said. "General Dimasio says the governor wants to meet me. I think he plans to give me a little banquet."

Call decided it would be worth dying just to strike the coward once—at least his body decided it. In a second, he was charging through the startled soldiers—he even managed to snatch a musket as he ran past, but he didn't get a good grip on it and the musket fell to the ground. He kept running. His wild charge spooked the high-strung buggy horses, both of whom leaped into the air, jerking the driver off the buggy, right under the horse's feet. It was a light buggy, and Call hit it while it was slightly tipped from the team's leap. Caleb and the General lurched forward on the buggy seat. Call leapt for Caleb and hit him once. Then, as the buggy was tipping, he grabbed the heavy glass jar the General had been drinking from and smashed Caleb with it, flattening his nose and also his fresh cigar. The jar broke in Caleb's face—blood and whiskey poured down his chest. Soon four men were squirming in the overturned buggy, which the frantic horses were dragging slowly forward on its side. The driver was caught under one of the wheels and groaned loudly every time the horses moved.

For a second, the whole Mexican camp was paralyzed. They all stood stunned while one Texan caused their General's buggy to tip over. General Dimasio was near the bottom of the pile, and Call was still pounding at Caleb with his bloody fist. After the first shock, though, the Mexicans regained their power of motion—soon fifty rifles were leveled at Call.

"Don't shoot!" Captain Salazar yelled, in Spanish. "You'll hit the General. Use your bayonets—stick this man, stick him!"

The nearest soldier did manage to bayonet Call in the calf, but before anyone else could stab him, General Dimasio struggled to his feet and ordered them to stop.

"*El Fiero!*" he said, looking at Call, whose hands were bleeding as badly as Caleb Cobb's face.

Several soldiers, all with their bayonets raised to deal the Texan a fatal wound, were startled by the General's order, but all obeyed it. The first blow with the whiskey bottle had rendered Caleb unconscious, but Call was still trying to strike him.

"I think Colonel Cobb's jaw is broken," Salazar said; though the man's face was very bloody, it seemed to him that his jaw had dropped at an odd angle.

Call wanted to kill Caleb Cobb, but he had no weapon—the few shards of glass around him were all too small to stab with, and before he could get a grip on Caleb's bloody neck to strangle him, the Mexicans began to drag him off. It was not easy—Call was bent on killing the man, and he flailed so that the soldiers kept losing their grip. Finally, one looped a horsehide rope over one of Call's legs and they pulled him off. A dozen men piled on him and finally held him steady enough that they could truss him hand and foot. Just before they pulled him off, Call pounded Caleb's head against the edge of the wagon-wheel seat, opening a split in his forehead. He failed in his purpose, though. Caleb Cobb was damaged, but he was not injured fatally.

Through the legs of the men standing over him, many of them panting from the struggle, Call saw several Mexicans help Caleb Cobb to his feet. Caleb's face and forehead were dripping blood, but once he cleared his head, he hobbled through the soldiers and broke into the circle where Call lay tied. Without a word he grabbed a musket from the nearest soldier and raised it high, to bayonet Call where he lay, but Captain Salazar was quicker. Before Caleb struck, he stepped in front of him and leveled a pistol at him.

"No, Colonel, put down the gun," Salazar said. "I must remind you that this man is our prisoner, not yours."

Call looked at Caleb calmly. He had done his best to kill the man, and was prepared to take the consequences. He knew that Caleb wanted his death—he could see the murderous urge in the man's eyes.

With difficulty, Caleb mastered himself. He turned the musket over, as if he meant to hand it back to the soldier he had borrowed it from. But then, in a whipping motion too quick for anyone to stop, he struck with the stock of the musket across both of Call's bound feet. The blow was so sudden and painful that Call cried out. Caleb immediately handed the musket back to the soldier he had borrowed it from, and hobbled back toward the buggy.

Call twisted in pain—through the legs of his captors he could see the buggy being righted. The horses, still jumpy, were being held by three men each. General Dimasio stood by the buggy, talking to Captain Salazar. Now and then, the General gestured toward Call. The company barber had been hastily summoned, to pick the glass out of Caleb's face and neck. The barber wiped the blood away with a rag as best he could, but several cuts were still bleeding freely— he took the rag from the barber and dabbed at the cuts himself.

General Dimasio climbed back into the buggy, and Caleb after him. The canopy was sitting a little crookedly. The driver had survived; he turned the buggy, and the eight cavalrymen fell in behind it again, as it left the camp.

The buggy went at a good clip—soon the General and Caleb Cobb were nearly to the mountains.

Captain Salazar strolled over and stood looking down at Call, who was still surrounded by soldiers ready to bayonet him if he gave them an excuse.

"You are a brave young man, but foolish," Salazar said. "Your Colonel had no choice but to surrender. His men had no food and no ammunition. If he hadn't surrendered, we would have killed you all."

"I despise him," Call said. "At least he won't look so pretty at his damn banquet."

"You're right about that," Salazar said. "But the governor's wife will enjoy him anyway. She likes adventurers."

"I despise him," Call said, again.

"I'm afraid you will not look so good either, once we have whipped you," Salazar said. "The General admired your mettle so much that he ordered one hundred lashes for you—a great honor."

Call looked at Captain Salazar, but said nothing. His feet still pained him badly. He had supposed there would be more punishment coming, too. After all, he had knocked the fat General out of his fancy buggy, turned the buggy over, caused the driver to get partly crushed by a wagon wheel, and bent the canopy of the buggy out of shape.

"Fifty lashes is usually enough to kill a man, Corporal," Captain

Salazar went on. "You will have to eat heartily before this punishment, if you hope to live."

"Why would I need to eat, especially?" Call asked.

"Because you won't have any flesh left on your ribs," the Captain said. "The whip will take it off."

Then he smiled at Call again, and turned away.

29.

GUS WAS WALKING UP the little slope toward the Ranger troop when suddenly a cheer went up. He looked up to see that the men were all waving their guns and hooting. At first he thought they were merely welcoming him back—but when he looked more closely, he saw that they were looking beyond him, toward the Mexican camp.

He turned to see what the commotion was about and saw that the General's buggy had been overturned, somehow—at first he supposed it was merely some accident with the horses. Good buggy horses were often too high strung to be reliable.

When he saw there was a melee, and that Call was in the middle of it, his stomach turned over. Call was in the overturned buggy, pounding at Caleb Cobb. Then he saw a soldier bayonet Call in the leg—several more soldiers had their bayonets up, ready to stab Call when they could. Gus didn't want to watch, but was unable to turn away. He knew his friend would be dead in a few seconds.

But then, to Gus's surprise, Salazar stepped in and stopped the stabbing. He saw Caleb come over and strike at Call with the musket stock. Why he struck his feet, rather than his head, Gus couldn't figure. He began to walk backward, up the ridge, so he could continue to watch the drama in the Mexican camp. Salazar came back and seemed to be having a talk with Call, while Call lay on the ground. Gus didn't know what any of it meant. All he could be sure of was that Caleb Cobb then left the camp with General Dimasio. Call was tied up—no doubt he was in plenty of trouble for attacking the General's buggy.

He soon gave up walking backward—the ground was too rough. The boys were close by, anyway—some were coming down the ridge to meet him. The Mexican infantry stood in a ring around them, just out of rifle range.

"So what's the orders, why did Caleb leave?" Bigfoot asked, when Gus walked up to the troop.

"The orders are to surrender our weapons," Gus said. "Call didn't like them—I guess that's why he knocked over that buggy."

"Well, he was bold," Bigfoot said. "I expect they'll put him up against the wall of a church, like they did Bes."

"They would have already, only there's no church available," Blackie Slidell said.

"Where did Caleb bounce off to, with that fat general?" Bigfoot asked.

Gus didn't know the answer to that question, or to most of the questions he was asked. He couldn't get his mind off the fact that Woodrow Call was probably going to be executed, and very soon. He had never had a friend as good as Woodrow Call—it was in his mind that he should have stayed and fought with him, and been killed too, side by side with his friend.

"Caleb is a damn skunk," Long Bill Coleman said. "He had no right to surrender for us—what if we'd rather fight?"

"What happens if we do surrender?" Jimmy Tweed asked. "Will they put all of us up against a church?"

"Oh, they'd need two churches, at least, for all of us," Bigfoot said. "That church where they shot Bes was no bigger than a hut. They'd have to shoot us in shifts, if they used a church that small."

"Shut up about the churches, they ain't going to shoot us," Gus said. He was annoyed by Bigfoot's habit of holding lengthy discussions of ways they might have to die. If he had to be dead, he wanted it to occur with less conversation from Bigfoot Wallace.

"We can have breakfast, as soon as we give up our guns," he added.

To the hungry men, cold, wet, and discouraged, the notion of breakfast was a considerable inducement to compromise.

"I wonder if they've got bacon?" Jimmy Tweed asked. "I might surrender to the rascals if I could spend the morning eating bacon."

"There's no pigs over there," Matilda observed. "I guess they could have brought bacon with them, though."

"What do you think, Shad?" Bigfoot asked.

Shadrach had picked up a little, at the prospect of battle. There was a keen light in his eyes that had been missing since he got his cough and had begun to repeat himself in his conversations. He was walking back and forth in front of the troop, his long rifle in his hand. The fact that they were completely surrounded by Mexican infantry, with a substantial body of cavalry backing them up, was not lost on him, though. He kept looking across the plain and then to the mountains beyond. The plain offered no hope. It was entirely open; they would be cut down like rabbits. But the mountains were timbered. If they could make it to cover, they might survive.

The problem with that strategy was that the Mexican camp lay directly between them and the hills. They would have to fight their way through the infantry, then through the cavalry, then through the camp. Several men were sickly, and the ammunition was low. Much as he wanted to sight his long rifle time after time at Mexican breasts, he knew it would be a form of suicide. They were too few, with too little.

"We could run for them hills—shoot our way through," he said. "I doubt more than five or six of us would make it. We'd give them a scrap, at least, if we done that."

"Not a one of us would make it," Bigfoot said. "Of course they might spare Matilda."

"I don't want to be spared, if Shad ain't," Matilda said.

"You're a big target, Matty," Bigfoot observed, in a kindly tone. "They might shoot you full of lead before they even realized you were female."

"Why do we have to fight?" Gus asked. "They have us surrounded and we're outnumbered ten to one—more than that, I guess. We can't whip that many of them, even if they *are* Mexicans. If we surrender we won't be hurt—Caleb said that himself. We'll just be prisoners for awhile. And we can have breakfast."

"I am *damn* hungry," Blackie Slidell said. "A few tortillas wouldn't hurt."

"All right, boys—they're too many," Bigfoot said. "Let's lay our guns down. Maybe they'll just march us over to Santa Fe and introduce us to some pretty señoritas."

"I think they'll line us up and shoot us," Johnny Carthage said. "I'm for the breakfast, though—I hope there's a good cook."

The Rangers carefully laid down their weapons, in full view of a captain of the infantry. They piled the guns in a heap, and raised their hands.

The captain who received their surrender was very young—about Gus's age. Relief was in his face when he saw that the Rangers had decided not to fight.

"*Gracias*, Señores," he said. "Now come with us and eat."

"There's one good thing about surrendering," Gus said to Jimmy Tweed, as they were marching.

"What?" Jimmy asked. "Señoritas?"

"No, weapons—lots of guns, and they've got that cannon," Gus said. "It ought to be enough to keep off the bears."

"Oh, bears," Jimmy said, casually.

"You ain't even seen one," Gus said. "You wouldn't be so reckless if you had."

30.

"THE WHIP WAS MADE in Germany," Captain Salazar said, as Call was being tied to the wheel of one of the supply wagons.

"I have never been in Germany," he added. "But it seems they make the best whips."

The whole Mexican force had been assembled, to watch Call's punishment. The Texans were lined up just behind him. Many of them were in a very foul temper, since the promised breakfast had turned out to consist of flavourless tortillas and very weak coffee.

None of them had had a chance to talk to Call, who was under heavy guard. He was marched by armed men with bayonets fixed to the wagon, where he was tied. His shirt was removed, too. One of the muleteers was to do the whipping—a heavyset man with only one or two teeth in his mouth. The whip had several thongs, each with a knot or two in them. The thongs were tipped with metal.

"I guess I won't be going to Germany, if they're that fond of whips," Long Bill said. "I wouldn't want to be Woodrow. A hundred times is a lot of times to be hit with a whip like that."

Matilda Roberts stood with the men, a look of baleful hatred in her eyes.

"If Call don't live I'll kill that snaggle-toothed bastard that's doing the whipping," she said.

Bigfoot Wallace was silent. He had seen men whipped before—black men, mostly—and it was a spectacle he didn't enjoy. He didn't like to see helpless men hurt—of course, young Call *had* knocked over the General's buggy. Dignity required that he be punished, to some extent, but a hundred lashes with a metal-thonged whip was a considerable punishment. Men had died of less, as Captain Salazar was fond of reminding them.

"If you'd like to say a word to your friend Corporal McCrae, I'll permit it," Salazar said.

"No, I'll talk to him later," Call said. He didn't like the tone of familiarity Salazar adopted with him. He did not intend to be friends with the man, and didn't want to enter into conversation with him.

"Corporal, there may be no later," Salazar said. "You may not survive this whipping. As I told you earlier, fifty lashes kills most men."

"I expect to live," Call said.

Mainly what he remembered of the whipping was the warmth of blood on his back, and the fact that the camp became very silent. The grunt of the muleteer who was whipping him was the only sound. After the first ten blows, he didn't hear the whip strike.

Gus heard it, though. He watched his friend's back become a red sheet. Soon Call's pants, too, were blood soaked. The muleteer wore out on the sixtieth stroke and had to yield the bloody whip to a smaller man. Call was unconscious by then. All the Rangers assumed he was dead. Matilda was restrained, with difficulty, from attacking the whipper. Call hung by his bound wrists, presenting a low target. The second whipper had to bend low in order to hit his back.

When they untied Call and let him slide down beside the wagon wheel they thought they were untying a corpse, but Call turned over, groaning.

"By God, he's alive," Bigfoot said.

"For now," Salazar said. "It is remarkable. Few men survive a hundred lashes."

"He'll live to bury you," Matilda said, giving Salazar a look of hatred.

"If I thought that were true, I would bury him right here and right now, alive or dead," Salazar said.

"Now be fair, Captain," Bigfoot said. "He's had his punishment. Don't go burying him yet."

No one could stand to look at Call's back except Matilda, who sat beside him that first night and kept the flies away. She had nothing to cover the wounds with—if too many of them festered, she knew the boy would die.

Gus McCrae had not been able to watch the whipping, beyond the first few strokes He sat with his back to the whipping ground, his head between his hands, grinding his teeth in agony. None of the Texans were tied, but a brigade of riflemen were stationed just beside them, with muskets ready. Their orders were to shoot any man who tried to interfere with the punishment. None did, but Gus fought with himself all through the whipping; he wanted to dash at the whipper. His friend was being whipped to death, and he could do nothing about it. He had not even been able to exchange a word with Call, before the whipping began. It was a terrible hour, during which he vowed over and over again to kill every Mexican soldier he could, to avenge his friend.

Now, though, with Call alive but still in mortal peril, he came and went. Every ten minutes he would walk over to Matilda and ask if Call was still breathing. Once Matilda told him Call was alive, he would go back to where the Texans sat, plop down for a minute, and then get up and walk around restlessly, until it was time to go check on Call again.

There was a small creek near the encampment. Matilda persuaded an old Mexican who tended the fires and helped with the cooking to loan her a bucket, so she could walk over to the creek and get water with which to wash Call's wounds. He was already delirious with fever—the cold water was the only thing she had to treat him with, or clean his wounds. When she went to the creek, three soldiers went with her, a fact that annoyed her considerably.

She didn't complain, though. They were captives—Call's life, as well as others, depended on caution now.

Shadrach had spread his blanket near where Matilda sat with Call. He and Bigfoot were the only Rangers who had watched the whipping through. Before it was over most of the men, like Gus, had turned their backs. "Oh, Lord . . . oh, Lord," Long Bill said many times, as he heard the blows strike.

"Was it me, I'd rather be put up against the wall," Blackie Slidell said. "That way's quick."

Captain Salazar had been right in his assessment of the damage the whip could cause. In several places, the flesh had been torn off Call's ribs. None of the Texans could stand to look at his back, except Bigfoot, who considered himself something of a student of wounds. He came over once or twice, to squat by Call and examine his injuries. Shadrach took no interest. He thought the boy might live—Call was a tough one. What vexed him most was that the Mexicans had taken his long rifle. He had carried the gun for twenty years—rare had been the night when his hand wasn't on it. For most of that time, the gun had not been out of his sight. He felt incomplete without it. The Texans' guns had all been piled in a wagon, a vehicle Shadrach kept his eye on. He meant to have his gun again. If that meant dying, then at least he would die with his gun in his hand.

Shadrach slept cold that night—Matilda stayed with Call, warming him with her body. He went from fever to chill, chill to fever. The old Mexican helped Matilda build a little fire. The old man seemed not to sleep. From time to time in the night, he came to tend the fire. Gus didn't sleep. He was back and forth all night— Matilda got tired of his restless visits.

"You just as well sleep," she said. "You can't do nothing for him."

"Can't sleep," Gus said. He couldn't get the whipping out of his mind. Call's pants legs were stiff with blood.

When dawn came Call was still alive, though in great pain. Captain Salazar came walking over, and examined the prisoner.

"Remarkable," he said. "We'll put him in the wagon. If he lives three days, I think he will survive and walk to the City of Mexico with us."

"You don't listen," Matilda said, the hatred still in her eyes. "I told you yesterday that he'd bury you."

Salazar walked off without replying. Call was lifted into one of the supply wagons—Matilda was allowed to ride with him. The Texans all walked behind the wagon, under heavy guard. Johnny Carthage gave up his blanket, so that Call could be covered from the chill.

At midmorning the troop divided. Most of the cavalry went north, and most of the infantry, too. Twenty-five horsemen and about one hundred infantrymen stayed with the prisoners. Bigfoot watched this development with interest. The odds had dropped, and in their favor—though not enough. Captain Salazar stayed with the prisoners.

"I am to deliver you to El Paso," he said. "Now we have to cross these mountains."

All the Texans were suffering from hunger. The food had been scanty—just the same tortillas and weak coffee they had had for supper.

"I thought we were supposed to get fed, if we surrendered," Bigfoot said, to Salazar.

All day the troop climbed upward, toward a pass in the thin range of mountains. The Texans had been used to walking on a level plain. Walking uphill didn't suit them. There was much complaining, and much of it directed at Caleb Cobb, who had led them on a hard trip only to deliver them to the enemy in the end. There were Mexicans on every side, though—all they could do was walk uphill, upward, into the cloud that covered the tops of the mountains.

"The bears live up here," Bigfoot mentioned, lest anyone be tempted to slip off while they were climbing into the cloud.

When Call first came back to consciousness, he thought he was dead. Matilda had left the wagon to answer a call of nature—they were in the thick of the cloud. All Call could see was white mist. The march had been halted for awhile and the men were silent, resting. Call saw nothing except the white mist, and he heard nothing, either. He could not even see his own hand—only the pain of his lacerated back reminded him that he still had a body. If he was dead, as for a moment he assumed, it was vexing to have to feel the pains he would feel if he were alive. If he was in heaven, then it was a disappointment, because the white mist was cold and uncomfortable.

Soon, though, he saw a form in the mist—a large form. He

thought perhaps it was the bear, though he had not heard that there were bears in heaven; of course, he might not be in heaven. The fact that he felt the pain might mean that he was in hell. He had supposed hell would be hot, but that might just be a mistake the preachers made. Hell might be cold, and it might have bears in it, too.

The large form was not a bear, though—it was Matilda Roberts. Call's vision was blurry. At first he could only see Matilda's face, hovering near him in the mist. It was very confusing; in his hours of fever he had had many visions in which people's faces floated in and out of his dreams. Gus was in many of his dreams, but so was Buffalo Hump, and Buffalo Hump certainly did not belong in heaven.

"Could you eat?" Matilda asked.

Call knew then that he was alive, and that the pain he felt was not hellfire, but the pain from his whipping. He knew he had been whipped one hundred times, but he could not recall the whipping clearly. He had been too angry to feel the first few licks; then he had become numb and finally unconscious. The pain he felt lying in the wagon, in the cold mist, was far worse than what he had felt while the whipping was going on.

"Could you eat?" Matilda asked again. "Old Francisco gave me a little soup."

"Not hungry," Call said. "Where's Gus?"

"I don't know, it's foggy, Woodrow," Matilda said. "Shad's coughing—he can't take much fog."

"But Gus is alive, ain't he?" Call asked, for in one of his hallucinations Buffalo Hump had killed Gus and hanged him upside down from a post-oak tree.

"I guess he's alive, he's been asking about you every five minutes," Matilda said. "He's been worried—we all have."

"I don't remember the whipping—I guess I passed out," Call said.

"Yes, up around sixty licks," Matilda said. "Salazar thought you'd die, but I knew better."

"I'll kill him someday," Call said. "I despise the man. I'll kill that mule skinner that whipped me, too."

"Oh, he left," Matilda said. "Most of the army went home."

"Well, if I can find him I'll kill him," Call said. "That is, if they don't execute me while I'm sick."

[314]

"No, we're to march to El Paso," Matilda said.

"We didn't make it when we tried to march to it from the other side," Call reminded her. Then a kind of red darkness swept over him, and he stopped talking. Again, the wild dreams swirled, dreams of Indians and bears.

When Call awoke the second time, they were farther down the slope. The sun was shining, and Gus was there. But Call was very tired. Opening his eyes and keeping them open seemed like a day's work. He wanted to talk to Gus, but he was so tired he couldn't make his lips move.

"Don't talk, Woodrow," Gus said. "Just rest. Matilda's got some soup for you."

Call took a little soup, but passed out while he was eating. For three days he was in and out of consciousness. Salazar came by regularly, checking to see if he was dead. Each time Matilda insulted him, but Salazar merely smiled.

On the fourth day after the whipping, Salazar insisted that Call walk. They were on the plain west of the mountains, and it had turned bitter cold. Call's fever was still high—even with Johnny Carthage's blanket, he was racked with a deep chill. For a whole night he could not keep still—he rolled one way, and then the other. Matilda's loyalties were torn. She didn't want Call to freeze to death, or Shadrach either. The old man's cough had gone deeper. It seemed to be coming from his bowels. Matilda was afraid, deeply afraid. She thought Shad was going, that any morning she would wake up and see his eyes wide, in the stare of death. Finally she lifted Call out of the wagon and took him to where Shadrach lay. She put herself between the two men and warmed them as best she could. It was a clear night. Their breath made a cloud above them. They had moved into desert country. There was little wood, and what there was the Mexicans used for their own fires. The Texans were forced to sleep cold.

The next morning, finding Call out of the wagon, Salazar decreed that he should walk. Call was semiconscious; he didn't even hear the command, but Matilda heard it and was outraged.

"This boy can't walk—I carried him out of the wagon and put him here to keep him warm," she said. "This old man don't need to be walking, either."

She gestured at Shadrach, who was coughing.

Salazar had come to like Matilda—she was the only one of the Texans he did like. But he immediately rejected her plea.

"If we were a hospital we would put the sick men in beds," he said. "But we are not a hospital. Every man must walk now."

"Why today?" Matilda asked. "Just let the boy ride one more day —with one more day's rest, he might live."

"To bury me?" Salazar asked. "Is that why you want him to live?" He was trying to make a small jest.

"I just want him to live," Matilda said, ignoring the joke. "He's suffered enough."

"We have all suffered enough, but we are about to suffer more," Salazar said. "It is not just you Texans who will suffer, either. For the next five days we will all suffer. Some of us may not live."

"Why?" Gus asked. He walked up and stood listening to the conversation. "I don't feel like dying, myself."

Salazar gestured to the south. They were in a sparse desert as it was. They had seen no animals all the day before, and their water was low.

"There is the Jornada del Muerto," he said. "The dead man's walk."

"What's he talking about?" Johnny Carthage asked. Seeing that a parley was in progress, several of the Texans had wandered over, including Bigfoot Wallace.

"Oh, so this is where it is," Bigfoot said. "The dead man's walk. I've heard of it for years."

"Now you will do more than hear of it, Señor Wallace," Salazar said. "You will walk it. There is a village we must find, today or tomorrow. Perhaps they will give us some melons and some corn. After that, we will have no food and no water until we have walked the dead man's walk."

"How far across?" Long Bill asked. "I'm a slow walker, but if it's that hard I'll try not to lag."

"Two hundred miles," Salazar said. "Perhaps more. We will have to burn this wagon soon—maybe tonight. There is no wood in the place we are going."

The voices had filtered through the red darkness in which Call lived. He opened his eyes, and saw all the Texans around him.

"What is it, boys?" he asked. "It's frosty, ain't it?"

"Woodrow, they want you to walk," Gus said. "Do you think you can do it?"

"I'll walk," Call said. "I don't like Mexican wagons anyway."

"We'll help you, Corporal," Bigfoot said. "We can take turns toting you, if we have to."

"It might warm my feet, to walk a ways," Call said. "I can't feel my toes."

Cold feet was a common complaint among the Texans. At night the men wrapped their feet in anything they could find, but the fact was they couldn't find much. Few of them slept more than an hour or two. It was better to sit talking over their adventures than to sleep cold. The exception was Bigfoot Wallace, who seemed unaffected by cold. He slept well, cold or hot.

"At least we've got the horses," he remarked. "We can eat the horses, like we done before."

"I expect the Mexicans will eat the horses," Gus said. "They ain't our horses."

Call found hobbling on his frozen feet very difficult, yet he preferred it to lying in the wagon, where all he had to think about was the fire across his back. He could not keep up, though. Matilda and Gus offered to be his crutches, but even that was difficult. His wounds had scabbed and his muscles were tight—he groaned in deep pain when he tried to lift his arms across Gus's shoulders.

"It's no good, I'll just hobble," he said. "I expect I'll get quicker once I warm up."

Gus was nervous about bears—he kept looking behind the troop. He didn't see any bears, but he did catch a glimpse of a cougar—just a glimpse, as the large brown cat slipped across a small gully.

Just then there was a shout from the column ahead. A cavalryman, one of the advance guard, was racing back toward the troop at top speed, his horse's hooves kicking up little clouds of dust from the sandy ground.

"Now, what's his big hurry?" Bigfoot asked. "You reckon he spotted a grizzly?"

"I hope not," Gus said. "I'm in no mood for bears."

Matilda and Shadrach were walking with the old Mexican, Francisco. They were well ahead of the other Texans. All the soldiers clustered around the rider, who held something in his hand.

"What's he got there, Matty?" Bigfoot asked, hurrying up.

"The General's hat," Matilda said.

"That's mighty odd," Bigfoot said. "I've never knowed a general to lose his hat."

31.

Two MILES FARTHER ON they discovered that General Dimasio had lost more than his hat—he had lost his buggy, his driver, his cavalrymen, and his life. Four of the cavalrymen had been tied and piled in the buggy before the buggy was set on fire. The buggy had been reduced almost to ash—the corpses of the four cavalrymen were badly charred. The other cavalrymen had been mutilated but not scalped. General Dimasio had suffered the worst fate, a fate so terrible that everyone who looked at his corpse bent over and gagged. The General's chest cavity had been opened and hot coals had been scooped into it. All around lay the garments and effects of the dead men. Both the fine buggy horses had been killed and butchered.

"Whoever done this got off with some tasty horse meat," Bigfoot said.

Except for the burned cavalrymen, all the dead had several arrows in them.

"No scalps taken," Bigfoot observed.

"Apaches don't scalp—ain't interested," Shadrach said. "They got better ways to kill you."

"He is right," Salazar said. "This is the work of Gomez. For awhile he was in Mexico, but now he is here. He has killed twenty travelers in the last month—now he has killed a great general."

"He wasn't great enough, I guess," Bigfoot said. "I thought he rode off with a skimpy guard—I guess I was right."

"Only Gomez would treat a general like this," Salazar said. "Most Apaches would sell a general, if they caught one. But Gomez likes only to kill. He knows no law."

Bigfoot considered that sloppy thinking.

"Well, he may *know* plenty of law," he said. "But it ain't his law and he don't mind breaking it."

Salazar received this comment irritably.

"You will wish he knew more law, if he catches you," he said. "We are all in danger now."

"I doubt he'd attack a party this big," Bigfoot said. "Your general just had eleven men, counting himself."

Salazar snapped his fingers; he had just noticed something.

"Speaking of counting," he said. "Where is your Colonel? I don't see his corpse."

"By God, I don't neither," Bigfoot said. "Where *is* Caleb?"

"The coward, I expect he escaped," Call said.

"More than that," Gus said. "He probably made a deal with Gomez."

"No," Salazar said. "Gomez is Apache—he is not like us. He only kills."

"He might have taken Caleb home with him, to play with," Long Bill suggested. "I feel sorry for him if that's so, even though he is a skunk."

"I doubt Caleb Cobb would be taken alive," Bigfoot said. "He ain't the sort that likes to have coals shoveled into his belly."

Before the burials were finished, one of the infantrymen found Caleb Cobb, naked, blind, and crippled, hobbling through the sandy desert, about a mile from where the Apaches had caught the Mexicans. Caleb's legs and feet were filled with thorns—in his blindness he had wandered into prickly pear and other cactus.

"Oh, boys, you found me," Caleb said hoarsely, as he was helped into camp. "They blinded me with thorns, the Apache devils."

"They hamstrung him, too," Bigfoot whispered. "I guess they figured he'd starve or freeze."

"I expect that bear would have got him," Gus said.

Even Call, beaten nearly to death himself, was moved to pity by the sight of Caleb Cobb, a man he thoroughly despised. To be blind, naked, and crippled in such a thorny wilderness, and in the cold, was a harder fate than even cowards deserved.

"How many were they, Colonel?" Salazar asked.

"Not many," Caleb said, in his hoarse voice. "Maybe fifteen. But they were quick. They came at us at dawn, when we had the sun in our eyes. One of them clubbed me with a rifle stock before I even knew we were under attack."

For a moment he lost his voice, and his ability to stand. He sagged in the arms of the two infantrymen who were supporting him. The leg that had been cut was twisted in an odd way.

"Fifteen ain't many," Gus said. He didn't like seeing men who had been tortured, whether they were alive or dead. He couldn't keep his mind off how it would feel to have the tortures happen to him. The sight of Caleb, with his leg jerking, his eyes ruined, and his body blue with cold, made him want to look away or go away— but of course he couldn't go away without putting himself in peril of the Apaches and the bears.

"Fifteen was enough," Bigfoot said. "I've heard they come at you at dawn."

Captain Salazar was thinking of the journey they had to make. He kept looking south, toward the dead man's walk. The quivering, ruined man on the ground before him was a handicap he knew he could not afford.

"Colonel, we have a hard march ahead," the Captain said. "I'm afraid you are in no condition to make this march. The country ahead is terrible. Even healthy men may not survive it. I am afraid you have no chance."

"Stick me in a wagon," Caleb said. "If I can have a blanket, I'll live."

"Colonel, we cannot take the wagons across these sands," Salazar said. "We will have to burn them for firewood, probably tonight. They have blinded you and crippled you."

"I won't be left," Caleb said, interrupting the Captain. "All I need is a good doctor—he can fix this leg."

"No, Colonel," Salazar said. "No one can fix your leg, or your eyes. We can't take you across the sands—we have to look to ourselves."

"Then send me back," Caleb said. "If I can be put on a horse, I reckon I can ride it to Santa Fe."

There was anger in his voice. While they all watched, he managed to get to his feet. Even crippled he was taller than Salazar—and he was determined not to die. Call was surprised by the man's determination.

"If he'd been that determined to fight, we wouldn't be prisoners," he whispered to Gus.

"He ain't determined for us . . . he's determined for himself," Gus pointed out.

Salazar, though, was out of patience.

"I cannot take you, Colonel," he said, "and I cannot send you back, either. If I sent you with a few men, Gomez would find you again, and this time he would do worse."

"I'll take that chance," Caleb said.

"But I won't take it, Colonel," Salazar said, drawing his pistol. "You are a brave officer—it is time to finish yourself."

The troops grew silent, when Salazar drew his pistol. Caleb Cobb was balanced on one leg; the other foot scarcely touched the ground. Call saw the anger rise in his face; for a second he expected Caleb to go for Salazar. But after a second, Caleb controlled himself.

"All right," he said. "I never expected to die in a goddamn desert. I'm a seaman. I ought to be on my boat."

"I know you were a great pirate," Salazar said, relieved that the man was taking matters calmly. "You stole much treasure from the King of Spain."

"I did, and lost it all at cards," Caleb said. "I know you need to travel, Captain. Give me your pistol and I'll finish it, and you can be on your way."

"Would you like privacy?" Salazar asked—he still held the pistol.

"Why, no—not specially," Caleb said, in a normal voice. "These wild Texas boys are all mad at me for surrendering. They'll hang me, if they get the chance. It will amuse me to cheat 'em, by shooting myself."

[322]

"All right," Salazar said.

"How was that you said I ought to do it, Wallace?" Caleb asked. "Are you here, Wallace? I know you think there's a sure way—I want to take the sure way."

"Through the eyeball," Bigfoot said.

"It'll have to be through the eye hole," Caleb said. "I'm all out of eyeballs."

"Well, that will do just as well, Colonel," Bigfoot said.

"I'll take the pistol now, if you please," Caleb said, in a pleasant, normal voice.

"Adios, Colonel," Salazar said, handing Caleb the pistol.

Caleb immediately turned the pistol on Salazar and shot him— the Captain fell backward, clutching his throat.

"Rush 'em, boys—get their guns," Caleb said. "I'll take down a few."

But in his blindness, Caleb Cobb fired toward the Texans, not the Mexicans. Two shots went wild, while the Texans ducked.

"Hell, he's turned around, he's shooting at *us!*" Long Bill said, as he ducked.

Before Caleb could fire a fourth time, the Mexican soldiers recovered from their shock and cut him down. As he fell, he fired a last shot—Shadrach, who had been standing calmly by Matilda, fell backwards, stiffly. He was dead before he had time to be surprised.

"Oh no! no! not my Shad," Matilda cried, squatting down by Shadrach.

The Mexican soldiers continued to pour bullets into Caleb Cobb —the corpse had more than forty bullets in it, when it was buried. But the Texans had lost interest in Caleb—Bigfoot ripped open Shadrach's shirt, hoping the old man was stunned but not dead. But the bullet had taken Shadrach exactly in the heart.

"What a pity," Captain Salazar said. He was bleeding profusely from the wound in his throat—the wound, though, was only a crease.

"Shad, Shad!" Matilda said, trying to get the old man to answer —but Shadrach's lips didn't quiver.

"This man had walked the dead man's walk," Salazar said. "He might have guided us. Your Colonel was already dead when he shot him—I suppose his finger twitched. We are having no luck today."

"Why, you're having plenty of luck, Captain," Bigfoot said. "If that bullet had hit your neck a fraction to the left, you'd be as dead as Shad."

"True," Salazar said. "I was very foolish to give Colonel Cobb my gun. He was a man like Gomez—he knew no law."

When Matilda Roberts saw that Shadrach was dead, she began to wail. She wailed as loudly as her big voice would let her. Her cries echoed off a nearby butte—many men felt their hair stand up when the echo brought back the sound of a woman wailing in the desert. Many of the Mexican soldiers crossed themselves.

"Now, Matty," Bigfoot said, kneeling beside and putting his big arm around her. "Now, Matty, he's gone and that's the sad fact."

"I can't bear it, he was all I had," Matilda said, her big bosom, wet already with tears, heaving and heaving.

"It's sad, but it might be providential," Bigfoot said. "Shadrach wasn't well, and we have to cross the Big Dry. I doubt Shad would have made it. He'd have died hard, like some of us will."

"Don't tell me that, I want him alive—I just want him alive," Matilda said.

She cried on through the morning, as graves were dug. There were a dozen men to bury, and the ground was hard. Captain Salazar sat with his back to a wagon wheel as the men dug the graves. He was weak from loss of blood. He had reloaded his pistol, and kept it in his hand all day, afraid the brief commotion might encourage the Texans to rebel.

His caution was justified. Stirred by the shooting, several of the boys talked of making a fight. Blackie Slidell was for it, and also Jimmy Tweed—both men had had enough of Mexican rule.

Gus listened, but didn't encourage the rebellion. His friend Call had collapsed, from being made to walk when he wasn't able. He was weaker than Salazar, and more badly injured. Escape would mean leaving him behind—and Gus had no intention of leaving him behind. Besides, Matilda was incoherent with grief—four men had to pull her loose from Shadrach's body, before it could be buried. The Mexican soldiers might mostly be boys, but they had had the presence of mind to kill Caleb Cobb—since they had all the guns, rebellion or escape seemed a long chance.

They had planned to shelter for the night in a village called San

Saba, but the burials and the weakness of Captain Salazar kept them in place until it was too late to travel more than a few miles.

That night a bitter wind came from the north, so cold that the men, Mexicans and Texans alike, couldn't think of anything but warmth. The Texans even agreed to be tied, if they could only share the campfires. No one slept. The wind keened through the camp. Matilda, having no Shadrach to care for, covered Call with her body. Before dawn, they had burned both wagons.

"How far's that village, Captain?" Bigfoot asked—dawn was grey, and the wind had not abated.

"Too far—twenty miles," Captain Salazar said.

"We have to make it tomorrow, we've got nothing else to burn," Bigfoot said.

"Call will die if he has to sleep in the open without no fire," Matilda said.

"Let's lope along, then, boys," Bigfoot said.

"I'll help you with Woodrow, Matty," Gus said. "He looks poorly to me."

"Not as poorly as my Shad," Matilda said.

Between them, they got Call to his feet.

32.

ALL DAY CALL STRUGGLED through the barren country. The freezing wind seemed to slide through the slices in his back and sides; it
seemed to blow right into him. He couldn't feel his feet, they were
so cold. Gus supported him some; Matilda supported him some;
even Long Bill Coleman helped out.

"How'd it get so damn cold?" Jimmy Tweed muttered, several
times. "I never been no place where it was this cold. Even that snow
wasn't this cold."

"You ought to leave me," Call said. "I'm slowing you down." It
grated on him, that he had to be helped along.

"Maybe there'll be a bunch of goats in this village," Gus said.
He was very hungry. The wind in his belly made the wind from
the north harder to bear. He had always had a fondness for goat
meat—in his imagination, the village they were approaching was
a wealthy center of goat husbandry, with herds in the hundreds
of fat, tasty goats grazing in the desert scrub. He imagined a

feast in which the goats they were about to eat were spitted over a good fire, dripping their juices into the flame. Yet, as he struggled on, it became harder to trust in his own imaginings, because there was no desert scrub. There was nothing but the rough earth, with only here and there a cactus or low thornbush. Even if there were goats, there would be no firewood, no fire to cook them over.

Captain Salazar rode in silence, in pain from his neck wound. Now and then the soldiers walking beside him would rub their hands against his horse, pressing their hands into the horsehair to gain a momentary warmth.

Except when she was helping Call, Matilda walked alone. She cried, and the tears froze on her cheeks and on her shirt. She wanted to go back and stay with Shadrach—she could sit by his grave until the wind froze her, or until the Indians came, or a bear. She wanted to be where he had died—and yet she could not abandon the boy, Woodrow Call, whose wounds were far from healed. He still might take a deep infection; even if he didn't, he might freeze if she was not there to warm him.

The cold had had a bad effect on Johnny Carthage's sore leg. He struggled mightily to keep up, and yet as the day went on he fell farther and farther behind. Most of the Mexican soldiers were freezing, too. They had no interest in the lame Texan, who dropped back into their ranks, and then behind their ranks.

"I'll catch you, I'll catch you," Johnny said, over and over, though the Mexicans weren't listening.

By midafternoon some of the other Texans had begun to lag, and many of the Mexican infantrymen as well. The marchers were strung out over a mile—then, over two. Bigfoot went ahead, hoping for a glimpse of the village they were seeking—but he saw nothing, just the level desert plain. Behind them there was a low bank of dark clouds—perhaps it meant more snow. He felt confident that he himself could weather the night, even without fire, but he knew that many of the men wouldn't—they would freeze, unless they reached shelter.

"I wonder if we even know where we're going—we might be missing that town," Bigfoot said, to Gus. "If we miss it we're in for frosty sleeping."

"I don't want to miss it—I hope they have goats," Gus said. He was half carrying Call at the time.

Bigfoot dropped back to speak with Salazar—the Captain was plodding on, but he was glassy eyed from pain and fatigue.

"Captain, I'm fearful," Bigfoot said. "Have you been to this place —what's it called?"

"San Saba," Salazar said. "No, I have not been to it."

"I hope it's there," Bigfoot said. "We've got some folks that won't make it through the night unless we find shelter. Some of them are my boys, but quite a few of them are yours."

"I know that, but I am not a magician," Salazar said. "I cannot make houses where there are no houses, or trees where there are no trees."

"Why don't you let us go, Captain?" Bigfoot asked. "We ain't all going to survive this. Why risk your boys just to take us south? Caleb Cobb was the man who thought up this expedition, and he's dead."

Captain Salazar rode on, still glassy eyed, for some time before answering. When he did speak, his voice was cracked and hoarse.

"I cannot let you go, Mr. Wallace," he said. "I'm a military man, and I have my orders."

"Dumb orders, I'd say," Bigfoot said. "We ain't worth freezing to death for. We haven't killed a single one of your people. All we've done is march fifteen hundred miles to make fools of ourselves, and now we're in a situation where half of us won't live even if you do let us go. What's the point?"

Salazar managed a smile, though the effort made his face twist in pain.

"I didn't say my orders were intelligent, merely that they were mine," he said. "I've been a military man for twenty years, and most of my orders have been foolish. I could have been killed many times, because of foolish orders. Now I have been given an order so foolish that I would laugh and cry if I weren't so cold and in such pain."

Bigfoot said nothing. He just watched Salazar.

"Of course, you are right," Salazar went on. "You marched a long way to make fools of yourselves and you have done no harm to my people. If you had, by the way, you would have been shot— then all of us would have been spared this wind. But my orders are still mine. I have to take you to El Paso, or die trying."

"It might be the latter, Captain," Bigfoot said. "I don't like that cloud."

Soon, a driving sleet peppered the men's backs. As dusk fell, it became harder to see—the sleet coated the ground and made each step agony for those with cold feet.

"I fear we've lost Johnny," Bigfoot said. "He's back there somewhere, but I can't see him. He might be a mile back—or he might be froze already."

"I'll go back and get him," Long Bill said.

"I wouldn't," Bigfoot said. "You need all you've got, to make it yourself."

"No, Johnny's my *compañero*," Long Bill said. "I reckon I'll go back. If we die tonight, I expect I should be with Johnny."

It took Gus and Matilda both to keep Call going. The sleet thickened on the ground, until it became too slippery for him to manage. Finally, the two of them carried him, his arms over their shoulders, his body warmed between their bodies.

As the darkness came on and the sleet blew down the wind like bird shot, doom was in the mind of every man. All of them, even Bigfoot Wallace, veteran of many storms, felt that it was likely that they would die during the night. Long Bill had gone loyally back into the teeth of the storm, to find his *compañero*, Johnny Carthage. Captain Salazar was slumped over the neck of his horse, unconscious. His neck wound had continued to bleed until he grew faint and passed out. The Mexican soldiers walked in a cluster, except for those who lagged. They had only one lantern; the light illumined only a few feet of the frigid darkness. As the darkness deepened, the cold increased, and the men began to give up. Texan and Mexican alike came to a moment of resignation—they ceased to be able to pick their feet up and inch forward over the slippery ground. They thought but to rest a moment, until their energies were restored; but the rest lengthened, and they did not get up. The sleet coated their clothes. At first they sat, their backs to the wind and the sleet. Then the will to struggle left them, and they lay down and let the sleet cover them.

It was Gus McCrae, with his keen vision, who first saw a tiny flicker of light, far ahead.

"Why, it's a fire," he said. "If it ain't a fire, it's some kind of light."

"Where?" Matilda asked. "I can't see nothing but sleet."

"No, there's a fire, I seen it," Gus said. "I expect it's that town."

One of the Mexican soldiers heard him, and prodded his captain awake.

Salazar, too, felt that he would not survive the night. The wound Caleb Cobb had given him was worse than he had thought—he had bled all day, the blood freezing on his coat. Now a soldier had awakened him with some rumour of a light, although the sleet was blowing and he himself could not see past his horse's head. There was no light, no town. The blood had dripped down to his pants, which were frozen to the saddle. Instead of delivering the invading Texans to El Paso and being promoted, at least to major for his valour in capturing them, his lot would be to die in a sleet storm on the frozen plain. He thought of shooting himself, but his hands were so cold he feared he would merely drop his pistol, if he tried to pull it out. The pistol, too, was coated in bloody ice—it might not even shoot.

Then Gus saw the light again, and yelled out, hoping somebody ahead would hear him.

"There's the light—there it is, we're close," he said.

This time, Bigfoot saw it, too.

"By God, he's right," he said. "We're coming to someplace with a fire."

Then he heard something that sounded like the bleating of sheep —the men who heard it all perked up. If there were sheep, they might not starve. Captain Salazar suddenly felt better.

"I remember the stories," he said. "There is a spring—an underground river. They raise sheep here—this must be San Saba. I thought it was just a lie—a traveler's lie, about the sheep and the spring. Most travelers lie, and few sheep cross this desert. But maybe it is true."

One by one, hopeful for the first time in days, the men plodded on toward the light. Now and then they lost it in the sleet, and their hopes sank, but Gus McCrae had taken a bead on the light, and, leaving Matilda to support Woodrow Call, led the troop into the little village of San Saba. There were not many adobe huts, but there were many, many sheep. The ones they heard bleating were in a little rail corral behind the jefe's hut, and the jefe himself, an old man with a large belly, was helping a young ewe bring forth her first kid. The light they had seen was his light. At first, he was surprised and alarmed by the spectral appearance of the Texans, all of them white with the sleet that covered their clothes. The old man had no weapon—he could do nothing but stare; also, the ewe was at her crisis and he could not afford to worry about the men who appeared out of the night, until he had delivered the kid. Although he had many sheep, he also lost many—to the cold, to wolves and coyotes and cougars. He wanted to see that the kid was correctly delivered before he had to face the wild men who had come in on a stormy night into the village. He thought they might be ghosts—if they were ghosts, perhaps the wind would blow them on, out of the village, leaving him to attend to his flock.

Captain Salazar, cheered by the knowledge that his troop was saved, became a captain again and soon had reassured the jefe that they were not ghosts, but a detachment of the Mexican army, on an important mission involving dangerous captives.

It was not hard to convince the jefe that the Texans were dangerous men—they looked as wild as Apaches, to the old man. Once the kid was delivered, the jefe immediately sprang to work and soon had the whole village up, building fires and preparing food for the starving men. Several sheep were slaughtered, while the women set about making coffee and tortillas.

Because it was Gus who had seen the light and saved the troop, Captain Salazar decreed that the Texans would not be bound. He was aware that he himself would have missed the light and probably the village, in which case all his men would have died. There would have been no medals, and no promotion. The Texans were put in a shed where the sheep were sheared, with a couple of good fires to warm them. Gus, sitting with Call, soon got to hear the very sound he had dreamt of: the sound of fat sizzling, as it dripped into a fire.

Some of the men were too tired even to wait for food. They took a little hot coffee, grew drowsy, and tipped over. The floor of the shed was covered with a coat of sheep's wool, mixed with dirt. The wool made some of the men sneeze, but that was a minor irritation.

"I guess we lost Long Bill," Bigfoot said.

"If we lost him, we lost Johnny too," Gus said. "He should have waited until we found this town. Maybe one of the Mexicans would have gone back with us and we could have found Johnny."

Matilda was silent by the fire. All she could think about was that Shadrach was dead. He had wanted to take her west, to California. He had promised her; but now that prospect was lost.

Long after most of the Texans had eaten a good hunk of mutton and gone to sleep, there was a shout from the Mexicans. Long Bill Coleman, his clothes a suit of ice, came walking slowly into the circle of fires, carrying Johnny Carthage in his arms. Johnny, too, seemed to be sheathed in ice—at first, no one could say whether Johnny Carthage was alive or dead.

He laid his friend down by the warmest campfire and himself stood practically in the flames, shaking and trembling from cold and from exertion. He held out his hands to the fire; he was so close that ice began to melt off his clothes.

"If that's mutton, I'll have some," he said. "I swear, it's been a cold walk."

33.

FOR THREE DAYS THE Texans, under guard again, never left their sheep shed, except to answer calls of nature. Captain Salazar's escort had been reduced by more than twenty men, lost and presumed frozen back along the sleety trail—six Texans failed to make the village. The weather stayed so cold that most of the men were glad of the confinement. They were allowed ample firewood, and plenty to eat. Blackie Slidell had to have two frostbitten toes removed—Bigfoot Wallace performed the operation with a sharp bowie knife—but no one else required amputations.

Once the people of the village realized that the Texans were not spectres, they were friendly. The old jefe, still much occupied with his lambing in the terrible weather, saw that they had ample food. The men could drink coffee all day—poor coffee, but warming. Noticing that Call was injured, one old woman asked to look at his back; when she saw the blackened scabs, she drew in her breath and hurried away.

A few minutes later the woman returned, another woman at her side. The other woman was so short she scarcely came to Bigfoot's waist. She had with her a little pot—she went quickly to Call, but instead of lifting his shirt as the first woman had, she put her thin face close to his back and sniffed.

"Hell, she's smelling you," Bigfoot said. "I wonder if you smell like venison."

Bigfoot's remarks were sometimes so foolish that Call was irritated by them. Why would he smell like venison? And why was the wizened little Mexican woman smelling him, anyway? He was passive, though—he didn't answer Bigfoot, and he didn't move away from the woman. The village women had been unexpectedly kind—the food they brought was warm and tasty; one woman had even given him an old serape to cover himself with. It had holes in it, but it was thickly woven and kept out the chill. He thought perhaps the tiny woman who was sniffing him was some kind of healer; he knew he was in no position to reject help. He was still very weak, often feverish, and always in pain. He could survive while in the warmth of the sheep shed, but if he were forced to march and was caught in another sleet storm, he might not live. He could not ask Gus or Matilda to carry him again, as they had the first time.

The little woman sniffed him thoroughly, as a dog might, and then set her pot in the edge of the nearest campfire. She squatted by it, muttering words no one could understand. When she judged the medicine to be ready, she gestured for Call to remove his shirt; she then spent more than two hours rubbing the hot ointment into his back. She carefully kneaded his muscles and spread the ointment gently along the line of every scar. At first the ointment burned so badly that Call thought he would not be able to stand the pain. The burning was far worse than what he could remember of the whipping itself. For several minutes, Gus and Matilda had to talk to him, in an effort to distract him from the burning; at one point, they thought they might have to restrain him, but Call gritted his teeth and let the little woman do her work. In time a warmth spread through his body and he slept soundlessly, without moaning, for the first time since the whipping.

The next day, through a crack in the wall, Gus saw the same woman applying ointment to Captain Salazar's neck. The Captain looked weak. He had taken a fever, which soared so high that he was sometimes incoherent; the jefe took him into his house and the little woman tended him until the fever dropped. Even so, the Captain was at first too weak to walk in a straight line. He wanted to stay and rest in San Saba, but when the weather warmed a little, he decided he had better take advantage of it and press on. He came to the Texans' shed, to inform them of his decision.

"Enjoy a warm night," he told them. "We leave tomorrow."

"How many days before we get across this dead man's walk?" Long Bill asked.

"Señor, we have not yet come to the Jornada," Salazar said. "The land here is fertile because of the underground water. Once we get beyond where the sheep are, we will start the dead man's walk."

The Texans were silent. They had all convinced themselves that the day of the sleet would be their worst day. They had forgotten that Salazar said the dead man's walk was two hundred miles across. They had grown used to the coziness of the shed, and the warmth of the campfires. Each of them could remember the bitter cold, the pain of marching on frozen feet, the sleet, and the hopeless sense that they would die if they didn't find warmth.

They had found warmth; but Salazar had just reminded them that the hardest part of the journey had not even begun. Some of the men hunched closer to the campfires, holding out their hands to the warmth—they wanted to hug the warmth, keep it as long as they could. Few of them slept—they wanted to sit close to the fires and enjoy every bit of warmth left to them. They wanted the warmth to last forever, or at least until summertime. Johnny Carthage, terrified that he would fall so far behind that Long Bill Coleman couldn't find him and rescue him, asked over and over again, through the night, how long it would be until morning.

Informed by the old jefe that there was neither food nor water enough for many horses in the barren region that awaited them, Salazar kept only one horse—his own—and traded several for two donkeys and as much provender as the donkeys could carry. On the morning of departure, abruptly, he decided to reduce the force to twenty-five men. He reasoned that twenty-five could probably hold off the Apaches, if they attacked—more than twenty-five would be impossible to provision on such a journey. The Texans alone would account for most of the provisions the donkeys could carry.

What that meant was that the Texans would slightly outnumber his own force; and the Texans, man for man, were stronger than his troops.

"Señores, you will have to be tied," he informed the Texans, when they were led out into the cold air. "I regret it, but it is necessary. I can afford no risks on this journey—crossing the dead man's walk is risk enough."

Bigfoot swelled up at this news—Gus thought he was going to make a fight. But he held on to his temper and let his wrists be bound with rawhide thongs, when his turn came. The other men did the same. Even Call was tied, though Matilda lodged a strong protest.

"This boy's hurt—he can't do nothing—why tie him?" she asked.

"Because he has fury in him," Captain Salazar said. "I saw it myself. He almost killed Colonel Cobb while he was riding in our General's buggy. If I had to choose only one of you to tie, I would tie Corporal Call."

"I suppose that's a compliment, ain't it?" Gus said.

"I don't care what it is," Call said. Since the old woman had treated him with her ointment he could at least stretch his muscles without groaning in pain. He glared at the young Mexican who tied him, although he knew the boy was simply doing his job.

Many of the women of San Saba broke into tears when they saw the Texans being tied. Some of them had formed motherly attachments to one prisoner or another. Some pressed additional food, tortillas or pieces of jerky into the men's hands as they were marched through the street, out of the village.

The fertile country lasted only three miles. By the fourth mile, only the smallest scrub grew. Soon even that disappeared—before them, as far ahead as they could see, was a land where nothing grew.

"This is the dead man's walk," Captain Salazar said. "Now we will see who wants to live and who wants to die."

"I intend to live," Gus said, at once.

Call said nothing.

"Even the Apaches won't cross it," Salazar said.

One-eyed Johnny Carthage looked at the emptiness before them, and was filled with dread.

"What's the matter, Johnny?" Long Bill said, noting his friend's haggard look. "It's warmer now, and we got food. We'll get across this like we got across the plains."

Johnny Carthage heard what Long Bill said, but didn't believe him. He looked at the great space before them and shivered—not from cold, but from fear.

He felt that he was looking at his death.

part III

1.

ON THE FOURTH NIGHT out from San Saba, a warm night that left the men encouraged, Captain Salazar's horse and both donkeys disappeared. Some of their provisions were still on the donkeys—they had traveled late and had only unpacked what they needed for the evening meal, corn mostly, with a little dried mutton.

Captain Salazar had tethered his horse so close to his pallet that the lead rope was in reach of his hand as he slept. He had only to turn over to reassure himself that his horse was there. But when he did turn over, in the grey dawn, all he had left was the end of the lead rope, which had been cut. The horse was gone.

"I thought you said Indians didn't come here," Bigfoot said, annoyed. He had wondered at the laxness of the Mexicans, in setting no guard. The foot soldiers had simply lain down and slept where they stopped, with no thought of anything but rest. The Texans did the same, but the Texans were tied—guard duty was not their responsibility.

Captain Salazar was silent, shocked by what had happened and what it meant. He stared for a long time across the dry plain, as if hoping to see his horse and the donkeys, grazing peacefully. But all he saw was the barren earth, with an edge of sun poking above it to the east.

Bigfoot had to repeat his statement.

"I guess those Indians that don't come here took your horse," he said.

"Gomez took my horse," Salazar said. "Gomez is not like the rest. He has no fear of this country. No one else would be so bold."

"That rope he cut was about three feet from your throat," Bigfoot remarked. "He could have cut your throat if he'd wanted to."

Captain Salazar was looking at the cut end of the lead rope. A scalpel could not have cut it more cleanly. Bigfoot was right: Gomez could easily have cut his throat.

"He could have, but there would have been little sport," he said. "We must walk."

By midmorning all the men felt the air, which had been warm, turn chill. The north wind picked up.

"Oh God, I don't want it to get cold," Johnny Carthage said. "I wouldn't mind to die if I could just do it warm." The great dread had not left him.

"Shut up your complaining, it's just a breeze so far," Long Bill said. "I carried you once and I'll carry you again, if it comes to that."

"No you won't, Bill—you can't carry me no hundred miles," Johnny said, but the wind was already howling at their backs, and no one heard him.

Call walked between Matilda and Gus—he was still unsteady on his feet and was swept, at times, by waves of fever that made his vision swirl. Matilda was the only one of the Texans who had not been tied. Captain Salazar had come to like her—from time to time, she consented to play cards with him. He would not fraternize to that extent with the prisoners, and his own men were mostly too young to be good cardplayers. An old bear hunter had taught him rummy—it was mostly rummy that he played with Matilda Jane.

As they were stumbling along, pushed by the cold north wind, Gus happened to look back, a habit he got into after his encounter with the grizzly bear. He could not get Bigfoot's story about the man who had been stalked while fishing out of his mind. It was worrisome that bears could be so stealthy.

When he glanced over his shoulder he got a bad start, for something large and brown was hurtling down toward them. Whatever it was was still far away—he could only see a shape, but it was a brown shape, the very color of a bear.

"Captain, get the rifles!" he yelled, in consternation. "There's a bear after us."

For a moment, the whole troop believed him—no one could clearly determine what was moving toward them, but something was, and fast. Salazar lined his men up and had them ready, their guns primed.

"I wish you'd let me shoot, Captain," Bigfoot said. "Your boys are so scared I expect half of them will miss."

"I expect it, too," Salazar said. He walked over to the nearest soldier and took his musket. He walked over to Bigfoot, untied his hands, and handed him the musket.

"The last time I handed a Texan a gun, he shot me," Salazar reminded him. "Please be honorable, Mr. Wallace. Shoot the bear. If we kill it we will have meat enough to make it across the dead man's walk."

Just then, Gus saw something that was even more unnerving: the bear leapt high in the air. It seemed to fly for several yards, before coming back to earth.

"Good Lord, it's flying," he said.

As he said it, the shape flew again—the whole troop was transfixed, even Bigfoot. He had heard many bear stories, but no one had ever told him that grizzly bears could fly. He squatted and leveled his musket, though the bear—if it was a bear—was still far away.

Some of the young Mexican soldiers became so nervous that they began firing when the hurtling brown object was still two hundred yards away. Salazar was irritated. The wind whirled dust from the plain high, so that it was hard to see anything clearly.

"Don't fire until I say fire," he said. "If you all fire now you will be out of bullets when the bear gets here, and he will eat us all."

"I'm saving my bullet," Bigfoot said. "I intend to shoot him right between the eyes—that's the only sure way to stop a bear."

Just then, the hurtling brown object collided with a hump of rocks and flew high in the air, above the dust. For the first time Bigfoot saw it clearly and he immediately lowered his rifle.

"Boys, old Gomez has got us rattled," he said. "That ain't a bear —that's a tumbleweed."

Salazar looked disgusted.

"Seven of you shot, and the tumbleweed is still coming," he said.

"Why, it's the size of a house," Gus said. He had never imagined a weed could grow so big. It hurtled by the company, rolling over and over, as fast as a man could run. From time to time it hit a bump or a small rock and sailed into the air. Soon it was a hundred yards to the south, and then it vanished, obscured by the blowing dust.

"Let us have no more talk of bears," Salazar said, looking at Gus.

They marched late into the night, with only a few bites of food. In San Saba the men had been given gourds, to use as water carriers —some of them had already drunk the last of their water, while others still had a little. The temperature had dropped and all the men longed for a fire, but there was nothing to burn, except the branches of a few thin bushes. The Texans gathered enough sticks to make a small blaze and were about to light it when Salazar stopped them.

"No fires tonight," he said.

"Why not?" Gus asked. "I'd like to warm my toes."

"Gomez will see it if he is still following us," Salazar said.

"Why would he follow us—he's done got our donkeys and most of our food," Bigfoot asked.

"He might follow us to kill us," Salazar replied.

"He could have killed you last night and he didn't," Bigfoot said. "Why would he walk another day just to do what he could already have done?"

"Because he is an Apache, Señor," Salazar said. "He is not like us. He may have gone home—I don't know. But I want no fires tonight."

By midnight, the cold had become so intense that the men were forced to huddle together for warmth. Even huddled, they were so cold that several of them ceased to be able to feel their feet. Johnny Carthage could not overcome his dread. He tried to think of the sunlight of south Texas, but all he could think of was the terrible white sleet that had nearly taken his life a few days before. He was squeezed up against Long Bill—he could feel his friend shivering. Long Bill shivered violently, but slept, his mouth open, his breath a cloud of white in the cold night. Johnny began to wish that Bill would wake up. Bill had been his pard—his *compañero*. Bill had risked his life to locate him and bring him out of the terrible sleet storm. Now the dread of the cold was overwhelming him—he wanted Long Bill to sense it and wake up, to talk him out of what he meant to do with the small knife he had just taken out of his pocket. He wanted his oldest and best friend to help him through the night. Johnny Carthage began to tremble even more violently than the man he was huddled against. He trembled so that he could scarcely hold the knife, or raise the blade. He didn't want to drop the knife. If he did, he might not have the strength to find it in the freezing night. He didn't want to wake his friend, so tired from the long day's march; yet, he needed his help and began to cry quietly, in despair. He didn't want to live, his hope was broken; no more did he want to die, without his friend to help him. There was no sound on all the plain except the breathing of the exhausted men around him. The darkness was spotted with little clouds—the white breath of his *compañeros*. Johnny's gimpy leg was aching terribly from the cold; his foot twitched, twitched, twitched; though he could not feel his foot he felt the twitching, regular as the ticking of a clock.

"Dern this leg," he whispered. "Dern this leg."

Then he opened the knife, and put the blade against his throat—but the blade was so cold that he withdrew it. He began to sob, at the knowledge that he hadn't the strength to push the cold knife blade into his throat and cut. It meant he would freeze, but he could not do it amid the Rangers, because they would insist on making him go on. They would not accept the fact that he didn't want to live anymore.

Johnny put the knife to his throat again, but again he withdrew it. The tip made a tiny cut in his neck and the cold seared the cut, like a brand. Johnny quietly moved an inch away from Long Bill, and then another. Slowly, waking no one, he eased out from the midst of the Rangers, a foot at a time. Even when he had slipped beyond the sound of their breathing, he merely scooted over the cold ground, a foot at a time.

Of all the Texans, only Matilda Roberts was awake. At night she had taken to sleeping between the two boys, making Call turn his torn back to her so she could warm it. Gus slept on the other side, squeezed up against her as close as he could get. Both boys slept, but Matilda didn't. She saw Johnny Carthage—he crawled right by her. As he was about to go into the night he felt her gaze, and turned to look at her for a moment. He could only see her outline, not her face; nor could she see him clearly, yet she knew who he was and where he was going. Johnny paused in his crawl. The two of them looked at one another, through the darkness. Matilda opened her mouth, but closed it again, without speaking. Johnny Carthage was beyond her words—but she did reach out and squeeze his arm. She heard him sob; he touched her arm for a moment, before he crawled away. "Oh, Johnny," she whispered, but she didn't try to stop him. Since Shadrach's death she had used her strength for the boys, Gus and Call—one was hurt, and the other was foolish. It would take all her strength, and perhaps more than her strength, to get them across the desert. She could not save them and Johnny Carthage, too—nor could Long Bill save his friend without losing his own chance to live. If the cold didn't take Johnny, the stony ground would grind at him until it broke him. If he wanted to make his own end, she felt it was wrong to stop him. His chances were slight at best; there was no point in his suffering beyond his strength.

Even so, it was hard to listen to the scraping of his poor leg, as he dragged himself over the hard ground, into the icy night. But the scraping grew faint, and then very faint. Soon she could hear nothing but the breathing of the two boys who slept beside her. Since the day when Caleb Cobb had struck his foot with the rifle barrel, Call had limped almost as badly as Johnny. Probably there were broken bones, somewhere in his foot—but he was young. The broken bones would heal.

Johnny Carthage crawled on until he figured he was almost two hundred yards from camp. He had worn one of his pants legs through and scraped one of his knees on the icy ground. Bigfoot had once told him that freezing men felt a warmth come over them, near the end; when he judged that he was far enough from camp not to be found, even if Long Bill should wake and miss him and come looking, he stopped and sat, shivering violently. He waited for the warmth in which he could sleep and die—he had been cold long enough; he was ready for the warmth, but the warmth didn't come—only a deeper cold, a cold that seeped inside him and chilled his lungs, his liver, even his heart.

Desperate for the warmth, he opened his little knife again and clutched it tightly, meaning to plunge it into his neck, where the great vein was. But before he could grasp the knife tightly enough in his shivering hands, he looked up and saw a shadow between himself and the starlight. Someone was there, a presence he felt but could not see. Before he could think more about it, Gomez struck. Johnny Carthage finally felt the longed-for warmth—a warm flood, flowing down his chest and onto his freezing hands. For a moment, he was grateful: whoever was there, between him and the cold stars, had taken a hard task off his hands. Then he slipped down and the shadow was astride him, opening his pants. Before Gomez struck again, one-eyed Johnny Carthage had ceased to mind the cold, or to feel the pain of the knife that had severed his privates. Oh, Bill, he thought—then all thoughts ceased.

Gomez wiped his knife on Johnny Carthage's pants leg, and moved quietly toward the Mexican camp. Long before he got there, he heard the snores of several sleeping men. He had planned to kill the shivering Mexican sentries and take their guns, but when he realized that the large woman was awake, he changed his mind. He did not want the large woman to know he was there. The night before, in the little cave where he rested, he had seen a snake, though it was much too cold for snakes to be moving about; worse, late in the night, he had heard the call of an owl, though he was far out on the malpais, where no owls flew. He knew it must be the large woman who summoned the snake and the old owl to places where they should never be. He knew the large woman must be a witch, for only a witch would be traveling through the malpais with so many men.

Gomez knew that the large woman had been the woman of Tail-Of-The-Bear, and Tail-Of-The-Bear had been a great man, perhaps a shaman. Gomez turned away from the camp at once; he did not want the witch to find out that he was near. If she knew, she might summon the owl again—the buu—and to hear the call of the buu twice meant death.

Gomez skirted the camp and walked several miles, to where he had left his two sons. One of them had found a wolf den that day—

they had made a little fire and were cooking the wolf pups they had caught. Gomez wanted to eat one of the young wolves—it would give him cunning, and protect him from the buu and the witch, the large woman who had traveled with Tail-Of-The-Bear.

2.

Long Bill Coleman was frantic, when he discovered that Johnny Carthage had left him in the night. He felt guilty for not having watched his friend more closely.

"I expect he just went for a walk, to keep warm," he said. "I ought to have kept him warmer, but it was hard, without no fire."

Bigfoot did not suppose that Johnny Carthage had merely walked into the night to keep his feet warm; nor did Captain Salazar believe it. A few hundred yards to the east, they saw four buzzards circling.

"Bill, he went off to die—got tired of this shivering," Matilda said, before Gus or anyone could comment on the buzzards. It was colder that day than it had been the day before. The whole troop was shivering.

Salazar allowed the Texans to burn their few pitiful sticks, but the blaze was not even sufficient to boil coffee. It died, and the only warmth they had was the warmth of their own breath—they all stood around blowing on their hands. When Long Bill saw the buzzards and realized what they meant, he had to be restrained from running to bury his friend.

"Bill, the buzzards have been at him," Bigfoot said. "Anyway, we got nothing to bury him with. Gus and me will go and take a look, just to be sure it wasn't some varmint that froze to death."

"Yes, go look," Salazar said. "But hurry. We can't wait."

When Gus saw the torn, white body of Johnny Carthage he immediately turned his back. Bigfoot, though, shooed the buzzards away and took a closer look. What he saw didn't please him. Johnny's throat had been slashed, and his privates cut off. The buzzards hadn't cut his throat, nor had they castrated him. Bigfoot circled the body, hoping to see a man track—something that would allow him to gauge the strength of their opponents. If several Apaches had been there, that would be one thing. It would mean that none of them could sleep safe until they moved beyond the Apache country. But if Gomez was so confident that he would come to the camp alone, take a horse, kill a man—or several men —then they were up against someone as formidable as Buffalo Hump—someone they probably could not beat.

As Gus stood with his back turned, trying to keep his heaving stomach under control, Bigfoot remembered the dream he had had back on the Pecos, the dream in which Buffalo Hump and Gomez were riding together, to make war on anyone in their path, Mexican or white. Now, in a way, that dream had come true, even though the two Indians might be hundreds of miles apart, and might have never met. Buffalo Hump had almost killed them on the prairie, and now Gomez was cutting them down in the New Mexican desert. If the two men, Comanche and Apache, ever did join forces, the little troop standing around in the cold would have no chance. Texans and Mexicans alike would be drained of blood like poor one-eyed Johnny Carthage, their throats cut, and their balls thrown to the varmints.

He looked across the long, barren plain, hoping to see some sign —a wolf, a bird, a fleeing antelope, anything at all that would tell him where the Apaches were. But the plain was completely empty —only the grey clouds moved at all. Gus McCrae had dropped to his knees—despite himself, his stomach turned over; he retched and retched and retched. Bigfoot waited for him to finish, and then led him back to camp. He didn't tell Gus what he knew, or what he feared. The troop was close to panic anyway—panic and despair, from the cold and hunger and the knowledge that they were on a journey that many of them would not live to finish.

"Did he freeze?" Long Bill asked, grief stricken, when Bigfoot came back.

"Well, he's froze now, yes," Bigfoot said. "We should get to walking."

Call's hurt feet were paining him even more than they had been. He had wobbled the day before, coming over a ridge; he hit his foot on a rock, and since then, had had a sharp pain in his right foot, as if a bone thin as a needle was poking him every time he put his foot down.

All that day he struggled to keep up, helped by Matilda and Gus. He noticed that Bigfoot kept looking back, turning every few minutes to survey the desert behind them. It became so noticeable that Call finally asked Gus about it.

"Did Johnny just freeze?" he asked.

"I don't know," Gus said. "All I seen was his body," Gus said. "The buzzards had been at him."

"I know the buzzards had been at him, but were the buzzards *all* that had been at him?" Call asked.

"He means did an Indian kill him," Matilda asked. She too had noticed Bigfoot's nervousness.

Gus had not even thought about Indians—he supposed that Johnny had just gone off to walk himself warm, but had failed at it and frozen. He had only glimpsed the body from a distance—it was blood splotched, like the body of Josh Corn had been, but he had supposed the buzzards had accounted for the blood. Now, though, once he tried to recall what he had seen, he wasn't sure. The thought that an Indian had found Johnny and killed him was too disturbing to consider.

"I expect he just died," Gus said.

The answer didn't satisfy Call—Johnny Carthage had survived several bitter nights. Why would he suddenly die, on a night that was no colder than the others? But Call saw that Gus was going to be of no help. Gus didn't like to look at dead bodies. He could not be relied on to report accurately.

Bigfoot was tempted to tell Captain Salazar what had happened to Johnny Carthage. He had a hard time keeping secrets. The day was bitter cold. The Texans were still bound at the wrists, and their hands began to freeze, from lack of circulation. As dusk came, Bigfoot felt his anger rising. Very likely, they were going to die on the dead man's walk—he reflected ruefully that the sandy stretch of country was accurately named. Why tie the hands of men who were all but dead anyway? His anger rose, and he strode up to Salazar and fell in beside him.

"Captain, Johnny Carthage didn't freeze to death," he said. "He was kilt."

Salazar was almost at the end of his strength—the pace he set was not a military pace, but the pace of a man unused to walking. His family had a small hacienda—all his life he had ridden. Without his horse, he felt weak. Also, he liked to eat—the cold, the wound on his neck, and the lack of food had weakened him. Now, just as they faced another day with little food and another night without fire, the big Texan came to him with unwelcome news.

"How was he killed?" he asked.

"Throat cut," Bigfoot said. "He was castrated, too, but I expect he was past feeling, when that happened."

"Why did you wait so long to tell me this, Señor Wallace?" Salazar asked. He kept walking, slowly; he had not looked at Bigfoot.

"Because this whole bunch is about to give up," Bigfoot said. "They'll panic and start deserting. Whoever killed Johnny will pick them off, one by one."

"Gomez," Captain Salazar said. "He's toying with us."

"Untie us, Captain," Bigfoot said. "Our hands will freeze this way. We'll fight with you, against the Apache—but we can't fight if our hands are frozen off. I couldn't hold a rifle steady now. My hands are too cold."

Salazar looked back at the stumbling Texans. They were weak and cold, but they still looked stronger than his own men. He knew that Bigfoot Wallace was right. His men wouldn't go much farther, unless they found food. They would flee toward the mountains, or else simply sit down and die. Gomez was the wolf who would finish them, in his own way.

He knew that if he freed the Texans, and they saw a chance, they would overpower his men, kill them, or else take their guns and leave them to their fate. To free them was to accept a large risk.

Yet, at least if it came to battle, the Texans would shoot—they wouldn't cut and run.

"No white man has ever seen Gomez," he told Bigfoot. "No Mexican, either. We caught his wife and killed her. We have killed two of his sons. But Gomez we have never seen. He cut my rope, not a yard from my head. And yet I have never seen him."

"I don't want to see the fellow," Bigfoot said. "If I can just avoid him, I'll be better off."

"Any Apache can be Gomez," Salazar said. "He might be dead. His sons might be killing for him now—we only killed two, and he has many. It is hard to fight a man you never see."

"I've seen him," Bigfoot said.

Salazar was startled. "*You've* seen him?" he asked.

"I dreamed him," Bigfoot said. "We was on the Rio Grande, trying to lay out the road to El Paso. I was with Major Chevallie— he's dead now. In my dream I seen Gomez and Buffalo Hump riding together. They were going to attack Chihuahua City and make all your people slaves—the ones they didn't kill."

Salazar kept walking.

"I'm glad it was only in Chihuahua City," he said.

"Why?" Bigfoot asked.

"Because I don't live in Chihuahua City," Salazar said. "If they had tried to take Santa Fe they would have done better than you Texans did."

"I expect so," Bigfoot said. "Will you untie us, Captain? We won't fight you. We might help save you."

"Why is this land without wood?" Salazar asked. "If we had wood and could make fires and be warm, we might survive."

"Just untie us, Captain," Bigfoot said. "We wouldn't be killing these boys of yours. Most of them ain't but half grown. We don't kill pups."

Salazar walked back through the Texans; he saw that they were suffering much, from their bound hands.

"Untie them," he told his men. "But be watchful. I want the best marksmen to stand guard at night and to flank these men during the day. Shoot them if they try to flee."

That night, again, there was no fire. All day they had looked for wood, without seeing even a stick. Six riflemen guarded the Texans, with their muskets ready. Late in the night, while Texans and Mexicans alike shivered in their sleep, two of the guards walked off a little ways, to piss.

In the morning their bodies, cut as Johnny Carthage's had been cut, were found less than fifty yards from camp.

This time there was no hiding the truth, from Gus McCrae or anyone.

"He's stalking us," Bigfoot said. "Ain't that right, Captain?"

"It is time to march," Salazar said.

3.

FOR THREE DAYS CALL could not put his right foot to the ground. Matilda and Gus took turns supporting him, alternating throughout the day. On the second day the whole company, Mexicans and Texans alike, were so weak they were barely able to stumble along. They made less than ten miles.

"If we can't make no better time than this, we might as well sit down and die," Bigfoot said. He himself could have made better time than that, but he did not want to desert his companions—not yet—not until he had to save himself.

In the afternoon of the second day, Jimmy Tweed, the gangly boy, gave up. He had turned his ankle the day before, crossing a shallow gully; now the ankle was so swollen that he could scarcely put his foot to the ground.

Salazar saw Jimmy Tweed sink down, and went over to him at once. He knew that the whole troop was ready to do what Jimmy Tweed had just done—sit down and wait to die. It was an option he could not allow his men, or the Texans, who, though no longer tied, were his captives. If the Texans began to give up, his own men might follow suit, and soon the whole party would be lost.

"Get up, Señor," Salazar said. "We will make camp soon. You can rest your ankle then."

"Nope, I'm staying, Captain," Jimmy Tweed said. "I'd just as soon stop here as a mile or two from here."

"Señor, I cannot permit it," Salazar said. "We would all like to stop—but you are a prisoner under guard, and I make the decisions about where we stop."

Jimmy Tweed just smiled. His lips were blue from the cold. He stared through Salazar, as if the man were not there.

Salazar saw that all his soldiers were watching him. Jimmy Tweed made no effort to stand up and walk. Most of the Texans were some ways ahead; they were not paying attention; each man had his own problems—none had noticed that Jimmy Tweed had stopped.

Wearily, Salazar drew his pistol and cocked it.

"Señor, I will ask you courteously to get up and walk a little farther," he said. "I would rather not shoot you—but I will shoot you if you do not obey me."

Jimmy Tweed looked at him—for a moment, he seemed to consider obeying the order. He put his hands on the ground, as if he meant to push himself up. But after a moment, he ceased all effort.

"Too tired, Captain," he said. "I reckon I'm just too tired."

"I see," Salazar said. He walked around behind Jimmy and shot him in the head.

At the shot, all the Texans turned. Jimmy Tweed had pitched forward on his face, dead.

Salazar walked quickly back to where the group waited, staring at the dead body of their comrade, Jimmy Tweed.

"His sufferings are over, Señores," Salazar said, the pistol still in his hand. "Let's march."

The Mexican soldiers made a show of raising their guns, in case the Texans chose to revolt—but in fact, none revolted. Bigfoot coloured, as if he were about to be seized with one of his great fits of rage, but he held himself in check. Several of the other Texans looked back at the body, sprawled on the dull sand, but in the main they were too numb to care. Several, whose feet were frozen stumps, felt a moment of envy, mixed with sadness. It was hard to dispute Captain Salazar's words. Jimmy's sufferings were over; theirs were not.

"That's two of us that ain't been buried proper," Blackie Slidell said. "I have always supposed I'd be buried proper, but maybe I won't. There's no time for funerals, out here on the baldies."

"Proper—they weren't buried at all," Bigfoot said. "Johnny and Jimmy both got left to the varmints."

Gus had the conviction that they were all going to die. As far as he could see—ahead, behind, or to the side—there was nothing. Just sky and sand. The dead man's walk was a hell of emptiness. His lips were blue from the cold, and his tongue swollen from thirst. Woodrow Call groaned whenever his broken foot touched the ground—even Matilda Roberts, the strongest spirit in the troop, except for Bigfoot, merely trudged along silently. She had not spoken all day.

Matilda had not looked back, when Jimmy Tweed was shot. She didn't want to think about Jimmy Tweed, a boy who had been sweet to her on more than one occasion, bringing her coffee from the campfire, helping her saddle Tom, when she still had Tom. Once he had asked her for her favors, but she had bound herself to Shadrach by then, and had turned him down. He pouted like a little boy at being refused, but got over it in an hour and continued to do her little favors. Now she regretted rebuffing him—Shadrach had been asleep and would never have known. Sweet boys rarely knew how little time they had; now Jimmy's had run out. Matilda put one foot in front of the other, helped Call as much as she could, and trudged on.

That night, Blackie Slidell and six of his chums disappeared. Blackie was of the opinion that there were villages to the west— often he pointed to columns of smoke that no one else could see.

"It's chimney smoke," Blackie said, several times; he was hoping to get the company to swing west.

"It ain't chimney smoke—it ain't smoke at all—it's just you hoping," Bigfoot said. "Gus McCrae has better eyesight than you, and he can't see no smoke over in that direction."

"It might be a piece of a cloud," Gus said. He liked Blackie and didn't want to flatly contradict him, if he could help it.

Blackie saw that he wasn't going to be able to convince Bigfoot or

Salazar that there were villages to the west. But he had become friendly with six boys from Arkansas, and he had better luck with them.

"Hell, I'd like to live to eat one more catfish from the old Arkansas River," one of them, a thin youth named Cotton Lovett, said.

"Or maybe one more possum," Blackie said. He had been down the Arkansas on occasion and remembered that the possums there were fat and easy to catch. The meat of the Arkansas possums was a trifle greasy—several of the Arkansas boys agreed to that—but they were all so hungry that the prospect of grease only made the venture more attractive.

That night, worried about Gomez, Salazar put all his men in a tight circle, facing out, their guns ready. They had crossed a flat lake that afternoon, mainly dry but with just enough smelly puddles to allow the men enough water to boil coffee. Several of the men were already cramping from the effects of the bad water. The Texans had drunk too, and were suffering. Blackie Slidell tried to interest several other men in escaping. He was sure the villages were there. But he found no takers and slipped off about midnight, with the six boys. Call and Gus watched them go—for a moment, Gus felt inclined to go with them, but Call talked him out of it.

"We don't know much about this country, but we do know the Apaches are that way," Call reminded him. "That's one good reason to stay with the troop."

"I would strike out with the boys, but I'm too cold," Gus said. "Anyway, I have to get you home. Clara will think poorly of me, if I don't."

Call didn't answer, but he was surprised—not by his friend's loyalty, but that cold, hungry, lost, and a prisoner, he was still hoping to gain the good opinion of a girl in a general store in Austin. He started to point out what seemed obvious: that the girl had probably forgotten them both, by this time. For all they knew, she could have married. Gus's hopes of winning her were as far-fetched as Blackie Slidell's hopes of finding a friendly village somewhere to the west.

He didn't say that, though; recent experience had shown him that men had to use what hope they could muster, to stay alive.

They sat together through the night, one on either side of Matilda Roberts. For several days the weather had been overcast, but when the dawn came, it was clear. Just seeing the bright sunlight made them feel better, although it was still cold and the prospects still bleak.

Captain Salazar had taken a little of the bad water the day before; he arose so tired and weak that he could scarcely walk to the camp-fire. When a cramp took him he had to bend almost double to endure the pain.

Bad as he was, his troop was worse. Several of his soldiers were too weak to rise. The fact that seven prisoners had escaped the night before didn't interest them—nor did it interest Salazar.

"Their freedom will be temporary," he told Bigfoot.

"How about *our* freedom, Captain?" Bigfoot asked. "Half your men are dying and half of ours too. What's the point of keeping us prisoners when we're all dying? Why can't you just turn us loose and let it be every man for himself? Maybe one or two of us will make it home, if we do it that way."

Call and Gus were there—and Long Bill. Captain Salazar could barely stand on his feet. Even a march of one mile might be beyond him, and they had far more than a mile to go. Bigfoot's request seemed reasonable, to them. If they were let go they might wander off in twos and threes and find food of some sort and live, whereas if the whole troop had to stay together they would probably all starve.

Salazar looked at his troops, many of them unable to rise. He still had at most eight soldiers who could be considered able-bodied men. The Texans had more, but not many more. The end of the dead man's walk was not in sight—it might be three days away, or four, or even five. He thought for a moment before answering Big-foot's request.

He took his pistol out of its holster, checked to see that it was fully loaded, and handed it butt first to Bigfoot Wallace.

"If you want to be free, kill me," he said.

Bigfoot looked at the sick, exhausted man in astonishment.

"Captain, I must have misheard," he said.

"No, you heard correctly," Salazar said. "I have decided that you can be free, if freedom is what you want most. But I am a Mexican officer, under orders to take you to El Paso. There is no one here to countermand my orders, and the General who gave them to me is dead. You saw what the Apaches did to him."

"Well, Captain, I know that," Bigfoot said. "But if the General was here and saw how weak we all are, he might change his mind."

"He might, but we cannot summon him up from hell and ask him," Salazar said. "My orders are still my orders. I cannot free you. But I will allow you the opportunity to free yourselves. All you have to do is shoot me."

Bigfoot held the gun awkwardly, not sure what to make of the Captain's odd decision. He looked at Call, at Gus, at Long Bill Coleman, and at Matilda Roberts. Now and then, throughout their time as prisoners, any one of them would have been happy to have the opportunity to kill Captain Salazar. When Call was being whipped, when they were chained, when Jimmy Tweed was shot— at such moments any of them might have killed him. But Salazar was no longer the cold Captain who chained them or tied them at his whim. He had suffered the same cold and the same hunger as they had, drunk the same bad water and been weakened by the same cramps. He was a weakened man, so weakened that he had calmly ordered his own death.

"Captain, I don't want to shoot you," Bigfoot said. "At times I could have done it easy, I expect, but now you're worse off than we are. I've got no stomach for shooting you now."

Salazar stood his ground. He looked the Texans over.

"If not you, then another," he offered. "Perhaps Corporal Call would shoot me. He endured the lash, and life has not been easy for him since. Surely he would like revenge. His feet are giving him pain, and yet I have kept him walking. Give him the gun."

"Caleb Cobb broke my feet," Call said. "You didn't. I'd shoot you if this was a fight, but I ain't gonna just take your damn gun and shoot you down."

"Corporal McCrae?" Salazar said. "Surely you hate me enough to shoot me," Salazar said, with a small smile.

"I used to, Captain, but I'm too cold and too tired to worry about shooting anybody," Gus said. "I'd just like to go home and get married quick."

Call was annoyed that once again the subject of marriage had come up, and at a time when a man's life was in the balance. They had no prospect of even getting home—why was he so convinced the girl would marry him, even if they did?

[360]

Salazar took his pistol back, and walked over to Matilda Roberts. He held the gun out to her.

"Kill me, Señorita," he said. "Then you will all be free."

"Free to what?" Matilda asked. "It ain't you I need to be freed of —I ain't a prisoner, anyway. What I'd like to be free of is this damn desert, and shooting you won't accomplish that."

"Then shoot me just for vengeance," Salazar said. "Shoot me to avenge your dead."

"I won't—they all died from foolishness," Matilda said. "All except my Shad—my Shad died from being in the wrong spot at the wrong time. Shooting you won't bring him back, or make me miss him no less."

Captain Salazar took the pistol, and put it back in its holster.

"Caleb Cobb would have shot you, if he was here," Bigfoot said, almost apologetically. He thought it bold of Salazar to take the risk he had just taken—any Texan, in the right mood, might have shot him. Of course, the Captain was as tired and hungry as the rest of them; his neck wound had never healed properly—there was pus on his collar. Perhaps he felt his end was coming, and wanted to hasten it. Still, it was bold. A man could perhaps and perhaps all day, and not find his way to the truth.

"Yes—no doubt—he *did* shoot me," Salazar said. "But in that, too, he failed."

Then he gingerly felt his neck—he looked, with a grimace, at the stain on his hand.

"Perhaps I am wrong," he said. "Perhaps he didn't fail. Perhaps he merely wanted me to walk two hundred hard miles before I died."

"He was blind at the time, Captain," Bigfoot said. "He just made a lucky shot—I expect he would have been happy to kill you where you stood."

Captain Salazar sighed—he looked for a moment at his weary troops.

"All right," he said. "Unfortunately you did not accept my terms, so you are still my prisoners. If you had killed me, I would have been a martyr—now I will only be disgraced."

"Not in my eyes—not if you're talking about military work," Bigfoot said. "You done your best and you're still doing it. You took on a hard job. I doubt Caleb Cobb would have even got us this far."

"I agree with that," Salazar said. "I have done my best, and Colonel Cobb would not have got you this far. He would have left, to banquet with the generals and perhaps seduce their wives."

He gestured for his soldiers to get up. Two or three merely stared at him, but most of them began to struggle to their feet.

"Unfortunately, you are not a Mexican officer, Señor Wallace," Salazar said. "You are not one of the men who will judge me. I lost most of my men and many of my prisoners. That is what the generals will notice, when I deliver you to El Paso. Where are the rest, they will ask."

"Captain, I've got some advice," Bigfoot said. "Let's get to El Paso and then worry about the generals."

Salazar smiled.

"It's time to march," he said.

4.

TOWARD NOON THAT DAY, as the company—strung out for almost two miles—struggled south, they came upon three dead cows, starved within a mile of one another. The buzzards were on the carcasses, but they hadn't been on them long; all the carcasses were stiff from the night's frost. Although all three cows were mostly just skin and bones, to the weary troop, at the point of starvation itself, their discovery seemed like a miracle. The men who lagged caught up—all the men were soon tearing at the thin carcasses with their knives, trying to scrape a few bites of meat off the cold bones.

Captain Salazar, with difficulty, restored order. He fired his pistol twice, to get the hungry men to back off. While they were making a fire and preparing to roast the bones and what little flesh remained, Bigfoot saw several specks rise into the air, from far to the south.

"I think them was ducks," he said. "If there's ducks there must be water. We can have us a fine soup, if that's the case."

"Well, we got the soup bones, at least," Gus said. He ran south with Bigfoot and sure enough found a creek, mostly dry but with several small scattered pools of water.

The troop camped for two days, until every bone of the three animals had been boiled for soup. Most of the bones were then split for their marrow. The food was welcome, and also the rest. Through the two days and night, the prairie scavengers, who had been deprived of their chances at the carcasses, prowled around the camp. Coyotes and wolves stood watching during the day. Two ventured too close, a coyote and a wolf. Bigfoot shot them both, and added their meat to the soup.

"I don't know about eating wolf," Gus said. "A wolf will eat anything. This one might have poison in its belly, you don't know."

"Don't eat it then, if you're scared," Bigfoot said. "There'll be more for the rest of us."

Call ate the wolf and coyote soup without protest. His bad foot, though still painful, was better for the rest. Near the little creek there were some dead trees—Matilda chopped off a limb with a fork in it, and made Call a rude crutch. She knew how much he hated having to be helped along by her and by Gus. He accepted it, because his only other option was death; but he accepted it stiffly. The look in his eyes was the look of a man whose pride was wounded.

"I thank you," he said, in a formal tone, when she presented him with the rude crutch. But the look in his eyes was not formal—it was a look of gratitude. Gus saw how fond Matty had become of Call, despite his rudeness—he felt very jealous. He himself had been cheerful and friendly, and had courted Matty as much as she would allow, and yet—since the death of Shadrach—she had fastened her attentions on his surly friend. It annoyed him so much that he mentioned it to Bigfoot. Call and Matty were sitting together, eating soup.

Neither Call nor Matilda was saying anything, but still, they sat together, sipping wolf soup that a young Mexican soldier had just dished out of the pot.

"Now what's the point of spending all that time with Call?" Gus asked. "Call don't care for women. It's rare that I could get him to go with a whore."

Bigfoot studied the couple for a minute, the large woman and the short youth.

"Matty's got her motherly side," he said. "Most cows will take a calf, if one comes up that needs her."

"Why, I need her, I guess," Gus said—now that his belly didn't growl quite so loudly, his envy had returned.

"I'm as much a calf as he is—we're the same age," Gus said.

"Yeah, but you're easy to get along with, and Woodrow ain't," Bigfoot said.

"Well, then, she ought to be sitting with me, not with that hard-headed fool," Gus said. "He ain't saying a word to her—I can out-talk him any day."

"Maybe it ain't talk she's after," Bigfoot suggested.

Long Bill Coleman had been stretched out on the ground, resting on his elbow, as he listened to the little debate.

"Why are you griping, Gussie?" he asked. "She ain't sitting with me, either, but you don't hear me complaining."

"Shut up, Bill—what do you know about women?" Gus asked, testily.

"Well, I know they don't always cotton to the easy fellows," Long Bill said. "If they did, I'd have been married long ago. But I ain't married, and it's going to be another cold night."

"Why, he's right," Bigfoot said. "Matty likes Woodrow *because* he's hardheaded."

"Oh, I suppose you two know everything," Gus said. He went over to where the two sat, and plopped himself down on the other side of Matilda.

"Matty and her boys," Bigfoot said, smiling at Long Bill. "I doubt she expected to be the mother of two pups when she headed west with this outfit."

Long Bill wished the subject of mothers had never come up. His own had died of a fever when he was ten—he had missed her ever since.

"If Ma was alive, I expect I would have stayed with farming," he said, with a mournful look. "She cooked cobbler for us, when she was well. I ain't et cobbler since that was half as good."

"I hope this starving is over," Bigfoot said. "I don't want to think about cobbler or taters until we get back to where folks eat regular."

The carcasses had been consumed completely—when the troop left, on the morning of the third day, they had no food at all. They were cheerful, though. The fact that they had seen ducks convinced many of the men that they were almost out of the desert. The Texans began to talk of catfish and venison, pig meat and chickens, as if they would be sitting down to lavish meals within the next few days.

Salazar listened to the talk with a grim expression.

"Señores, this is still the dead man's walk," he said. "We have far to go before we come to Las Cruces. Once we make it there, no one will starve."

They marched three days without seeing a single animal; they had water, but no food. On the second evening, they used the last of their coffee. The brew was so thin it was almost colorless.

"I could read a newspaper through this coffee, if I had a newspaper," Long Bill said, squinting into his cup.

"I didn't know you could read, Bill," Bigfoot said.

Long Bill looked embarrassed; the fact was, he couldn't read. Usually, if he were lucky enough to come by a newspaper, he had a whore read it to him.

Call was as hungry as the rest of the troop, but because of his crutch, he was in better spirits, even though the crutch was rough and soon rubbed his underarm raw. He had nothing to pad the crutch with, though. Matilda offered to tear off a piece of her shirt and pad the crutch for him, but he refused her. By the end of the third day, his shoulder was paining him almost as much as his foot had. Matilda, tired of his stubbornness, ripped off a piece of her shirt and padded the crutch anyway, while Call slept.

Even so, Call lagged behind the rest of the Texans. He was not quite at the rear of the column, though; three of the weakest of the young Mexican soldiers lagged far behind him. Though Call could not speak their language, he had ceased to regard the young soldiers as enemies. They had starved and frozen, just like the Texans; he didn't think they would shoot him, even if he hobbled right past them and tried to escape.

From time to time he glanced back, to see that the boys were still following him. He was afraid they might collapse and die, and he knew that if the company was too far in advance of them when they collapsed, Salazar would not go back for them. The Apaches had not bothered them for four nights; the assumption around the campfire was that they had given up, or decided the pursuit of such a miserable band wasn't worth it. There were no horses to take, only a few weapons.

Captain Salazar was not convinced. He didn't share the Texans' optimism, in regard to Gomez.

"If he stopped, it is because he has other business," he told Bigfoot. "If he has no other business, he will follow us and try to kill us all. I don't think he will attack—he will wait and take us, one by one."

He posted as strong a guard as he could muster, knowing, even so, that half his soldiers would fall asleep on duty. But four nights passed, and no corpses were found in the morning.

"He wouldn't wait four nights, if he was still after us," Bigfoot said.

"He would wait forty nights," Salazar told him. "He is Gomez."

The wrapping on Call's crutch had come loose—he stopped to rewrap it and, when he did, glanced back at the young Mexicans. It was then that he saw the Apache, a short, stumpy-legged man, with a bow in his hand, about to release an arrow. Before he could move, the arrow hit him in the right side. Call had no weapon—all he could do was yell, but he yelled loudly and the troop turned. Call gripped his crutch, prepared to defend himself if the Apache came closer, but the Apache had vanished, and so had the three Mexican soldiers who had been trailing behind. The plain to the north was completely empty.

Bigfoot came running up, and looked at the arrow in Call's right side.

"Why, he nearly missed you," he said. "The arrow's barely hanging in you."

Before Call could even look down, Bigfoot had ripped the arrow out—it had only creased his ribs. Blood flowed down his leg, but he didn't feel it. The shock of seeing the Apache, only fifty yards behind him, left him dizzy for a minute.

Captain Salazar came running back to Call.

"Where did he go?" he asked.

Call, still dizzy, couldn't tell him. He pointed to the spot where the short Indian had been, but when Bigfoot and Salazar and a few of the Mexican troops ran in that direction, they found no Indians.

The three Mexican soldiers who had trailed Call were dead, each with two arrows in them. They lay face down, fully clothed.

"At least they didn't get cut," Long Bill said.

"No, he was in a hurry," Salazar said. "He wanted Corporal Call —and he almost had him. You are a very lucky man, Corporal. I think it was Gomez, and Gomez rarely misses."

"I saw him," Call said. "He would have been on me in another few steps, if I hadn't turned. I expect he would have put an arrow right through me."

"If it was Gomez and you saw him, then you are the first white to see him and live," Salazar said.

"He won't like that," Bigfoot said. "We'd best watch you close."

"You don't have to—I'll watch myself," Call said.

"Don't be feisty, Woodrow," Bigfoot said. "That old Apache might come back and try to finish the job."

"I hate New Mexico," Gus said. "If it ain't bears, it's Indians."

That night Call was placed in the center of the company, for his own safety; even so, he slept badly, and was troubled by dreams in which Gomez was carrying Buffalo Hump's great hump. One moment the Apache chief would be aiming an arrow at him, so real and so close that he would awaken. Then, the minute he dozed off again, it would be the Comanche chief that was aiming the arrow.

In the grey morning, cold but glad to be alive, Call remembered that a long time back Bigfoot had had a dream in which Buffalo Hump and Gomez rode together into Mexico, to take captives.

"Didn't you dream about Buffalo Hump and Gomez fighting together?" he asked.

"Yes, I hope it don't never come true," Bigfoot said. "One of them at a time's plenty to have to whip."

"We ain't whipping them," Call pointed out. "We ain't killed but two of them, and they've accounted for most of our troop."

"I admit they're wild," Bigfoot said. "But they're just men. If you put a bullet in them in the right place, they'll die, just like you or me. Their skins ain't the same colour as ours, but their blood's just as red."

Call knew that what Bigfoot said was true. The Indians were men; bullets could kill them. He himself had fired a bullet into Buffalo Hump's son and the son had died, just as dead as the three Mexican boys who had fallen to Apache arrows.

"It's hitting them that's hard," he said. "They're too smart about the country."

So far the Indians had won every encounter, and not because bullets couldn't hurt them: they won because they were too quick, and too skilled. They moved fast, and silently. Both Kicking Wolf and Gomez had taken horses, night after night—horses that were within feet of the best guards they could post.

"The Corporal is right," Salazar said. "We are strangers in this country, compared to them. We know a little about the animals, that's all. The Apaches know which weeds to eat—they can smell out roots and dig them up and eat them. They can survive in this country, because they know it. When we learn how to smell out roots, and which weeds to eat, maybe we can fight them on even terms."

"I doubt I'll ever be in the mood to study up on weeds," Gus said.

"This is gloomy talk, I guess I'll walk by myself awhile, unless Matty wants to walk with me," Bigfoot said. He didn't like to hear Indians overpraised, just because the Rangers found them hard to kill. There *were* exceptional Indians, of course, but there were also plenty who were unexceptional, and no harder to kill than anyone else. He himself would have welcomed an encounter with Gomez, whom Call described as short and bowlegged.

"I expect I can outfight most bowlegged men," he remarked to Long Bill Coleman, who found the remark eccentric.

"I wish I still had my harmonica," Long Bill said. "It's dreary at night, without no tunes."

5.

THE NEXT DAY THEY saw a distant outline to the west—the outline of mountains. Captain Salazar's spirits improved at once.

"Those are the Caballo Mountains," he said. "Once we cross them we will soon arrive at a place where there is food. Las Cruces is not far."

"Not far?" Gus said. Even with his eyesight the distant mountains made only the faintest outline, and his stomach was growling from hunger.

"What does he think far is?" he asked Call. "We might walk another week before we come to them hills."

Call's shoulder had become so sensitive from the rough crutch that he had to grit his teeth every time he put his weight on it. His foot was better—he could put a little weight on it, if he moved cautiously—but he was afraid to discard the crutch entirely. The mountains might be another seventy-five miles away, and even then, they would have to be crossed.

That day, despite Captain Salazar's optimism, the Mexican troops began to desert. They were hungry and weak. At noon the Captain called a rest, and when it was time to resume the march, six of the Mexican soldiers simply didn't get up. Their eyes were dull, from too much suffering.

"You fools, you are in sight of safety," Salazar said. "If you don't keep walking, Gomez will come. He will kill you all, and you may not be so lucky as the three he killed with arrows. He may make sport of you—and Apache sport is not nice."

None of the men changed expression, as he talked. After a glance, they did not look up.

"They're finished," Bigfoot said. "We've all got a finishing point. These boys have just come to theirs. The Captain can rant and rave all he wants to—they're done."

Captain Salazar quickly came to the same conclusion. He looked at the six men sternly, but gave up his efforts at persuasion. He took three of their muskets and turned away.

"I am leaving you your ammunition," he said. "Three of you have rifles. Shoot at the Apaches with the rifles. If you do not win, drive them back, then use the pistols on yourselves. Adios."

Leaving the six men was hard—harder than any of the Texans had expected it to be. In the time of their captivity, they had come to know most of the Mexicans by their first names—they had exchanged bits of language, sitting around the fires. Bigfoot learned to say his own name, in Spanish. Several of the Mexican boys had started calling him "Beegfeet," in English. Gus had taught two of the boys to play mumblety-peg. Matilda and Long Bill had taught them simple card games. On some of the coldest nights they had all huddled together, moving cards around with their cold hands. As the weary miles passed, they had stopped feeling hostile to one another—they were all in the same desperate position. One of the Mexicans, who had some skill with woodwork had, the very night before, smoothed the crack in Woodrow Call's crutch, so that it would not rub his underarm quite so badly.

Now they were leaving them—Salazar and the other Mexicans were already a hundred yards away, plodding on toward the far distant mountains.

"I'm much obliged," Call said, to the boy who had smoothed his crutch.

Several of the Texans mumbled brief good-byes, but Matilda

didn't—she felt she couldn't stand it: boys dying, day after day, one by one. She turned her back and walked away, crying.

"Oh Lord, I wish we'd get somewhere," Long Bill said. "All this walking on an empty belly's wore me just about out."

That afternoon the company—what was left of it—stumbled on a patch of gourds. There were dozens of gourds, their vines curling over the sand.

"Can we eat these, Captain?" Bigfoot asked.

"They're gourds," Salazar said. "You can eat them if you want to eat gourds."

"Captain, there's nothing else," Bigfoot pointed out. "Them mountains don't look no closer. We better gather up a few and try them."

"Do as you like," Salazar said. "I will have to be hungrier than this before I eat gourds."

That night, though, he was hungrier than he had been in the afternoon, and he ate a gourd. They made a little fire and put the gourds in it, as if they were potatoes. The gourds shriveled up, and the men nibbled at their ashy skins.

"Mine just tastes like ashes," Gus said, in disappointment.

"It might taste better if it were served on a plate," Long Bill said, a remark that amused Bigfoot considerably. Though he had strongly recommended gathering the gourds—after all, there was nothing else to gather—he had not yet got around to tasting one.

Several of the men were so hungry they ate the scorched gourds without hesitation.

"Tastes bitter as sin," Gus observed, after chewing a bite.

"I wouldn't know what you mean," Bigfoot said. "I'm a stranger to sin."

Matilda stuck a knife into her gourd, and a puff·of hot air came out. She sniffed at the gourd, and immediately started sneezing. Annoyed, she flipped the gourd away.

"If it makes me sneeze, it's bad," she said.

Later, though, she found the gourd and ate it.

One of the Mexican soldiers had gathered up the gourd vines, as well as the gourds. He scorched a vine and ate it; others soon followed suit. Even Salazar nibbled at a vine.

"When will we hit the mountains, Captain?" Bigfoot asked. "There might be game, up there where it's high."

Salazar sighed—his mood had darkened as the day wore on. He had scarcely any of his company left, and only a few of his prisoners. It would not sit well with his superiors.

"The Apaches may not let us cross," he said. "There are many Apaches here. If there are too many, none of us will get through."

"Now, Captain, don't be worrying," Bigfoot said. "We've walked too far to be stopped now."

"You'll be stopped if enough arrows hit you," Salazar said.

The night was clear, with very bright stars. Salazar could not see the distant mountains, but he knew they were there, the last barrier they would have to cross before they reached the Rio Grande and safety. He knew he had done a hard thing—he had crossed the Jornada del Muerto with his prisoners. He had lost many soldiers and many prisoners, but he was across. In two days they could be eating goat, and corn, and perhaps the sweet melons that grew along the Rio Grande. None of his superiors could have done what he did, and yet he knew he would not be greeted as a hero, or even as a professional. He would be greeted as a failure. For that reason, he thought of Gomez—it would be worth dying, with what men he had left, if he could only kill the great Apache. Then, at least, he would die heroically, as befitted a soldier.

"I think the Captain's lost his spunk," Gus said, observing how silent and melancholy the man had been around the campfire. Even the amusing sight of his whole company attempting to eat the bitter gourds had not caused him to smile.

"It ain't that," Bigfoot said—then he fell silent. He had been around defeated officers before, in his years of scouting for the military. Some had met defeat unfairly, through caprice or bad luck; others had been beaten by such overwhelming numbers that survival itself would have brought them glory. And yet to military men, circumstances didn't seem to matter—if they didn't win, they lost, and no amount of reflection could take away the sting.

"It ain't that," he said, again. The young Rangers waited for him to explain, but Bigfoot didn't explain. He drew circles in the ashes of the campfire with a stick.

The next morning the mountains looked closer, though not by much. The men were weak—some of them looked at the mountains and quailed. The thought that there was food on the other side of the mountains brought them no energy. They didn't think they could cross such hills, even if the whole plain on the other side was covered with food. They marched on, dully and slowly, not thinking, just walking.

When the mountains were closer, no more than a few miles away, Call saw something white on the prairie ahead. At first he thought it was just another patch of sand—but then he looked closer, and saw that it was an antelope. He grabbed Gus's arm and pointed.

"Tell the Captain," he said. "Maybe Bigfoot can shoot it."

When the antelope was pointed out to Captain Salazar, he immediately gave Bigfoot his rifle. Bigfoot was watching the antelope closely. He cautioned the troop to be quiet and still.

"That buck's nervous," he said. "We better just sit real still, for awhile. Maybe he'll mistake us for a sage bush."

All the men could see that the antelope was nervous, and a minute later they saw why: a brown form came streaking out of a patch of sage bush and leapt on the antelope's neck, knocking it down.

"What's that?" Gus said, startled. He had never seen an animal run so fast. All he could see was a ball of brown fur, curled over the antelope's neck.

"That's a lion," Bigfoot said, standing up. "We're in luck, boys. I doubt I could have got close enough to that buck to put a bullet in him. The cougar done my work for me."

He started walking toward the spot where the cougar was finishing his kill. The rest of the troop didn't move.

"He's bold, ain't he—that lion might get him next," Gus said.

Before Bigfoot had gone more than a few yards, the cougar looked up and saw him. For a second the animal froze; then he bounded away. Bigfoot raised his rifle, as if to shoot, but then he lowered it. Soon they saw the spot of brown moving up the shoulder of the nearest mountain.

"Why didn't you shoot it?" Call asked, when he came up to Bigfoot. He would have liked a closer look at the cougar.

"Because I might need the bullet for an Apache," Bigfoot said. "We got a dead antelope—that's better eating than a lion. When there's food waiting to be et it's foolish to be wasting bullets on cats you can't hit anyway."

They skinned the antelope, and soon had a fire going and meat cooking. The smell of the meat soon revived the men who had been ready to die. Next day, they jerkied the meat they hadn't eaten, lingering in camp between the mountain and the plain. The more they ate the better their spirits rose; only Captain Salazar remained despondent. He ate only a little of the antelope meat, silent. Bigfoot, confident that what remained of the troop would now survive, tried to draw Salazar out about the future, but the Captain answered him only briefly.

"El Paso is not far," Salazar said. "We are all about to end our journey."

He said no more.

Bigfoot was allowed to leave and seek the best route through the mountains—in four hours he was back, having located an excellent low pass, not ten miles to the south. The troop marched all afternoon and camped in the deep shadow of the mountains, just at the lip of the pass.

That night, everybody felt restless. Long Bill Coleman, unable to abide the lack of tunes, cupped his hands and pretended he was playing the harmonica. Gus kept looking at the mountains—their looming presence made him a little apprehensive.

"Don't bears live in mountains—I've heard they sleep in caves."

"Why, bears live wherever they want to," Bigfoot told him. "They go where they please."

"I think most of them live in mountains," Gus said. "I'd hate to be eaten by a damn bear when we're so close to all them watermelons."

No one slept much that night. Matilda rubbed Call's sore foot with a little antelope fat she had saved. Call was walking better— his stride was almost normal again. He hadn't abandoned the crutch, but mainly carried it in his hand, like a rifle.

A blue cloud, with a rainbow arched across it, was over them when the troop started through the pass. It snowed for an hour, when they were near the top, but the light flakes didn't stick. Ahead, as they approached the crest, they could see brilliant sunlight, to the west beneath the clouds.

By noon the cloud was gone, and the bright sunlight shone on the mountains. The troop walked through a winding canyon for three hours and began to descend the west side of the mountains. Below them, they saw trees, on both sides of the river. To the south, Gus once again saw smoke, and this time he was not merely wishing. There was a village beside the river—they saw a little cornfield, and some goats.

"Hurrah, boys—we're safe," Bigfoot said.

Everyone stopped, to survey the fertile valley below them. Some of the Mexican soldiers wept. There was even a little church in the village.

"Well, we made it, Matty," Bigfoot said. "Maybe we'll see a stage-coach, heading for California. Maybe you'll get there yet."

He had continued to carry Captain Salazar's rifle, in case he encountered game. When they started down the hill, toward the Rio Grande, Captain Salazar quietly took it from him.

"Why, that's right, Captain—it's yours," Bigfoot said.

The Captain didn't speak. He looked back once, toward the Jornada del Muerto, and walked on down the hill.

6.

When the tired troop made its way into the village of Las Palomas, the doves for which the village was named were whirling over the drying corn, its shuck now brittle from the frost. An old man milking a goat at the edge of the village jumped up when he saw the strangers coming. A priest came out of the little church, and immediately went back in. In a moment, a bell began to ring, not from the church, but from the center of the village, near the well. Some families came out of the little houses; men and women stopped what they were doing to watch the dirty, weary strangers walk into their village. To the village people they looked like ghosts —men so strange and haggard that at first no one dared approach them. The Mexicans' uniforms were so dirty and torn that they scarcely seemed like uniforms.

Captain Salazar walked up to the old man who had been milking the goats, and bowed to him politely.

"I am Captain Salazar," he said. "Are you the jefe here?"

The old man shook his head—he looked around the village, to

see if anyone would help him with the stranger. In all his years he had never left the village of Las Palomas, and he did not know how to speak properly to people who came from other places.

"We have no jefe," he said, after awhile. "The Apaches came while he was in the cornfield."

"Our jefe is dead," one of the older women repeated.

The old man looked at her with mild reproach.

"We don't know that he is dead," he said. "We only know that the Apaches took him."

"Well, if they took him, he'd be luckier to be dead," Bigfoot said. "I wonder if it was Gomez?"

"It was Apaches," the old man repeated. "We only found his hoe."

"I see," the Captain said. "You're lucky they didn't take the whole village."

"They only take the young, Captain," the bold old woman said. "They take the young to make them slaves and sell them."

"That is why we are all old," the old man with the goat said. "There are no young people in our village. When they are old enough to be slaves, the Apaches take them and sell them."

"But there are soldiers in El Paso," Salazar said. "You could go to the soldiers—they would fight the Apaches for you. That is their job."

The old man shook his head.

"No soldiers ever come here," he said. "Once when our jefe was alive he went to El Paso to see the soldiers and asked them to come, but they only laughed at him. They said they could not bother to come so far for such a poor village. They said we should learn to shoot guns so we could fight the Apache ourselves."

"If the soldiers won't help you, then I think you had better do what they suggested," Captain Salazar said. "But we can talk of this later. We are tired and hungry. Have your women make us food."

"We have many goats—we will make you food," the old man said. "And you can stay in my house, if you like. It is small, but I have a warm fire."

"Call the priest," Salazar said. "These men are Texans—they are prisoners. I want the priest to lock them in the church tonight. They look tired, but they fight like savages when they fight."

"Are we to give them food?" the old man asked.

"Yes, feed them," Salazar said. "Do you have men who can shoot?"

"I can shoot," the old man said. "Tomas can shoot. Who do you want us to shoot, Captain?"

"Anyone who tries to leave the village," Salazar said.

Then he turned, and went into the little house the old man had offered him.

Despite Salazar's warning, the people of Las Palomas had little fear of the Texans. They looked too tired and hungry to be the savage fighters the Captain claimed they were. Even as they were walking to the church, the women of the village began to press food on them—tortillas, mostly. The little church was cold, but not as cold as the great plain they had crossed. Several old men with muskets stood outside, as guards. When the night grew chill, they built a fire and stood around it, talking. Long Bill walked out to warm his hands, and the old men made way for him. Bigfoot joined him, and then a few others. Gus went out a few times, but Call did not. The women brought food—*posole* and goat meat, and a little corn. Call ate with the rest, but he didn't mix with the crowd around the fire. He sat with Matilda, looking out of one of the small windows at the high stars.

"Why won't you go get warm?" Matilda asked. He was a tense boy, Woodrow Call. All that was easy for Gus McCrae was hard for him. He didn't mix well with people—any people. Though he had come to depend on her help, he was wary, even with her.

"I'm warm enough," Call said.

"You ain't, Woodrow—you're shivering," Matilda said. "What's the harm in sitting by a fire on a cold night?"

"You ain't sitting by it," Call pointed out.

"Well, but I'm fleshy," Matilda said. "I can warm myself. You're just a skinny stick. Answer my question."

"I don't like being a prisoner," Call said, finally. "I might have to fight those old men. I might have to kill some of them. I'd just as soon not get friendly."

"Woodrow, those men ain't bad," Matilda said. "They sent their women to feed us—we ain't been fed as well since we left the last village. Why would you want to kill them?"

"I might have to escape," Call said. "I ain't going to be a prisoner much longer. If I can't be free I don't mind being dead."

"What about Salazar?" Matilda said. "He's the one keeping you prisoner. We walked all this way with him. He ain't so bad, if you ask me. I've met plenty of worse Mexicans—and worse whites, too."

Call didn't answer. He didn't welcome the kind of questions Matilda asked. Thinking about such things was foolish. He could think about them all through the night, and be no less a prisoner when the sun came up. It was true that the old men of Las Palomas had been kindly, and that the women were generous with food. He didn't wish them ill—but he didn't intend to remain a prisoner much longer, either. If he saw a chance to escape, he meant to take it, and he didn't mean to fail. Anyone who stood in his way would have to take the consequences; he didn't want to feel friendly toward people he might have to fight.

Later, when the chill deepened, the women brought blankets to the church. Call wrapped up in his as tightly as he could. But he didn't sleep. Out the church door he could see Gus McCrae, yarning with Long Bill Coleman and Bigfoot Wallace. No doubt, now that he was warm and full, Gus had gone back to telling lies about his adventures on the riverboat; or else he was telling them how he was going to marry the Forsythe girl, as soon as he got back to Austin. Matilda had gone to sleep, with her head bent forward on her chest. Call felt that he had been rude, a little, in not being able to answer her questions any better than he had. He didn't understand why women had such a need to question. He himself preferred just to let life happen, and act when opportunity arose.

Finally, though, as Matilda slept, he did get up and go out of the church, not so much to warm himself—the old men kept the fire blazing—as to hear what lies Gus McCrae was telling. Long Bill was pretending his hands were a harmonica again; he was whistling through them. Bigfoot Wallace had gone to sleep, his back against the wall of the church. Several of the old men were watching Gus, as if he were a new kind of human, a kind their experience had not prepared them for. A few of the village women, wrapped in heavy shawls, stood back a little from the fire.

"Hello, Woodrow—did you freeze out, or did you want to listen to Long Bill whistle on his fingers?" Gus asked.

"I came out to whip you, if you don't shut up," Call said. "You're talking so loud it's keeping this whole town awake."

"Why, stop your ears, if you think I'm loud," Gus said. But he made way for his friend, and Call sat down. The blaze felt good on his sore feet. Soon he bent forward, and napped a little. Gus McCrae was still talking, and the yarn had something to do with a riverboat.

7.

In the morning, with frost on the cornfields and on the needles of the chaparral, Salazar provisioned his few troops for the march south. There were no horses in the village, but there were two mules, one of which Salazar requisitioned to carry their provisions. The Texans emerged from the church blinking in the strong sunlight. They had been given coffee, and a little cheese made from goat's milk, and were ready to march.

"I'm in a hurry to see El Paso," Bigfoot said. "We couldn't get to it coming the other way, but maybe we'll make it coming from the north."

"Yes, you will make it," Salazar said. "Then, I expect, they will send you on to the City of Mexico. There is a lake with many islands, and all the fruit is sweet—that is what I have been told."

The people of Las Palomas were anxious to see that none of the troop—Texans or Mexicans—went hungry on the march south to El Paso. Though they knew that the party would be following the river, where there were several villages that could supply them, they piled so many provisions on the mule that the animal was scarcely visible, under the many sacks and bags. Several of the Texans even had blankets pressed on them, as protection against the chill nights.

Captain Salazar was just turning to lead the party out of the village, when they heard the sound of horses—the sound came from the south.

"Reckon it's Indians?" Gus asked. Even though he was feeling more confident of his survival, thanks to a good meal and a night beside a warm fire, he knew that they were not yet beyond the Apache country. What the villagers had had to say about their stolen children was fresh in his mind.

Captain Salazar listened for a moment.

"No, it is not Indians," he said. "It's cavalry."

"Lots of cavalry," Bigfoot said. "Maybe it's the American army, coming to rescue us."

"I'm afraid not, Señor," Salazar said. "It's the Mexican army, coming to march you to El Paso."

All the villagers were apprehensive—they were not used to being visited by soldiers, twice in two days. Some of the women crept back inside their little houses. The men, most of them elderly, stood where they were.

In a few minutes, the horses they had been hearing clipped into town, forty in all. The soldiers riding them were wearing clean uniforms; and all were armed with sabres, as well as rifles and pistols. At their head rode a small man in a smart uniform, with many ribbons on his breast.

The sun glinted on the forty sabres in their sheaths.

Beside the cavalry were several men on foot, so dark that Call couldn't tell whether they were Mexican or Indian. They trotted beside the horses—none of them looked tired.

The Mexican soldiers who stood with Salazar looked embarrassed. Their own uniforms were torn and dirty—some had no coats at all, only the blankets that had been given them by the people of Las Palomas. Some of them remembered that when they had started out from Santa Fe to catch the Texans they had been as smartly dressed as the approaching cavalry. Now, in comparison to the soldiers from the south, they looked like beggars, and they knew it.

The small man with the ribbons rode right up to Captain Salazar and stopped. He had a thin mustache that curled at the ends to a fine point.

"You are Captain Salazar?" he asked.

"Yes, Major," the Captain said.

"I am Major Laroche," the small man said. "Why are these men not tied?"

The Major looked at the Texans with cold contempt—the tone of his voice alone made Call bristle.

The thing that surprised Gus was that the Major was white. He did not look Mexican at all.

Captain Salazar looked discouraged.

"I have walked a long way with these men, Major," he said. "Together we walked the dead man's walk. The reason they are not tied is because they know I will shoot them if they try to escape."

Major Laroche did not change expression.

"Perhaps you would shoot at them, but would you hit them?" he asked. "I think it would be easier to hit them if they were tied—but that is not my point."

Captain Salazar looked up, waiting for the Major's point. He did not have to wait very long.

"They are prisoners," the Major said. "Prisoners should be tied. Then they should be put up against a wall and shot. That is what we would do with such men in France, if we caught them."

The Major looked at the dark men who trotted beside the horses. He said something to them—one of the dark men immediately went to the pack mule and came back with a handful of rawhide thongs.

"Tie him first," the Major said, pointing at Bigfoot. "Then tie the one who turned over the General's buggy. Which is he?"

Salazar gestured toward Call. In a moment, two of the dark men were beside him with the thongs.

Bigfoot had already held out his hands so that the men could tie them, but Call had not. He tensed, ready to fight the dark men, but before his rage broke Bigfoot and Salazar both spoke to him.

"Let it be, Woodrow," Bigfoot said. "The Major here's ready to shoot you, and it's too nice a morning to get shot."

"He is right," Salazar said.

Call mastered himself with difficulty. He held out his hands, and one of the dark men bound him tightly at the wrists with the rawhide thongs. In a few minutes, all the Texans were similarly bound.

"Perhaps you should chain them, too," Salazar said, with a touch of sarcasm. "As you know, Texans are very wild."

Major Laroche ignored the remark.

"Where is the rest of your troop, Captain?" he asked.

"Dead," Salazar said. "The Apaches followed us into the Jornada del Muerto. They killed some. A bear killed two. Six starved to death."

"But you had horses, when you left Santa Fe," the Major said. "Where are your horses?"

"Some are dead and some were stolen," Salazar admitted. He spoke in a dull tone, not looking at the Major, who sat ramrod stiff on his horse.

When all the prisoners were bound, the Major turned his horse. He looked down once more at Captain Salazar.

"I suggest you go home, Captain," he said. "Your commanding officer will want to know why you lost half your men and all your horses. I am told that you were well provisioned. No one should have starved."

"Gomez killed General Dimasio, Major," Salazar said. "He killed Colonel Cobb, the man who led these Texans. He is the reason I lost the men and the horses."

Major Laroche curled the ends of his mustache once more.

"No officer in the Mexican army should be beaten by a savage," he said. "One day perhaps they will let me go after this Gomez. When I catch him I will put a hook through his neck and hang him in the plaza in Santa Fe."

"You won't catch him," Call said.

Major Laroche looked briefly at Call.

"Is there a blacksmith in this village?" he asked.

No one spoke. The men of the village had all lowered their eyes.

"Very well," the Major said. "If there were a blacksmith I would chain this man now. But we cannot wait. I assure you when we reach Las Cruces I will see that you are fitted with some very proper irons."

Salazar had not moved.

"Major, I have no horses," he said. "Am I to walk to Santa Fe? I am a captain in the army."

"A disgraced captain," Major Laroche said. "You walked here. Walk back."

"Alone?" Salazar asked.

"No, you can take your soldiers," Major Laroche said. "I don't want them—they stink. If I were you I would take them to the river and bathe them before you leave."

"We have little ammunition," Salazar said. "If we leave here without horses or bullets, Gomez will kill us all."

The priest had come out of the little church. He stood with his hands folded into his habit, watching.

"Ask that priest to say a prayer for you," Major Laroche said. "If he is a good priest his prayers might be better than bullets or horses."

"Perhaps, but I would rather have bullets and horses," Salazar said.

Major Laroche didn't answer. He had already turned his horse.

The Texans were placed in the center of the column of cavalry—the cavalrymen behind them drew their sabres and held them ready, across their saddles. Captain Salazar and his ragged troop stood in the street and watched the party depart.

"Good-bye, Captain—if I was you I'd travel at night," Bigfoot said. "If you stick to the river and travel at night you might make it."

The Texans looked once more at the Captain who had captured them, and the few men they had traveled so far with. There was no time for farewells. The cavalrymen with drawn sabres pressed close behind them.

Matilda Roberts had not been tied. She passed close to Captain Salazar as she walked out of the village of Las Palomas.

"Adios, Captain," she said. "You ain't a bad fellow. I hope you get home alive."

Salazar nodded, but didn't answer. He and his men stood watching as the Texans were marched south, out of the village of Las Palomas.

8.

Major Laroche made no allowance for weariness. By noon, the Texans were having a hard time keeping up with the pace he set. The pause for rest was only ten minutes; the meal just a handful of corn. The mule that the villagers had so carefully provisioned had become the property of the Major's cavalry. The Texans hardly had time to sit, before the march was resumed. While they ate their hard corn, they watched the Mexican cavalrymen eat the cheese the women of Las Palomas had provided for them.

Gus was puzzled by the fact that a Frenchman was leading a company of Mexican cavalry.

"Why would a Frenchie fight with the Mexicans?" he asked. "I know there's lots of Frenchies down in New Orleans, but I never knew they went as far as Mexico."

"Money, I expect," Bigfoot said. "I never made much money fighting—I've mostly done it for the sport, but plenty do it for the pay."

"I wouldn't," Call said. "I'd take the pay, but I've got other reasons for fighting."

"What other reasons?" Gus asked.

Call didn't answer. He had not meant to provoke a question from his companion, and was sorry he had spoken at all.

"Can't you hear? I asked you what other reasons?" Gus said.

"Woodrow don't know why he likes to fight," Matilda said. "He don't know why he turned that buggy over and got himself whipped raw. My Shad didn't know why he wandered—he was just a wandering man. Woodrow, he's a fighter."

"It's all right to fight," Bigfoot said. "But there's a time to fight, and a time to let be. Right now we're hog-tied, and we ain't got no guns. This ain't the time to fight."

They marched all afternoon and deep into the night, which was cold. Call kept up, though his foot was throbbing again. Major Laroche sent the dark men ahead to scout. He himself never looked back at the prisoners. From time to time they could see him raise his hand, to curl his mustache.

In the morning, there was thin ice on the little puddles by the river. The men were given coffee; while they were drinking it Major Laroche lined his men up at rigid attention, and rode down their ranks, inspecting them. Now and then, he pointed at something that displeased him—a girth strap not correctly secured, or a uniform not fully buttoned, or a sabre sheath not shined. The men who had been careless were made to fall out immediately; the Major watched while they corrected the problem.

When he was finished with his own troops, the Major rode over and inspected the Texans. They knew they were ragged and filthy, but when the Frenchman looked down at them with pitiless eyes they felt even dirtier and more ragged. The Major saw Long Bill Coleman scratching himself—most of the men had long been troubled by lice.

"Gentlemen, you need a bath," he said. "We have a fine ceremony planned for you, in El Paso. We will be there in four days. I am going to untie you now, so that you can bathe. We have a fine river here—why waste it? Perhaps if you bathe in it every day until we reach our destination, you will be presentable when we hold the ceremony."

[388]

"What kind of ceremony would that be, Major?" Bigfoot asked.

"I will let that be a surprise," Major Laroche said, not smiling.

Gus had taken a strong dislike to Major Laroche's manner of speaking—his talk was too crisp, to Gus's ear. He didn't see why a Frenchman, or anyone, needed to be that sharp in speech. Talk that was slower and not so crisp would be a lot easier to tolerate, particularly on a cold morning when he had enough to do just keeping warm.

"I'm going to release you now, for your bath," the Major said. "I want you to take off those filthy clothes—we're going to burn them."

"Burn 'em?" Bigfoot said. "Major, we've got no other clothes to put on. I admit these are dirty and smelly, but if you burn them we won't have a rag to put on."

"You have blankets," the Major pointed out. "You can wrap those around you, today. Tomorrow we will reach Las Cruces—when we get there we will dress you properly, so that you won't disgrace yourselves when we hold the ceremony."

He nodded to the dark men, who began to cut the rawhide thongs that bound the Texans.

With the cavalry behind them, the Texans were marched to the Rio Grande. They were all apprehensive—none of them trusted the French Major. Besides that, they were cold, and the green river looked colder. The frost had not yet melted from the thorn bushes.

"Strip, gentlemen—your bath awaits," Major Laroche said.

The Texans hesitated—no one wanted to start undressing. But Major Laroche was looking at them impatiently, and the cavalry was lined up behind him.

"I guess you boys think you're gents," Matilda said. "I'm tired of stinking, so I'll be first, if nobody cares."

There was a titter from the cavalry, when Matilda began to shed her clothes, but Major Laroche whirled on his men angrily and the titter died. Then he turned back, and watched Matilda walk into the water.

"Hurry, gentlemen," the Major said. "The lady has set you an example. Hurry—we have a march to make."

Reluctantly, the Texans began to strip, while the Mexican cavalry watched Matilda Roberts splash in the Rio Grande.

"I reckon it won't hurt us to get clean," Bigfoot said. "I'd prefer a big brass tub, but I guess this old river will do."

He undressed; so, finally, did the rest of the men. They were encouraged slightly by the fact that Matilda, skinnier than she had been when she lifted the snapping turtle out of the Rio Grande, but still a large woman, splashed herself over and over, rubbing her arms and breasts with sand scooped from the shallows where she stood.

"It might hurt us if we freeze," Gus said.

"Oh, now, it's just water," Long Bill said. "If it ain't froze Matty, I guess I can tolerate it."

The water, when Call stepped in, was so cold he felt as if he had been burned. It sent a pain so deep into his sore foot that he thought for a moment the foot might have died. Gradually, though, wading up to his knees, he came to tolerate the water a little better, and began to follow Matilda's example, scooping sand from the shallow riverbed and rubbing himself. He was surprised at how white the bodies of the men were—their faces were dark from the sun, but their bodies were white as fish bellies.

While the Texans splashed, Major Laroche decided to drill his troops a little. He put them through a sabre drill, and then had them present muskets and advance as if into battle.

Wesley Buttons, the youngest and most excitable of the three Buttons brothers, happened to glance ashore just as the cavalry was advancing with their muskets ready. Seeing the advancing Mexicans convinced Wesley that massacre was imminent. They had been expecting death for weeks—from Indians, from bears, from Mexicans, from the weather—and now here it came.

"Run, boys, they mean to shoot us all!" he yelled, grabbing his two brothers, Jackie and Charlie, by the arms.

Within a second, panic spread among the Texans, though Bigfoot Wallace at once saw that the Mexicans were merely drilling. He yelled out as loudly as he could, but his cry was lost—half the Texans were already splashing deeper into the river, desperate suddenly to get across.

The Mexican cavalry, and even Major Laroche, were startled by the sudden panic which had seized the naked men. For a moment the Major hesitated, and in that moment Bigfoot ran toward the shore, meaning to run to where the Major sat on his horse and explain that the men had merely taken a fright.

Call, Gus, and Matilda were downriver slightly, near the bank where the Mexicans were assembled. Gus had cut his foot on a mussel shell. Call and Matilda were helping him out of the water when the panic started. Long Bill Coleman had already had enough of the freezing water. He had walked back toward the pile of clothes, hoping to find a clean shirt or pants leg to dry himself with.

"Boys, come back—come back!" Bigfoot yelled, turning to look as he splashed ashore; but only the five or six men nearest him understood the command. One of the dark men had been attempting to burn the Texans' clothes—he was holding a stick of firewood to a shirt, hoping the filthy garment would ignite.

At that moment Major Laroche saw Bigfoot coming, and realized the Texans were merely scared.

He motioned his cavalry forward, disgusted at the delay this foolish act of ignorance would cause him—then, a second later, the cavalry, primed to shoot, and excited by the fact that half the prisoners seemed to be escaping, rushed past the Major before he could stop them, firing at the fleeing men.

"No! no! you stupids! Don't kill them—don't kill them!" he yelled.

But his words were lost in the rush of hooves, and the blast of muskets. He sat, helpless and in a cold fury, as his men spurred their horses into the river, some trying to reload their muskets, others slashing at the fleeing Texans with their sabres.

Bigfoot, Call, Matilda, Gus, Long Bill and a few others struggled back to where the Major sat, hoping he could call off his troops. The dark men at once covered them with their guns. None of them —Texans, the Major, the dark men—could do anything but watch. Both Bigfoot and the Major were yelling, trying to call off the cavalry before all the fleeing Texans were shot or cut down.

Bigfoot, holding up his hands to show that he meant no harm, walked as close to Major Laroche as the dark men would let him get.

"Major, ain't there no way to stop this?" he asked. "Don't you have a bugler, at least?"

Major Laroche had taken out a spyglass, and put it to his eye. Some of the naked men had made it across the narrow river, but many of the cavalrymen had crossed it, too, and were pursuing the running Texans through the cactus and scrub, slashing and shooting.

Major Laroche lowered the spyglass, and shook his head.

"I have no bugler, Monsieur," he said. "I had one, but he became familiar with the alcalde's wife, and the alcalde shot him. It was a great annoyance, of course."

When Gus looked back toward the river, all he could see were horses splashing and men trying to wade or swim, trying to escape the Mexican cavalry anyway they could. But there was no way. As he watched, Jackie Buttons tried to dive under the belly of a horse —but the river was too shallow. Jackie came up, his face covered with mud, only to have a cavalryman shoot him down at point-blank range.

"Oh God, they're killing the boys—they're killing them all!" Matilda yelled.

Quartermaster Brognoli stood beside her, uncomprehending, his head jerking slightly, as it had jerked the whole of the long trek from the Palo Duro. Sometimes Matilda led him, but mostly Brognoli walked alone—now, naked, he watched the destruction of the troop without seeming to understand it.

Call watched too, silent. The men had been fools to run, when the cavalry had only been practicing; but it was a folly that could not be corrected now. Charlie Buttons crawled out on the opposite shore, and was at once hacked down by two soldiers. He fell back in the river and the river carried him downstream, spilling blood into the water like a speared fish.

"Major, can't you stop them?" Bigfoot yelled again. "There won't be a man of them left."

"I am afraid you are right," Major Laroche said. "It will mean a much smaller ceremony, when we reach El Paso. I expect the alcalde will be disappointed, and General Medino too."

"Ceremony! ceremony! Those men weren't nothing but scared," Bigfoot said. There were floating bodies and swirls of blood all over the surface of the green water. John Green, a short Ranger from Missouri, managed to wrest a sabre from one of the cavalrymen, but when he tried to stab the soldier he missed, and stabbed the horse in the belly. The horse reared and fell, smashing John Green and the soldier he had tried to stab; the horse continued to flounder, but neither John nor the soldier rose again.

"Monsieur, I have no bugler, as I said," Major Laroche remarked, watching them coolly. "My men are soldiers and they smell blood. It would take a cannon shot to stop them now, and I was not provided with a cannon."

Across the river, Call and Gus could see men running. Some of them had managed to get a hundred yards or more from the river, but there were several cavalrymen for every Texan and none escaped. Guns fired, and sabres flashed in the bright sunlight. The few Texans on the east bank of the river watched the final stages of the massacre silently. Gus felt weak in the stomach—Call felt numb. Matilda Roberts had gone blank. She stared across the river, but her gaze was fixed on nothing. Long Bill Coleman stopped looking. He sat down and heaped sand on his naked legs, as a child might. Major Laroche smoked.

Finally, when all the Texans were dead, the Mexican troops began to return. Some had gone almost a mile west of the river, in their pursuit of the Texans. Some were still in the water, stabbing or shooting at any white body that seemed to have life in it. Major Laroche looked at the sun, and finally rode his horse down to the river. He didn't yell or gesture; he merely sat there, but one by one, his men noticed him. Slowly, they came to themselves. One or two looked embarrassed. They looked to the east bank, and saw that only a few Texans were left alive. A young soldier had just thrust his sabre into one of the floating bodies—Call knew the man only as Bob. The sabre stuck in Bob's breastbone, and the young cavalryman was unable to pull it out. He yanked harder and harder, lifting Bob's body completely out of the water at one point. But the sabre was stuck—he could not pull it free, and he was aware that the Major was watching him critically as he smoked.

"Poor Bob, he's gone, and that boy can't get him off his sword," Bigfoot said. He walked down to the water, and motioned for the soldier to pull the body to shore. Nervously, the young cavalryman did as Bigfoot asked. The body trailed a ribbon of blood, which was quickly carried downstream.

When the soldier drew the body to shore, Bigfoot took it and carried it a few yards up the bank. He motioned for Call and Gus to come help him, and they did. The young Rangers held the cold body of the dead man steady—Bigfoot carefully put his foot on the dead man's chest and, with a great heave, pulled the sabre out.

"Why, that wasn't near as hard as getting that Comanche lance out of your hip," Bigfoot observed. He handed the sabre to the young soldier, who took it with a hangdog look.

Major Laroche slowly rode his horse across the river, looking upstream and down, as he counted the corpses. Then he rode up on the west bank and began to bring back his soldiers. As they rode back across the river, they swished their bloody sabres in the water before shoving them back in their scabbards. While they were crossing, the horse with the sabre stuck in its belly floundered out of the river and stumbled past Call and Gus. Call made a lucky grab, and pulled the sabre free. For a moment, looking at the bodies of his friends dead on the far bank or in the river, he felt a rage building. Four Mexican soldiers were in the river, coming right toward him; Call looked at them, the sabre in his hand. The soldiers saw the look and were startled. One of them raised his musket.

"Don't, Woodrow," Gus said, as another of the soldiers lifted his gun. "They won't just whip you this time. They'll kill you."

"Not before I kill a few of them," Call said.

But he knew his friend was right. The Mexican cavalry, led by the stern Major, was coming back across the Rio Grande. He could not fight a whole cavalry without giving up his life. The rage was in him, but he did not want to give up his life. When the Major rode up, Call held the sabre out to him; the Major took it without comment.

Gus was looking across the river. The Mexicans had made no effort to bring back the bodies of the dead Texans—some of those killed in the river had floated downstream, almost out of sight. Jackie Buttons's body was stuck on a snag, near the far bank. Jackie floated on his back, the green water washing over his face.

"I'll miss Jackie," Gus said, to Matilda. "He was slow at cards—maybe that's why I liked him so."

Matilda was still naked, mud on her legs. "I wish I'd never looked, when the killing started," she said. "I don't like to look at killings, not when it's boys I know."

"Matty, I don't either," Gus said. He was wishing that the body of Jackie Buttons would come loose from its snag and float on down the river. He had often cheated Jackie at cards—not for much cash, but steadily, over the months of their travels—now, he regretted it. He knew Jackie Buttons was a little slow minded—it would have been better just to deal the cards fairly. Perhaps, now and again, Jackie would have won a hand or two.

But he had not dealt the cards fairly, and in all their playing, Jackie Buttons had not won a single hand. Now he never would, because he was floating on his back in a river, water coursing over his dead eyes and through his open mouth.

"Oh, dern," he said, and began to cry. He cried so hard he knelt down, covering his face with his arm. He was hoping that when he looked up again the body of the comrade he had cheated would be gone.

Matilda came out of her trance, and put her hand on Gus's shoulder.

"Are you crying for one of them, or for all of them?" she asked.

"Just for Jackie," Gus said, when he was calmer. "I cheated him at cards. He wasn't no cardplayer, but every single time I played him I cheated."

"Well, Jackie won't mind now," Matilda said. "But you ought to stop dealing them cards so sly, Augustus. Someday you'll meet somebody who'll be as quick with a gun as you are with an ace."

"No, I won't," Gus said. "I'm always slyer than anybody, when it comes to cards."

Matilda looked over at Call—he had given up his sabre, but not his rage. He looked as he had looked the day he turned the General's buggy over, in order to get at Caleb Cobb.

"I'll be glad to get you boys home," she said. "Woodrow's a fighter and you're a cheat. If I can just get you home, I don't want to hear of you joining no expeditions."

Gus sat down by the water's edge—he suddenly felt very tired.

"All right, Matty," he said.

"Get up, let's go—the Major's waiting," Matilda said. The Mexican cavalry passed so close that water from the horses' legs splashed on them.

Gus didn't think he *could* get up; his legs had simply given out. But Matilda Roberts offered her strong hand—Gus took it, and got to his feet. Call was still standing as if frozen, looking at the corpses in the river.

"I don't expect there'll be no burying," Bigfoot said, as Gus and Matilda came up.

His guess was right—there was no burying.

Woodrow Call stood where he was, looking at the blood-streaked river, until the dark men came to tie his wrists and lead him away.

9.

Major Laroche was a believer in cold-water bathing. He himself bathed every morning at dawn, in the Rio Grande. Three cavalrymen were required to shield him with a ring of sheets, while he sat in the icy river, breathing deeply. When he finished he insisted that each horse be led into the river, where they could be brushed until their coats shone. Often, while the horses were being brushed, the Major would mount and practice with his own fine sabre, slashing at cactus apples while racing at full speed.

The Texans were allowed blankets and a good fire, but they still had no clothes. Though Call despised Major Laroche, he could not help being impressed by the Major's skill with the sabre. Sometimes he would have his men throw gourds in the air, for him to slash as he raced. His horsemanship was also a thing of skill—the Major could turn his mount in midstride, if one of the gourds was thrown too far to the right or the left. His saddle was polished to a high gleam—he seemed to enjoy this morning practice more than the

[397]

rest of his duties. All day he rode at the head of his column of cavalry, seldom looking back.

Once, as they were nearing Las Cruces, a jackrabbit sped beneath the Major's horse—in a second the Major was after the rabbit. He overtook the jack within fifty yards, and with one stroke severed its head. Then he handed the sabre to his orderly to clean, and resumed his ride at the head of the column.

"I don't like them dandified little saddles," Gus remarked.

"Why not?" Call asked. "That Frenchie sits his like he was glued to it."

"He won't be glued to it if Buffalo Hump gets after him," Gus said. He knew that they were close to El Paso—beyond it was the wilderness where Buffalo Hump had killed Josh Corn and Zeke Moody. Lately, the thought of the big Comanche had been often in his mind.

Call didn't answer—he had not been listening very closely. He thought himself to be an adequate rider, but he knew he could not control a horse as well as the little French Major—nor as well as the humpbacked Comanche, who had raced across the desert holding a human body across his horse while he rode bareback. The Frenchman, running at full speed, had sliced the jackrabbit's head off as neatly as if he were sitting at a table, cutting an onion. The Comanche had scalped Ezekiel Moody, while racing just as fast.

No Ranger that Call had yet seen could ride as well as either the Comanche or the Frenchman. Gus McCrae was a better rider than he was, but Gus would be no match for either the Major or Buffalo Hump, in a fight. Call resolved that if he survived, he would learn as much as he could about correct horsemanship.

"The Major's better mounted," Call said. The Major rode a bay thoroughbred, deep chested and fast.

"Buffalo Hump would get him with that lance," Gus said. "He nearly got me with that lance, remember?"

"I didn't say he couldn't," Call said.

But the next day, he watched the Major as he put his horse through his morning paces. Gus was annoyed that Call would bother watching such a man exercise his horse.

"I don't like the way he curls his damn mustache," Gus said. "If I had a mustache I'd just let it grow wild."

"Let it grow anyway you want," Call said. "I got no opinion."

[398]

At the village of Mesilla, just south of Las Cruces, the surviving Texans—there were only ten, not counting Matilda—were finally given clothes: shirts that fell to their knees, and pants that were baggy and rough.

Then, as Major Laroche watched, an old blacksmith put the ten Texans in leg irons. The leg irons were heavier than the ones they had worn in Anton Chico, and the chains were too short for any of the men to take a full stride.

"Major, I could crawl to El Paso faster than I can walk in these dern ankle bracelets," Bigfoot said.

"You won't have to walk, Monsieur," the Major said. "We have a fine wagon for you to ride in. We want you to be rested for our little ceremony."

The fine wagon turned out to be an oxcart, drawn by an old black ox. The ten men fit in the wagon, but Matilda didn't. Gus offered to give her his place, but Matilda shook her head.

"I've walked this far," she said. "I reckon I can walk on into town."

Ahead, northeast of the river, they could see a grey mountain looming. Although the men were chained, and the oxcart bumped along at a slow pace, the cavalrymen kept pace around it with their sabres drawn. After two hours of bumping along, Gus's bladder began to trouble him—but when he started to slide out of the wagon to take a piss, the soldiers leveled their sabres at him.

"All right then, if that's the rule, I'll just piss over the side," Gus said, standing up. "I don't want to wet my new pants."

He stood up and peed off the end of the oxcart, watched by the soldiers with the sabres. In time, several of the Texans did the same.

It was dusk when the cart bumped into the outskirts of El Paso. A strong wind was blowing, whirling dust into their faces. They could not see the mountain ahead or the river to the west. As night came, the wind rose higher and the dust obscured everything. Now and then, they passed little huts—dogs barked, and a few people came out to look at the soldiers. Matilda kept her hand on the side of the oxcart; the dust was blowing so thickly that she was afraid she might lose her way and be without her companions.

In the cart, the men hid their heads and waited for the journey to be over. Now and then, Call looked out for a minute. He saw a few more buildings.

"I guess they call it the Pass of the North because all this dern wind out of New Mexico blows through it," Bigfoot said. "If it gets much stronger, it'll be blowing pigs at us."

As he said it, they heard over the keening wind a faint sound that they could not identify.

"What's that?" Bigfoot asked.

Call, whose hearing was as keen as Gus McCrae's sight, was the first to identify the sound.

"It's a bugle," he said. "I guess they're sending the army now."

Ahead, through the dust, they saw what seemed to be moving lights; soon a line of infantrymen with lanterns, led by a captain and a bugler, met the cavalrymen. The bugler continued to blow his horn, although the wind snatched the sound away almost before the notes were sounded. The soldiers with the lanterns formed a line beside the oxcart as it bumped along toward the town. One soldier, startled by the sudden appearance of a large woman at his side, dropped his lantern, which smashed on a rock. The infantry captain yelled at the soldier; then he in turn was startled as Matilda Roberts appeared, almost at his elbow. Then they heard shouts and the sound of snarling dogs—there was a shot, and several of the cavalrymen galloped ahead. The snarling got louder, there were more shots, and then a squeal from one of the dogs. A minute later Major Laroche, his sabre drawn, rode close to the oxcart and peered in at the Texans.

"The dogs here are hungry," he said. "Stay in your wagon, and you will be safe."

Then Matilda yelled.

"There's a dog got me—there's dogs all in with these horses," she cried.

Major Laroche turned, and disappeared. Bigfoot, Gus, and Long Bill Coleman managed to pull Matilda into the wagon.

"One of them dogs bit my leg," Matilda said, gasping. "I'm bloody."

Just as she said it the black ox turned, and the cart almost tipped. Three wild dogs jumped in it, snarling and biting.

"Why, this is dog town, I guess," Bigfoot said—he managed to heave one of the dogs out of the cart. The other two, after snarling and snapping at the men, leaped out themselves.

Matilda Roberts sobbed and clung to Gus—the dogs had rushed out at her so quickly that it unnerved her.

Through it all, the bugler continued to play, although the snatches of sound came from farther away.

"I think that bugler's lost," Gus said. "He'll be lucky if them dogs don't get him."

The wind rose higher—lanterns only a few feet from the wagons were hard to see. Now and then, a horse neighed. So much sand had blown into the oxcart that the men were sitting in it. Sand had sifted down the men's loose clothes—it coated their hair.

Then, abruptly, the wind stopped—the cart had turned a corner near a high wall. The sand still swirled above the wall, but for a moment the men were protected. When they lifted their heads, sand from their hair and their collars fell inside their shirts.

Through the dusty air they saw a nimbus of light approaching— it was Major Laroche, with a soldier beside him carrying a large lantern. The Major was wrapped in a great grey cloak, with a hood that came over his head. His mustache was still neatly curled—he seemed not at all affected by the storm.

"Welcome to the Pass of the North, Messieurs," he said. "I have brought you to the Convent of San Lazaro. In the morning the alcalde of El Paso will be here, with his staff, to watch the little ceremony we have planned. We have a warm room waiting for you, and you will be well fed."

"When do we get to know what this ceremony is all about?" Big-foot asked. "It might be one of those things I'd rather sleep through."

"You will not sleep through this one, Monsieur Wallace," the Major said. "This is what you have walked across Texas and New Mexico for. I assure you—you would not want to miss it."

Then the Major was gone, and the light with him. A gate creaked open—several figures stood beside it in the darkness, but the sand swirled through as the cart passed inside the walls. Call couldn't see well enough to tell whether the figures were men or women.

The cart they had been traveling in was so cramped that several of the Texans had to stretch their legs slowly before they could walk. When they were all mobile they were marched across a dusty, windy courtyard by the shadowy figures who had opened the gate.

[401]

A few of the cavalrymen, with their lanterns, came into the court-yard with the Texans, but they stayed close to the men and avoided the dim figures who led them. All the people inside the walls were wrapped in heavy cloaks; they led the Texans across the courtyard silently. All of the figures had the cloaks wrapped closely around their faces.

Bigfoot Wallace had so much sand in his boots that he found it difficult to walk. Big as his feet were, he considered them to be appendages to be cared for correctly; they had taken him across Texas and New Mexico successfully, and now they yet might have to take him farther, to Mexico City, it was rumoured. Sand often contained sand-burrs; he had once got a badly infected toe because he had neglected the prick of a sand-burr. The others marched into the room they were shown to, but Bigfoot calmly sat down and emptied his boots, one by one. He wanted to do it outside, rather than risk emptying burrs into the quarters they were being shown into. Some of the boys were nearly barefoot, as it was—he didn't want to bring burrs inside, where one of them could get stepped on and infect someone else.

As he sat, one of the dim figures, with a very small light, a candle whose flame flicked in the wind, came and stood beside him. Bigfoot was grateful for the light, small though it was. Sand-burrs were small, and not easy to see. He didn't want to miss any. He wiped off the soles of his feet carefully and prepared to pull his boots back on when he happened to glance toward the small, flickering light of the candle. Whoever was holding the candle cupped a hand around it, to shield the flame from the puffs of wind. That, too, was consid-erate, but what caught Bigfoot's eye was the hand itself—the hand was the hand of a skeleton, just bone, with a few pieces of loose, blackened flesh hanging from one of the fingers.

In all his years on the frontier, Bigfoot Wallace had never had such a shock. He had seen many startling sights, but never a skele-ton holding a candle. He was so shocked that he dropped the boot he had been about to put on. His hands, steady through many fierce battles, began to shake and tremble—he could not even locate the boot he had just dropped.

The presence holding the candle—Bigfoot was not sure he could call it a person—bent, in an effort to be helpful, and held the candle closer to the ground, so that Bigfoot could pick up his boot. When he fumbled, the presence bent even closer with the candle; Bigfoot looked up, hoping to see a human face, and received an even greater shock, for the person holding the candle had no nose—just a dark hole. Where he had expected to see eyes, he could see nothing. A hand that was mostly bone held the candle, and the form the hand belonged to had no nose. Then the wind rose higher, and the candle flickered.

Bigfoot was so shaken that he forgot the sand-burrs—he even forgot his boots. He stood up and walked barefoot straight through the doorway, into the room where his companions were. He almost ran through the door, running into Matilda Roberts and knocking her into Gus. There was no light at all in the room. The wind whooshed past the door, and the sand blew in—then someone outside closed the door, and a key grated in the lock.

When Matty knocked Gus down, Gus fell into Long Bill—no one knew what was happening, in the pitch-dark room.

"Woodrow, where are you?" Gus cried—"Someone knocked Matty down."

"It was nobody but me," Bigfoot said.

He realized at that moment that he had forgotten his boots and he turned to go back for them, only to find the door locked. He didn't know whether to be relieved or frightened that he was inside. It was so dark he could see no one—he had only known he shoved Matilda Roberts because none of the Rangers were that large.

"Oh Lord, Matty," he said. "Oh Lord. I seen something bad."

"What?" Matty asked. "I didn't see nothing but folks wrapped in serapes."

"It was so bad I don't want to tell it," Bigfoot said.

"Well, tell it," Matilda insisted.

"I seen a skeleton holding a candle," Bigfoot said. "I guess they've put us in here with the dead."

10.

ALL NIGHT THE RANGERS huddled in pitch darkness, not knowing what to expect. Bigfoot, when questioned, would only say that he had seen a skeleton holding a candle, and that when he looked up he had seen a face with no nose.

"But how would you breathe, with no nose?" Long Bill said.

"You wouldn't need to breathe," Gus said. "If it was just a big hole there, the air would go right into your head."

"You don't need it in your head, Gus—you need it in your lungs."

"What about eyes?" Long Bill asked.

"That's right, didn't it have eyes?" Don Shane asked. The mere sound of Don Shane's deep voice startled everyone almost as much as Bigfoot's troubling report. Don Shane, a thin man with a black beard, was the most silent man in the Ranger troop. He had walked all the way across Texas and Mexico, enduring hunger and cold, without saying more than six words. But the thought of a person with no nose brought him out of his silence. He felt he would like to know about the eyes. After all, Comanches sometimes cut the noses off their women. A barber in Shreveport had once slashed Don's own nose badly. The barber had been drunk. But a person without eyes would be harder to tolerate, at least in Don Shane's view.

"I didn't see eyes," Bigfoot said. "But it had a sheet wrapped over its head. There could have been eyes, under that sheet."

"If there weren't no eyes, that's bad," Long Bill said.

"It's bad anyway," Gus said. "Why would a skeleton be wanting to hold a candle?"

No one had an answer to that question. Call was in a corner—he took no part in the discussion. He thought Bigfoot was probably just imagining things. Gus's question was a good one. A skeleton would have no reason to light their way to their prison cell. Perhaps Bigfoot had gone to sleep in the oxcart, and had a dream he hadn't quite waked out of—skeletons were more likely in dreams than in Mexican prisons. It was true that the Mexican soldiers had seemed a little nervous when they brought them into the prison, but that could well have been because the wild dogs had attacked them. Wild dogs ran in packs; they were known to be worse killers than wolves. They sometimes killed cattle, and even horses. The fact was they were locked in until morning and wouldn't find out the truth about the skeleton until the sun came up.

There was no window in the room they had been put in. When the sun did come up, they only knew it because of a thin line of light under the door.

When the door opened Major Laroche stood there, in a fancier uniform than he had worn during the journey from Las Palomas. His mustache was curled at the ends, and he wore a different sabre, one with a gold handle, in a scabbard plated with gold.

Through the door they could see a line of chairs, and five men with towels and razors waiting behind the chairs. In front of the chairs were small tables with wash-basins on them.

"Good morning, Messieurs," the Major said. "You all look weary. Perhaps it would refresh you to have a nice shave. We want you to look your best for our little ceremony."

The Rangers came out, blinking, into the bright sunlight. The wind had died in the night; the day was clear, and no dust blew. Bigfoot stepped out cautiously. He had almost convinced himself that the skeleton with the candle had been a dream. When he sat down to get the sand-burrs out of his boots he might have nodded for a moment, and dreamed the skeletal hand.

"I guess a shave would be enjoyable," he said, but before the words were out of his mouth a shrouded figure walked up and held out the boots he had left in the courtyard last night.

This time the whole company, Matilda included, saw what he had seen in the courtyard. The hand that held the boots was almost skeletal, with just a little loose flesh hanging from one or two fingers. Such flesh as there was, was black. The figure turned quickly and the hood was wrapped closely around it—no one could see whether it had eyes or a nose, but all had seen the bony hand, and it was enough to stop them in their tracks. They looked, and around the edge of the large courtyard, back under the balconies, there were more figures, all of them wrapped in white sheets or white cloaks.

The Texans looked at the barbers standing behind the five chairs, with their towels and razors. They looked like normal men, but the white figures under the balconies made the Texans feel uneasy. Long Bill did a hasty count of people in sheets, and came up with twenty-six.

"Go on, gentlemen—you'll feel better once you've been shaved and barbered," the Major said.

"I guess I wouldn't mind a shave," Bigfoot said. "What worries me is these skeletons—one of them just brought me my boots."

Major Laroche curled the ends of his mustache. For the first time that any of the Texans could remember, he looked amused.

"They aren't skeletons, Monsieur Wallace," he said. "They are lepers. This is San Lazaro—the leper colony."

"Oh Lord," Long Bill said. "So that's it. I seen a leper once—it was in New Orleans. The one I seen didn't have no hands at all."

"What about eyes?" Gus asked. "Can they see?"

Major Laroche had already walked off, leaving Long Bill to deal with the technical questions about lepers.

"It was awhile ago—I think it could see," Long Bill said.

"These can see," Bigfoot said. "It seen my boots and brought them to me."

"Yeah, but what if the leprosy is in your boots now?" Bill asked. "If you put them boots on, your foot might rot off."

Bigfoot had just started to pull on his right boot—he immediately abandoned that effort, and the boots, too.

"I'll just stay barefoot for awhile," he said. "I'd rather get a few sand-burrs in my feet than to turn into a dern skeleton."

Gus was more disturbed than the rest of the troop by the white figures standing around the courtyard. They had a ghostly appearance, to him.

"Well, but what are lepers, Bill?" Gus asked. "Are they dead or alive?"

"The one I seen looked kind of in-between," Long Bill said. "It was moving, so I guess it wasn't full dead. But it didn't have no hands—it was like part of it had died and part of it hadn't."

Major Laroche had been giving his troops a brief inspection. He turned back impatiently, and gestured for the Texans to hurry on out to the row of barbers.

"Come, your shaves," he said. "The alcalde will not like it if he comes here and finds you looking like shaggy beasts."

"Major, we're a little nervous about them lepers," Bigfoot admitted. "Bill here's the only one of us who has ever seen one."

"The lepers are patients here," the Major said. "They will not hurt you. Those of you who stay here will soon get used to them."

"I hope I ain't staying here, if it means living around people without no skin on their bones," Gus said.

The Major looked at him with amusement.

"Who stays will depend on the beans," the Major said. Then, without explaining, he walked away.

Call studied the lepers as best he could. In the night the notion of dead people walking had been fearful, but in the daylight the lepers, seen at a distance, were not so frightening. One leper noticed that Call was looking at him, or her, and seemed to shrink back deeper into the shadows under the balconies. Some were very short—perhaps they were the ones without feet.

Half the Texans sat down in the barber chairs to be shaved, while the others stood watching. The warm sun felt good—so, in time, did the warm water the barbers used. While Call, who was in the first group, was being wiped clean, he happened to look up, to the walkway that ran around the second story of the convent. There he saw several figures, draped in white, grouped around a smaller figure: the smaller figure was dressed entirely in black. The black figure was not draped, as the others were. She was veiled and gloved. Call saw gloved hands gripping the railing of the walkway.

They were small hands—he supposed the black figure must be a woman, but as he was getting up from the barber chair, the great gates to San Lazaro swung open and a large, fancy carriage swept in, preceded and followed by cavalrymen on freshly brushed horses.

Major Laroche rushed over and spoke rapidly to the barbers, instructing them to hurry with the second group of Texans. Matilda had been given a wash-basin and warm water; she washed her face and arms while the Texans were being shaved.

In the carriage was a fat man in the most elaborate uniform they had yet seen, and four women. Cavalrymen with drawn sabres flanked the carriage, and Major Laroche motioned an orderly to help the alcalde out.

Several comfortable chairs were placed in the courtyard—the alcalde and his women sat in them, and infantrymen opened large parasols and held them over the alcalde and his ladies, to protect them from the sun.

The barbers, made nervous by the presence of the alcalde and under orders to hurry, did hastier work with the second group of Texans. Both Bigfoot and Long Bill suffered small nicks as the result of this haste; but it was not the hasty barbering that worried the Texans—it was what was going to happen to them next. The ceremony that Major Laroche had mentioned to them several times was about to happen. The fat alcalde and four women, all dressed in gay clothes, had come to watch it; and yet, the Texans had no idea what the ceremony might consist of.

Call noticed, though, that ten Mexican soldiers with muskets had lined up in front of a wall, in one corner of the courtyard. They stood there in the sun, holding their muskets. Near them stood a priest in a brown habit.

"They're gonna shoot us," Call said. "There's the firing squad. We should have run with the boys, when they charged up the river."

Bigfoot looked at the soldiers, and drew the same conclusion.

"If we wasn't chained up at the ankles we might jump the wall—one or two of us might make it out, but I figure they'd run us down in a day or two. Or them dogs would eat us."

"Me, I'd just as soon be shot as to be eaten by a damn bunch of curs," Long Bill said.

"Oh, they ain't going to shoot us—we're supposed to be marched to Mexico City," Gus said. "This here's just a show of some kind, for that big Mexican."

Call was skeptical.

"They don't need a priest and a firing squad if it's just a show," he said.

When the last Texan was barbered, they were lined up behind the tables where the basins sat. Then the stools were removed, and all but one of the tables.

Major Laroche stepped crisply toward them, carrying an earthen jar. He sat the jar on the table. It had a cloth over it, which he did not at first remove.

"At last we come to the moment of our ceremony," he said. "You are all guilty of attempting to overthrow the lawful government of New Mexico. By the normal laws of war you would all be shot. But the authorities have decided to be merciful."

"Merciful how?" Bigfoot asked.

"Some will live and some will die," the Major said. "There are ten of you, not counting the woman. The woman we will spare. But the ten of you are soldiers and must take the consequences of your actions."

"Most of us already have," Call said. They were going to shoot them all—he was sure of that. He saw no reason to stand there and listen to a French soldier make fancy speeches at them, for the benefit of a fat Mexican.

The Major paused, and looked at him.

"We started from Texas with nearly two hundred men," Call said. "Now we're down to ten. I'd call that punishment—I don't know what you'd call it."

"That is but the fortunes of war, Monsieur," Major Laroche said. "Here is how our ceremony will work. In the jar I have placed before you are ten beans. Five of them are white, and five are black. Each of you will be blindfolded. You will come to the bowl and draw a bean. The five who draw white beans will live. The five who draw black beans will die. We have a priest, as you can see. And we have a firing squad. So, gentlemen, who would like to be the first to draw a bean?"

There was a pause—Gus and Long Bill glanced at Bigfoot Wallace, but Bigfoot had his eyes fixed on the nearest soldier with a musket. He was not thinking about white beans or black—not yet.

He was thinking that he might try to grab a musket, shoot the Major or the fat alcalde, and try to get over the wall with a few of the boys. The leg irons were the deuce to cope with, but if a few of them could get over the wall with a musket or two, at least they would have a chance to die fighting. He didn't trust the Mexicans, in the matter of the beans. It might be that all the beans in the bowl were black—it was probably just a ruse to give them hope, when there was no hope.

Call didn't trust the beans either, but he didn't intend to stay like a coward and wait for someone to move—so he stepped forward, in front of the table that held the bowl. A soldier with a black bandana in his hand stood near the table.

"Ah, good—our first volunteer," the Major said.

He looked for a moment at the soldier with the bandana.

"Be sure that you blindfold him well," the Major said.

The bowl with the beans in it had a white cloth over it. The soldier came up behind Call and put the bandana over his eyes; he pulled it tight and knotted it quickly in place. The soldier knew his job—Call couldn't see a thing. The bandana let through no light at all.

The blindfold alone did not satisfy Major Laroche. He picked up the jar of beans, took the cloth off it, and walked around behind Call.

"A blindfold can slip," he said. "I am going to hold the jar behind you, just below your left hand. When you are ready, reach in and pick your bean."

Call felt his hand bump the side of the jar. He didn't know what to expect, but he put his hand in the bowl anyway. It occurred to him that it was just a trick of some kind. There could be spiders or scorpions in the bowl—even a small snake. Bigfoot had pointed out to him that the smallest rattlesnakes were often the deadliest. Perhaps the firing squad was just for show.

Immediately, though, he realized that his suspicions were foolish. In the bottom of the bowl were a few beans. There was no way to choose between them so he took one, and pulled his hand out of the bowl. The soldier immediately began to untie the blindfold.

"You were brave enough to start, Monsieur, and your courage has been rewarded," Major Laroche said.

Call looked in his palm, and saw that the bean was white.

"You will live," the Major said. "Step to the side, please. We need another volunteer."

Bigfoot Wallace immediately stepped forward. Call's luck had persuaded him that there really were beans in the brown jar. He abandoned his plan to try and steal a musket and leap the wall. Mostly, through the years, in situations that were life and death, his luck had held. Call had drawn a white bean; he might also. There was no point in flinching from the gamble.

Bigfoot had a head to match his more famous appendages. The blindfold, which had been easy to knot around Call's head, would barely go around Bigfoot's. By pulling hard, the soldier assigned to do the blindfolding could just get the ends of the bandana to meet, but he could not pull it tight enough to knot it.

"We should have cut your hair, Monsieur Wallace," the Major said. "The blindfold won't fit you."

"I can just squinch up my eyes," Bigfoot said. "The beans are behind me, anyway. I can't see behind myself."

"Maybe not, but rules are rules," the Major said. "You must be blindfolded."

He motioned to another soldier, who held the other end of the bandana—the two soldiers pressed the blindfold tightly against Bigfoot's eyes.

"I couldn't see a bolt of lightning if one was to strike right in front of me," Bigfoot said.

"The bowl is below your left hand," Major Laroche said. "Please draw your bean."

Bigfoot took out a bean, and held it in his palm. Even before the soldier dropped his blindfold he heard a cry from one of the ladies who sat with the alcalde. When he looked in his palm, he saw that the bean was black.

"The count is one and one," Major Laroche said.

One of the ladies sitting with the alcalde had fainted at the sight of the black bean. Two of the other women were fanning her. The alcalde paid no attention to the women. He did not seem very interested in the Texans, or in the drama of life and death that was unfolding in front of him. A boil on his hand seemed to interest him more. He picked at it with a tiny knife, and then wiped it with a fine white handkerchief.

Bigfoot looked at the bean in his hand, and then put it in his pocket. Two soldiers moved him a short distance, in the direction of the wall where the firing squad waited. Bigfoot glanced back at his comrades, the Texans still waiting to draw.

"Good-bye, boys—I guess I'll be the first to be shot," he said.

As he waited, he pulled the black bean out of his pocket several times and looked at it. In his years on the frontier he had been in threat of his life many times, from bullets, tomahawks, arrows, lances, knives, horses, bears, Comanche, Apache, Kiowa, Sioux, Pawnee—yet his life had finally been lost to an unlucky choice of beans, in the courtyard of a leper colony in El Paso.

The Rangers still waiting were stunned. Bigfoot, more than any other man, had led them to safety across the prairies. He had outlasted their commanders, and taught them the tricks of survival. He had helped them find food, and had located rivers and water-holes for them. Yet now he was doomed.

"Bye, Matty," Bigfoot said, waving to Matilda. Then he had a thought.

"Will you sing over me, Matty?" he asked. He remembered that his aunts had sung beautifully, back in old Kentucky, long ago.

"I'll sing a song for you—I'll try to remember one," Matilda said. "I'll do it—you were a true friend to my Shad."

Don Shane stepped up next, and drew a black bean. Silent as usual, Don didn't speak or change expression. Quartermaster Brognoli, who was still glassy eyed and whose head still jerked, stood at attention while being blindfolded; he drew a white bean. Joe Turner, a stocky fellow from Houston who spoke with a slow stutter, came next and drew a black bean. He and Don were marched over to stand with Bigfoot. Brognoli moved over and stood with Call.

Gus stood by Long Bill Coleman. Wesley Buttons stood with two cousins named Pete and Roy—no one could remember their last names. Neither Wesley, nor Pete, nor Roy, seemed inclined to advance to the table where the jar waited. Long Bill turned, and looked at Gus.

"Well, do you want to go and draw?" he asked. He himself was not anxious to step forward and be blindfolded, but the Texans' ranks were thinning. A turn could not be avoided much longer.

Gus knew he ought to take a bold approach to the gamble ahead —the sort of approach he had always taken at cards or dice. But this was not cards or dice—this was life or death, and he did not feel bold. He looked at Matty, who was crying. He looked at Major Laroche, and at the fat alcalde, who was still picking at his boil.

"Woodrow went first, maybe I'll be the last," Gus said.

"I expect you're hoping somebody will use up all them black beans before you get there," Long Bill said. "The way I count it there's two of them damn black ones left."

Gus didn't answer. He felt very frightened, and a good deal annoyed with Woodrow Call, for being so quick to volunteer. If he himself had been given a moment to steady his nerves, he might have gone first and drawn the same white bean that Woodrow drew. Woodrow Call was too impatient—everyone agreed with that.

Wesley Buttons went next, while Long Bill was thinking about it; he drew a white bean—Gus and Long Bill were both chagrined that they had not stepped forward more quickly. Now Wesley was safe, but they weren't.

Long Bill felt a terrible anxiety growing in him; he could not stand the worrying any longer. He bolted forward so quickly that he almost overturned the table where the jar with the beans sat.

"Calm, Monsieur, calm," the Major said. "There is no need to bump our table."

"Well, but I'm mighty ready now," Long Bill said. "I want to take my turn."

"Of course, you shall take your turn," the Major said.

The blindfold was tied in place, and the bowl moved below Long Bill's left hand. He quickly thrust his hand into the bowl and felt the beans. Before he could choose one, though, an anxiety seized him—it gripped him so suddenly and so strongly that he could not make his fingers pick out a bean. He froze for several seconds, his hand deep in the jar. He wondered if black beans felt rougher than white beans—or whether it might be the other way around.

Major Laroche waited a bit, then cleared his throat.

"Monsieur, you must choose," he said. "Come. Be brave, like your comrades. Choose a bean."

Desperately, Long Bill did as he was told—he forced his trembling fingers to clutch a bean, but no sooner had he lifted it free of the pot than he dropped it. The soldier with the bandana bent to pick it up. Then he took the blindfold off, and handed the bean to Long Bill—the bean was white.

Pete went next; he turned his blindfolded face up to the sky as if seeking instruction, before he drew. He didn't seem to be praying, but he held his face up for a moment, to the warm sun. Then he drew a black bean.

That left two men: Gus, and the skinny fellow named Roy.

At the thought that he might be the last to draw, which would condemn him for sure if Roy was lucky enough to draw a white bean, Gus jumped forward almost as quickly as Long Bill had. When he put his hand in the jar he realized that the Mexicans had not been lying about the number of beans. There were only two beans left—one for him, and one for Roy. One had to be white, the other black. He pushed first one bean and then the other with his finger, remembering all the times he had thrown the dice. He always threw quickly—it didn't help his luck to cling to the dice.

He took a bean and pulled his hand out, but when the soldier removed the blindfold, he could not immediately bring himself to open his eyes. He held out his hand, with the bean in his palm—everyone saw that it was white before he did.

Roy went pale, when he saw the white bean in Gus's palm.

"I guess that does it for me," he said quietly, as if speaking to himself. But he went through the blindfolding calmly, and drew the last black bean; then he walked with a steady step over to join the men who were to die.

Gus stepped the other direction, and stood by Call.

"You shouldn't have waited so long," Call told him.

"Well, you went first, and nobody told you to," Gus said, still annoyed. "There were five black beans in there, when you went, and there wasn't but one when I went. I figure I helped my chances."

"If I had had a weapon I wouldn't have stood for it," Call said—their five comrades were even then being marched toward the wall where the firing squad waited.

As he watched, the same soldier who had blindfolded them as they drew the beans went over with five bandanas and soon had the unlucky Texans blindfolded—all, that is, except Bigfoot Wallace, whose head, once again, was too large for the blindfold that had been provided.

Major Laroche, annoyed by the irregularity, yelled at one of the soldiers behind the alcalde, who hurried into the building, followed by one of the shrouded figures. A moment later the soldier came back with part of a sheet, which had been cut up to make a blind-fold.

"Monsieur Wallace, I am sorry," the Major said. "A man doesn't like to wait, at such a time."

"Why, Major, it's not much of a thing to worry about," Bigfoot said. "I've seen many a man die with his eyes wide open. I guess I could manage it too, if I had to."

The men who were to live were marched over and offered the chance to exchange last words with those who were to die—but in fact, few words were exchanged. Bigfoot handed Brognoli a little tobacco, which he had accepted from one of the men in the oxcart. Joe Turner was shaky—he gripped Call's hand hard, when Call reached out to exchange a last shake.

"Matty, have you picked a song?" Bigfoot asked. "I expect a hymn would be the thing—I don't know none myself, but my ma and her sisters knew plenty."

Matilda was too choked up—she couldn't reply. Now five of the ten boys were to be shot—soon there would be no one left at all, of all the gallant boys she had set out from Austin with.

Gus, likewise, was tongue tied. He looked at Roy, at Joe, at Don Shane, at Pete, and couldn't manage a word. He shook their hands —since they were in leg irons already, Major Laroche had decided that their hands did not need to be tied. The five who were to live waited a moment in front of the five who were condemned, thinking they might want to send messages to their loved ones, or exchange a few last words, but the five blindfolded men merely stood there, silent. Pete turned his face to the sky, as he had just before drawing the black bean.

"So long, boys," Bigfoot said. "Don't waste your water on the trip home—it's dry country out there."

The five who had drawn white beans were then moved back. The fat alcalde got out of his chair and made a speech. It was a long speech, in Spanish—none of the Texans could follow it. None even tried. Their friends stood with their backs against the wall, blind-folded. When the alcalde finished his speech, Major Laroche spoke to the firing squad—their muskets were raised.

Major Laroche nodded: the soldiers fired. The bodies of the Tex-ans slid down the wall. Bigfoot Wallace stayed erect the longest, but he, too, soon slid down, tilting as he did. He lay with his head—the

[415]

head that had been too big for the blindfold—across stuttering Joe Turner's leg.

Call felt black hatred for the Mexicans, who had marched many of his friends to death, and now had shot five of them down right in front of them. Gus felt relieved—if he hadn't marched forward and drawn the bean when he did, he was sure he would now be with the dead. Brognoli, his head still jerking, chewed a little of Bigfoot's tobacco. When he saw the men fall he felt a jerking inside him, like the movement of his head. He had no voice; he could not comment on the death of men, which, after all, was an everyday thing.

The Mexicans brought the same oxcart, with the same black ox, into the courtyard and were about to begin loading the Texans' bodies in it when, to everyone's surprise, a voice was raised in song, from the balcony above the courtyard. It was a high voice, sweet and clear, yet not weak—it carried well beyond the courtyard, strong enough to be heard all the way to the Rio Grande, Gus thought.

Everyone in the courtyard was stilled by the singing. The alcalde had been about to get in his carriage, but he stopped. Major Laroche looked up, as did the other soldiers. There were no words with the sound, merely notes, high and vibrant. Matilda stopped crying—she had been trying to think of a song to sing for Bigfoot Wallace, but a woman was already singing, for Bigfoot and the others—a woman with a voice far richer than their own. The sound came from the balcony, where the woman in black stood. It was she who sang for the dead men; she sang and sang, with such authority and such passion that even the alcalde dared not move until she finished. The sound rose and swooped, like a flying bird; some of the tones brought a sadness to the listeners, a sadness so deep that Call cried freely and even Major Laroche had to wipe away tears.

Gus was transfixed; he liked singing, himself, and could bawl out a tune with the best of them when he was drunk; but what he heard that day, as the bodies of his comrades were waiting to be loaded into an oxcart, was like no singing he had ever heard, like none he would ever hear again. The lady in black gripped the railing of the balcony as she sang. As she was finishing her song, the notes dipped down low—they carried a sadness that was more than a sadness at the death of men; rather it was a sadness at the lives of men, and of women. It reminded those who heard the rising, dipping notes, of notes of hopes that had been born, and, yet, died; of promise, and the failure of promise. Gus began to cry; he didn't know why, but he couldn't stop, not while the song continued.

Then, after one long, low tone that seemed to hang soft as the daylight, the lady in black ended her requiem. She stood for a moment, gripping the railing of the balcony; then she turned, and disappeared.

The alcalde, as if released from a trance, got into his carriage with his ladies; the carriage slowly turned, and went out the gate.

"My Lord, did you hear that?" Gus asked Call.

"I heard it," Call said.

The soldiers, too, had come to life. They had begun to load the bodies in the oxcart. Matilda came over to where the five survivors stood.

"We ought to go with them, boys," she said. "They're our people. I want to see that they're laid out proper, in their graves."

"Go ask the Major if we can help with the burying," Call said, to Gus. "I expect if you ask him he'll let us. He likes you."

"Come with me, Matty," Gus said. "We'll both ask."

The alcalde had stopped a moment, to have a word with Major Laroche, who stood by the gate. Through the gate Gus could see the long, dusty plain to the north. The Major saluted the alcalde and bowed to his women—the carriage passed out. The oxcart, with the bodies of the Texans in it, was creaking across the courtyard, toward the same gate.

"We'd like to help with the burying, Major," Gus said. "They was our friends. We can't do much for them now, but we'd like to be there."

"If you like, Monsieur," the Major said. "The graveyard is just outside the wall. Follow the cart and return when the work is finished."

Gus was a little startled that the Major meant to send no guard.

"I suggest you hurry back," the Major said, with a look of amusement. "The dogs here are very bad—I don't think you can outrun them, with those chains. You saw a few of them last night, but there are many more. If you try to escape you will soon meet with the dogs."

Matilda could not get the singing out of her mind. She wished

Bigfoot could know what wonderful singing there had been, after his death and the deaths of the others. She had tried to get a good look at the woman in black, but the veils were too thick and the distance too great.

"I never heard singing like that, Major," Matilda said. "Who is that woman?"

"That is Lady Carey," the Major said. "She is English. You will meet her soon."

"What's an English lady doing in a place like this?" Gus asked. "She's farther off from home than we are."

Major Laroche turned, as if tired of the conversation, and motioned for one of the soldiers to bring his horse.

"Yes, and so am I," Major Laroche said, as he prepared to mount. "But I am a soldier and this is where I was sent. Lady Carey is here because she is a prisoner of war, like yourselves. I will tell my men to let you help with the burial. I suggest you pile on many, many rocks. As I said, the dogs here are very bad, and they don't have much to eat."

Gus motioned to the others—they all filed out, behind the oxcart. As soon as they were out the gate, Major Laroche and his ten cavalrymen galloped out and were soon enveloped in the dust their horses' hooves threw up.

"I asked about that woman who done the singing," Gus told Call. "The Major says she's a prisoner of war, like us."

Call didn't answer—he was looking at the bodies of his dead comrades. Blood leaked out the bottom of the crude oxcart, leaving a red line that was quickly covered by blowing sand.

"Lord, it's windy here, ain't it?" Wesley Buttons said.

11.

THE MEXICAN SOLDIERS WERE glad to allow the Texans to bury their comrades. One of the soldiers had a bottle of white liquor, which he handed around among his friends. Soon the Mexicans were so drunk that all but one of them passed out in the oxcart. None of them had weapons, so it made little sense to think of overpowering them and attempting to escape, though Woodrow Call considered it.

Gus saw what direction his friend's thoughts were taking, and quickly pointed out what the Major had said about the dogs.

"He said they'll eat us, if we try to run with these chains on," Gus said.

"I don't expect to be eaten by no cur," Call said—but he knew the Major was probably right. Packs of wild dogs could bring down any animal less fierce than a grizzly bear.

Matilda Roberts had saved a broken piece of tortoiseshell comb through the long journey—she was attempting to comb the dead men's hair, while the Mexican soldiers finished the bottle of liquor.

The Texans were laid in one grave, by the walls of San Lazaro.

A dust storm had blown up. When they began the burial they could see the river, but the river was soon lost from view. Once the graves were covered the Texans stumbled around, gathering rocks. Several dogs had already gathered—Gus and Wesley threw rocks at them, but the dogs only retreated a few yards, snarling.

While they worked, another smaller cart, drawn by an old mule, made its way around the wall. It, too, was a vehicle of burial—on it were the bodies of two lepers, wrapped tightly in white shrouds. The cart passed close to where the Texans were working; the person driving the cart was also shrouded.

"Look, it's that one without no meat on his fingers," Gus said— all that was visible of the driver was the same two bony hands that had given Bigfoot his boots, only a few hours earlier. The leper did not look their way; nor did he make any pretenses. He merely tipped them out of the cart, and turned the cart back toward the gate. Soon the dogs were tearing at the shrouds. The sight saddened Matilda even more. She didn't imagine that they could find enough rocks to make the bodies of Bigfoot and the others safe for very long.

Call led the ox back into San Lazaro. Most of the Mexican soldiers were sleeping in the oxcart; one would have thought them as dead as the Texans, but for the snores. The two soldiers who could still walk kept close to the Texans, for fear of the dogs.

Once inside the gates the Texans, though still chained, were allowed the freedom of the courtyard. They were served a simple meal of beans and *posole*, on the table where the jar they had drawn from had been set.

An old man and an old woman served them—both were lepers, yet neither was shrouded, and the dark spots on their cheeks and arms looked no worse to the Texans than bad bruises. Both seemed to be kindly people; they smiled at the Texans, and brought them more food when they emptied their dishes. The only soldiers left in San Lazaro were the drunks in the oxcart. In midafternoon, they began to awake. When they did, they picked up their weapons and drove the oxcart out of the walls. All of them looked frightened.

"They're scared of them dogs," Gus said. "Why don't the Major get up a dog hunt and kill the damn curs?"

"There'd just be more," Call said. "You can't kill all the dogs."

He watched the lepers, as they came and went at their tasks. All of them kept themselves covered, but now and then a wind would riffle a cloak, or blow a shawl, so that he could glimpse the people under the wraps. Some were bad: no chins, cheeks that were black, noses half eaten away. Some limped, from deformities of their feet. One old man used a crutch—he had only one foot. There were a few children playing in the courtyard; all of them seemed normal to Call. There was even a little blond boy, about ten, who showed no sign of the disease. Some of the adults appeared to be not much worse than the old man and the old woman who served them. Some had dark spots on their cheeks and foreheads, or on their hands.

Once the soldiers were gone, San Lazaro did not seem a bad place. Many of the lepers looked at the Texans in a friendly way. Some smiled. Others, whose mouths were affected, covered themselves, but nodded when they passed.

Overhead, the dust swirled so high they could barely see the mountain that loomed over the convent.

Gus felt such relief at being alive, that his appetite for gambling began to return. He had ceased to mind the lepers much—at night they might be scary, but in the daylight the place they were in looked not much worse than any hospital. He began to wish he had a pack of cards, or at least some dice, though of course he had not one cent to gamble with.

"I wonder how long the Mexicans mean to leave us here?" he asked.

Brognoli's head was going back and forth, like the pendulum of a clock, as it had ever since his fright in the canyon. He watched the lepers with dispassion, and the little blond boy with curiosity. Once, he looked up at the balcony where the lady in black had been and saw a short stout woman standing there. She spoke, and the little blond boy reluctantly left his play and ran upstairs.

Call was thinking about a way to rid them of the leg irons. If he had a hammer and a chisel of some sort, he felt certain he could break the chains himself. The Major had said nothing about coming back, and the last of the soldiers had gone. They were alone with the lepers—the only impediments to their escape were the chains and the dog packs. If he could get the chains off, there would be a way to brave the dogs.

Wesley Buttons, though he had held up bravely during the long march and the drawing of the beans, was feeling keenly the loss of his two brothers, and of the rest of the troop.

"I remember when we left—I got to drive the wagon with old General Lloyd in it," he said. "We had an army. There was enough of us to hold off the Indians and whip the Mexicans. Now look—there's just us, and we're way out here in the desert, locked in with these sick 'uns."

"It's a long way home, I reckon," he added. "Ma's going to be sad, when she hears about the boys."

Brognoli's head swung back and forth, back and forth.

"I barely know which way *is* home," Long Bill said. "It's so dusty it's all I can do to keep my directions. I guess I could go downriver, but it would be a pretty long walk."

Gus remembered that it was the same river they had camped on when Matilda caught the big green snapping turtle.

"Why, if it's the Rio Grande, we could just stroll along it easy," he said. "Matty could catch us turtles, when we get hungry."

Matilda shook her head—she didn't welcome the prospect of another long walk.

"It's just the six of us got across New Mexico," she pointed out. "If we have to walk the rest of the way, I doubt any of us will make it. That big Indian knows that river—he might get us yet."

"We'd have to have weapons," Call said. "None of us would make it, without weapons."

"I don't see what the hurry is," Gus said. "We've had a long hike, as it is. I'd like to laze around here and rest up, myself. These lepers ain't bothering us. All you got to do is not look at them too close."

He had been inclined to try escape, until Matilda had mentioned Buffalo Hump. Memory of the fierce Comanche put a different slant on such a trip. Better to stay inside the walls of San Lazaro and rest with the lepers, than to expose themselves to Buffalo Hump again—especially since they only had five men.

"I want to leave, if we can get these chains off," Call said. "What if the Major comes back and has us draw some more beans?"

He was tired, though, and didn't urge escape immediately. When the wind was high, his back still sometimes throbbed, and his sore foot pained him. A day or two's rest wouldn't hurt—at least it wouldn't if the Mexicans didn't decide to eliminate them all.

As the evening wore on, the Texans rested and napped—they had been assigned the little room where they had spent the night before, but no one really wanted to go into such a dark hole. The courtyard was sunny; those who didn't want sun could rest under the long barricades.

Gus was determined to gamble—he had asked several of the Mexicans who worked in the convent if they had any cards; one woman with only three teeth took a shine to him and managed to find an incomplete deck. It was missing about twenty cards, but Gus and Long Bill soon devised a game. They broke a few straws off a broom to use for money.

While they were making up rules for a card game involving only thirty-three cards, a black woman taller than Gus came across the courtyard. She didn't seem to be a leper—her face and hands were normal. She approached them in such a dignified manner that the men straightened up a little. Gus hid the cards.

"Gentlemen, I have an invitation for you," the Negress said, in English better than their own. "Lady Carey would like to ask you to tea."

"Ask us to what?" Gus asked. He was taken by surprise. Although he had just shaved the day before, the dignity and elegance of the black woman made him feel scruffy.

"Tea, gentlemen," the Negress said. "Lady Carey is English, and in England they have tea. It's like a little meal. Lady Carey's son, the viscount Mountstuart, will be taking it with us. I'm sure you've seen him playing with the Mexican children. He's the one who's blond."

Call, too, was startled by the black woman's courtesy and poise. He had never seen a Negress so tall, much less one so well spoken. Few black women in Texas would dare to speak to a group of white men so boldly, and yet the woman had not been rude in any way. She had an invitation to deliver, and she had delivered it. Like Gus, he felt that the few Rangers left were a rugged lot, hardly fit to take food with an English lady.

While he and Gus and Wesley and Long Bill were looking at one another, a little uncertain as to how to respond, the black woman turned to Matilda Roberts and smiled.

"Miss Roberts, Lady Carey knows you've traveled a long way across a dusty land," the Negress said. "She was thinking you might appreciate a bath and a change of clothes."

Matilda was surprised by the woman's serenity.

"I would . . . I would . . . mainly I've just had a wash in the river, when we were by the river," Matilda said.

"That river comes out of the mountains," the woman said. "I expect it's cold."

"Ice cold," Matilda confirmed.

"Then come along with me," the Negress said. "Lady Carey has a tub, and the water is hot. These gentlemen can wait a few minutes —tea will be served in about half an hour."

Matilda looked a little uncertain, but she followed the black woman across the courtyard and up the stairs.

"I wonder what kind of meal it will be," Wesley Buttons said. "I hope it's beefsteak. I ain't had no beefsteak in a good long while."

"For it to be beefsteak there'd have to be cattle," Gus remarked. "I ain't seen no cattle around here, and I don't know how a cow would live if there was one. It would have to eat sand, or else cactus, and if it wasn't quick the dern dogs would get it."

A problem they considered as they waited for it to be time to go to Lady Carey's was that Brognoli's condition seemed to be getting worse. He turned his head more and more rapidly, back and forth, back and forth, and he had begun to drool; now and then he emitted a low, thin sound, a sound such as a rabbit might make as it was dying.

A little later, the black woman appeared on the balcony above them and motioned for them to come. Gus had doubts about taking Brognoli, but it seemed unfair to leave him, since food was being offered. It was true that the Mexicans who ran San Lazaro had been generous with soup and tortillas, but Wesley Buttons had put the notion of beefsteak in their minds. It seemed wrong to exclude Brognoli from what might be a feast.

"Come on, Brog," Gus said. "That lady that did that singing over Bigfoot and the boys is up there waiting to give us grub."

Brognoli got up and came with them, walking slowly and still swinging his head.

None of them knew what to expect, as they went up the stairs and along the narrow balcony that led to Lady Carey's quarters. Gus kept brushing at his hair with his hands—he had meant to ask Matty for her broken comb, but forgot it. Of course, he had not expected Matilda to be led away by a tall black woman who spoke better english than any of them.

Suddenly, the little blond boy jumped out of the shadows, pointing a hammerless old horse pistol at them.

"Are you Texans? I am a Scot," the boy said.

"Why, I'm part Scot myself," Gus said. "That's what my ma claimed. You're as far away from home as I am."

"But that's why my mother wants to see you," the boy said. "She wants you to take us home. She told me we could leave tomorrow, if you would like to take us."

Call and Gus exchanged looks. The little boy was handsome and frank. Perhaps he was merely fibbing, as children will, but there was also the chance that his mother, Lady Carey, had told him some such thing. Call didn't mean to stay a prisoner of the Mexicans long, but neither had he expected to leave in a day.

"If we were to take you home, what would we ride?" he asked. "Our horses got stolen a long time back."

"Oh, my mother has horses," the boy said. "There's a stable in the back of the leprosarium."

"In the back of the what?" Gus asked.

"The leprosarium—aren't you lepers?" the little boy asked. "My mother's a leper, that's why I never get to see her face. But her hands are not affected yet—she can still play the violin quite well, and she's teaching me."

"When we get home I shall have the finest teacher in Europe," he added. "Someday I may play before the Queen. My mother knows the Queen, but I haven't met her yet. I'm still too young to be presented at court."

"Well, I'm not as young as you—I'd like to meet a queen," Gus said. "Especially if she was a pretty queen."

"No, the Queen is fat," the little boy said. "My mother was beautiful, though, until she became a leper. She was even painted by Mr. Gainsborough, and he's a very famous painter."

Just then a door opened, and the tall Negress stepped out.

"Now, Willy, I hope you haven't been pointing that gun at these gentlemen," the woman said. "It's very impolite to point guns at people—particularly people who might become your friends."

"Well, I *did* point it, but it was just in fun," the boy said. "I couldn't really shoot them because I have no bullets."

"That doesn't make it less impolite," the woman said.

Then she looked at the group.

"Of course I've been impolite, too," she said. "I failed to introduce myself. I'm Emerald."

"She's from Africa and her father was a king," the boy said. "She's been with us ever so long, though. She's been with us even longer than Mrs. Chubb."

"Now, Willy, don't bore the gentlemen," Emerald said. "Tea is almost ready. You may want to come in and wash your hands."

"We washed once, when they barbered us," Gus pointed out. "It's been quite a few months since we washed twice in one day."

"Yes, but you are now under the protection of Lady Carey," Emerald said. "You may wash as often as you want."

"Ma'am, if there's grub, I'm for eating first and washing later," Wesley Buttons said. "I've not had a beefsteak for awhile—I feel like I could eat most of a cow."

"Goodness, you don't serve beefsteak at tea," Emerald said. "Beefsteak belongs with dinner, never with tea. Lady Carey is quite unconventional, but not *that* unconventional, I'm afraid."

The Texans were led into a room where there were five wash-basins; the water in the basins was so hot that five columns of steam rose into the room. There were also five towels, and more extraordinary still, five hairbrushes and five combs. The brushes were edged in silver, and the combs seemed to be ivory. At a slight remove was another table, with another wash-basin, a towel, and another silver-edged brush and ivory comb.

"That's the hottest water I've seen since we left San Antonio," Gus remarked. "We'll all scald ourselves, if we ain't careful."

The sixth wash-basin was for Willy, the young viscount. The Texans were left to scrub themselves after their own inclinations, but while they were watching the water steam in the wash-basins, a short, fat woman in grey clothes burst through a door and grabbed Willy before he could elude her.

"No, no, Mrs. Chubb," Willy said, trying to squirm out of her grip; but his squirming was in vain. In a second, Mrs. Chubb had Willy bent over his own wash-basin; she gave his face a vigorous scrubbing, ignoring his protests about the scalding water.

"Now, Willy, try not to howl, you'll upset our guests," Mrs. Chubb said. She didn't take her eye, or her hands, off her young charge until she considered him sufficiently washed; once her task was done to her satisfaction, the young boy's face was red from scrubbing and his hair shining from a skillful application of comb and brush. Then the plump woman surveyed the Texans with a lively blue eye.

"Here, gentlemen, your water's cooling—plunge in," she said. "Lady Carey has a glorious appetite, and your Miss Roberts is eating as if she's been starved for a month."

"Two months," Long Bill said. "Matty ain't had a good meal since we crossed the Brazos."

"Well, she's having a splendid high tea, right now," Mrs. Chubb said. "If you gentlemen want anything to eat between now and dinner, I suggest you wash up quickly. Otherwise there won't be a scone left, or a sandwich, either."

Willy rushed through the door Mrs. Chubb had just emerged from.

"Mamma, I *must* have a scone," he said. "Do wait—I'm coming."

The Texans, under the urging of Mrs. Chubb, hastily splashed themselves with the hot water and rubbed themselves with the towels. Though they had shaved and washed just that morning, the towels were brown with dust when they finished their rubbing. Gus took a swipe or two at his hair with the silver brush—the rest of the Texans felt awkward even picking up such unfamiliar instruments, and left themselves uncombed.

Mrs. Chubb, unfazed, shooed them toward the door, much as a hen might shoo her chickens.

When the Texans entered Lady Carey's room they were shocked to see Matilda Roberts, pink-faced, and with wet hair, in a clean white smock, sitting on a stool eating biscuits.

Beside her, in a chair, was the lady in black, the one who had sung so movingly over their fallen friends. Gus had hoped to get a glimpse of her face, but he was disappointed: Lady Carey was triply veiled, and the veils were black. Nothing showed at all, not her hair, not her face, not her feet, which were in sharp-toed black boots. Call supposed the woman's face must be badly eaten up, else why would she cover herself so completely? He could get no hint even of the color of her eyes. Yet she was eating when they came in, eating a small thing that seemed to be mostly bread. When Lady Carey wanted to eat, she tilted her head forward slightly, and slipped the little bite of bread under the three veils—just for a second he saw a flash of white teeth, and a bit of chin, which seemed unblemished.

"Excuse me, gentlemen," Lady Carey said, in a low, friendly voice. "When I'm hungry I have no manners—and I always seem to be hungry, in San Lazaro. I expect it's the wind. When I'm eating, I don't mind it quite so much."

"It blows, don't it?" Long Bill said—he was surprised that he had been able to utter a word, to such a great lady. They were in a large room whose walls had been hung with patterned cloth. The two windows were tightly shuttered. In one corner was a large, four-poster bed with a little dog sitting on it; beside it was a smaller bed where Willy slept.

"Certainly does—it blows," Lady Carey said. "Eat, gentlemen. Don't be shy. I expect it's been awhile since you've sat down to a tea such as this."

Lady Carey's hands, too, were gloved in black—she reached down with two gloved fingers, took another small piece of the bread, and popped it under the veils and into her mouth.

Gus felt that it was his turn to speak—he had been about to address Lady Carey when Long Bill rudely jumped in ahead of him, and only to make a pointless comment about the wind. Before them on the table was an array of food, and all of it was rather small food, it seemed to him: there were little pieces of bread, cut quite square, with what seemed like slices of cucumber stuck between the squares of bread. Then there were biscuits and muffins, and larger, harder muffins with raisins stuck in them: he thought those might be the things called scones that Willy had referred to. Besides the various muffins and biscuits there were little ears of corn, with a saucer of butter and salt to dip them in; there were tomatoes and apricots and figs, and a plate of tiny fish that proved very salty to the taste. Gus had every intention of saying something complimentary about the food, but something about Lady Carey intimidated him, preventing him from getting even a word out of his mouth. He looked at her and opened his mouth, but then instead of speaking, put a bit of biscuit in his mouth and ate it.

The Texans were shy in the beginning—most of the foods they were being offered were foods they had never tasted. They stuck, at first, to what was safest, which were the biscuits—but, in part because they stuck to them so strictly, the biscuits were soon gone. Then the muffins went, then the scones, then the corn, and, finally, the various fruits. All the Texans, though, avoided the cucumber sandwiches, even preferring the salty fish. All the while, Mrs. Chubb supplied them with large cups of hot, sweet tea; the tea was sweet because Mrs. Chubb dropped square lumps of sugar into it with a pair of silver tongs.

"Lord, that's sweet," Gus said. None of the Texans had ever tasted pure sugar before. They were amazed by the sweetness it imparted to the tea.

"Oh well . . . that's the nature of sugar," Lady Carey said. She, too, was having tea, but instead of drinking it from a cup, she was sipping it through a hollow reed of some kind, which she delicately inserted under her veils.

"This was refined by my chemist, the learned Doctor Gilley," Lady Carey said. "It came from sugarcane grown on my plantation, in the islands. I do think it's very good sugar."

"That's where Mamma caught leprosy," Willy said. "On our plantation. I didn't catch it and neither did Emerald and neither did Mrs. Chubb."

"Poor luck, I was the only one afflicted," Lady Carey said.

"Well, Papa *might* have had it, but we don't know, because the Mexicans shot him first," Willy said. "That's when we were made prisoners of war—when they shot Papa."

"Now, Willy—these gentlemen have traveled a long way and lost many friends themselves," Lady Carey said. "We needn't burden them with our misfortunes."

"I lost my Shad," Matilda said. "It was a stray bullet, too. If he'd been sitting anywhere else I expect he'd still be alive."

"Well, Matty, that's not for sure," Gus said. "We walked a far piece, after that, through all that cold weather."

"Cold wouldn't have kilt my Shad," Matilda said. "I would have hugged him and kept him warm."

"It is cold in our castle," Willy said. "There aren't many fires. But we have cannons and someday I will shoot them. When will we go back to our castle, Mamma?"

"That depends on these gentlemen," Lady Carey said. "We'll discuss it as soon as they've finished their tea. It's *very* impolite to discuss business while one's guests are enjoying their food."

"We can talk now, I guess," Call said. "If you've a plan for leaving here, I'm for talking now."

"Fine, there's nothing left but the cucumber sandwiches anyway," Lady Carey said. "I suppose cucumbers are not much valued in Texas, but we Scots have a fine appetite for them. Come help me, Willy, and you too, Mrs. Chubb. Let's finish off the sandwiches and plan our expedition."

Call was enjoying the breads and muffins and fruit. Everything he put in his mouth was tasty, particularly the small, buttery ears of corn. After the cold, dry trip they had made, across the prairies and the desert, it seemed a miracle that they had come through safe and were eating such food in the company of an English lady, her servants, and her little boy. He was startled, though, when she mentioned an expedition. The country around El Paso was as harsh as any he had seen. Five Rangers, four women, and a boy wouldn't stand much chance, not unless the Mexican army was planning to go with them.

"First, we need proper introductions," Lady Carey said. "I'm Lucinda Carey, this is Mrs. Chubb, this is Emerald, and this is Willy. You know our names, but we don't know yours. Could you tell us your names, please?"

Gus immediately told the lady that his name was Augustus McCrae. He was determined that Long Bill Coleman not be the first to speak to the fine lady who had fed them such delicious food.

"Why, Willy, he's Scot, like us," Lady Carey said. "I expect we're cousins, twenty times removed, Mr. McCrae."

The news perked Gus up immediately. The other Rangers introduced themselves—Woodrow Call was last. Long Bill took it upon himself to introduce Brognoli, whose head was still swinging back and forth, regular as the ticking of the clock. None of them knew how to behave to a lady—Long Bill attempted a little bow, but Lady Carey didn't appear to notice. She divided the cucumber sandwiches between herself, Mrs. Chubb, and Willy, who ate them avidly.

All the while Emerald, the tall Negress, stood watching, near the bed. The little dog had gone to sleep and was snoring loudly.

"Throw a pillow at him, Willy—why must we hear those snores?" Lady Carey said, when the last cucumber sandwich was gone. Willy immediately grabbed three pillows off a red settee and threw them at the sleeping dog, which whuffed, woke up, shook itself, and ran off the bed into Lady Carey's arms.

"This is George—he's a smelly beast," Lady Carey said. The little dog was frantically attempting to lick her, but the best he could do was lick her black gloves.

Call was watching the tall Negress, Emerald. She stood by the four-poster bed, keeping her eye on the company. She wasn't unfriendly, but she wasn't familiar, either. She was wrapped in a long, blue cloak. Call wondered if she had a gun under the cloak, or at least a knife. He could see that she was protective of Lady Carey and the little boy; he would not have wanted to be the one who attacked them, not with Emerald there.

While he was sipping the last of his tea, he happened to look up and see the head of a large snake, raised over the canopy of the four-poster bed. In a second the snake's long body followed—it was far and away the largest snake Call had ever seen. He looked around the table, hoping to see a knife he could kill it with, but there was no knife, except the little one they had used to spread butter. He grabbed one of the little stools and was about to run over and try to smash the big snake with it when the Negress calmly stretched out a long black arm and let the big snake slide along it. All the Rangers gave a start, when they saw the snake slide onto Emerald's arm. Soon it was draped over her shoulders, its head stretching out toward the table where the tea had been.

"No cause for alarm, gentlemen," Lady Carey said. "That's Elphinstone—he's Willy's boa."

"Only he's too big for me," Willy said. "Mamma and Emerald play with him now. Mrs. Chubb doesn't care for snakes. She hides her eyes when Elphinstone eats his rats."

Emerald walked over and handed the boa to Lady Carey, who let it slither over her lap and off under the table.

"I think he wants George," Lady Carey said. "Cake crumbs don't satisfy a boa, but I expect a smelly little beast such as George would be a treat."

"But Mamma, he can't *have* George!" Willy insisted. "He finds quite a lot of rats—I shouldn't think he'd need to eat our dog."

"Who knows what a boa needs, Willy?" Lady Carey said. "I'm afraid we've let all these beasts distract us. Willy and I want to go home, gentlemen, and the Mexican government has agreed to release us. What they won't do is provide us with an escort, and we're rather a long way from a seaport."

"I'll say," Long Bill said. "It's so far I wouldn't even know which one to head for."

"Galveston is the most feasible, I believe," Lady Carey said. "I'd rather try for Galveston than Veracruz. If we travel through Mexico the greedy generals might decide they want more ransom—my father has already paid them a handsome sum. He didn't pay it for me, of course—father wouldn't waste a shilling on a leprous daughter. He paid it for the young viscount here. Willy's the one he needs —Willy's the heir."

The Rangers listened silently to what Lady Carey said. Call looked at Gus, who looked at Long Bill. Brognoli continued to swing his head, and Wesley Buttons, who was a slow eater, was still consuming the last crumbs of one of the big scones with raisins in it. The others had accepted that the big snake was a pet, but Wesley didn't trust snakes, particularly not snakes that were longer than he was tall. This one had slithered off somewhere, but it could always slither back and take a bite out of him. He was careful to keep both feet on the rungs of his stool, and did not pay much attention to the talk of ransoms and seaports. He would go where the boys went —he was happy to let them decide.

"Ma'am, we'll be pleased to take you to Galveston," Call said. "If we can find the way. It's a far piece, though, and we've got no mounts and no gear. Our horses got stolen, and the Mexicans took our guns."

"Fortunately, we aren't poor yet, we Careys," Lady Carey said. "I didn't expect you to walk across Texas barefoot, in leg irons. We have our own mounts, and we'll soon find some for you. You look like honest men—I'll send you to town with enough gold to equip us properly. Don't skimp, either. Buy yourselves reliable weapons and warm clothes and trustworthy mounts. We have a tent large enough for ourselves and Miss Roberts—but I'm afraid you men will have to sleep out, if it's not too inconvenient."

"We don't know how to sleep no way *but* out," Gus said. "If we can get some slickers and some blankets we'll be cozy, I guess."

Just then, the snake emerged and began to glide up one of the bedposts. Soon it disappeared, back onto the canopy over the big bed. Wesley Buttons cautiously put his feet back on the ground.

"I expect it's a little too late to send you to town today," Lady Carey said. "Emerald, tell Manuel to get the irons off these men. I want them to get into town early tomorrow. I want to leave San Lazaro quickly—these greedy Mexicans might change their minds."

"Come," Emerald said. "We've fixed a room for you. The mattresses are just corn shuck, but it will be more comfortable than the place the Mexicans put you."

When they left the room, Willy had seated himself next to his mother and was helping her select from a bunch of storybooks, piled beside the low settee where Lady Carey sat. She raised her head to them, as they left the room, but all they could see were her veils.

"I wonder how bad she is, with the leprosy?" Gus asked, as the Texans were following Emerald along the balcony to their quarters. "Wouldn't it be awful if she didn't have no nose?"

"Yes, it would be awful, but I like her anyway," Call said. "She's going to get us out of here. I never supposed we'd be this lucky."

Gus thought of the long miles they had to travel, over the dry, windy country, to get even as far back as the settlements around Austin. It was a long way, even to the mountains where Josh Corn and Zeke Moody had been killed. And if they got that far, they would be in the land of Buffalo Hump.

"We don't know yet if we're lucky," he said. "We got to go right across where that Comanche is."

"It still beats being a prisoner and wearing these damn chains," Call said.

part

IV

1.

BUFFALO HUMP CAUGHT KIRKER, the scalp hunter, in a rocky gully just east of the Rio Pecos. Kirker had forty scalps with him at the time. Buffalo Hump judged the scalps to be mostly Mexican scalps, but he tortured Kirker to death anyway. The man had not been easy to take. He had managed to get in amid some rocks and delayed them a whole day, an annoying thing to the war chief. The Comanche moon was full—he wanted to follow the old trail, down into Mexico, and bring back captives, children they could use as slaves, or sell to the half-breed traders, in the trading place called the Sorrows, near the dripping springs where travelers on the llano stopped to rest and water their animals.

Buffalo Hump did not like having to slow his raid to catch one scalp hunter, a man so weak that he only killed Mexicans and rarely even attempted to take an Apache scalp, or a Comanche. At first he considered leaving three men, to hide and wait. When Kirker thought he was safe and came out of his hiding place in the rocks, the men could kill him and then follow the raiding party south.

Kicking Wolf, though, protested so vigorously that Buffalo Hump gave in. Kirker had killed two of Kicking Wolf's wives, and one of his sons; he had taken their scalps and sold them. Kicking Wolf was not a man who forgave or forgot; he wanted to take part in Kirker's death. The Comanche moon had only just turned full—they could easily sweep on into Mexico and take their captives. Kicking Wolf even had an idea that would help drive Kirker out of his hole in the rocks, and he put it into practice at night, just before moonrise. He had his young warriors catch several snakes and tie their tails together so tightly that they couldn't rattle well. Of course the rattlers' heads had to be held down with a stick—they grew angry at the mistreatment they received. There were seven snakes in all. Once the seven were bound together by their tails, a young brave named Fast Boy climbed up on the rocks above Kirker and threw the bundle of snakes down on top of him. Kirker screamed when the first snake bit him—when he screamed, revealing his position, Buffalo Hump himself jumped down on him and knocked his gun away before he could kill himself. Fortunately, the snake had only bitten Kirker in the leg; the wound would not kill him, or weaken him enough to spoil the torture. Even before they got Kirker back to camp, Kicking Wolf, who could not be restrained when he was angry, poked a sharp stick in Kirker's ear, destroying his eardrum and causing much blood to run out of his head. Kirker snarled and howled, like a tied wolf. He spat at the Comanches so many times that Buffalo Hump took a needle and a thread and sewed his lips together; after that he could not scream loudly, though he rolled and writhed and made gurgling sounds as he was being burnt and cut by Kicking Wolf, who insisted on doing most of the torturing himself. Some of the braves were in favor of saving Kirker; they wanted to send him back to the main camp, so the squaws could torture him. One squaw named Three Seed was better at torture than any man. She could bite off a man's fingers or toes as neatly as if she were merely biting a willow twig.

Buffalo Hump, though, was impatient. It was true that Kirker was a bad man who deserved to be tortured by the squaws, but the squaws were four days' ride to the north, and the raiders' business lay to the south. Kicking Wolf might not be as expert at torture as Three Seed, but he was good enough to make Kirker writhe and gurgle through a whole afternoon. He had been burned and cut and blinded when they took him to a small tree near the Pecos and tied him upside down. They built a small fire beneath his dangling head, and prepared to ride off; the greasewood would burn all night. Long before the sun rose, Kirker's head would be cooked.

Even so, when Buffalo Hump mounted and indicated that it was time to take advantage of the Comanche moon and get on with the serious business of the raid, Kicking Wolf refused to leave. He was determined to enjoy Kirker's torture to the end. He jabbed a thorny stick into Kirker's other ear, and let blood from his head drip into the fire.

Buffalo Hump was irritated, but Kicking Wolf, as a warrior, could do as he pleased, up to a point. The man knew the way to Mexico as well as anyone. It was not likely that Kirker would last until the morning—Kicking Wolf would follow and catch up the next day.

Still, before he left, Buffalo Hump made sure Kicking Wolf knew he was expected in Mexico soon. Kicking Wolf was the best horse thief in the tribe, and also the best stealer of children. He moved without making any sound at all. Once or twice he had reached through a window and taken a child while its parents were right in the room, eating or quarreling. Buffalo Hump did not want Kicking Wolf lingering too long, just to torture one scalp hunter. The man was already too weak to respond strongly to torture, anyway. He only jerked a little, and made a weak sound behind his sewn lips when the flames touched his head.

Kicking Wolf paid little attention to Buffalo Hump and the other warriors, as they rode off to the south. He was glad the war chief was gone—Buffalo Hump was a great fighter, but he was too impatient for the slow business of torture. For the same reason, Buffalo Hump was not an especially good hunter—he often jumped too soon. Torture took patience, and Buffalo Hump didn't have it. Before the warriors were even out of sight, Kicking Wolf took a stick or two off the fire and touched them to Kirker here and there, causing the man to jerk like a speared fish. The jerking made Kicking Wolf happy. It was good to be rid of the impatient war chief, good to be alone to hurt the man who had scalped his wives and his little son. In a little while, he cut the bloody threads that Buffalo Hump had used to sew Kirker's lips together. Then he stoked the fire a little and grabbed Kirker by the hair, so he could hold the man's face right over the flames. He wanted to hear the man scream.

After the first screams were over, Kicking Wolf scattered the fire a little and let Kirker's head hang down again. He got up and walked a short distance to a pile of rocks, carrying one of the burning sticks, to give him a little light. He wanted to find some little scorpions and put them on the white man. The scorpions would hurt him but would not kill him, and the torture could go on.

2.

CALL WAS SURPRISED BY Lady Carey's riding. She rode sidesaddle, of course, but handled her black gelding as expertly as any man. She could even make the horse jump, putting him over little gullies and small bushes while at a gallop. Call thought that was foolish, but he had to admit it was skillful, and pretty to watch. Willy tried to get his pony to jump like his mother's gelding, but of course the pony wouldn't. Mrs. Chubb rode a donkey, and protested constantly about its behaviour, though Gus pointed out to her that her donkey behaved no worse than most donkeys.

"In England they behave better, sir," Mrs. Chubb insisted. "This one tried to bite my toe."

Emerald, the tall Negress, rode a large white mule; she astonished Gus when she told him that the mule had sailed over from Ireland, along with Willy's pony and Lady Carey's black gelding.

"I doubt I could get fond enough of a mule to bring one on a ship," Gus said. He himself was riding a lively bay, procured in El Paso. In fact, thanks to Lady Carey's largesse, they were all better mounted than they had been at any time during their journeying. Each man had two horses, and there were four pack mules. One carried Lady Carey's canvas tent; the others carried provisions, including plenty of ammunition. They all had first-rate weapons, too —brand-new rifles and pistols, and a pretty shotgun for shooting fowl. Gus was eager to try the shotgun on prairie chickens—he had acquired a taste for the birds, but traveling east out of El Paso, they saw no prairie chickens, only desert. Gus did manage to bring down a lean jackrabbit with the shotgun, but upon inspecting the rabbit, Emerald declined to cook it.

"Lady Carey doesn't care for hares, unless they're jugged," she said. Lady Carey had raced far ahead. She was still completely veiled, so veiled that Call didn't know how she could see prairie-dog holes and other dangers of the trail. But she rode fast, her veils flying, and the black gelding rarely stumbled.

At four, to the Rangers' astonishment, the party stopped so that tea could be served. A small table was set up, covered with a white damask cloth. A fire was made; while Emerald sliced a small ham and made little sandwiches, Mrs. Chubb brewed the tea. The sugar bowl was brought out and sugar tonged into the cups. All the Rangers liked the tea and drank several cups; they decided they approved of English customs. Call, though he enjoyed the tea, thought it was foolish to waste an hour of daylight sitting around a table in the desert. The boys could drink all the tea they wanted at night—why waste the daylight? But he had to admit that otherwise Lady Carey's arrangements had been excellent. The saddles were the best that could be located in El Paso; also, mindful that winter was approaching, Lady Carey had insisted that they buy slickers, warm coats, and plenty of blankets. If Caleb Cobb's expedition had been half so well equipped, it might have succeeded, at least in Call's view. With proper equipment, it would have had a chance.

At night, with Long Bill's help and Gus's, Emerald set up Lady Carey's tent. While the tent was being anchored, Lady Carey sat by the campfire and read Willy stories from one of the storybooks they had with them. Some of the Rangers, unused to having a lady handy who would read, listened to the stories and enjoyed them as much as Willy. Matilda Roberts, for her part, enjoyed them more than Willy—the young viscount, after all, had had the stories read to him many times. But Matilda had never heard of Little Red

Riding Hood, or Jack and the Beanstalk. She sat entranced, letting her tea grow cold, as Lady Carey read.

Even more entrancing than the stories was Lady Carey's singing. Mostly she sang light tunes, "Annie Laurie," "Barbara Allen," and the like—the light tunes suited the men best. But now and then, as if bored with the sentimental tunes, Lady Carey would suddenly let her voice grow and grow, until it seemed to fill the vastness of the desert. She sang in a tongue none of them knew—none, that is, except Quartermaster Brognoli, who suddenly stood up and attempted to sing with her. He had not emitted an intelligible sound in so long that his voice was hoarse and raspy, but he was trying to sing and there was life in his eyes again. A vein stood out on his forehead as he attempted to sing with Lady Carey.

"Why, he's Italian and he knows his operas," Lady Carey said. "Now that he's found his voice again, I expect he'll be singing arias in a day or two."

That prediction proved wrong, for Quartermaster Brognoli died that night. Call looked at him in the morning, and saw at once that he was dead. His head was twisted far around on his back and neck.

"I guess that jerking finally killed him," Gus said, when the sad news was reported.

"No, it was the opera," Lady Carey said. "Or perhaps it was just hearing his native tongue."

Quartermaster Brognoli was buried in the hard ground—the four remaining Rangers took turns digging. Lady Carey sang the same piece she had sung when the Mexican firing squad cut down Bigfoot and the others. All the men cried, although Wesley Buttons had never been fond of Brognoli. Still, they had traveled a long way together, and now the man was dead. In the vastness of the desert, each reduction of the group made them realize how small they were, how puny, in relation to the space they were traveling through.

"We're back where it's wild again," Call said.

Lady Carey happened to overhear the remark—she drew rein for a moment, looking toward a faint outline of mountains in the east.

"Yes, it's wild, isn't it," she said. "It's like a smell. I smelled it in Africa and now I smell it here."

"It means we have to be careful," Call said.

Lady Carey looked again at the distant mountains.

"Quite the contrary, Corporal Call," she said. "It means we have to be wild, like the wild men."

She turned her head toward him, and sat watching him for a moment. Call couldn't see her eyes, through the several dark veils, but he knew she was watching him. One of her shirtsleeves had ridden up a bit—he could see just a bit of her wrist, between the shirtsleeve and her black gloves. He and Gus had speculated a little, about how affected Lady Carey was by the leprosy. She had no trouble handling her horse, and she was dexterous with her hands, when it came to pouring tea, or buttering muffins. The wrist he saw was a creamy white—much whiter than Matilda's. Matty was brown from the sun.

Although she had been always polite, Call felt nervous, knowing that her hidden eyes were fixed on him.

"Are you wild enough, Corporal Call?" Lady Carey asked. "I have a feeling you are."

"I guess we'll see," Call said.

3.

THE COMANCHES STRUCK DEEP into Mexico, under the bright moon. In Chihuahua Buffalo Hump struck a ranch, killed the rancher and his wife and all the vaqueros, and took three children and seventy horses. He ordered three young braves, led by Fast Boy, back up the war trail with the horses. He wanted the horses safely back in the main camp, in the Palo Duro Canyon, before the worst of the winter ice storms came. They could eat the horses, if buffalo proved scarce.

Then, with the shivering, terrified children tied on one horse, he struck east, taking only those children that were old enough to be useful slaves. The others he killed, along with their parents. At one hacienda he tied the whole family, threw them on their own haystack, and burned them. The Comanches rode on, striking hard and fast. Once they saw a little militia in the distance, perhaps twenty men. The young braves wanted to attack, but Buffalo Hump wouldn't let them. He told them they could come back and fight

Mexican soldiers anytime. Now they were on a raid, and needed to concern themselves with captives and horses.

They soon had ten children—four boys and six girls—none of them older than eight or nine years. They also had twenty more horses, which they drove with them as they turned north. Buffalo Hump was satisfied. They had taken almost a hundred horses, and ten children who were strong enough not to die on the hard journey. Kicking Wolf had failed to appear. Some of the braves speculated that he had caught another white to torture.

More than thirty Mexicans had been killed on the raid. Now the wind was growing colder—Buffalo Hump wanted to go to the trading place, the Sorrows, to trade his captives for tobacco and blankets and ammunition. He himself had the fine gun the Texans had given him, but he didn't use it to kill Mexicans. The fine gun he kept for buffalo hunting. The Mexicans he merely struck with his lance, or put an arrow through. He wanted guns, though—not for himself but for his braves. There were more Texans than ever, moving west on the creeks and rivers, cutting trees and making little farms. They were easy to kill, the Texans, but there were many of them, and most of his warriors still only had bows and arrows. All the Texans had guns—some of them could shoot well. It would be better if his young men learned to use the gun. Otherwise, the Texans might come all the way into the Comancheria and start killing the buffalo.

A day south of the Rio Grande, Buffalo Hump took a girl, a pretty Mexican girl who was caught while washing clothes on a rock in a little creek. There was a village not too far distant, but Buffalo Hump was on the girl so quickly that she did not have time to scream. He drew his knife to kill her, but in the brief struggle her young breasts spilled out of her tunic and he decided to keep her. He had had Mexican women before, but none so appealing as the slim girl he had just caught. He gagged her with a piece of rawhide, and put her over his horse.

Later, when they were many miles north and not far from the river, one of the braves came and informed him that a foolish young warrior named Crow was missing. Buffalo Hump didn't wait. Probably Crow had gone into the outskirts of the village and attempted to steal a girl for himself—Crow had always been jealous of Buffalo Hump. Though only sixteen, he wanted everything the war chief had. The young braves became restive. They didn't want to leave

Crow; he was known to be foolish. An old witch woman had told Crow that he would not die, and Crow believed her. Yet, he was brave in battle, and the young warriors didn't want to leave him. Buffalo Hump finally sent two of them to find their friend. They arrived back late at night with long faces and bad news. Crow had attacked the Mexican village single-handedly, convinced that he could scare away all the cowardly Mexicans and take what he wanted from the town. The braves who went back caught a boy and made him tell them what had happened, for they had not met Crow along the trail. The boy said Crow had ridden around the village, drinking and shooting off an old gun he had found. He did scare the Mexicans away for awhile, but he enjoyed frightening the village people so much that he grew careless. A vaquero roped him from a rooftop. While he was spinning in the air, the village men came back and hacked him to death with their machetes.

Buffalo Hump took the Mexican girl, though she struggled violently. He decided to take her for a wife. It might be that when they got to the trading place one of the traders would offer him a very high price for the girl; unless it was very high he resolved to keep her, although he would have to be careful when he took her back to the tribe. His old wives were jealous and would beat the girl severely, with firewood or sticks, unless he made it clear to them that they would suffer from his hand if the girl was too much damaged.

Crow's loss he did not lament. It was true that Crow had been brave, but he was not respectful. Several times already, Buffalo Hump had been tempted to put a lance through him, in response to an insolent look.

The girl, Rosa, whimpered from cold and fright. Buffalo Hump went to her, and took her again. Then he stuffed the rawhide gag back in her mouth; he didn't like the sounds frightened women made.

The next day, one warrior short, the Comanches crossed the Rio Grande. That day they caught two whites, an old man and an old woman, traveling west in a little wagon. They were people of God —they prayed loudly to their Jesus, but Buffalo Hump burned them anyway, in their own wagon. They screamed more loudly than they prayed. As the Comanches were riding off, a cougar jumped out of a little spur of rocks and raced away. Several of the young braves gave chase—it would be a great thing, if one of them could kill a cougar. But Buffalo Hump let them go—he had once longed to kill a cougar or a bear himself, and finally *had* killed a bear, near the headwaters of the Cimarron. But it had only been an old she-bear with a wounded paw; he could not claim much credit for having killed it. Once he had put his lance in a male grizzly, but the grizzly had treated the lance like a burr, and had chased Buffalo Hump for a mile. If he had not been on his best horse that day, the bear would have killed him.

Of course, the young braves did not manage to catch the cougar. Their horses were a little tired, from the swift raid. The cougar outran them easily.

Later that day, Kicking Wolf appeared. Buffalo Hump was angry with him, for missing the raid, but they had taken so many horses and so many captives that he didn't bother complaining. Kicking Wolf was a very contrary man—he did as he pleased. He told Buffalo Hump he had decided to wait for them on the trail, because he was enjoying the feeling he had after torturing Kirker to death.

It was a feeling of great power and calm, Kicking Wolf said. He didn't want to lose it just to catch a few Mexican children and run off a few horses. He explained that he had tortured Kirker for another day, after they hung him over the fire. After Kirker died, Kicking Wolf cut off all of his fingers—he meant to take them to the main camp and make them into a necklace. The fingers of the scalp hunter should not be wasted.

When Kicking Wolf saw Rosa, the Mexican girl, he became immediately jealous. He began to wish he had taken time to go on part of the raid. His only wife was old and smelly—Buffalo Hump had three young wives already, too many, in Kicking Wolf's view. He was a lustful man and could only watch enviously when Buffalo Hump went to the girl and took her. He ought to have gone to Mexico and taken a girl himself—it was only that he had been patiently torturing Kirker and didn't want to lose the feeling of great peace that came to him when the scalp hunter died.

4.

"It's a lurchy way to travel, if you ask me," Call said. "It's still a long way to Galveston and we ain't near through the Comanche country, yet. Why is she stopping, just to paint a hill?"

"You can't rush a lady like her, Woodrow," Gus said. He, too, thought it was eccentric of Lady Carey to stop the trip for a whole day, just so she could paint the colours of a desert sunset as they appeared on the line of bluffs to the north. They had happened to be traveling below a kind of rim-rock the day before, and had camped just at sunset. Lady Carey had not been able to get her easel and her paint-brushes out in time to capture the colours of rose and gold that the sun threw on the cliffs.

"Why, there's nothing like it in the world," she said. "I must paint —Willy, you might try, too. We'll wait until tomorrow and both have a go at it."

"That's a good plan—I'm tired of my pony," Willy said.

Gus had managed to shoot an antelope that afternoon; he was immensely proud of himself. Emerald, the Negress, walked out and butchered the animal, very precisely and in half the time it would have taken Gus. Before they could even set Lady Carey's tent up properly, Emerald returned with the best cuts of antelope. That night she cooked what she referred to as the saddle, with some corn and a few chilies they had brought from El Paso. Gus thought it was the best meal he had ever eaten; Call had to admit it was mighty tasty. Emerald had struck up a friendship with Matilda Roberts—she showed Matilda some of the finer points of cooking game. Lady Carey had a little chest containing nothing but salts and peppers, spices, and herbs. While Emerald cooked, Lady Carey sang, plucking her mandolin. That evening the great boa, Elphinstone, was let out of its basket. It curled around Lady Carey's shoulders, as she sang.

Call thought Lady Carey fearless to the point of folly. She ordered no guard, but he and Gus and Long Bill stood one anyway, taking turns through the chilly nights. Wesley Buttons was exempt from guard duty—it was well known that he could not stay awake even ten minutes, unless someone was talking to him, and Wesley's conversation was so dull that no one wanted to attempt to talk to him through the night. He was put in charge of the saddling and packing instead; Call and Gus usually helped him take down Lady Carey's tent.

During the day of rest, while they waited for the sunset colours to come, Lady Carey amused herself by sketching the Rangers. She drew quickly, and made such good likenesses of the men that it startled all of them. None of them felt that his own sketch was quite accurate, but contended that Lady Carey had captured the other men perfectly.

Toward evening, as the sun sank, the cliffs to the north reddened. Lady Carey prepared her colours and began to paint. Willy, the young viscount, had a small easel; his attempts at capturing the sunset were done in watercolour. Matilda stood beside Lady Carey, watching. Seeing the red cliffs form on the canvas fascinated her, much as the stories had. She had never known anyone who could do such things.

Lady Carey painted until nightfall, but Willy tired of art and walked off with Gus, in search of game. He had a small fowling piece, and would pop away at anything that moved; this evening, though, nothing moved. Willy wanted to keep looking, but as the shadows lengthened, Gus grew apprehensive and insisted that they return to camp. They had seen nothing to provoke unease, but Gus knew how quickly that could change, in such a wild place.

"There could be an Indian not fifty feet from us," he told Willy.

"But if there's an Indian I *want* to see him," Willy said. "Why can't you find him and show him to me?"

"If I found an Indian I wouldn't have to show him to you," Gus told him. "He'd be shooting arrows at us quicker than you can think. If I didn't kill the Indian, he'd kill us."

"Of course, you *would* kill him, I'm sure," Willy said, moving a little closer to Gus as they walked toward camp.

Call was prepared for an early start, and was up before sunrise— but to his surprise, Lady Carey had risen ahead of him. She was standing beside her easel, waiting for the first light from the east.

"I know you're restless, Corporal Call," she said. "I painted the sunset—now I want to paint the dawn. Go and ask Emerald to cook the bacon."

It was almost midday before Lady Carey was content to pack up her easel and her oils and mount the black gelding.

For three days more they moved eastward, past the line of the rim-rock but not beyond the desert or the mountains. On the afternoon of the third day, Call, Gus, and Long Bill all began to feel uneasy. There was no reason for their unease, yet they had it. Call debated scouting ahead, to see if he could detect any sign of Indians; in the end he decided against it. There were only the four of them to fight, in case of attack, and Wesley Buttons was a notably unreliable shot, at that. It was probably better to stay together, in case of trouble.

Toward evening, they passed a solitary mountain—a lump of rock, mainly. Lady Carey rode off toward the mountain, to have a closer look. Despite many warnings about the Indians, she still darted off at will, now ahead and now behind. She took a keen interest in the desert plants and would sometimes dismount, with her sketch pad, and draw a cactus or a sage bush. Once or twice, she had galloped so far away that Call had ridden out, protectively, to be in a position to help if he needed to help. Lady Carey, though, made it clear that she did not welcome even the best-intentioned supervision.

"I'm not a chicken, Corporal Call," she said to him once. "You needn't act like a hen."

Gus felt a deep disquiet, not about Lady Carey but about the place. Looking at the high, rocky hump he suddenly realized that he had looked at it before—only before, he had been racing toward it from the east, in the hope of killing mountain sheep. Now they were coming toward it from the west—the sloping ridge the Comanches had hidden themselves behind was just ahead of them.

Call had the same recognition, at the same time. They had gone east from El Paso, and come back to the bluff where Josh Corn and Zeke Moody had been killed.

"I hope there ain't no mountain sheep up there," Gus said. "If there are, we'll know they're Comanches and that big one is somewhere around."

"Maybe he's still north," Call said, remembering the day when the Comanches had walked their horses along the face of the Palo Duro Canyon.

"No, he ain't north—I feel him," Gus said.

"Now, that's mush," Call said. "You didn't feel him the first time, and he was closer to us than I am to Willy."

"I don't say he's close, but he's somewhere around," Gus said. "I feel funny in my stomach."

"At least Major Chevallie would be proud of us if he could see us now," Call said.

"Why would he?" Gus asked. "He never even made us corporals."

"No, but now we've found the road to El Paso," Call said. "It's south of them high bluffs. If he was alive, he could start up a stagecoach line."

Gus was still thinking about Buffalo Hump—how quickly he could strike. Lady Carey was almost out of sight, at the base of the mountain. If Buffalo Hump was close, even the fast gelding wouldn't save her.

"Look at her," Gus said, to Call. "If he was here, he'd get her."

"Not just her," Call said. "He'd get us all, if he was here."

5.

When Buffalo Hump rode into the trading place, the valley called the Sorrows, with his captives and the last group of Mexican horses, the old slaver, Joe Nibbs, was there waiting, with Sam Douglas and two wagons full of goods. A band of Kiowa had been there the day before, but they had only raided one settlement: the only captives they had to offer were a nine-year-old girl, and a little Negro boy. Joe Nibbs wouldn't take the girl—she had a sickly look; very likely she would be dead within the month. Joe Nibbs had come west with the first trappers to leave St. Louis—he was too experienced a slaver to be wasting trade goods on a sickly girl.

Joe had been coming to the Sorrows for ten years; he had seen mothers kill themselves because he sold their children away; more than one husband had tried to kill him, because he had sold a wife. But Joe was a decisive man—he kept a hammer stuck in his belt and used it to dispatch troublesome captives quickly, silently, and cheaply. He knew where the human skull was weakest—he rarely had to strike twice, when he pulled his hammer. Bullets he normally saved for buffalo, or other game too big and too swift to be dispatched with a hammer. When the Kiowa arrived, with one sickly girl, Joe Nibbs upbraided them for laziness. The Texas settlements were creeping westward, up the Brazos and the Trinity. If the Kiowa didn't want to make the long ride into Mexico for captives, they could at least be a little more active around the new settlements. Most of them weren't really settlements anyway, just groups of scattered farms, always poorly defended. They ought to yield more than a sick girl and a small Negro boy.

In the wagons were blankets and beads, knives, mirrors, a few guns, and some harmless potions and powders that Joe passed off as medicine. He did not trade liquor. Life was risky enough on the Comancheria without pouring liquor into wild men skilled at every form of killing.

He traveled in the Indian lands with Sam Douglas, a youth of twenty-two, reedy but strong. He kept the wagons repaired and the captives secured. Sam had come from a whaling family, back in Massachusetts—he was so skilled with knots that in the three years he had been helping Joe Nibbs, not a single captive, male or female, had escaped. Sometimes, if the Comanche seemed restive, Sam would entertain them by tying intricate knots. Kicking Wolf was particularly fascinated by this skill—he would sit by Sam and encourage him to run through his whole repertory of knots; then he would want Sam to untie all his knots and tie them again, over and over.

Sam Douglas had grown up by the sea; he was used to cool, moist air. He had hated the West, with its sand and its dust, and had no fondness at all for Joe Nibbs, a greedy, profane, violent old man with black teeth, and a blacker heart. More than twenty times Sam had seen Joe Nibbs fly into a rage, yank out his hammer, and crack the skull of some man or woman who could' perfectly well have been sold for a fine profit, if only Joe had been able to hold his temper. But Sam stayed with the old slaver because he was handicapped by a clubfoot and a harelip, both impediments to the satisfying of his considerable lust. In the settlements women shied from him, but traveling with a slaver solved that problem; there were always budding girls amid the captives, and sometimes grown women, too. Since it was Sam's job to tie the women and to guard them, he had access to many females he could not have approached or succeeded with, had he met them in Massachusetts. Many of them writhed and squirmed, or begged and wept, or cursed and spat, while Sam was enjoying his access; but he paid no attention. They were slaves, and he was their slaver; they had to submit and most did, without him having to whack them or whip them or tie their legs to opposite sides of the wagon bed. Even if he had to beat the women a little, he was still kinder to them than Joe Nibbs. Joe was apt to whip them for no reason, or torment them with the handle of his hammer, or to tie them over a wagon wheel and rut at them from behind, like the rough old billy that he was.

The moment Buffalo Hump and Kicking Wolf rode into the Sorrows with their bunch of Mexican children, Sam noticed the girl, Rosa. Joe Nibbs noticed her, too. She had a beauty not often seen in captives.

"Why, he's caught a pretty one," Joe Nibbs said. "Them lazy Kiowas could ride for a year and not catch a girl that rare."

"Let's buy her, Joe," Sam Douglas said. "Maybe the Apaches would buy her. They'd give us silver for her. They take lots of silver off them Mexicans they kill."

What Sam was really thinking was that they would get to keep the girl for awhile. Old Joe could go first and rut at her from the back, if he wanted to. Then it would be Sam's turn, and he might take it two or three times a night, under the pretense of seeing that the girl was properly bound.

"Ssh . . . hush about the 'Paches," Joe instructed. "Buffalo Hump hates everybody but his own tribe, and he don't like too many of them. We don't need to let on what we aim to do with this gal."

They watched closely as the Comanche raiders rode down into the shallow valley—just a cleft between two ridges, really. In the distance, they could see a curve of the Rio Rojo. The wind was blowing hard from the north; spumes of sand curled over the lip of the ridge to the north and blew into the eyes of the Mexican captives. The Mexican children appeared to be well fed, Sam noted. Some of them were as plump as the little Negro boy who was tied in the first wagon. Several of the Mexican girls looked to be eight or nine years old—they could be used, if there was no one better, but Sam Douglas didn't figure on having to drop that low, not if the wily Joe Nibbs could talk Buffalo Hump out of the young woman.

Joe had bought captives from most of the major chiefs, north of the Santa Fe trail and south. He knew a route through the Carlsbad Mountains that allowed him to slip back and forth between Comanche and Apache, desert and plain. He was the oldest slaver on the plains, good at figuring out what a given Indian would take for a prize captive. The girl who rode behind Buffalo Hump, her wrists tied with a rawhide thong, was the prettiest woman to come up the Comanche war trail since Sam had been driving a wagon for Joe.

Joe Nibbs was rarely nervous, when among the red men. He cheated white men freely, but he didn't cheat Comanches or Apaches, or Kiowa or Pawnee or Sioux. A trader who cheated Indians might survive a year, or even two—but Joe Nibbs had survived almost twenty, by saving his tricks for the whites. Even an Indian who didn't speak a word of the white man's tongue would know when he was being cheated—it was a practice that didn't pay.

Buffalo Hump, though, was one Indian who made Joe Nibbs nervous. He dealt with the humpback because Buffalo Hump raided deepest into Mexico and brought back the most captives. But with Buffalo Hump, Joe was always careful, always aware that he was doing something not quite safe, not quite within the normal range of hazards that went with the slaving trade on the wild Texas prairies. Joe Nibbs was always aware that the day might come when Buffalo Hump would rather kill than trade. In his dealing with the humpback, he had only once looked the war chief in the eye. What an eye! What he saw then unnerved him so that he immediately gave the war chief a brand-new rifle and several fine blankets. As soon as the Comanches had gone, he warned Sam Douglas to keep his eyes to himself, when dealing with the big Comanche. No wise man met the eye of a mad dog or a wolf, a bear or a panther. The animal might come out, and blood be spilled, over nothing more than a glance.

"Hell, I won't look at him at all," Sam said. "That damn hump is an ugly thing, anyway."

Buffalo Hump saw immediately that the slavers wanted Rosa, the Mexican girl. He had once come upon the slavers while the old one was tormenting a dead missionary's wife. He had watched from a distance as Joe Nibbs beat the woman with the handle of his hammer—beat her and did more. That night the woman died from the beating and abuse—she had not been young.

What he mainly wanted from the slaver was knives and needles. It would soon be time for the fall hunt—they needed to kill many buffalo before the winter came. Often ice storms came, coating the plain for several days at a time, making hunting difficult. The white men made good knives, far better than the stone knives his people had had to use when he was a boy. After the hunt, there would be much cutting—the women would need knives, and also needles, for sewing leggins from deerskin, and stitching buffalo robes. The white man's blankets Buffalo Hump mostly scorned—buffalo robes were warmer. But he liked the yellow cloth that shed the rain and allowed his braves to hunt on wet days and yet be dry like ducks. The rifles he was offered were cheap, and his young braves were rough with guns: soon half would be broken, and the ammunition used up. It was not worth giving up good captives for weapons that would be broken in a month. He himself had the fine gun the white chief Caleb Cobb had given him. He was careful with the gun—no one in the tribe was allowed to touch it. Kicking Wolf was bitterly jealous that Buffalo Hump had such a gun, but he knew better than to disobey the edict. Buffalo Hump only rarely shot the gun; he had not even taken it with him on the raid, preferring to depend on his bow and his lance. But once he had shot it at an antelope, a very great distance away, and the antelope fell.

But if the old trader, Joe Nibbs, thought he could trade a few cheap weapons for the Mexican girl, he would have to think again. Buffalo Hump was willing to give him several of the Mexican children for a box full of good, sharp knives. The girl he meant to keep. It might be a cold winter—a fresh young wife to lay with would be good to have on days when the ice covered the plains.

"Now, don't be mentioning that girl—don't even look at her," Joe Nibbs warned Sam Douglas. "I'll trade for the brats first. And remember what I said. Don't look him in the eye."

"Why would I want to—he's a goddamn stinking Indian," Sam said.

Kicking Wolf at once wanted the Negro boy. When the boy was brought out of the wagon, naked, and saw Buffalo Hump, he was so frightened that he tried to run away, speeding on his little legs toward the ridge the sand spumed over. The Comanche braves followed, curious; Kicking Wolf and the others had seen few blacks. They thought the boy might be some kind of small black animal—

perhaps he could be trained to gather firewood, or just be kept as a pet, like a bear cub. Just as the little black boy was about to get to the ridge, Kicking Wolf picked him up, screaming, and brought him back to the wagons.

"That's my brat, give him back," Joe Nibbs said. Kicking Wolf, too, was a man to be wary of—everyone on the plains knew what a good thief he was. Joe and Sam had two extra donkeys with them, besides the horses that pulled the wagons. He meant to see that the donkeys were close hobbled that night, else Kicking Wolf would come back and take them.

Kicking Wolf motioned toward two of the captives, indicating that he would trade them for the black boy. Before Joe Nibbs could even walk over and inspect the children, to be sure that they were healthy, Buffalo Hump lowered his lance and put it in front of the children. Kicking Wolf had not set foot in Mexico. Who was he to be offering the captives in trade? While they had been raiding he had lingered near the Pecos, torturing one scalp hunter to death. Of course, Kicking Wolf had made many raids and taken many children—he would have to be allowed some booty. But he could not simply trade away children that were not his. Fast Boy had taken the two children in question—if anyone had the right to dispose of them, it should be he.

Kicking Wolf was very annoyed by Buffalo Hump's intervention. He himself, not Buffalo Hump, was the great child thief. He had taken more than fifty children from their homes, and brought them north. It was because of his skill as a child thief that the tribe had had plenty of knives the last few winters. Who was Buffalo Hump to deny him two children, when all he wanted in exchange was the small black animal?

"Even swap—even swap," Joe Nibbs said, pointing at a Mexican boy who was about the same size as the little Negro. He didn't like trading blacks, not on the plains. He had only given a packet of needles and a small blanket for the black boy. In the south it was profitable to trade little blacks, but not on the plains, and even less so west of the Carlsbad Mountains. The Apaches had superstitions about blacks—they usually killed them.

Buffalo Hump allowed the trade—one Mexican child for the black cub Kicking Wolf held. He had merely lowered his lance to remind Kicking Wolf that he was not the war chief. Of course,

Kicking Wolf was an unusually good raider; the need to torture Kirker had distracted him; but his pride had to be considered. He could have the black cub.

Joe Nibbs produced tobacco, and the trading went quickly. Buffalo Hump kept four captives, including the girl, Rosa. The other three were Mexican boys old enough to be useful slaves. The others he traded for three boxes of knives, many needles, some mirrors, a box of fishhooks, and four rifles. Several of his younger braves considered themselves to be great marksmen. It was well enough to take a few guns for them to break.

"He don't like guns much," Sam said, to Joe. "He only took four. How are we going to get this girl if he won't take guns?"

Rosa, still tied, sat by a little bush near Buffalo Hump's horse. She had seen the two traders looking at her—she felt no hope. Either the white men or the Comanches would use her and kill her. She watched the sand spuming over the ridge as the wind gusted. She wished she could simply lie down and be covered with sand; be dead; be at peace. She watched the sand come, and tried not to think.

Joe Nibbs was wondering the same thing as Sam—what could he offer Buffalo Hump that might make him part with the girl?

"I've got that old Gypsy glass," he said. Some months before he had found a wagon and a dead man, an old Gypsy, on the Kansas plain near Fort Lawrence. Probably the old man had been killed by Pawnees, who had ripped up his body and his wagons, taken his whiskey, and left. Joe had happened to notice something shining through a crack in the wagon bed, and had discovered a ball of glass, or crystal, hidden so well that the Pawnees had not noticed it.

"He might want that glass," he said, going to his wagon and taking the glass from a blanket he had wrapped it in. It was the size of a small melon. When you looked into it, it made your face elongated.

"It's Gypsy glass—take it to your medicine man, he can use it for prophesying," Joe said, offering the ball of glass to Buffalo Hump.

All the warriors crowded around, exclaiming at the way the glass made their faces long. Buffalo Hump thought the glass a very odd thing—he turned it over and over, and let his young braves handle it. It was clearly a thing of power, but he was not convinced that it could be used for prophesying.

"Yes, it's a prophecy glass, that's what it is," Joe insisted. "Take it to your medicine man. It'll tell him where the buffalo are, and when's the best time to hunt. It'll tell you when to go to war, and when to stay home."

Buffalo Hump was not convinced, but as the afternoon waned, he began to want the glass. He wanted to take it home to his main camp and study it. Perhaps he would come to understand its power. His mother was old, and knew much. Perhaps she would understand why the glass made faces long.

He decided, though, to kill the traders, the old one and the young one, too. He meant to take all the knives; there were several more boxes in the wagons. With so many knives they would not need the traders for several winters; he did not want Joe Nibbs coming into his country with such a thing as the glass. If it was a prophecy glass, then it could do much evil. Some of his people grew sick and died, just from meeting with the whites. With such a glass the old trader might cause many deaths. The glass might be a trick, to spread death among the Comanches, to get their robes and their horses and their hunting lands. The whites were always coming, up the rivers and creeks, always north and west, toward the Comancheria. Buffalo Hump thought the glass was a bad sign. He would take it to the main camp and let the old ones see it—perhaps one of them would know what to do.

Buffalo Hump left them the Mexican girl and took his braves over the ridge, where the sand spumed. Then he told his braves that he had decided to kill the traders, take back the captives, and get all the knives. Kicking Wolf wanted to go back with him and catch the white men and torture them, but Buffalo Hump wouldn't let him. Instead, he gave him the glass that might be evil, and rode back alone. When he crossed the ridge of blowing sand, the old white man had already tied the girl to a wagon wheel and was abusing her. The young white man sat on the tailgate of the wagon and waited his turn. Buffalo Hump walked quietly, over the soft sand. He had his lance, and a knife.

Sam Douglas sat on the wagon, trying to decide whether to take one of the nine-year-old Mexican girls, or wait for night, when old Joe would be sleeping. Then he could do what he pleased with Rosa. He had meant to leave the nine-year-olds alone, but after all, why should he? They were slaves. They were there. Old Joe was tiresome, when he had a new slave to abuse. He might keep Rosa tied to the wagon wheel for hours.

Then, before he knew it, Sam Douglas found himself doing the one thing he had vowed not to do: he looked straight into Buffalo Hump's eyes.

It was a mistake: he knew it. He had thought the big Indian was gone. But there he was: the animal, the panther, the bear.

The next second, Buffalo Hump drove his knife straight down through Sam Douglas's skull. One of the Mexican captives screamed. The old trader, Joe Nibbs, had his hammer in his hand. When he turned, Buffalo Hump threw the lance—the distance was short. Half the lance came out the other side of Joe Nibbs's body and stuck in the ground, so that his torso was tilted slightly back. He was still alive; he dropped his hammer. Buffalo Hump picked it up and hit him at the base of the neck. Joe Nibbs's head flopped back, like a chicken's.

Then the warriors came back; they took the captives, the knives, the donkeys. They decided to burn the wagons and camp for the night; they could eat all the white men's food.

Buffalo Hump could not get his knife out of Sam Douglas's skull. It was stuck so deep that not even his strength was enough to pull it out. The braves laughed. Their own war chief had stuck a perfectly good knife into a white man's skull so deeply that he could not get it out. Finally, Buffalo Hump smashed the skull with the old slaver's hammer and freed his knife.

Rosa, the young captive, could not stop weeping. She hurt from what the man with the hammer had done to her. She wanted to be with her mother, her brother, and little sisters; but she knew she could not go home. She had been with the Comanche; the people of her village would consider her disgraced, if she went home. She wept, and listened to the sand; she wished that she could sleep beneath the sand, breathe it into her, and die. But she could not; she could only weep, and be cold, and wait for the big Comanche who sat nearby, holding the rawhide string that bound her wrists.

Later, not long before dawn, one of the donkeys began to whinny. The wind had shifted; now it blew from the west, and the donkey had smelled something. The horses pointed their ears to the west, but did not whinny. The braves around the campfire thought it was an animal. Donkeys were cowards—they would whinny at a coyote, or even a badger. Fast Boy, who slept little, decided that the animal was probably a cougar. Perhaps the cougar they had seen earlier was following them, hoping to eat a donkey. The other braves laughed at Fast Boy, and laughed even more when he mounted his horse and loped off to look for the cougar. They thought it was ridiculous for Fast Boy to suppose he could find a cougar in the darkness.

When Fast Boy returned, running his horse, the sun was just rising. The wind was high; the sun was ringed with a haze of sand. Buffalo Hump was annoyed, when Fast Boy raced into camp. He did not approve of such behaviour. They were cooking horse meat from one of the old slaver's horses. Fast Boy's horse kicked dust on the meat, which was gritty enough, anyway.

But Buffalo Hump forgot his irritation when Fast Boy told him that a party of whites was camped only three miles to the west. It was a small party, mostly women, Fast Boy said. There were only four men and a boy, besides the women. But the news that made Buffalo Hump forgive the reckless riding and the gritty meat was that one of the men was Gun-In-The-Water, the young Ranger who had killed his son. When Buffalo Hump heard that, he began to put on his war paint—most of the other warriors put on their war paint, too. Kicking Wolf declined to bother—he did not like to paint himself. He made the point to Buffalo Hump that he himself could sneak over the hill and kill Gun-In-The-Water and all the whites in less time than it would take for Buffalo Hump and the other braves to paint themselves. Buffalo Hump ignored Kicking Wolf. Kicking Wolf had always thought his way of doing things was best. Buffalo Hump didn't care what Kicking Wolf thought. He intended to paint himself properly. Then he would ride to where the whites were and do to Gun-In-The-Water what he had done to the old slaver: throw his lance so hard that it would go through him without killing him at once. Then, before he died, Buffalo Hump intended to scalp him and cut him. The scalp he would take home to his son's mother, so she would know the boy had been correctly avenged.

When Buffalo Hump mounted, he made a speech in which he warned all the braves to leave Gun-In-The-Water alone. He himself would kill Gun-In-The-Water.

Kicking Wolf didn't like the speech much. He rode off in the middle of it, in a hurry to have a look at the women. Perhaps one of them would be as pretty as the Mexican girl, or even prettier. He wanted to be the first to see the women, so he would get the best. Maybe he would find one who smelled better than his wife.

6.

THE HORSES SMELLED THE Indians first. Call was about to throw the sidesaddle on Lady Carey's black gelding, when the gelding began to nicker and jump around. Gus's bay did the same, and even the mules acted nervous. Lady Carey's tent had been folded and packed —they were all about ready to start the day's ride. Emerald was brushing her white mule; she brushed the mule faithfully, every morning.

Call scanned the horizon to the east, but saw nothing unusual— just the bright edge of the rising sun. Lady Carey still had a teacup in her hand. Willy was eating bacon. Mrs. Chubb was trying to wash his ears, pouring water out of a little canteen onto a sponge that she kept with her, just for the purpose of washing Willy. Wesley Buttons had his boots off—he was prone to cramps in his feet, and liked to rub his toes for awhile in the morning, before he put his boots on. If he took a bad cramp with the boot on, he would have to hop around in pain until the cramp eased.

Matilda Roberts walked her mare around in circles. The mare was skittish in the mornings, with a tendency to crow-hop. Matilda was no bronc rider; she liked to walk off as much of the mare's nervousness as she could. Twice already, the mare had thrown her; once she had narrowly missed landing on a barrel cactus, which was all the more reason to walk the mare for awhile.

Gus McCrae and Long Bill had walked off from camp a little ways, meaning to relieve themselves. Long Bill was much troubled by constipation, whereas Gus's bowels tended to run too freely. They had formed the habit of answering nature's call together—they could converse about various things, while they were at it. One of the things Gus had on his mind was whores; now that he was eating better and not having to walk until he dropped, his sap had risen. A subject of intense speculation between himself and Long Bill was whether Matilda Roberts intended to take up her old profession, now that they were back in Texas—and if so, when? Gus was hoping she would resume it sooner, rather than later. He was of the opinion that anytime would be a good time for Matilda to start being a whore again, even if he and Long Bill were her only customers.

"Well, but Lady Carey might not approve," Long Bill speculated, as he squatted. "Matty might want to wait until we're shut of all these English folks."

"But that won't be till Galveston," Gus said. "Galveston's a far piece yet. I would like a whore a lot sooner than Galveston."

Long Bill had no comment—he noticed, as he squatted, that there was commotion back at the camp. Woodrow Call and Lady Carey were standing together, looking to the east. Long Bill could see that Call had his rifle. Matty had come back to stand near the others. Long Bill felt a strong nervousness take him—the nervousness clamped his troubled bowels even tighter.

"Something's happening," he said, abruptly pulling his pants up. "This ain't no time for us to be taking a long squat."

The two hurried back to camp, guns in their hands. It seemed a peaceful morning, but maybe it wasn't going to be as peaceful as it looked.

"Here's Gus, he's got the best eyes," Call said.

Lady Carey went to her saddlebag, and pulled out a small brass spyglass.

"Help me look, Corporal McCrae," she said. "Corporal Call thinks there's trouble ahead, and so does my horse."

Lady Carey looked through her telescope, and Gus did his best to scan the horizons carefully with his eyes, but all he saw was a solitary coyote, trotting south through the thin sage. He, too, had begun to feel nervous—he didn't fully trust his own eyes. He remembered, again, how completely the Comanches had concealed themselves the day they killed Josh and Zeke.

Emerald walked over, leading her white mule.

"The wild men are here, my lady," she said, calmly.

"Yes, I believe they are," Lady Carey said. "I believe I smell them. Only they're so wild I can't see them."

Then they all heard a sound—a high sound of singing. Buffalo Hump, in no hurry, walking his horse, appeared on the distant ridge, the sun just risen above him. He was singing his war song. As the little group watched, the whole raiding party slowly came into view. All the braves were singing their war songs, high pitched and repetitive. Gus counted twenty warriors—then he saw the twenty-first, Kicking Wolf, somewhat to the side. Kicking Wolf was on foot, and he was not singing. His silence seemed more menacing than the war songs of the other braves.

Call looked around for a gully or a ridge that might provide them some cover, but there was nothing—only the few sage bushes. They had camped on the open plain. The Comanches held the high ground, and had the sun behind them, to boot. They were four fighting men against twenty-one, and Wesley Buttons couldn't shoot. Even if he had been a reliable shot, the Comanches could in any case easily overrun them, if they chose to charge. Four men, four women, and a boy would not look like much opposition to a raiding party, singing for death and torture. Call wondered if the English party knew what Comanches did to captives; he wondered if he ought to tell Lady Carey, and Emerald, and Mrs. Chubb how to shoot themselves fatally, if worse came to worst. Bigfoot's instructions about putting the pistol to the eyeball came back to him as he watched the Comanches. No doubt Bigfoot had known exactly what he was talking about, but would the English lady, the nanny, and the Negress be capable of performing such an act? Would Matilda Roberts, for that matter?

Lady Carey stood watching the Indians calmly. As always, she was dressed only in black, and wore her three veils. She did not seem frightened, or even disturbed.

"What do you think, Corporal Call?" she asked. "Can we whip them?"

"Likely not, ma'am," Call said. "They beat us when we had nearly two hundred men. I don't know why they wouldn't beat us now that we've only got four."

"It's interesting singing, isn't it?" Lady Carey said. "Not so fine as opera, but interesting, nonetheless. I wonder what it means, that singing?"

"It means death to the whites," Gus said. "It means they want our hair."

"Well, they may want it, but they can't have it," young Willy said. "I *need* my hair, don't I, Mamma?"

"Of course you do, Willy," Lady Carey said. "And you shall keep it, too—Mamma will see to that. Corporal Call, will you saddle my horse?"

"I will, but I don't think we can outrun them, ma'am," Call said.

"No, we won't be running," Lady Carey said. "I think the best thing would be for me to try my singing. I will be leading us through these Comanches, gentlemen. I'll be mounted, but I want the rest of you to walk and lead your mounts. Saddle my horse, Corporal Call—and don't look at me. None of you must look at me now, until I say you may."

"Well, but why not, ma'am?" Gus asked—he was puzzled by the whole proceedings.

"Because I intend to disrobe," Lady Carey said. "I shall disrobe, and I shall sing my best arias—besides that, I shall need my fine snake, Elphinstone. Emerald, could you bring him?"

Calmly, not hurrying, Lady Carey began to sing scales, as she undressed. She let her voice rise higher and higher, moving up an octave and then another, until her high notes were higher than any that came from the Comanches. Emerald took the boa from its basket on the mule, and let it drape about her shoulders as Lady Carey undressed.

"I think, Willy, you should mount your pony," Lady Carey said. "The rest of you walk. Matilda, would you take my clothes and carry them for me? I shall want them, of course, once we have dispersed these savages. You haven't saddled my horse yet, Corporal Call. Please cinch him carefully, so he won't jump—I've got to be a regular Lady Godiva this morning, and I don't want any trouble from this black beast."

Call saddled the horse and handed the reins to Matilda, along with his pistol. He had no belief that anything they could do would get them through the Comanches. Lady Carey could undress if she wanted—Buffalo Hump would kill them anyway.

He kept his eyes down, as Lady Carey undressed—so did Long Bill, and Wesley Buttons. They had come to like Lady Carey—to revere her, almost—and were determined not to offend her modesty, though they were much confused by the undressing.

Gus, though, could not resist a peep. So normal did she seem that he had almost forgotten that she was a leper, until he caught the first glimpse of black, eroded flesh as she turned to hand a garment to Matilda. Her neck and breasts were black; bags of yellowing skin hung from her shoulders. Gus was so startled that he almost lost his breakfast. He didn't look at Lady Carey again, though he did notice that her legs, which were very white, did not seem to be affected by the disease, except for a single dark spot on one calf.

"Oh Lord," he said—but no one else was looking, and no one heard him.

Lady Carey kept on her hat, and the three veils that hid her face. She also kept on her fine black boots. Matilda looked at Lady Carey's body, and felt bad—the English lady had been nicer to her even than her own mother. To see her young body blackened and yellowish from disease made Matilda feel helpless. Yet, she took the garments, one by one, as Lady Carey handed them to her, and folded them carefully. Mrs. Chubb was calm, as was Emerald—neither of them had seen what Comanches could do, Matilda reflected.

When Lady Carey had disrobed she mounted the black gelding, settled herself firmly in the sidesaddle, and reached for her snake.

"All right now, keep in line," she said. "You too, Willy—keep in line. I want you Texans in the middle, right behind Willy. Matilda, Mrs. Chubb, and Emerald will bring up the rear. Emerald, if you don't mind, I think you might want to carry my husband's sword.

[468]

Unsheath it, and hold the blade high—remember, it's sharp. Don't cut yourself."

The Negress smiled, at the thought that she might cut herself. Call had often noticed a fine sword in the baggage, but had not known that it was Lady Carey's husband's. Emerald took it and unsheathed it. She went to the rear, and waited.

"All right now, front march," Lady Carey said. "I am going to sing very loudly—after all, I'm one voice against twenty. Willy, you might want to stop your ears."

"Oh no, Mamma," Willy said. "You can sing loud—I won't mind."

Lady Carey, on the fine black gelding, started up the long ridge toward the Comanches, the boa draped over her shoulders. She was still singing her scales, but before she had gone more than a few feet she stopped the scales and began to sing, high and loud, in the Italian tongue—the tongue that had caused Quartermaster Brognoli to rouse himself briefly, and then die.

The line of Comanches was still some two hundred yards away. Lucinda Carey, watching from behind her three veils, rode toward them slowly, singing her aria. When she had closed the distance to within one hundred yards, she stretched her arms wide; Elphinstone liked to twine himself along them. She felt in good voice. The aria she was singing came from Signor Verdi's new opera *Nabucco* —he had taught her the aria himself, two years ago in Milan, not long before she and her husband, Lord Carey, sailed together for Mexico.

Ahead, the line of Comanches waited. Lady Carey glanced back. Her son, the four Rangers, and the three women all walked obediently behind her. Emerald, the tall Negress, at the end of the line, had undraped one breast—she held aloft Lord Carey's fine sword— the keen blade flashed in the early sunlight. Emerald paused, on impulse, and shrugged off her white cloak. Soon she, too, was walking naked toward the line of warriors.

As she came nearer, close enough to see the Comanche war chief's great hump and the ochre lines of paint on his face and chest, Lucinda, Lady Carey, opened her throat and sang her aria with the full power of her lungs—she let her voice rise high, and then higher still. She pretended for a moment that she was at La

[469]

Scala, where she had had the honor of meeting Signor Verdi. She filled her lungs, breathing as Signor Verdi had taught her in the few lessons she had begged of him—her high, ripe notes rang clearly in the dry Texas air.

Ahead, the war chief waited, his long lance in his right hand.

7.

KICKING WOLF GREW TIRED of listening to the war songs. He ran ahead, meaning to make the first kill. He would leave Buffalo Hump the Texan called Gun-In-The-Water, since Gun-In-The-Water had killed his son; it would not do to cheat the war chief of his vengeance. The man Kicking Wolf meant to kill was the tall one who always walked beside Gun-In-The-Water. Kicking Wolf was short; he would kill the tall one; Buffalo Hump, who was tall, could kill the short one.

So Kicking Wolf ran ahead, and squatted beside a small clump of chaparral—he had an arrow in his bow, ready to shoot. He heard a death song coming from the Texans, but because he wanted to surprise them, he did not look up once he was in his ambush place behind the chaparral. Of course, it was appropriate for the whites to sing a death song—they would all be dead very soon, unless one or two could be caught for torture. But it was a little surprising; Kicking Wolf could not remember any instances in which whites sang death songs. Once in awhile, when there was cavalry, a man

[471]

might blow a short horn, to make the soldiers fight; he had actually killed such a person once, near the San Saba, and had taken the horn home with him. But it was not a good horn; when he tried to play it, it only made a squawking sound, like a buffalo farting. He eventually threw it away.

Then Kicking Wolf realized that he was hearing no ordinary death song—the voice that he heard lifted higher toward the sky than any Comanche voice could go. The notes rose so high and were so loud that, as the singer came near him, the song seemed to fill the whole air, and even to turn off the far cliffs and come back. Astonished at the power of the death song, Kicking Wolf stood up, ready to kill the person who was singing it.

His arrow was in his bow; he could tell from the power of the song that the person was near—but what Kicking Wolf saw when he rose from his ambush place chilled his heart, and filled him with terror: there, on a black horse, was a woman with a hidden face, black breasts, and shoulders that were only yellowing flesh and white bone. Worse, this woman who poured a song from beneath the cloth that hid her face had twined around her naked arms a great snake—a snake far larger than any Kicking Wolf had ever seen. The head of the snake was extended along the horse's neck. Its tongue flickered out, and it seemed to be looking right at Kicking Wolf.

So frightened was Kicking Wolf, that he would have immediately sung his own death song had his throat not been frozen with fear. The woman on the black horse was Death Woman, come with her black flesh and her great serpent, to kill him and his people.

Kicking Wolf let the arrow fall from his bow—then he dropped the bow itself, and turned and ran as fast as his short legs could carry him, toward the war chief. Behind him he heard the high, ringing voice of Death Woman, and could imagine the head of the great serpent coming closer and ever closer to him. In his panic, he stepped on a bad cactus; thorns went through his foot, but he did not stop running. He knew that if he slowed the slightest bit, the great snake of Death Woman would get him.

When the Comanches sitting with Buffalo Hump saw Kicking Wolf running toward them they thought it was just some clever plan the stumpy little man had thought up, to lure the whites closer to their arrows and their lances. But the strange, high song seemed to come with Kicking Wolf, to ring in the air like an old witch woman's curse. Some of the Comanches began to be a little apprehensive—they looked to their war chief, who sat as he was. It was only when Kicking Wolf ran up and Buffalo Hump saw the terror in his face, that he knew it was not a ruse. Kicking Wolf was fearless in battle—he would attack anyone, and had once killed six Pawnees in a single battle. Yet, now he was so frightened that he had cactus thorns sticking through his foot and blood on his moccasins, and he was still running. He ran right past Buffalo Hump without stopping—also, Buffalo Hump saw that Kicking Wolf had even dropped his bow; not since Kicking Wolf was a boy had he seen him without his bow in his hand.

Buffalo Hump had been listening to the death song with admiration—he had never heard one so loud before. The song came back off the distant hills, as if the singer's ghost were already there, calling for the singer to come. But something was wrong—Kicking Wolf was terrified, and the ringing, echoing death song was causing panic among his warriors. Then Buffalo Hump saw Death Woman, with her rotting black body; he saw the great snake, twisting its head above her horse's neck. He was so startled that he lifted his lance, but didn't throw it. Behind Death Woman, at the far back, was a naked black woman with a lifted sword; the black woman led a white mule.

At the sight of Death Woman, with her great serpent, the Comanche warriors broke, but Buffalo Hump held his ground. Worse even than the snake twisted around the shoulders of Death Woman was the white mule that followed the tall black woman with the sword. Long ago his old grandmother, who was a spirit woman, had told him to flee from a woman with a white mule; for the coming of the white mule would mean catastrophe for the Comanche people. The great snake he didn't fear; he could kill any snake. But there before him was the white mule of his grandmother's spirit prophecy: he could not kill a prophecy.

It was doom, he knew. His warriors were fleeing; Kicking Wolf had fled. Buffalo Hump lowered his lance, but he did not flee. He could not kill the Texans, not even Gun-In-The-Water, not then; they were under the protection of Death Woman. But they would not escape him; he would kill them later, when Death Woman was sleeping and when the white mule was gone.

[473]

He rode a little higher on the hill and waited. If Death Woman tried to come at him, he would fight, and if he could keep his face toward her he might win, for there was a prophecy, too, that he could only be killed by a lance that pierced him through his hump. He must not let the woman with the white mule and the flashing sword get behind him. As long as his hump was protected, even Death Woman could not kill him.

"Don't look at him," Call said, as he and Gus walked slowly past. "She's spooked most of them, but she ain't spooked him. Just don't look at him. If he comes at us, the rest of them might come back, and we ain't no match for twenty Comanches, even if they're scared."

Slowly, not looking up, the Texans and the women passed the ridge where Buffalo Hump sat. Lady Carey sang even louder as they passed almost beneath the great humpbacked Comanche. Her voice rose so high, it was as if she were trying to cast it into the clouds. She draped her reins over her horse's neck, and spread her arms as she sang.

Buffalo Hump sat above them, immobile, the desert wind blowing the feathers he had tied to his lance. Call did not look up, but he felt the war chief's hatred, as he passed below him. He tensed himself, in case the lance came flying as it had at Gus, on a stormy night not far to the south.

When they had passed the ridge and deemed it safe to stop, Lady Carey dismounted. Matilda brought her clothes. The men dropped their eyes, while she dressed. The boa, Elphinstone, was returned to its basket on the donkey. Emerald put her cloak back on, and returned Lord Carey's sword to its fine sheath. During the excitement the donkey had managed to pull Mrs. Chubb's straw bonnet out of the baggage pack, and had eaten half of it.

"There, who says opera isn't useful?" Lady Carey asked, when she remounted. "I shall have to write Signor Verdi and tell him his arias were not appreciated by the wild Comanche."

When they resumed their journey they saw a strange thing: Buffalo Hump was backing his horse, step by step, across the desert toward the north. His warriors were nowhere in sight, but he had not turned his horse to go and find them. His face was still toward the Texans—step by step, he backed his horse.

"We didn't kill him," Call said. "We should have."

"That's right," Gus said. "We should have. He's still out there—I reckon he'll be back."

"If he does come back, he won't find me," Long Bill said. "If I ever get to a town, I aim to take up carpentry and sleep someplace where I can lock my doors. I've had enough of this sleeping outside."

"I wonder why he's backing his horse?" Call said. "We got no gun that could shoot that far. We couldn't hit him if we tried."

"Go ask him, Woodrow, if you're that curious," Gus said.

8.

W‌HEN THEY RODE IN at dusk to San Antonio, two barefoot friars were bringing a little herd of goats within the walls of the old mission by the river. Somewhere within the walls, another priest was singing.

"Why, it's vespers," Lady Carey said. "Isn't it lovely, Mrs. Chubb? It rather reminds me of Rome."

"A plain English hymn will do for me," Mrs. Chubb said.

"A plain English hymn and no donkeys," she added, a bit later. "I'm afraid I will never be reconciled to donkeys."

Ten days later, on a pier in Galveston, Mrs. Chubb was still complaining of donkeys, to any sailor who would listen.

"Not only did it bite my toe, it ate my best bonnet," she said, but no one listened.

Lady Carey paid the Texans one hundred dollars each, a sum so large that none of the four could quite grasp that they had it. She gave Matilda two hundred dollars, a sum that made Gus jealous— after all, what had Matilda done that he hadn't? Then, as Call and

[476]

Gus, Matilda, Wesley, and Long Bill stood on the pier in the warm salty breeze, the English party boarded a boat whose mast was taller than most trees. Young Willy waved, and Lady Carey, still triply veiled, waved her hand. Mrs. Chubb was gone, still complaining, and Emerald, the tall Negress, looked at the shore but did not wave.

The Texans stood watching as the boat pulled away and began its journey across the great grey plain of the sea. Gus was talking of whores again, as the boat pulled away, but Call was silenced by the immense sweep of the water. He had not expected the sea to be so large: soon the boat containing Lady Carey and her party began to disappear, as a wagon might as it made its way across a sea of grass.

Woodrow Call could be subdued by the ocean if he wanted to— Gus McCrae, for his part, had never felt happier: he was rich, he was safe, and the port of Galveston virtually teemed with whores. He had already visited five.

"I guess this is where I quit the rangering, boys," Long Bill said, with a sigh. "It's rare sport, but it ain't quite safe."

Woodrow Call said nothing; the little ship had vanished. He was watching the sea.

Wesley Buttons knew that he could no longer avoid going home and telling his mother that his two brothers were dead, killed by Mexican soldiers in New Mexico.

Matilda Roberts was thinking that she was farther from California than ever—but at least she had money in her pocket.

"Now, Woodrow, come on," Gus said, taking his friend's arm. "Let's whore a little, and then lope up to Austin."

"Austin—why?" Call asked.

"So I can see if that girl in the general store still wants to marry me," Gus said.